THE
BORDER

ROBERT McCAMMON

Subterranean Press 2015

First Edition

Limited Edition ISBN
978-1-59606-702-8

Trade Edition ISBN
978-1-59606-703-5

Subterranean Press
PO Box 190106
Burton, MI 48519

subterraneanpress.com

To Uncle Carlos

ONE.

LAST STAND
AT PANTHER RIDGE

ONE.

THE BOY WHO WAS RUNNING RAN INTO THE RAIN.

He came suddenly into its stinging shower. Within seconds it became a small storm of torment, like the fierce prick of a hundred hot needles. He looked back as he ran and saw through the moving haze the tops of mountains explode in the distance. He saw chunks of rock as big as buildings fly into the diseased air, crash back upon the earth and crack into tumbling fragments. Above the mountains flickered the electric blue lightning that put terror into the heart of the bravest man and made the weaker man fall to his knees.

The boy kept running, into the rain.

The field was wide and long. The field was barren. Its mud began to pull at the boy's shoes. He was wearing dirty Pumas, once white. He couldn't remember where they had come from, or when he'd put them on. He couldn't remember where his dirty jeans had come from, or his grimy dark red shirt that was missing its right sleeve. He couldn't remember much at all.

He knew, though, that he had to run. And he had to hope he would live through this day.

For though his memory flapped like a tattered flag, he knew what was behind him. He knew he was in Colorado. He knew why the mountains, as old as time, were being torn to jagged pieces. He knew what the blue lightning was, and why soon there would be pulses of red flame floating up from tortured earth to angry sky. They were fighting there. They had found another border to contest. And between them, they would destroy it all.

He ran on, breathing hard, and sweating in the sultry air, as the rain began to hammer down.

The mud took him. It trapped his shoes and made him stumble and down he went into its embrace. It was sticky and hot and got on his face and up his nose. Dark with mud, he struggled up to his knees. Through the curtains of rain, he saw the movements on both sides of him, to left and right in the wide barren field, and he knew one army was on the march.

The boy flattened himself in his muddy pool. He lay like the dead, though his heart was very much alive in its pounding and twisting on a root of terror. He wished he could cover himself with the mud, that he could sink into it and be protected by its darkness, but he lay still and curled up like an infant just out of the womb and stunned by life itself.

He had seen them before. Somewhere. His mind was wrecked. His mind had crashed into some event that had left him half-brainless and groping for memory. But to left and right he saw the blurred smears of their presence as they moved across the field like swirls of gray smoke, like formless but deadly ghosts.

He lay still, his hands gripped into the earth as if in fear of being flung into nothingness.

And suddenly he realized one of them had stopped its advance, and in stopping its body caught up with itself and took form, and suddenly one of them was standing only a few feet to his left and was staring at him.

The boy couldn't help but stare back, his face freighted with mud. There was no protection to be found here. There was no protection to be found anywhere. The boy's blue eyes stared into the black featureless slope of the creature's face, or mask or helmet or whatever it might be. The creature was thin to the point of skeletal, its body about seven feet tall. It was similar to the human body in that it had two arms and two legs. Black-gloved hands with ten fingers. Black boots on human-shaped feet. Whether this was a construction or a real thing born from egg or womb, the boy did not know and could not guess. The black skin-tight suit showed no inch of flesh, and small veins laced the suit carrying rushes of dark reddish fluid. The creature did not seem to be breathing.

The creature held a weapon. It was black also, but it looked fleshy. It had two barrels, and was connected to the body by the fluid-carrying veins.

The weapon was held down at the creature's side, but aimed at the boy. A finger was on a spiky pod that might be a trigger.

The boy knew his death was very close.

A vibration keened the air. It was felt rather than heard, and it made the hairs on the back of the boy's neck ripple. It made his skin crawl and his scalp of unruly brown hair tighten, for he knew what was to come without knowing how he knew.

The creature looked behind it, and upward. Other creatures halted their blurred, ghostly motion and became solid. They too looked upward and their weapons raised in unison toward the enemy.

Then the boy heard it, through the noise of falling rain. He turned his head and angled his face up into the downpour, and through the low yellow clouds came the thing that made a noise like the quiet movement of gears in a fine wristwatch or the soft ticking of a time bomb.

It was huge, two hundred feet across in a triangle shape, and mottled with colors like the hide of a prehistoric predator: brown, yellow, and black. It was as thin as a razor and had no ports nor openings. It was all muscle. It glided forward with what the boy thought was an awesome and nearly silent power. Yellow tendrils of disturbed air flowed back from the flared wingtips, and four electric-blue orbs the size of manhole covers pulsed at its belly. As the craft continued to advance slowly and almost silently, one of the creatures on the ground fired its weapon. A double gout of flame that was not exactly flame, but had something white-hot at the center of its two scorching red trails, shot up toward the craft. Before it reached meat or metal—whatever the craft was made of—a blue spark erupted and snuffed out the flames and its two centers of destruction as easily as damp fingers on a matchhead.

11

Instantly, as the boy watched and shivered in spite of his frozen posture, the creatures turned their weapons on the craft and began to fire…
faster and faster, the gouts of alien flame flaring up in dazzling incandescent ropes, hundreds of them, all to be extinguished by the leaping and
sizzling blue spark.

The boy knew, without knowing how he knew. His mind echoed
with things he could not exactly hear nor understand. He seemed to have
come a long way from where he'd started, though where that had been
he did not remember.

But he knew this, though he could not remember his own name or
where he'd been running from or to or where his parents were: *The creatures with the weapons…soldiers of the Cyphers.*

The craft above…piloted by the Gorgons.

Names humans had given them. Their real names unknown. Their
silence impenetrable.

The blue spark jumped and danced, putting out the white-hot
flames with almost dismissive ease. The rain poured down and the yellow clouds swirled. The Cypher soldiers began to lower their ineffective
weapons and vibrate again into blurs, and suddenly the boy was alone
in the muddy field. The monstrous craft floated above him, its blue
orbs pulsing. He felt as small as an insect on a windshield, about to be
smashed into pulp. He tensed to jump up and run again, as far as he
could get in this mud and downpour, and then the craft drifted on past
him and he felt its force diminish as it gained speed. In his mouth there
was the taste of mud and something like the tang of running the tongue
across rusted metal. He heard a sharp sizzling noise—bacon in a frying
pan—and turning his head in the direction of the parting craft he saw
bolts of electric-blue energy striking out from the vehicle's underside.
Small explosions—bursts of black matter—showed hits on the Cypher
soldiers even as they blurred themselves into near-invisibility.

The boy decided it was time to get up and run some more, in another direction.

He staggered to his feet and fled across the field, away from the
battle. The rain struck his head and shoulders and the mud tried to pull

him down. He fell to his knees once, but when he got up he vowed he would not fall again.

Onward through the rain and across the mud he ran, toward a yellow mist that hung across the horizon. He passed and leaped over smoking craters that held things at their bottoms that were burnt black and twisted like old tree roots. The breath was rasping hard in his lungs, which pained him as if they'd been punched by heavy fists; he coughed up a spool of red blood and kept going.

From the mist before him appeared a dozen or more Cypher soldiers, all thin and black-garbed in material that was not of this earth. They all held the weapons that seemed to be growing from their bodies, and they all wore the black featureless masks that might have been the faces of robots, for all the boy knew. Before he could change direction he was aware of something coming at him from behind with a metallic noise like piano wires being plucked in a high register. He veered to the left and dove into a fresh crater, while above him incandescent blue spheres of tight fire skimmed over his refuge at tremendous speed and tore into the Cyphers, spinning out whips that looked to be made of flaming barbed-wire. The boy crawled up to the crater's edge to see the Cyphers being ripped to pieces by this new weapon, and though some of the Cyphers shot down a few of the fireballs with their own energy weapons or blurred away into the mist the battle was over in a matter of seconds. Twitching arms and legs lay upon the black-splattered battlefield and the fireballs like burning eyes powered on into the yellow mist beyond, seeking more victims.

A movement in the crater with him caught the boy's attention. He felt the hairs rise on the back of his neck, and his heart pounded.

Across from him, a faceless mud-splattered Cypher soldier was reaching for its energy gun, which had been torn off its veins and lay shrivelled like dying flesh a few feet away. The black-gloved hands scrabbled to regain the diminished weapon, but could not quite reach it since some other encounter had nearly cut the creature in half. The legs were still twitching, the boots pushing futilely against the ravaged earth. In the body cavity glistened black intestines streaked with yellow and red like the bodies of the grasshoppers the boy remembered, yet did not know how he remembered. He smelled an acrid odor akin to the smell of the liquid the grasshoppers shot out upon rough fingers. Only this was maybe twice as strong. The Cypher lay in a pool of it. The creature still struggled to reach the weapon, but the severed body would not obey.

The boy spoke, in a voice he'd never heard before.

"I thought you were supposed to be so tough," he said.

The faceless creature continued its struggle for the weapon. The boy got up in a crouch, mindful of other soldiers or flying things that might take his head off, and dared to touch the energy gun. It had a sticky feel, like rubber left out too long under a burning sun. The veins had ceased to pump fluid. The weapon was crumpling and collapsing inward on itself even as he watched. The Cypher soldier's spidery hand reached for his ankle, and he feared the grip because he had the quick mental image of being paralyzed with pain. Avoiding the soldier's hand, he stood up and ran again because he knew that sitting still in one place too long was death.

He also knew that he wanted to live. Knew that he *needed* to live, and so he'd better find himself a place of shelter before it was too late.

As he ran the rain thrashed into his face. From his pressured lungs he began to cough and spit up more threads of blood. He asked himself who he was and where he had come from, but to those questions only returned blankness. He had no memory beyond running across this field, as if his mind had been turned off and then on again by a jittery hand on a lightswitch. Father? Mother? Home? Brother or sister? Nothing, not even the shadow of a shadow.

He was hurting. His lungs, heart and stomach, yes, but his bones too. He felt rearranged. He felt as if in that weird old song about the thigh bone being connected to the kneebone and all that shit, his thigh bone was connected to his collarbone and his kneebone to his buttbone. Something about him was messed up, but he was good to run. For now, that was enough.

The monstrous triangular shape moved above him. He looked up and saw the massive Gorgon craft, mottled like a prehistorical reptile, gliding from the ugly yellow clouds. It was still firing its electric-blue bolts of energy to hit unseen figures on the ground. It was oblivious to him; he was nothing, worth not even a spark of destruction.

Suddenly the bright blue bolts began to flare out to the left and right, seeking other targets. The Gorgon craft might have given a shiver of dread, and in another few seconds the boy saw why.

From both sides came thin ebony missiles maybe twenty feet in length. There were ten of them, moving fast and silently. Four of them were hit by the bolts and exploded into flying black ribbons, but the remaining six grew claws and teeth as they pierced the meat of the Gorgon ship, and forming into shapes like voracious, glistening spiders, they began to rapidly eat and tear their way through the mottled hide.

Six more of the hungry missiles came at the ship, launched from somewhere beyond sight. Two were shot down, the other four became ebony spider-shapes that winnowed themselves into the alien flesh, if it could be called that. Chunks of the Gorgon ship began to fall away, revealing an interior of purplish-red meat veined with what looked like hexagonal corridors. The missile-spiders continued to claw and chew, faster and faster, as the blue bolts fired crazily in every direction. The boy dodged as an energy bolt sizzled the earth maybe forty feet to his right, but he couldn't pull his gaze away from the hideous feast and the death of a giant.

Surely the Gorgon ship was dying. Its bulk shivered and writhed as the Cypher spiders penetrated deeper into the heart of the mystery. Dark red liquid was pouring out from a dozen wounds. Pieces of the craft fell to the earth and yet still writhed and convulsed. The machine screamed. There was a high-pitched sound that seemed to the boy a cross between fingernails on a blackboard and the sinister rattling of a timber viper. He had to put his hands to his ears, to block the noise out before it overcame him and made his knees buckle. A huge chunk of the craft fell away, spiralling fountains of the dark liquid. Within the cavity, the black spider-shapes were feasting, ripping through the alien meat and the inner corridors with claws and fangs that the boy thought could likely tear through concrete and metal. The Gorgon ship pitched to the right, spilling its insides in great falling sheets of liquid and fleshy pieces the Cypher-spiders had not fully consumed.

The machine-scream went on and on, as the ship crashed down upon the earth. The spiders swarmed over the twitching hide. The boy turned and fled.

Where there was any safety anymore, he didn't know. The ear-piercing noise ceased. *Score one for the Cyphers*, he thought. He ran through the yellow mist and onward, and suddenly found broken concrete under his feet.

He was in a parking lot. Around him in the thickened air were the rusted and weather-beaten hulks of eight abandoned vehicles. The rain had ceased. Puddles of water filled cracks and craters. A long building of red bricks stood before him, with not an unshattered window remaining. To the left was a sagging goalpost and the weeds of a football field. The bleachers had collapsed. A sign had stayed up in the parking lot, valiant in its declaration of a message from the past.

ETHAN GAINES HIGH SCHOOL read the permanent black letters. And below those, the moveable red ones: Senior Pl y A ril 4-6 'The Ch ngeling'

The boy saw blurs approaching from his left, across the football field. A few of the Cypher soldiers stopped and regained their bodily forms for a few seconds before they sped up again. He thought there might be forty or fifty of them, coming like a dark wave. He started to run to the right, but even as the impulse hit him he knew he wouldn't have time to escape; they would be on him too soon.

He slid to the concrete and under a smashed pickup truck that used to be black but was now more red with rust and still had a Denver Broncos decal on the remains of the broken rear window.

Dark blurs entered the parking lot. The Cypher soldiers were on the move, from somewhere to somewhere. The boy pressed himself against the cracked concrete. If any of them sensed him here...

Something was coming.

The boy felt it, in a shiver of his skin. He smelled some form of pulsing power in the tainted air. From his hiding place he saw the legs of several of the soldiers materialize, as they stood motionless; they too were feeling this yet-unknown approach.

There was silence but for the dripping of water from the car hulks. Then something passed overhead with a noise like a whisper of wind, and there was a bright flash of blue light that lit up the parking lot and made the boy squint and then whatever it was had gone.

The boy waited, blinking. Spots spun before his eyes. Some of the soldiers blurred out again, while others remained in cautious and stationary—and maybe stunned—visibility.

Above the boy, the pickup truck moved.

It gave a shudder that made its rusted seams groan, and the boy heard that same groaning of metal echo across the parking lot, and suddenly the underside of the pickup was changing from metal to red and brown scales, and its moldy tires were changing into stubby scaled legs from which grew red spikes tipped with gleaming black.

He realized the pickup truck was coming to life.

In a matter of seconds a breathing belly was over his head. He saw the shape over him broaden and thicken, with a noise that was a combination of bones slipping into sockets and metal crackling as it formed itself into flesh.

With a burst of panic he rolled out from under the thing, and found himself on his knees amid what was now not a parking lot of abandoned vehicles but a menagerie of creatures from the darkest depth of nightmares.

The boy realized that whatever had passed over and released its energy beam in its eye-stunning blue burst had the power to create life. And the life it had created here, from the rusted and abandoned hulks, were either born from real creatures of the Gorgons' domain, or from the imagination of an alien warlord. Bulky, muscular shapes began to rise up from the concrete. The boy was in their midst, among their clawed feet and legs that seethed with red and black spikes. Horned heads with multiple eyes and gaping mouths scanned the battleground, as the Cypher soldiers opened fire. The red coils of otherworldly flame flailed out, striking and burning the newborn and monstrous flesh. The creatures that were hit roared and yowled, shaking the earth, and others rushed forward with tremendous speed upon the soldiers. As the boy watched in

17

stunned horror while the Gorgon creations struck left and right with spiked arms and claws into the mass of soldiers, he noted that one of the thickly-muscled beasts had a Denver Broncos decal on the reddish scales at juncture of shoulders and neck. It appeared to be just underneath the armored flesh, like the faded remnant of an earthly tattoo.

The soldiers fired their weapons, scaled flesh burned and smoking, the creatures crushed and tore apart and trampled the long slim figures in their black uniforms, and intestines that smelled of grasshopper juice flew through the air and splattered where they hit. One monster's triple-horned head with six deepset crimson eyes burst into flame from a Cypher weapon, and the creature rampaged around the parking lot blindly striking out as its craggy face melted like gray wax. The Cyphers were being overwhelmed and crushed beneath the monsters, and some blurred away but a few remained standing their ground and firing into the beasts until they too were ripped to dripping shreds. Some on all fours and some on two legs, the creatures began to give pursuit after the retreating soldiers. Three dying Gorgon beasts lay on the concrete being eaten up by the Cypher flames, and they shrieked and beat futilely at the alien fire and tried to rise up from their impending deaths. One got to its knees, its burning triangular head on a thick stalk of a neck turned, and its ebony eyes found the boy, who crawled backwards away from the thing even as the eyes burned out, the flames rippled across its scales and spikes and it fell back upon the concrete with a gasp of life released.

The boy got up, staggering, and ran again.

———✖———

It was all he could do to stay upright, but as he entered the haze of yellow mist he knew he could not—*must not*—fall. He could hear the roaring of the monsters behind him, off in the distance, and his dirty Pumas nearly flew him off the ground. He was no longer on concrete, but again on a field of mud and weeds. Crumpled and smoking bodies of Cypher soldiers lay around him, where another battle had passed. Score one for the Gorgons, he thought.

He hadn't gone another hundred yards when he knew something was coming up fast behind him.

He was terrified to look back. Terrified to slow down. Terrified, to know he was about to be destroyed in this muddy field.

Whatever it was, he sensed that it was almost upon him.

Then he did look back, to see what was after him, and he was about to juke to the right when a rider on a gray-dappled horse emerged from the mist, reached down and grabbed the boy's arm in a lockgrip. He was pulled off his feet and upward, and a hard human voice growled, "Get up here!"

The boy got up behind the man and held on tightly to his waist, seeing the man was wearing at his left side a shoulder holster with what looked like an Uzi submachine gun in it. The horse and its two riders swept on across the field, while in the distance the Gorgon monsters roared like a chorus of funeral bells on the last day of the world.

TWO.

B UT IT WAS NOT THE LAST DAY OF THE WORLD.

It was a Thursday, the 10th of May. Some may have wished it was the last day of the world, some may have prayed for it to be and wept bitter tears that it would be so, but others had prepared for yet another day to follow this one, and so the boy found himself on horseback, approaching a fortress.

On the road that led up to this Colorado hilltop on the southern edge of Fort Collins was an aged and weather-battered sign that showed the stylized emblem of a prowling panther and the tarnished brass lettering *Panther Ridge Apartments*. At the top of the hill, with a panoramic view of all around, were the apartments themselves. There were four buildings constructed of bricks the color of sand with gray-painted balconies and sliding glass doors. Built in 1990 and at one time a desired address for swinging singles, the Panther Ridge Apartments had fallen on hard times since the crash of 2007, and the investment company that owned it had sold it off to another company in the beginning of a downward spiral for maintenance and managers. The boy knew none of this. He saw only four dismal-looking buildings surrounded by a fifteen-foot high wall of mortared rocks topped with thick coils of barbed wire. Wooden watchtowers with tarpaper roofs stood behind the wall at

21

east and west, north and south. He couldn't fail to note heavy machine guns set up on pivoting stands at each tower. As the horse and its riders continued up the road to the north, a green signal flag was flown from the south-facing tower. The boy saw a large wooden door covered with metal plates begin to open inward. As it opened wider the horse galloped through and immediately the men and women who had pulled the heavy door open began to push it shut. It was locked by two lengths of squared-off timber manhandled across the door through iron brackets and into grooves in the walls. But by this time the boy was being lifted from the horse by a husky man on the ground who had run up alongside to do just this task. The husky man had a long gray beard and wore leather gloves and held the boy before him like a sack of garbage as he ran deeper into the apartment complex and down a set of stairs. A door was opened, the boy was nearly thrown inside, and the door closed again. The boy heard a key turning in the lock.

He was, as he discovered within a few seconds, imprisoned.

The floor was bare white, scarred linoleum. The walls, painted a yel-lowish-gray, also bore scars. They looked to the boy, as he sat on the floor and examined his surroundings, like claw marks. And bullet holes here and there, too. The door was reinforced with metal plates, as the front gate had been. The sliding door to the balcony was covered with sheet metal and barbed wire. One small square of window allowed in a weak shaft of light. There was no furniture. The light fixtures had been removed but of course there was no electricity so the bare wires hanging down were just reminders of what had been. He saw on the walls and floor what might have been the faint brown remnants of bloodstains.

The boy said, "*Okay,*" just to hear his own voice again.

And it was more than that. *Okay.* If he had made it across that field and out of that parking lot with the Gorgons and Cyphers all around, then he was going to survive. He knew he had a survivor's instinct, though he had no idea who he was or where he'd come from. So...*okay.* And *okay* because at least he was with humans, and maybe they were going to stick him in a pot, boil him, and eat him, but...well, maybe thinking that way wasn't so *okay,* so he let that go. But at least he was with humans, right? And *okay* because for the moment—just for this moment—he felt safe here in this little apartment prison, and he didn't have to do any more running right now, and he was tired and hurting and it was *okay* just to sit here and wait for what was coming next.

What was coming next was not very long in coming. Within a few minutes the boy heard the key in the lock again. His heartbeat quickened. He tensed and slid himself across the floor to press his back against the wall behind him, and he waited as the door opened and three men came into the dimly illuminated room. One of the men carried an old-timey black doctor's bag and a burning oil lamp, which he held toward the boy as he entered. The other two men were armed with submachine guns, which they also aimed at the boy.

The door was closed and locked behind them.

"Stand up," commanded one of the men with a machine gun. "Take off your clothes."

"What?" the boy asked, still dazed from his run.

"*Up*," came the rough voice. "And your clothes *off*."

The boy got to his feet. The man who had spoken to him was the same who had heaved him up upon the horse. This man was maybe forty years old, was of medium build, but obviously strong for his size. He had a hard-lined face with a hawk's beak of a nose and deep-set, wary, dark brown eyes. He looked like he'd never known what a smile felt like. Such a thing might break his face. The man wore faded jeans, brown work-boots, a gray shirt with rolled-up sleeves, and on his head was a grimy dark blue baseball cap. He had a brown beard edged with gray. Around his left shoulder and hanging down close at his side was the holster for his very deadly weapon. On his left wrist was a battered-looking watch that had no crystal.

"Go ahead, son," the man with the doctor's bag urged. He was older, probably in his mid-sixties, was white-haired and clean-shaven, thin and dressed more neatly than either of the others in a blue shirt and faded khakis. He was holding onto whatever he could of his life as it had been. His face maybe had once been friendly and open, but now was strained and tense. The boy noted a holster around his waist with a revolver parked in it, and this man wore a wristwatch that looked to be in fairly good working order.

"Are you going to kill me?" the boy asked, speaking to the elder man.

"If we have to," replied the hard-faced man. "Get your clothes off. *Now.*"

The third man, thin and sallow and black-bearded, stood aside near the door. The boy figured he was there in position to get a clear line of fire. The boy began to undress, slowly because his bones ached and he felt so weary he could sleep for a hundred years. When he was out of his clothes and they had dropped around him to the floor, he stood motionlessly while the three men stared at him in the light of the oil lamp.

"Where'd you get all those bruises?" asked the doctor-man, in a quiet voice.

The boy looked down at himself. He hadn't realized. Across his chest was a massive, ugly black bruise. It covered from shoulder to shoulder. Black bruises were streaked across his sides, his stomach and his thighs. He had no memory of what had caused those injuries, but now he knew why he was aching and he was spitting up blood. Something had hit him, very hard.

"Please turn around," said the doctor-man. "Let's see your back."

The boy did. The black-bearded man at the door gave a low grunt and the hard-faced man spoke in nearly a whisper to the third one.

"My question again," said the doctor-man. "Where'd the bruises come from?"

"I don't know," came the still-stunned answer, as the boy turned to face them again.

"You have an equally large bruise across your back and down your spine. Your contusions look to be *very* severe. You've been through an extremely violent incident…not like falling down some stairs or skinning a knee. I mean…*violent.*" He stepped forward, shining the lamp into the boy's eyes.

"Careful, doc!" warned the hard-faced man. His Uzi was trained on the boy's midsection, and did not waver.

"Are you spitting up blood?"

"Yes sir."

"I'm not surprised. What's surprising me is that your lungs didn't burst and that you still *can* breathe. Your hearing all right?"

"Got a little ringing in my ears. They kind of feel stopped up. That's all."

"Hm. Interesting. I think you've been through…well, I won't say right now." He offered a thin, crinkly smile, which was maybe the best he could do.

"Can I put my clothes back on?"

"Not yet. Hold your arms out to your sides, will you?"

The boy did as he was asked.

The doctor gave his medical bag to the hard-faced man and neared the boy again. He shone the lamp over the boy's body, and seemed to be looking for something in particular. He frowned as he examined the huge black bruise across the boy's chest. "You can lower your arms," he said, and the boy did. Then the doctor reached back and opened the medical bag. From it he brought a hypodermic needle, which he uncapped ready for use. "Left arm, please," he said.

The boy hesitated. "What's this for?"

"A saline solution."

"What's it *for*?" the boy asked, with a little irritation.

"We're checking to see," said the doctor, "whether you're fully human or not. The saline solution causes a reaction in the alien blood. It heats it up. Then things happen. Left arm, please."

"I'm human," the boy said.

"Do what you're told," the hard-faced man spoke up. "We don't want to shoot you for no reason."

"Okay." The boy managed a tight smile. He offered his left arm. "Go ahead."

The needle sank into a vein. The doctor stepped back. Both of the other men were ready with their weapons. The doctor checked the time on his wristwatch. About a minute slipped past. "Dave," the doctor said to the hard-faced man, "I think he's clean."

"Sure about that?"

The doctor stared into the boy's face. His eyes were blue, nested in wrinkles, but were very clear. "No nodules I can see. No abnormalities, no growths. No reaction to the saline. Let's give a listen to the heart and take a bp reading." The doctor retreived a stethoscope from his bag, checked the boy's heartbeat and then used a blood pressure cuff. "Normal," was the conclusion. "Under the circumstances."

"What about the bruises?"

"Yes," said the doctor. "What about those." It was a statement, not a question. "Son, what's your name?"

The boy hesitated. He was tired and hurting, and he could still taste blood in his mouth. A name? He had none to give. The men were waiting. He decided he'd better offer them something, and he thought of a name he'd recently seen. "Ethan Gaines," he answered.

"*Really*?" Dave cocked his head to one side. "Funny about that. One of our lookouts spotted you through her binocs running into that high school parking lot. Funny, that it's Ethan Gaines High School. *Was*, I mean. So that's your name, huh?"

The boy shrugged.

"I think," the doctor said, "he doesn't know his name. He's suffered a very violent concussive event. An explosion of some kind. Might have been caught in a shockwave. Where are your parents?"

"Don't know," the boy said. He frowned. "I just seemed to wake up, all of a sudden. I was running. That's all I remember. I know I'm in Colorado…in Fort Collins, I think? But everything else…" He blinked and looked around the little prison. "What's this place for? What did you mean…about the alien blood heating up?"

"That's for later," Dave said. "Right now, we're the ones asking the questions…like where you came from?"

The boy had reached his limit with Dave. Whether the man was holding an Uzi on him on not, he didn't care. He took a solid step forward, which made both guns train on him, and he thrust his chin out and his blue eyes glinted with anger and he said, "I *told* you. I don't remember who I am, or where I came from. All I know is, I was running. From *them*. They were fighting over my head. All around me." He had to pause to draw a breath into his sore lungs. "I don't know who *you* people are. I'm real glad you got me out of where I was, but I don't like guns aimed at me. Either yours or the Cyphers'." He let that hang for a few seconds, and then he added, "Sir."

The weapons were lowered. Dave glanced quickly at the doctor, who had stepped to one side and was wearing a small, amused smile.

"*Well*," said the doctor. "Ethan, I think you can put on your clothes now. As for who *we* are, *I* am John Douglas. Was a pediatric surgeon in my previous life. Now, mostly an aspirin-pusher. This is Dave McKane," he said, motioning toward the hard-faced man, "and Roger Pell."

"Hi," said Ethan, to all three of them. He started putting his clothes back on…dirty white socks, underwear that was the worse for wear, muddy jeans, the grimy dark red shirt with the torn-off right sleeve, and the dirt-caked Pumas. He thought to check the pockets of his jeans for anything that might be a clue, but searching them brought up nothing. "I don't remember these clothes," he told the men. And he felt something break inside him. It was sudden and quiet, and yet it was like an inner scream. He had been about to say *I don't remember who bought them for me*, but it was lost and fell away. He trembled and his right hand came up to press against his forehead, to jar loose the memories that were not there, and his eyes burned and his throat closed up and everywhere he turned there seemed to be a wall.

"Hell," Dave McKane said, "sometimes I forget my own name too." His voice was quieter now, not so harsh. There was a quaver in it that he killed by clearing his throat. "It's just the times. Right, Doc?"

"Right," said John Douglas. He reached out and touched Ethan's arm; it was the gentle touch of a pediatric surgeon. "The times," he said, and Ethan blinked away his tears and nodded, because tears would win no battles and right no wrongs.

"She'll want to see him," Dave said, speaking to the doc. "If you're *sure?*"

"I'm sure. Ethan, you can call me JayDee. Okay?"

"Yes sir."

"All right. Let's get out of this hole."

27

They took him out through the metal-reinforced door and into the yellow-misted light. A half-dozen people—thin, wearing clothes that had been patched many times and washed only a few—were standing around the door, waiting for the little drama within to play out, and they retreated up the stairs as Ethan emerged.

"This way." JayDee directed Ethan to the left as they reached what had been the lowest building's parking lot. The rain had stopped and the sun was hot through the jaundiced clouds. The air smelled of electricity before a thunderstorm. That and the air itself was heavy and humid. There was no hint of a breeze. As Ethan followed the three men across the parking lot, past a disused set of tennis courts and a swimming pool that had debris in it but only a small puddle of rainwater at its deepest end, he saw that people of many different generations were gathered here in the protection of this makeshift fortress. There were women of many ages holding babies and young children, there were older children and teenagers and on up to the elderly, people maybe in their seventies. Some of these people were working, the strong-backed chopping wood and stacking the lengths in neat piles, others laboring on the outer walls to strengthen places that looked damaged, and doing various other tasks in this fortress community. Most of the inhabitants paused in their work to watch Ethan and the men pass by. Everyone was thin and moved slowly, as if in a bad dream, their expressions blank and hollow-eyed, but they were survivors too. Ethan counted eight horses grazing in a corral on a brown-grassed, rocky hillside up near the highest point. A small wooden barn, surely not original to the apartment complex, stood nearby. With no gasoline available, true horsepower would be the only way to travel.

"Up here," said JayDee, motioning Ethan up another flight of stairs at the central building. The walls had been painted with graffiti slogans in red, white and blue that proclaimed among other silent shouts *We Will Not Die*, *This World Is Ours*, and *Tomorrow Is Another Day*. Ethan wondered if the people who had painted those slogans were still alive.

He climbed the stairs behind JayDee, with Dave McKane and Roger Pell following him, and on the next level the doctor stopped at a door with the number 227 on it and knocked. Just before it opened something screamed past overhead, so fast it was nearly invisible, just the quickest impression of a yellow-and-brown-blotched triangular shape cutting through the air and then gone, and everyone but Ethan flinched because he was tired of running and if he was going to die today it would be without shrinking from his fate.

The door opened and a slim, pallid-faced man with a mass of curly reddish hair and a ginger-colored beard peered out. He was wearing glasses held together with electrical tape. The lenses magnified his gray eyes. He wore a pair of dirty overalls and a brown-checked shirt, and he was holding at his side a clipboard with a pad of yellow paper on which Ethan caught sight of lines of numbers. He had the stub of a much-chewed-upon pencil clenched in the left side of his mouth.

"Afternoon, Gary," JayDee said. He motioned toward Ethan. "We have a new arrival."

The man's magnified eyes studied Ethan. His reddish brows went up. "Fell in some mud?" he asked, and Ethan nodded.

"Someone new?" came a woman's voice from behind Gary, who wore a pistol in a holster at his waist just as did John Douglas. "Let's have a look."

Gary stepped aside. JayDee let Ethan enter the apartment first. There was a woman sitting behind a desk and behind her there was a wall with a large, expressionist painting of wild horses galloping across a field. The glass sliding door that led to the balcony and facing the distant mountains that had exploded behind Ethan not long ago was reinforced with a geometry of duct tape. On the floor was a crimson rug, there were two chairs, a coffee table and a brown sofa. Everything looked like junk shop stuff, but at least it made the place comfortable. Or maybe not. On another wall was a rack of three rifles, one with a scope. A few oil lamps were set about, their wicks burning low. A second woman was sitting in a chair in front of the desk, and before her was another clipboard and a pad of yellow paper with figures written on it. Evidently some kind of meeting had been in progress that involved number crunching, and as Ethan approached the desk he had the distinct feeling that the numbers were not good.

Both women stood up, as if he were worth the respect. He figured maybe he was, for getting here without being killed by either Gorgon monsters or Cypher soldiers. The woman who was behind the desk was the older of the two. She was dressed in a pale blue blouse and gray pants and around her neck she wore a necklace of turquoise stones with a silver crucifix in the middle. She said, "What do we have here?" Her dark brown eyes narrowed and quickly went to JayDee.

"He's human," the doctor said, answering her unspoken question. But in his voice there was something else. *As far as I can tell*, was what Ethan heard. "One problem, though. He doesn't know his—"

"My name is Ethan Gaines," said the boy, before JayDee could get that out.

"His *history*," the doctor went on. The apartment door had been closed by Gary, after Dave and Roger had come in. The noise of work outside was muffled. "Ethan has no memory of where he came from or where his parents are. He is...shall we say...a mystery."

"Hannah saw him through her binoculars," Dave added. His voice was less gruff but still hard-edged. He removed his baseball cap, showing brown hair that stuck up with multiple cowlicks and had streaks of gray at the temples. "I made the decision to go out after him. Didn't have time to bring it to you or anybody else."

"Brave or crazy, which one is it?" said the woman behind the desk, speaking to Dave with a hint of irritation as if she valued his life greater than a horseback jaunt into the battlefield. Her gaze went to the boy again. "Ethan," she said. "I am Olivia Quintero. I suppose I'm the leader here. At least that's what they tell me. I guess I should say...welcome to Panther Ridge."

Ethan nodded. He figured there were plenty of places worse to be. Like anywhere out there beyond the walls. He took a good long look at Olivia Quintero, who radiated a comforting confidence, or a strength of will and purpose. He thought that was why she was the leader here. She looked to be a tall woman, slimly built and likely made more slim by lack of food. But she was sinewy and tough in the way she held herself, her face placid and composed, her forehead high under a crown of short-cut white hair. Ethan thought she was maybe in her mid-fifties, her skin tone slightly darkened by her Hispanic heritage. Her forehead was lined and there were deeper lines at the corners of her eyes, but otherwise she wore the roads and travels of her life well. She looked like what he thought she must have been before all this happened: a high school principal, but one who had experienced some "stuff" in her own younger years and might let things slide if you explained yourself the right way. Maybe she'd been the principal at Ethan Gaines High, who knew? Or a businesswoman, maybe. Someone who had come up from a poor family and made a fortune selling real estate, the kind of houses that used to look like little castles before there was a need for fortresses. And how he knew this about the little castles he couldn't remember, so he just let it go because no daylight was breaking through his night.

He felt her examining him, too. And she saw him as a muddied boy about fourteen or fifteen years old with a mop of unruly brown hair that hung over his forehead and nearly into his eyes, which were the light blue color of the early morning sky at the ranch she had owned with her deceased husband Vincent about twenty miles east of here, back when there was sanity in the world. She noted Ethan's sharp nose and chin and the equally sharp—nearly piercing—expression in those eyes, and she thought he was an intelligent boy who must have been born under a very lucky star, to have survived what he must've gone through out there. Or...*tal vez no tan afortunado*, because maybe the lucky ones had all died early, along with their loved ones and their memories of what Earth had been.

Thinking about that too much was a dark path to Hell, and God only knew all of the survivors here had suffered aplenty, with more suffering yet to come. The suicide rate was getting higher. There was no way to stop someone who wanted to leave, and with so many guns around...

The loss of hope was the worst, Olivia knew. So she could let no one else know how close she was to taking a gun, putting it to her head in the middle of the night and joining her husband in what must surely be a better place than this.

But Panther Ridge needed a leader, someone who pressed on and organized things and said *tomorrow is another day* and would never show her terror and hopelessness. And she was it, though deep in her soul she wondered how much longer she could be, and why there was any point to any of it.

"Have you ever killed anyone?" Ethan suddenly asked her.

"*What?*" she replied, a little startled by the question.

"Killed anyone in that room I was put in," Ethan went on. "I saw claw marks and bullet holes in the walls. What looked like bloodstains, too. I'm thinking people were taken in there and killed."

Dave stepped closer, between Ethan and Olivia. "Yeah, we've killed some *things* in there. Maybe they were people once, but they sure weren't when we killed them. It had to be done. Then we scrubbed up the blood the best we could. Don't you *know?*"

"I know about the Gorgons and the Cyphers. I know they're fighting. Tearing the world apart. That's all I can remember."

"And you don't remember *how* you know?" Olivia asked. "Not anything?"

"Nothing," said the boy.

Olivia glanced at John Douglas, who lifted his white eyebrows and shrugged, saying *I have no idea.* She directed her attention back to the new arrival. "I don't know where you've been or how you survived out there, but I think there's a lot you need to *grasp.* And much more than about the Cyphers and Gorgons. Are you hungry? I hope you don't mind horse meat."

"I don't mind."

"We do what we can here. Make do or do without. Mostly do without. But we keep going." *Why?* she asked herself even as she said it. *What is it that we think will change the way things are?* She quickly pushed those questions away. She also saw no point in mentioning yet that on some nights true Hell was visited upon the wrack and ruin of this Earth. "Dave, take him to the mess hall. Get him fed. Find him a place to stay."

"Sure," said Dave, stone-faced. "Another happy addition to our little family."

"How many people are here?" Ethan asked the woman.

32

"A hundred and twelve by last count. It changes sometimes, day to day."

Ethan's gaze went to the yellow pad on the desk. He saw that numbers had been written, scratched out and scrawled again by a nervous hand.

"That's not people," Olivia said, noting Ethan's interest. "That's circumstances. We've been here nearly two years. Our supplies are running out."

"Food and water?" Ethan asked.

"Canned food and bottled water, both stockpiles pretty low. That's why we've had to start eating the horses, and we don't trust the rainwater. So, that's how things are," she finished.

Bad, Ethan thought. He could see the end of things, deep in her eyes. As if she felt that, she looked away at Dave once more. "Take him and get him fed. Ethan, I'll see you later. Okay?"

He nodded, and Dave and Roger led him out of the room and shut the door.

John Douglas stayed behind, as Kathy Mattson took her chair again and Gary Roosa regarded his clipboard and yellow pad with all the figures of doom upon them. Olivia sat down, but she knew there was a reason the doctor had stayed and so she said, "What is it?"

"Interesting young man," said JayDee.

"Tough to think what he must've gone through. But others have made it too. We had a few survivors in a couple of a days ago, didn't we?"

"We did. Hard to survive out there, but not impossible." The doctor frowned. "It's just that...I wish I had a decent lab set up. Wish I had some way to really give Ethan a thorough exam."

"Why?" A trace of fear tightened her mouth. "Because you think he may not be—"

"I *think*," JayDee interrupted, "he's human and clean. But I also think—and this stays in this room, please—that he sustained some injuries that...well, I don't know how he's walking around, with all the bruises he has under his clothes. And *ought* to have, at least in my opinion, some major internal injuries. I think he was caught in a shockwave. It's just...very strange, that he's so..."

33

"*Alive?*" Olivia prompted.

"Maybe that," JayDee admitted. "From the outside, it looks like he had a massive chest injury. That alone would be enough to…" He shrugged. "But I can't really say, because I can't do a proper exam."

"Then do what you *can* do," Olivia said, her gaze steady. "*Watch* him. If it turns out he's a different kind of lifeform…good enough to get past the saline…then we'd better know that *fast*. So watch him, do you hear me?"

"I hear." JayDee started for the door.

"Keep your gun loaded," she reminded him, as she turned her attention to the numbers of the dwindling stockpiles and the ideas of further rationing that Kathy and Gary—both ex-accountants from the previous world—had advanced.

"Yes," JayDee replied heavily, and he went out of the room into the sick sunlight.

THREE.

Dave and JayDee watched the boy eat a small bowl of horse-meat stew at a table in the room that served as the mess hall. Meals were usually staggered so as not to overwhelm the three cooks, who were doing the best they could with what they had. Everything had to be cooked outside over woodfires, then brought in. Beyond the double-locked storage room doors, the canned foods were getting low and the bottled water was almost gone. Afternoon light filtered through two windows that were reinforced with duct tape. A few oil lamps and candle lanterns were set about on the other tables. It was a dreary-looking room, but across one wall someone had painted in bright red *We Will Survive*. The paint had been applied with fierce—or frantic—resolve, and had dripped down in red rivulets to the linoleum-tiled floor.

The boy ate as if there were no tomorrow. He'd been given a paper cup with three swallows of water and told it was all he could have, so he was taking it easy on that. The horsemeat stew, though, was quickly history.

"Take a deep breath," said John Douglas.

Ethan paused in his licking of the bowl to do as the doctor said.

"No pain in your lungs?"

"A little tight. Sore right in here," Ethan answered, touching the center of his chest. He went back to getting every shred of meat his fingers and tongue could find.

"Sore neck too, I'd think."

"Little bit."

"I'm surprised you aren't in more pain." The doctor rubbed his chin; unlike most of the other men, he tried to shave as often as possible and he used deodorant. He had been fastidious about his appearance and his habits as a younger man, and as an older man in the world that used to be. It was tougher now, and the point was unclear about why one would wish to maintain as many old habits as possible, but he was a creature of order and neatness and it kept him connected to the man he used to be. It also probably kept him sane and wanting to live. "I'd think," he offered, "that you could hardly *walk* after such traumas, much less *run*. Then again, you *are* a young boy. Fifteen years old, would be my guess. But *still*..." He paused, unable to come to any conclusion about this without a proper examination lab, and that fact made him very uneasy. Though he was certain this boy was human. Almost certain. At least the saline test hadn't set the boy's blood burning, and made him burst into a spiked monstrosity or a howling spider-like nightmare as had happened in previous tests when so-called 'humans' were brought in.

"But still," Dave growled, though it wasn't meant as a growl, "your story is...can I say...fucked up." A brickmason in his previous life, also a bouncer at a Fort Collins country music bar and an all-around rough-ass dude who didn't mind throwing himself into any kind of action that called for a bad attitude, Dave McKane minced no words. He had dirty fingernails and dirty hair and dirt in the creases of his face and he carried his responsibilities in this fortress—this last stand—very, very seriously. "If you have no memory, how come you know about the Gorgons and Cyphers? How come that wasn't blanked out?"

Ethan sipped at his cup of water. He met Dave's stare. "I guess I haven't got any memory of most things, but *that*...I know they're fighting."

"Then you know how it started? You remember it? The day?"

Ethan concentrated. Nothing was there. He sipped at his water again, and found with his tongue a shred of horsemeat between two teeth. "No, I don't remember that."

"The third day of April, two years ago?" said Dave. He folded his hands together atop the table, and recalled praying at a kitchen table similar to this one with his wife and two sons in the little house not many miles from here yet worlds away. He had gone out alone one morning a couple of months after getting here, riding the dappled gray horse Pilgrim, daring fate and maybe wishing to commit suicide by alien weapon. They didn't fight over one place very long but you could never tell when they would come back. The battleground shifted, and nothing was ever resolved. As far as he knew, it was the same all over the world.

Dave had ridden Pilgrim to the piece of land he and Cheryl had owned, and stood at the crater where the charred debris of the house lay. He had seen the shards of that kitchen table down at the bottom, and then he had turned away and thrown up and gotten back on his horse because Panther Ridge was his home now and Cheryl and the boys were dead. And…a Gorgon ship was coming, sliding through the yellow air, which meant the Cyphers would not be far away either.

"April the third," JayDee said, picking up the recollections and emotions. He felt a hammer blow to his heart, and he thought he had progressed past that pain, but he had not. There was so much pain, for everyone. His wife of thirty-two years had died in their apartment here, in March. He had watched her slowly lose her mind, cry for her mother and father and tremble like a little child when the aliens were fighting in this area and their explosions shook the earth. Deborah had stopped eating and dwindled away, a victim of lost hope. He had tried to feed her, tried his best, but she lay in bed day after day and stared at the stained ceiling and the part of her that had known joy and freedom was already gone. And as he sat at her bedside and held her hand in the deepening twilight with the oil lamps lit, she had looked at him with her weary and watery eyes and asked one question in the voice of a child imploring her father: *Are we safe?*

He had not known what he was about to say, but he had to say something. Though before he could speak he heard the wave of them coming, the shriek of their approach, the thunder of their headlong rush against the walls of Panther Ridge, and he heard the first rifle shots and the chatter of machine guns, and when he looked at Deborah again she had left this earth because she could no longer bear what it had become.

At that moment John Douglas had faced a choice. It involved either the rifle or the pistol he owned. It involved what he intended to do in the next few minutes, as he stared at the dead woman who had been the love of his life and had raised for them two daughters and a son. It involved whether he had the strength to go out there and join the fight, or whether he needed in his heart and soul to follow Deborah to whatever Promised Land lay beyond life, because this one had become a blighted and corrupted nightmare.

The minutes had passed slowly, and not without its thorny seconds. But in the end he had left Deborah sleeping alone, and he had taken his rifle and pistol out to defend his fortress.

"That day," JayDee said quietly. "April the third. It was about ten in the morning. Oh, I remember the time exactly. It was eighteen minutes after ten. I was in my office, doing some paperwork. One of my nurses ran in, said for me to come look at the TV out in the waiting room. CNN, Fox, MSNBC, all the local channels were covering it. Huge explosions in the skies across the world. What looked like fiery meteors blowing up, and out of them were coming…those Gorgon ships. Nobody was calling them 'Gorgon' yet, I mean. That was later. But they were coming out of the blasts…just gliding out, and then the fighter planes went up and they were shot to pieces, and that went on for…I don't remember how long."

"Two days," Dave offered. He flicked his Bic and lit a cigarette without asking permission, because nobody gave a damn anymore whether you smoked or not. "It was over in two days. I know you don't remember Nine-Eleven," he said, speaking to Ethan, "but this was…like…a thousand Nine-Elevens, one after another. The Gorgons finished off our Air Force and the Army and Navy, too." He blew smoke through his nostrils, like a furious dragon, though his eyes were blank and nearly dead. "It was the same all over the world. Nothing could hurt those ships. At least nothing *we* had. Nothing created on earth. The Gorgons hit some of the cities, but not all. New York was blasted, so was Atlanta and Dallas and Los Angeles…Moscow…Tokyo…Berlin…Beijing. A show of power, is what the big dogs at the Pentagon said. But the big dogs were suddenly not so big. Suddenly…nobody was very big." He focused once more on the boy through the drift of smoke. "You don't remember any of this?"

"No," said Ethan. If it had ever been there, it was all gone. And maybe, he thought, it was better that way.

"A cloaking device," said JayDee, "is what the scientists said got the Gorgons close enough to our atmosphere to enter without being detected. And by then they were calling them 'Gorgons', so that name stuck."

"Why that name?"

"Somebody at Fox News came up with it," Dave answered. "Supposed to be so terrible to look at you'd turn to stone. The idea was there…that the Gorgons must be so different from us…it would drive a person insane to see one. Anyway, once that name was out there, it was used in all the newscasts."

JayDee remembered images of the worldwide panic. People were running, but where would they run to? The President of the United States urged calm, and then he disappeared into a "secure location", as did every other elected official in Washington. Elsewhere around the world, the so-called leaders fled their positions and roles. All civil order broke down and all police forces were overwhelmed. The television networks and radio stations hung on as long as they could. Within forty-eight hours of the first Gorgon ship being documented as it slid from its fiery womb, amateur videos were taken of what appeared to be swirling black portals opening in the air, and from them emerged the huge, sleek bat-like shapes of what came to be known as the Cypher ships.

"An enigma," JayDee said, almost to himself. "The unknowable." He blinked, bringing himself back to the moment. "The Cyphers," he said to Ethan, "came from what looked like black holes opening in the sky. Then…those two forces went to war. Humans were puny. We're the bugs to be stepped on…or played with," he added. "But their battle is with each other. Soon after the Cyphers came, power grids around the world started failing. The cell towers went out. I suppose the communications satellites were destroyed. The Cyphers must've done that, to silence the chatter I guess. Or another display of power."

Ethan finished his meager cup of water and was still thirsty but satisfied at least that he'd gotten this much. He was trying to take everything in, and it was a lot to take. Dave smoked his cigarette in silence for a moment, and then he said, "I talked to somebody who heard one of the last radio broadcasts." He regarded the cigarette's glowing tip, and blew on it to make it flare. "Some scientists and military men were talking. Giving their ideas on what was happening. That these two civilizations—whatever they are—have been at war...like...forever. And maybe it's the Earth they're fighting over, and maybe not, because—"

"It's the border," said Ethan, who heard himself speak those words as if from a distance.

Dave and JayDee said nothing, but they both stared at Ethan with renewed interest.

"The border," Ethan repeated. "Between them. Their worlds, or their universe or dimension or wherever they come from. Earth is on the border, and that's what they're fighting over." He realized, almost startled, that he he had no doubt what he was saying was true. "They're going to keep fighting until one destroys the other. That may never happen, because..." He felt a sudden panic rise up inside him; he felt he was floating away from himself, into an area unknown. It took him a moment to draw a deep breath that hurt his lungs, and to calm himself. "They're in an—" He cast about for the right term. "An arms race," he said.

The silence went on, as the two men stared at the boy who had named himself after a high school.

It was JayDee who spoke first, in a tight and cautious voice. "Now... tell us...how would you *believe* all that, if you can't remember anything else? Did you hear that from someone? One of your parents?"

"No." Ethan felt hot and sweaty, uncomfortable in his own skin. His bones were aching like sore teeth. "I don't know who told me. I just..." He met the doctor's puzzled stare. His own blue eyes glinted with a nearly feverish intensity. "I just know that's the truth. We're on the border between them, and it's not the Earth they want. It's a line in space."

Dave and JayDee looked at each other, and Ethan read their unspoken question: *Are you believing what you're hearing?*

"I'm really tired," Ethan said. "Can I get some sleep somewhere?"

It took a few seconds for the spell of Ethan's comments to break. Dave cleared his throat and said, "Sure. There are plenty of empty apartments." He did not say that most of them had been occupied by people who had over time come to the end of their hope and killed themselves. A cemetery behind the third building held dozens of white-painted wooden crosses. Whole families had decided to let go of their lives, and who could blame them? There were two ministers—a male Presbyterian and a female Methodist—among the survivors at Panther Ridge, and they still led religious services and did what they could, but sometimes the voice of Christ could not be heard over the distant explosions and the shrieking of the nightime army.

Which Dave decided Ethan didn't need to hear about right now. They didn't come every night, but if they came tonight...the boy would find out soon enough.

"Come on, then." Dave kept the stub of his cigarette between his teeth as he stood up. "Let's get you settled in. Get you a bucket of sand to scrub some of that mud off, too." Water being too precious a commodity to waste on washing. He would not yet tell Ethan any more about the things they had killed—exterminated would be the better word—in the Security Room, and what they had burned that at first had appeared to be human but was in reality nearly demonic.

His Uzi and its holster was never far away from him. He picked it up off the table and put it on, and he, JayDee, and the boy left the mess hall to find an apartment without human bloodstains somewhere on the walls, the floor or the furniture.

FOUR.

ETHAN.

He woke up. It seemed that someone had called him, in the name he had chosen for himself to give him some kind of identity. Not loudly, but quietly. Enough to make him lie on the bed in the apartment he'd been given, his eyes open, and listen to the dark.

It was not entirely dark in Apartment 246. Two candle lanterns burned low. The walls were a cheap brown plasterboard, the carpet the color of wheat. On one wall was a decoration of metal squares painted blue and silver. Someone's artistic touch, he thought. He sat up on the bed, his back against the pillows. He was hungry, thirsty, and edgy. He was wearing the dark green p.j. bottoms of somebody who was probably dead. His bones still ached, and his bruises felt heavy with gathered blood. He wanted to return to sleep, back to its peace and stillness, but he could not…because something was on his mind…something important…and he couldn't figure out what it was.

He felt like an empty hole, waiting to be filled. With what? Knowledge? Memory? There was nothing beyond his waking up, into running across that field in the rain. *Water*, he thought. *Thirsty*. But he understood that the last of the water was being rationed, and that the people here did not want to drink the rainwater because it brought with it chemicals or poisons. They were eating the horses; the horses ate grass, and the grass was watered by the rain. So they were getting chemicals in the rain anyway. He guessed that even boiling the rainwater over a fire wasn't enough for them to fully trust it. So the bottled water was going down and down, and when it was gone they would have to drink the rain no matter what.

Ethan understood why they feared being caught in one of the battles between the Gorgons and Cyphers, but what else was it they feared that made them cower here behind the stone walls?

He had no idea how long he'd slept. JayDee had brought him the p.j.s and some other clothes, two pairs of jeans with patched knees and a couple of t-shirts, one gray and the other purple with the clenched fist logo of the band Black Destroyer, which Ethan had never heard... or never remembered hearing. He'd scrubbed the mud off himself in the yellow-tiled bathroom with a bucket of sand. He had looked at his injuries in the mirror, by the candle's light. His chest was black, from shoulder to shoulder. And turning around, he could angle his head and see in the mirror the mass of black bruises on his back. They looked soul-deep. He thought that maybe it was best he had no memory of what had caused them, because it seemed to him he'd been through a world of pain.

Thirsty, he thought. But there was no water in the empty taps of either kitchen or bathroom and the toilet was a dry hole. Dave had told him he was supposed to do his business in the same bucket of sand he'd been given. To get any water, he'd have to go to the mess hall where the rations were given out, and that place—Dave had told him—was locked up tight and guarded by men with guns after the nighttime meal, such as it was.

Ethan found himself staring at the blue and silver squares on the wall opposite his bed.

He could imagine them melting, and becoming streams of clear, fresh and pure water that ran down the wall and puddled on the floor.

As he stared at them, the blue and silver squares seemed to shimmer and merge into a glistening pool.

The swimming pool, he thought. *Something...about the swimming pool.*

But he didn't know what. The swimming pool was mostly empty, except for some debris that looked like broken lawn furniture and a few inches of murky rainwater in the deep end.

Still…he had a strong sensation that he should get up from this bed and go to the swimming pool, and there he might understand what was drawing him. He got up, pulled on the Black Destroyer t-shirt and his Pumas, and he went out of the apartment onto an exterior corridor that led to a concrete stairway. Halfway down the stairs he saw on the horizon blue flickers of what might have been lightning but might also have been the never-ending battle. He continued down to the parking lot and walked along the curving roadway in the direction of the pool.

Quiet had fallen upon Panther Ridge. It was a warm and humid night, with the threat of more rain coming. Through the windows of some of the apartments he saw the comforting sight of little flames of oil and candle lamps, and he knew he was not the only one awake. He saw lights up on the watchtowers too; the towers were likely manned around the clock, the watchers at their machine guns. He came upon a group of six people sitting in the parking lot, with a few oil lamps at the center of their circle. They were holding hands and praying, their heads bowed. He went on. He passed a man with shoulder-length hair and no shirt or shoes, just wearing a pair of jeans, sitting on the pavement with his knees pulled up to his chin. "They might be comin' tonight," he said to Ethan. "But they ain't gonna eat *me*. No, they ain't." And so saying, he lifted the automatic pistol that lay at his side, and he put its barrel to his temple.

Ethan saw the man grin. There was madness in it, and Ethan went on.

He came in another moment to the swimming pool, which was surrounded by what had once been a decorative iron fence and gate. Most of it had been knocked down, all of it rusted by the corrosive rain. The gate was open, hanging by a hinge. Ethan thought that many of the people here were also hanging by a hinge. He went to the side of the pool and looked down into it, and saw only what he'd briefly seen when he'd passed by here before: what looked like broken pieces of wooden chairs and maybe some other junk in a few inches of water in the deep end— 5 FEET, NO DIVING, the pockmarked sign read—otherwise nothing else.

45

Nothing here, he thought.

But still…

…*something.*

He had the image of the blue and silver squares in his mind, as they merged and glistened and became clear water.

Ethan walked down the steps into the pool's shallow end. The blue paint covering the bottom had gone dark and scabby and was coming up in wrinkled sheets. Exposed beneath it was gray concrete. He walked in a straight line at the center of the pool, down the slight decline into the deep end. His shoes found about four inches of dirty rainwater around the drain.

What was here? he asked himself.

Nothing, was the answer.

His motion in the water caused the debris to float away from him. He sloshed in a circle around the drain, because it seemed to him the thing to do. *Was there something here after all?* he wondered. *A deep, secret movement…like the flowing together of the blue and silver squares upon the wall?* He stood for awhile in the deep end, his senses questing for something he wasn't sure of, and then he walked back up to the shallow end along the middle of the pool. He had the distinct feeling that something hidden was very near, and yet…

"What in the name of Jack Shit are you doing out here?" a hard voice suddenly asked.

Ethan looked to his right, where the figure of Dave McKane stood with his Uzi at his side, pointed somewhere just east of the boy. "I heard your door open and close," Dave said. "My place is next to yours. What are you doing? Getting water?"

"No, sir." Ethan saw that Dave might not have done much sleeping tonight, because he was still dressed in what he'd been wearing today and he had his baseball cap on. "I just came out walking."

"That's a bag of bull's balls."

Ethan decided the truth was best. The truth, at least, as he understood it. "I felt like I needed to come here."

"Yeah? Midnight swimming?"

"No, sir. I just needed to come here, that's all."

"What? To get a drink?"

Ethan shook his head. "I'm thirsty, but Olivia said not to trust the rainwater. That's why you only drink the bottled water." He thought of the prison room, and the inspection he'd endured. What John Douglas had said: *We're checking to see whether you're fully human or not.* Ethan knew, but he wanted to hear it. "You think the rainwater's poison, don't you? Because of all the alien stuff up there?" He tilted his chin toward the lightning-shot sky. "What does it do to people? Turn them into things you have to kill?"

"We don't know that yet," Dave said. "We don't know why some *things* come in here looking like humans. Maybe they were humans once, and they're being engineered by *them*." He made a motion toward the horizon's flickering lightning. "Playing with the human toys, maybe. There's just a hell of a lot we don't know."

"But that's not *all*, is it?"

"No," Dave said. "Not all."

"Tell me."

"First get out of there." Dave aimed his Uzi at the ground and retreated a few paces as Ethan came up the pool's steps.

"What else?" Ethan prompted.

Dave said, "The Gray Men come at night."

"The Gray Men," Ethan repeated. He didn't like the sound of that, not from Dave's mouth or from his own. And then he had to ask: "What are they?"

"Mutated humans." Dave pulled no punches and he wasn't about to start now. "Some of them are…way mutated…into things that don't look human anymore. We don't know what causes it. Maybe it's something in the atmosphere, in the rain, maybe it's a disease *they* brought. The Gray Men come at night. Not every night, but when they *do* try to get in here…it's bad. We think—JayDee thinks—their skin can't take sunlight anymore. Or something that keeps them hidden during the day. Like I say, we don't know for sure and we haven't met anybody who does."

Ethan had a jumble of questions in his mind, all trying to be first. He started with, "Why are they called Gray Men?"

"Because they *are* gray. Or near enough. They've lost all their flesh color. I don't know who first called them that, but it suits 'em. They started coming about three months ago. Only a few at first...then more and more. *I* think they have some kind of radar or sense or whatever that draws them together...maybe they can *smell* each other." Dave offered a thin, pained smile. "We don't have much ammo left. Glad you joined our happy group?"

"Better than being out *there*."

"Uh-huh. Well, the Gray Men try to get at us because they're meat eaters. They drag their dead away, so we figure they eat the corpses. That keeps them satisfied for awhile."

Ethan nodded. "But I'm not gray and I'm not mutated. So why did you take me to that room where you've killed *things*?"

"We took you to the Secure Room because we've had...let's call them *intruders*. They're creatures who look like humans, and maybe they used to be or they still think they are...but now they're another kind of lifeform. JayDee's opinion—and Olivia's too—is that they're humans who've been picked up by the aliens and experimented on. Then they're let loose. Like alien time-bombs, I guess. Let's just say we've had some real interesting reactions to the saline. We had another doctor here. He killed himself and his wife and son last December, but it was his idea to get something in the bloodstream to test all new arrivals. Thank God he came up with that, or we would've let some real horrors in here without knowing it until too late."

"The rain," Ethan said. "You think that's what makes the Gray Men? If that's so, hasn't anybody here ever started changing?"

"Yes, they have. It starts out as gray, ashy-looking blotches. The blotches get bigger, fast...and then the bones start changing. We kept the first victim under watch while it happened. We had to chain her up, which was cruel as hell but we had to." Dave stared darkly at the boy before he went on. "After a couple of days, when she was twisted and deformed, she started growing a second head that was all mouth and little needle teeth. That's when her father stepped in and shot her. She was twelve years old."

"*Oh*," said Ethan, or thought he did.

"We had four others. They had to be taken care of before it got too bad. There *has* to be poison in the atmosphere," Dave said. "Sometimes the rain falls dirty brown or piss yellow, but we're not sure that causes the mutations. Nobody's sure of anything. But yeah…that's why we're depending on the bottled water. We shelter the horses but we know they're getting exposed to the rain, and we're eating the horses, and the rain's eating through the roofs and walls and leaking in…so there's no way to avoid it. The doc thinks it takes time for the effects to show up, and maybe it depends on a person's chemistry too. Like any virus, or cancer. Some get it, some don't." Dave shrugged. "What are you gonna do?" He answered his own question: "Die, eventually. It's just…how long you want to wait."

"Why have *you* waited?" Ethan glanced pointedly at the submachine gun.

Dave held the Uzi up before his face and examined it as if it were a piece of deadly art. Then he let it fall back to his side. "Good question," he allowed. "I've known a lot of people in here who decided not to wait. Decided that between the Gorgons, the Cyphers, the Gray Men and plain old hopelessness, it was best to pass on through the gates." He paused for a moment, pondering an answer. "I guess," he said at last, "I'm not ready yet. But tomorrow, I might be. Just depends on the—"

Weather, he was about to say, but he was interrupted by a red flare suddenly shooting skyward from the watchtower at the western corner of the wall.

It was followed within seconds by the wail of a crank-driven siren from somewhere else in the complex. Dave said, "Lucky you. They're coming tonight," in a voice both hollow and haunted.

As Dave started running toward the wall and others with pistols and rifles began to emerge from their dwellings wearing whatever had come quickly to hand, Ethan heard the sounds of the Gray Men.

It was distant at first, a strange murmur of discordant music, steadily growing louder. Ethan had already seen that wooden walkways had been built along the top of the wall a few feet below the coils of barbed wire, and now the defenders of Panther Ridge were using ladders to climb up. A second red flare shot from the southernmost watchtower, which Ethan figured meant the Gray Men were attacking from two directions. He had to see for himself, so he started running away from the pool, down the road and to the wall's nearest ladder. Just as he reached it, a tall and slender older woman with a crown of short-cut gray hair got in his way to climb up first. She paused to look him in the face. Olivia Quintero had a rifle under her arm and a holstered revolver around the waist of her jeans. She had pulled on a yellow western-style blouse with blue cornflowers stitched across the shoulders.

"Get away from here." Her dark brown eyes were nearly ebony. *"Move!"* She climbed up without waiting to see if he obeyed or not. Ethan let a man with another rifle go up next. Then he climbed up to the walkway himself, because he had to see.

The shrieking hit him like an oncoming wave. The rock wall was as high as his upper chest. As he stared out through the barbed-wire coils, he saw that the earth itself seemed to be in motion. Were there a hundred of them? More than that? They were scrabbling up the hillside toward the wall. A white star shell flare was fired from the southernmost watchtower. As it sizzled and drifted down Ethan saw that some of the attackers wore the rags of clothing but many were naked, and their nakedness revealed ashy gray flesh that drooped in gobbets off the bones like the dissolving of a nasty jelly, or ashy gray flesh that looked to be covered with scales, or ashy gray flesh that rippled with what looked to be spines or bony plate armor. The full impact of horror hit Ethan like a blow to the belly. Here were sinewy creatures with flattened skulls and hunched backs, like human battering rams. There were things that ran on legs as thick as tree trunks, things that hobbled on jellying limbs and things that crawled as decaying crablike torsos under the legs of the others.

From the front of the unhuman wave came leaping creatures with armored backs and clawed hooks for hands. They grappled the wall and began to scramble up toward the barbed wire. Frozen with shock, Ethan saw one of the climbers look up and grin in a gray, slit-eyed face with a nose that had collapsed inward and thin lips parted from teeth like little sawblades. Then the face exploded with one of the first machine-gun bursts and the body hung twitching a few feet below the barbed wire with its hooks driven into the mortar between the rocks.

The other rifles, pistols, and machine guns opened up. Though the bodies of the Gray Men were torn by the hail of bullets, the creatures continued onward in their crashing wave against the walls of the fortress of Panther Ridge. Something hit the metal-covered door with a force that made the walkway under Ethan's feet tremble. Dust flew from between the stones. Shots were directed at whatever was down there, and that monstrous strength hit the door again but with less power and then more shots seemed to finish it off.

Before Ethan in the white flarelight was a sea of malformed, grotesque creatures that used to be human beings. He saw men, women, and children turned to hissing and shrieking monsters by either an alien disease or poison in the rainwater. He saw hump-backed shapes with greedy eyes and skeletal figures with gray, paper-thin flesh that looked like…

The Visible Man.

He remembered.

Building his model of the Visible Man, with its clear plastic skin that displayed all the internal organs, veins, and arteries of a human being. Got it from…where? Wal-Mart? No, Amazon. Sitting at his desk in his room…a house somewhere…under a green desklamp…the plastic organs lined up in the order he wanted to paint them…carefully because he wanted everything about the anatomy kit to be right…a school project… and a woman coming into the room…dark-haired…and saying—

"Get back!" shouted the woman at Ethan's side. He realized a scale-skinned, thin monstrosity with black, sunken eyes in one head and a grapefruit-sized growth of a second head with white sightless eyes on the stalk of its neck had climbed up to the wire and was reaching through the coils for his throat, and then Olivia Quintero pushed him aside and shot the thing in the temple of its larger head so that its brains flew out and the second head chattered and gnashed its sharp little baby teeth as the body slithered down and away.

She gave Ethan a look that would've cracked a mirror, and then she chambered another bullet and fired again into the mass of Gray Men bodies that were climbing relentlessly up the wall with their spiked fingers and toes. Some were getting to the wire and reaching through to grasp at whatever their claws could find before they were shot down. A gray-fleshed froglike figure with bulging eyes and the long ebony hair of a woman suddenly came leaping up and landed in the barbed wire to Ethan's left, crushing it down, and following it was a male creature with four arms—two normal-sized and two spindly things growing from its rib cage—that moved in a frenzy, tearing the wire from its frame. Ethan saw Dave McKane fire his Uzi right in the thing's face, but as soon as that bloodied creature fell away it was replaced by two others, one rail-thin and its ashy flesh covered with small, sharp spines, and the other a thick behemoth with a distorted skull like a hammerhead and a face that looked to be all gaping sharp-toothed mouth with eyes the size of black beads.

The hammerhead monster gave from its hideous mouth a roar that no longer had a sound anywhere near human. It pushed itself over the barbed wire onto the walkway. Only a few feet to Ethan's left, it grasped with spiked fingers the shoulders of a young man whose revolver went off into the monster's chest, but the gaping mouth was already tearing hunks of flesh from the young man's face. As the creature was shot by every weapon that could bear on it, its mouth expanded to engulf the man's entire head, and with a violent and sickening twist, it ripped the head from the body. Then the lead storm finally sent the beast falling back over the barbed wire and the headless body toppled the other way to the ground.

Other things were clambering up, faster and faster. They were tearing the wire loose from its framing, taking bullets and falling, and then more climbed up to take their places.

Guns were starting to click empty. Desperate hands searched for bullets in holsters, pockets and ammo boxes. Some of the defenders had brought axes, and now they were reduced to flailing and chopping. Ethan could feel the cold spread of panic. Creatures that resembled human beings only in the depth of tortured nightmares were tearing the wire down and coming over the top. Dave McKane's Uzi fired and fired and suddenly went silent as he frantically dug into his pockets for more clips. Olivia Quintero's rifle spoke, knocking a dark spidery shape off the wall. She paused to slap another ammo clip into her weapon and was almost seized by a slim creature with long white hair, jellied flesh, and the jagged-toothed grin of a shark. She hit the thing in the chest with the rifle's butt and followed that blow with a bullet to the forehead that sent it reeling off and downward, shrieking like the sound of fingernails across a chalkboard. The sweat of effort and fear glistened on Olivia's face. She drew her pistol, took aim, and began firing slowly and methodically into the shapes that were relentlessly climbing up.

Ethan saw.

There were too many. Tonight the Gray Men were going to defeat this last stand at Panther Ridge. The watchtower machine guns were still firing and so too were the rifles and the pistols along the walls, but Ethan knew that soon the bullets would be gone and all guns reduced to clubs. He saw dozens of the things climbing up the walls, and dozens more out there swarming forward—a malignant army of them—so that again the earth itself seemed in turbulent motion.

They needed to be thrown off the walls, he thought. They needed to be shaken off the hillside, devoured by the earth itself, and what power could do that?

It came to him, amid the shooting and the shrieking and the screams as one of the female defenders near him was attacked, that he should press his hands against the rocks of the wall before him, as if touching the earth itself beyond the wall. Of shaping the earth, or molding it. Of commanding the earth and demanding from it, and seeing in his mind the vision of what he wanted to happen.

It was a sharp, clear inner voice that told him to do this, that it was the right thing, just as walking down into the swimming pool had been the right thing. *Just touch the rocks*, this voice—his own voice, but a stronger and surer voice—said; *just touch the rocks, and see in your mind the power...*

...of an *earthquake.*

I'm just a boy! he thought. *I can't! I can't do that!*

But even as he thought this, Ethan knew the Gray Men were coming over the wall and more were climbing up and the bullets were running out and time was short because in just a little while they would all be dead.

Earthquake, he thought.

You can, said the voice. His own, but different. An older voice, maybe. One that knew things he did not, and maybe he was afraid to know. Because the fact was, he was scared almost to immobility. Paralyzed, waiting for the end.

You can, said the voice. *Obey. And try. Do it* now, *before the time is gone.*

He had no idea how to do this, but he realized something was expected of him. And yes, it seemed crazy to him, but he had to try. He placed his palms against the stones. He looked out upon the seething mass. He drew a long deep breath into his still-sore lungs, and when he exhaled, he saw vividly in his mind the hillside moving like the skin of a snake, and he fixed firmly upon that, and a second went by and another and another and nothing happened but the clicking of the guns going empty and the shrieks of the Gray Men climbing up and the sound of axes hitting deformed flesh...nothing...nothing at all. And when he was about to take his hands away from the stones and prepare for his own death maybe he felt a startling heat suddenly rise up from his deepest part and seem to scorch his flesh from the inside, or maybe it was like a surge of electricity that burned his ears and crackled in his hair, or maybe it was like none of these things but a sense of firm belief that he could do this, if he wanted to save himself and the others, and just that fast in the midst of this tumult and violence Ethan felt some part of him—some mystery part he did not understand—gather ferocious strength. He felt it leave his body like a whirlwind and and cast its will upon the earth.

The earth groaned like the awakening of an old man from a long and troubled slumber. And then the old man stretched and tossed, and in that instant the entire hilltop shifted.

It was not a gentle shifting. Cracks shot across the roadway and glass shattered in apartment windows behind Ethan. The Panther Ridge

Apartment buildings made noises of wood splintering and balconies popping loose from their supports. But the walls shook off a few of the climbers and blew rock dust and fragments into the deformed faces of those below. Many of the defenders fell to their knees and some fell off the walkway, and Ethan also went to his knees but staggered up, still with his hands pressed against the stones. He had the sense of being part of the earth himself, of directing its throes through the earth element of rock, but otherwise his heart was pounding like crazy and he had already bitten blood from his lower lip. One of the watchtowers crashed over, its machine-gunner leaping out to safety. The hilltop shook again, more violently still, and more of the Gray Men lost their grips on the wall. The Gray Men fell down, monstrosity tangled up with monstrosity. The third tremor was the most violent. Dozens of rocks in the walls broke apart with the noise of small explosions. More glass blew from the apartment windows. The whole of Panther Ridge shifted, with the noise of ancient mountain stones shattering to pieces. Fissures cracked open and snaked down the hillside. Some of the Gray Men staggered and stepped into them as the fissures widened two or three feet. Many were still caught within when the fissures closed again, rock grinding against malformed flesh and crushing the alien-infected bones. Clawed hands reached up from their new graves and grasped at the air until they were still.

This assault by the earth, which continued with more minor quakes, was enough to show that the Gray Men for the most part retained their survival instincts. They turned and fled down the hillside, many dragging dead bodies with them for later feasting. They had come shrieking but they departed silently, as if in shame. Some looked back over their spiny shoulders, and their message was nearly the same as the graffiti declaration written on the wall of the Panther Ridge Apartments: *Tomorrow Is Another Night.*

Then they were just a mass of misshapen figures running and hobbling and shambling across the nightscape down at the bottom of the hill, and in another moment they were gone from sight.

The quakes had ended.

Ethan had taken his hands away from the stones. His task—however incredible it had been—was done. His palms and fingers felt burning hot. He had broken out in a cold sweat and was breathing hard, he was scared to death, he was dazed and disoriented but he had felt the awesome power that had emerged slide back into its hiding place deep within himself and become still and silent. And whatever he had been for the last few moments, he was once again only the boy who had wanted to build a very cool Visible Man.

FIVE.

"SEVEN DEAD, TWELVE WOUNDED," SAID JOHN DOUGLAS IN THE yellow lamplight. "Got six people with broken bones. Jane Petersen is not going to survive her wounds. And I think we should move Mitch Vandervere's body as soon as possible, don't you?"

"Yes," said Olivia, her eyes weary and dark-circled. She was sitting at the desk in her apartment, with the damning yellow legal pads before her and a few ballpoint pens in a black leather holder. She had taken from a bottom drawer of her desk something that Vincent had given her as a joke on her fiftieth birthday four years ago: the Magic Eight Ball with its black ink inside and its floating icosahedron. She had set it before her on the desk, just as an element of the past. An element that had survived many terrors and tumults up until now. An element of Vincent, and their life together that now seemed like a magical fantasy, a time of joy that was very hard to remember. Yet the Magic Eight Ball brought some of it back. A little bit. *La parte más pequeña.* She made no decisions using it, but sometimes...sometimes...she thought she might, because it could be Vincent trying to speak to her, to guide and comfort her, through the black ink of the unknown.

"I liked Jane very much," she heard herself say, hollowly. "A very kind woman. Yes, we should move Mitch's body. Will you take care of that?" She was asking Dave McKane, who had sprawled himself out on the tattered brown sofa and was staring up at the cracked ceiling. The series of bizarre quakes had knocked the hell out of the old buildings. Some of the stairs had given way, part of the eastern wall had crumbled, just about every window was broken and was held together only by the duct tape, and some of the roofs had fallen in. Dave had already seen the dozens of cracks in the walls of his own apartment. He figured it was only a matter of time before the damned place collapsed. The floor of his bedroom had gone so crooked it was like walking across the deck of a ship at sea pitched at a dangerous angle by a rogue wave.

"I'll get to it," he said listlessly.

JayDee had splotches and streaks of other people's blood on his shirt and his khaki trousers. The hospital—two apartments with the wall removed between them—was in the lower building and was being staffed by two nurses, one who had worked for a veterinarian in Fort Collins and one who had been a dental assistant when she was a young woman in Boise, Idaho, about thirty years ago. The make-do medical resources consisted of Band-Aids in various sizes, bottles of aspirin and sedatives, antiseptic, some plaster bandages to make casts, some wooden splints, a few surgical instruments such as probes and forceps and some dental tools, and a few bottles of pain-killers like Demerol and Vicodin.

"We need to do another bullet count," Olivia said. She was trying very hard to keep her voice strong and steady. There were three other people in the room beside Dave and JayDee, all of whom shared some measure of responsibility for keeping track of supplies and the ammo. "Find out what everybody's got left."

"I've got five clips," Dave answered. "Thirty-two bullets each. After that, I'm done." He sat up on the sofa and took his baseball cap off. His face was deeply lined and his eyes dazed. "We can't take another one like that. There are too many now. If those quakes hadn't happened...they would've gotten in. No way we could've turned 'em back."

"The quakes," said Carmen Niega, a thin Hispanic woman who'd been a tax attorney in Denver. She had lived here a little less than four months, arriving with a half-dozen other wanderers. "Has anything like that ever happened before?"

"Never," Olivia said. She looked toward the door, which hung open because it was now impossible to close in the crooked frame. Ethan Gaines was standing on the threshold, peering in. Behind him, the first dank yellow light of dawn had begun to filter through the thick soup of clouds. "You all right?" she asked him.

He nodded, his face wan and rock dust whitening his hair and clothes.

"Told you to get away from there," she said. She glanced at the doctor. "John, I think he's in shock. Would you—"

"No, I'm not," Ethan replied before JayDee could speak. He came into the room, stumbling a little bit because he realized he probably *was* in shock. "I wanted to tell you. Tell all of you." He paused, trying to figure out exactly what it was he wanted to say.

"Tell us *what*?" Dave prompted, the harshness back in his voice because he was dead tired, and he had to go put together a detail to bury people including the headless body of a pretty good guy who used to remember a few jokes and play poker with him and some of the others.

Ethan said, "I think...I caused the earthquakes." He frowned. "I *know* I caused them."

There was a moment's silence. Then JayDee said quietly, "Ethan, let's go to the hospital where you can lie down and rest, and I can give you some water and a seda—"

"I said...I *caused* the quakes," Ethan repeated.

"Sure you did." Dave put his cap back on and ran a hand across his bearded chin. "Oh yeah, you did a great job. Ran the Gray Men off, yeah. Also almost destroyed our complex here, but...hey...I don't mind sleeping in a room that's about to fall in. If my ceiling doesn't collapse first. What's wrong with you, kid? You lost your marbles along with your memory?"

"Stop it, Dave," Olivia cautioned. She stood up. "Ethan, I want you to go with the doctor. Will you—"

"No, I won't go." Ethan came forward into the room with such a deliberate stride and such a determined expression that Carmen Niega, Russ Whitcomb and Joel Shuster backed away to give him room. He passed JayDee and walked up to the edge of Olivia's desk. In the lamp-light his eyes were bright blue and nearly frightening to Olivia in their fierce intensity. "I'm telling you. I knew to touch the rocks in the wall and...I don't know, exactly...but...I saw what would happen, in my head. It was like I was making a command, and the earth did what I wanted. What I saw. Only...it was stronger than I thought it would be. Does that make any sense?"

"No, Ethan...it doesn't. It just happened, that's all. Why it happened at that moment, I don't know. We were very lucky. But *you* didn't cause the quakes. Now, I really do want you to go to the hospital. I want you to be quiet and rest down there, if you can."

JayDee gave a grunt. It was going to be hard to rest, with all those injured people in there needing attention. Still, he could give the boy a swallow of the precious bottled water and two sleeping pills and that would take care of him for about twelve hours.

"Hey...listen!" Kitt Falkenberg had come to the door. She was about thirty years of age, had dirty blonde hair and a tall, lean physique and had been a star volleyball outside hitter at the University of Colorado. In her voice was the high, breathless strain of both excitement and tension. "I heard it from Tommy Cordell and then I saw it myself! The swimming pool! The quakes cracked it right down the middle. Only...it's filling up!"

"*What?*" Dave roused himself to his feet.

"The pool," Kitt repeated, her green eyes nearly luminous in her dirt-smudged face. "Water's flooding in...coming up through the crack! Come on, you've gotta see it!"

It took them a few minutes to get out of the crooked apartment and down the hill. Olivia was first. JayDee walked at the back of the group alongside Ethan. About forty people had already gathered around the pool. In the yellow light of oncoming dawn Olivia pushed through the throng, with Dave behind her. They saw what Kitt had already seen: the pool had a jagged crack right along its center, from the drain to the shallow end, and water was streaming up from below. A man—Dave and Olivia recognized him as Paul Edson, who in his previous life had been a musician in a jazz band and played a very mean saxophone—was standing in the shallow end, and was leaning over to touch the water as it gurgled up.

"It's *cold*," Paul said. He cupped a handful and tasted it. "My God!" he said. "I think it's spring water!"

Others entered the pool to also touch and taste the water. Olivia descended the steps and cupped a handful, then put it to her mouth. Her eyes found Dave. She said, nearly as breathlessly as Kitt had spoken, "We've been living here with a spring under the swimming pool. All this time. Clean water." She brought herself back to her leadership role, and she pulled herself up straight and took on the mask again. "Everyone, get bottles or buckets or whatever you can find and fill them! Come on, hurry! Tell everyone else you see to get over here!" She didn't have to tell anyone twice, and from the strength of the water rising from its underground channel there was really no need to hurry, except to beat the next contaminated rainfall. She thought they needed some kind of covering for the pool, something to keep the rain out, and she looked to Dave again to tell him that but Dave had retreated from the pool's edge.

He was standing a few feet to Ethan's right, staring at the boy. It had occurred to Dave that Ethan had said *I felt like I needed to come here* after Dave had seen him walking the length of the pool. Dave had realized that the crack had followed Ethan's trail; the pool had broken open directly where the boy had been walking.

Ethan watched, his eyes heavy-lidded, as the water continued to stream in. He felt very tired, drifting toward sleep. Is this what shock feels like? he wondered. He watched the other people moving quickly to go get their bottles and buckets, and then he was aware of Dave McKane standing at his side, staring fixedly at him as if he had never really seen the boy before.

"What is it?" Ethan asked.

"I'm just looking," Dave answered.

"At what?"

"I don't know yet," said Dave, and it was the truth. He turned away to get to his misshapen apartment and find whatever bottles he could.

There was still the task of burying Mitch to take care of, as well as burying the other dead.

John Douglas decided it was time to guide the obviously dazed boy to the hospital and get him sedated and resting, and then with the help of his nurses tend to the broken bones and other wounds. It was going to be a rough morning…but then again, they all were.

Olivia came out of the pool and asked a couple of the men to devise some kind of canopy that might deflect the rain, but even as she proposed this idea she thought of the dwindling supply of food and ammunition, the damaged walls and the growing hoardes of Gray Men. Panther Ridge could not hold out much longer, even with an unlimited supply of clean water. She looked up at the dull yellow clouds of dawn. Somewhere out there, and all around what remained of the world, the Cyphers and Gorgons were still fighting. Maybe it would be an endless war, she thought; at least it would be a war that she and likely none of the defenders of Panther Ridge would ever see ended.

"All right," she said to herself. There was so much to do, so much to take care of. She could not break, on this misty yellow morning. The pool was yielding a bounty of fresh water. That was kind of a miracle, wasn't it? Just a little pond of hope, growing deeper by the moment.

"All right," Olivia repeated, because it sounded good and strong. And then she turned away from the pool and went off to find her own bottles with which to collect a little of a liquid miracle.

The dead were buried by a detail of men, among them Dave McKane, who thought they were used to such a task but they never were. Dave worked hard and steadily and spoke to none of the others, and when the new graves were filled he lit a cigarette and walked over to the pool to smoke in silence and watch the water gush forth. He liked the noise it made, like the sound of a stream moving through a quiet forest. He had six cigarettes left and he was down to his last Bic lighter. *Nasty habit anyway*, he thought; *ought to give it up someday*. A low peal of thunder echoed off in the clouds above. Either that, or one side had just scored a hit on the other.

At the hospital, Ethan slept in a darkened room with the aid of two zaleplon capsules. In another room, John Douglas and the two nurses worked on the injured. The morning moved on. The fallen watchtower was being rebuilt, and the eastern wall repaired, and workers began to fill in damaged places in the other walls with more rocks and mortar. The sun remained a faint smear. Around noon a light rain began to fall, but by then a green canvas canopy had been put up on a wooden frame over the pool, which continued to be filled by the underground spring.

In his apartment, Dave McKane had looked up at the pipes and dead wires that hung from the cracked ceiling over his bed and he had crossed the crooked floor to the closet and gotten out his sleeping bag. He had taken off his shoes and baseball cap, unrolled the sleeping bag onto his gray sofa and pushed himself into it. One hour after trying to get some sleep, he was still awake and thinking.

He had been born into a hardscrabble farmer's life by no-nonsense parents who believed in God, the Devil, and the pride of a job well done. He'd worked for years in the family's corn and soybean fields. When the Gorgons had appeared just after ten o'clock on the morning of April third, he'd called his mom and pop at the farm outside Cedar Rapids, Iowa, to tell them he, Cheryl, and the boys would be there in a couple of days, that everything was going to be all right and it was not the end of the world and it was crazy, sure, and scary as hell but the military was going to take care of business.

Then CNN had shown the jets bursting into flames and falling like dead leaves, and the missiles exploding as they hit some kind of force field that protected the crafts, and the President in the Oval Office telling everyone to remain calm before he and all the rest of the government officials vanished. Around the world, panicked mobs searched for leadership and found that no one was there. Police and military forces disbanded to protect and shelter their own families and find a way to survive. Then the Cypher ships had arrived, and all cell phones, landlines, the Internet, televisions, radios, and electric power had gone dead.

Dave, Cheryl, and his two sons had never made it to Cedar Rapids. Nor to her parents' home south of Colorado Springs, and they had never found out what happened to them or to Cheryl's sister in San Francisco. It had been so fast it was still unreal. It was night, they were packing to leave the house in the glow of candles and the battery-powered lanterns, and Dave was carrying a couple of suitcases through the front room out to the camper parked on the other side of their pickup truck. In the next instant faceless, black-suited soldiers with weapons growing out of them were not only in the house, but were moving through the walls like shimmering ghosts. Cheryl was in the back room with Mike and Steven, and Dave had shouted for everyone to get to the camper *now*, and he dropped the suitcases and was reaching for his shotgun next to the open door when a blue flash licked at the windows. He remembered an ear-cracking blast and a sensation of first being kicked in the back by a heavy boot and then falling as if into a black pit...a great distance, falling, falling...falling, it seemed, from one world into another...and when he came to he was lying on the ground next to the scorched camper with his clothes smoking, the burning house and the pickup truck had collapsed into a crater and every tree in the woods all around had become a torch that burned with an eerie blue flame.

He had tried to get up, but his body was trembling, his nerves out of control, he couldn't make anything work. His nose was bleeding and blood was crawling from his eyesockets. He had grabbed fistfuls of dirt and dragged himself across the ground as best he could, screaming the names of his wife and sons. In the sky above his torment, things left glowing blue and red trails that some might have called beautiful as they zigzagged across the dark.

How long it was Dave stayed at the house, after the fire had died and he had crawled down into the crater and found the blackened bodies, he didn't know. It was a murky light, he was sitting amid the bodies in the smoking ruins trying to remember where the camper's keys were and how he could change the four melted tires when the Cypher soldiers moved through again, silent and ghostly, on some unknown mission to an unknown destination. A couple of them looked at him as they passed by the crater's edge, or rather their faceless, helmeted heads turned toward him and downward for the briefest of seconds. But he was nothing for them to contend with, in his burned rags with his blood-crusted nose and his bloody half-insane eyes and his mouth hanging open drooling threads of saliva.

He was nothing, on the scale of this war.

He remembered thinking that it was time to move. Time to go, if he was going. And he had looked at the very nice Bulova wristwatch Cheryl had given him on their tenth anniversary and seen that the crystal was gone and the hands were frozen at 9:27, and that had nearly killed the last part of his mind. But something must have kicked in to get him moving, because after that he remembered staggering along the highway in what must have been the dark of another night, with the smoke of burning trees, houses, and fields shrouding the earth. Headlights stabbed through the smoke as cars and vans with panicked people inside missed him by inches. He kept walking to his own unknown destination, and maybe he was shouting and raving about the end of the world because he thought in his ravaged mind, *yes it really is.*

His path had eventually brought him here to the fortress that the Panther Ridge Apartments had become, and though every day he prodded himself to take some supplies, saddle up a horse and go out on a journey to Cedar Rapids to see if his mother and father were still alive, the truth was he thought they were dead and any journey out there would be a torturous trip through an unbelievable Hell. He figured he wouldn't make it two nights out, with the Gray Men on their search for fresh meat. Either that, or he might be caught in some battle between the aliens, and he would die burned to black ashes as Cheryl, Mike, and Steven had died.

Did that mean he was at heart a coward? he had asked himself. That for all his bar fights and bad-assedness and bravado, he was inside a frightened little shadow of what he portrayed himself to be?

Because, really…he *was* afraid. He was terrified. His friends were here. He was useful in this place. It was where he knew he would die, eventually. And from the numbers of Gray Men that had stormed the fortress last night, death was only a matter of using up five Uzi clips. Then it would all be over for him. Would it be tonight? Tomorrow night? One night next week? Impossible to know, but soon. And when it was over for him, it would likely be over for everyone else here, because not for very long would even freak earthquakes banish hunger for human meat from the bellies of those monsters.

Dave lay in his sleeping bag on his sofa and wished he had the last bottle of Jim Beam he'd finished off about a month ago. He could not make himself sleep. He could not let go of two things.

Ethan, saying with fierce conviction *The earth did what I wanted*.

And the fact that where the boy had walked at the bottom of the swimming pool, a crack had opened up to give them clean water.

They didn't have to worry about rationing the bottled water anymore. Sure, there was plenty to worry about, but...not about water anymore.

The earth did what I wanted, he'd said.

And only Dave knew about Ethan walking the length of the pool, and when challenged the reply was *I felt like I needed to come here*.

A simple statement. But...there was something more to it. Much more. Dave had his own feelings, and abruptly he got out of his sleeping bag and put on his shoes and cap. He had seen black-helmeted soldiers glide through the walls of his house and seen monstrous things that used to be God-fearing, hard-working American citizens tearing at barbed wire for the taste of human meat and seen the glowing trails of alien battleships in the night sky, and he realized that things he had never dreamt could possibly be true *were* true, and forevermore nothing in this nightmare world could be considered impossible. Dave left his apartment and started down the hill toward the hospital, because he had some questions to ask a mysterious boy.

SIX.

EVEN IN THE STRONGHOLD OF SLEEP, ETHAN WAS NOT SAFE.

He was standing atop the wall again, watching the multitude of distorted, disfigured and decaying figures swarming forward up the hillside. Guns were firing all around him and cut many of them down, but just as many of the Gray Men caught hold of the rocks, hooking spiked toes and fingers into the cracks and climbing up with the speed and determination of rabid hunger. They began to climb over the barbed wire, some pressing the coils down with their bodies so more could get over, others tearing with maddened fury through the wire to get at the defenders beyond.

The walls were about to be conquered. Guns were running out of ammo and falling silent. Some of the defenders were caught between ripping claws and torn by saw-blade teeth, others jumped in panic from the platform to the ground and fled to find shelter. Ethan backed away from spiny figures crawling over the wire before him. He was balanced on the edge of the platform, and suddenly an ashen-colored hand darted through the coils and caught him by the throat. Ethan saw a slender thing that might have been half-human and half-serpent pushing itself over the wire, and he was pulled toward it with terrible strength. A yellow-eyed face blotched with warty gray scales and topped with a shock of black hair stared into Ethan's own face, and the thin-lipped mouth opened to show teeth already sharpened and broken by gnawing on human bones.

The mouth opened. The teeth glinted.

The creature spoke, in a rattling whisper.

"*Go,*" it said, "*to the white mansion.*" Then a bullet hit the side of its head and the black blood ran. The yellow eyes blinked, as if in indignant surprise. The hook-nailed hand released Ethan's throat and the creature fell back across the barbed wire leaving pieces of gray flesh hanging from the barbs.

"*Ethan? Ethan?*"

Someone was shaking his shoulder. He felt himself flinch, and realized in his darkness that he was coming out of a solid sleep. He opened his eyes to the glow of an oil lamp on the table next to him. Curtains had been drawn over the windows to filter the afternoon's hazy light. Rain was falling outside, thrashing at the broken glass which had been covered over with sheets of styrofoam. Water dripped from the ceiling at a half-dozen places. Ethan had no idea how long he'd been sleeping in this narrow bed in the small room that was part of the hospital. Someone had pulled a chair up next to his bed. Ethan saw a hard-lined face with a hawk's beak of a nose. Dave McKane had removed his baseball cap, his multiple cowlicks sticking up. The man smelled like a wet dog.

"JayDee let me in," Dave explained quietly. The door between this room and the other part of the hospital was closed, mostly. "Said you'd had enough rest, you oughta be okay."

Ethan sat up on the bed. His body still ached and his mind was a little foggy. Three words were echoing around in his brain: *the white mansion.* He nodded. "I'm okay. Better, I guess."

Dave grunted. He wore the pained expression of someone in desperate need of either a cigarette or a drink of whiskey, and the doctor had forbidden him to smoke in here and that last bottle of Beam was a golden memory. "I have to ask you some questions." His voice was not harsh, but rather imploring. He paused and studied the knuckles of his hands for a moment. Rainwater glistened on the baseball cap, which was hung on the back of his chair. The rain itself had felt oily and hot on Dave's skin as he'd walked from his apartment to the hospital, and he wondered how many alien poisons were in it.

"Go ahead," Ethan said, sensing the man's indecision of where to begin.

"Yeah," Dave answered. "Okay. You said you caused the quakes. How is that possible? I mean…you're a boy, right? A human? *Aren't* you?"

"You must think so. You didn't bring your machine gun."

"I'm going to *believe* you're human. Not something that *looks* human. Some experiment the Cyphers or the Gorgons made. But…*if* you caused the quakes, how did you do that?"

"I don't really know," Ethan said, and in his mind he thought *the white mansion*. He was trying to push that away, but it would not be pushed away, and stronger and stronger it was becoming. "I wanted it to happen. I put my hands on the wall. I wanted the earth to shake the Gray Men off. That's all I could think to do."

"You put your hands on the wall? And you just thought of what you wanted to happen, and it *did*?"

"Yes."

"Uh-huh. Okay, then. Move my hat off the back of the chair and put it on my head."

Ethan almost laughed, but the stony expression on Dave's face said it would be a bad idea. "That would be a trick, wouldn't it? I don't think I can do that."

"Why not? You caused a freakin' earthquake! Using your mind, is that what you're saying? And now you can't use your mind to move a little *hat*?"

"I had to want to do it…like…because it was the only way. I don't know how I did it. I just knew…right then…that minute…I had to try, because I didn't want to die. I didn't want anybody else to die. I had to do what I could…whatever I could. So…it just came out of me. I felt it. Then when it was over I felt it go back into me, and it went to sleep."

"What did you feel? What came out of you and then went back in?" There was a note of sarcasm in the man's voice.

"I guess…power. That's all I can say."

"*Power.*" Now the sarcasm dripped. "Yeah, right. A fifteen-year-old boy with the power to make an earthquake happen, but he can't move a hat a couple of feet. Can you levitate yourself off the bed? See the future? Can you tell me how all this hell comes to a happy ending?"

"No," Ethan said, his face shadowed in the lamplight. "No. And no, I can't."

Dave ran a hand across his forehead. He listened to the rain hammering down outside. He stared intensely into the boy's eyes. "Did you know about the spring under the pool?"

"No."

"Then what were you doing? Why were you walking around in there?"

"I thought it was where I ought to be."

"Something told you that? Something *spoke* to you? Is that it?"

Ethan shrugged. "I don't—"

"Why *don't* you know?" Dave had almost shouted it, but he was holding himself back with a massive effort. "Or better yet...what the hell *do* you know? Not your real name, where you came from, or where your folks are. You just 'woke up' and you were running, isn't that what you said? And suddenly you can make an earthquake, and a swimming pool cracks open right where you've been walking and clean water flows out? Because you thought it was where you *ought* to be?" Dave grinned crazily, with fury and frustration behind it. "Christ!" he said. "Okay, you found us some water! How about more food? More bullets, too. That's what we need, because we're not going to be able to hold off another attack. So conjure us up some more ammo, Ethan! Can you do that for us? If you can't...we're done for. Got it?"

Ethan frowned. He knew the seriousness of what Dave was saying, but something else was working at him and it was relentless. "The white mansion," he said. "Have you ever heard of it?"

"*What*? Do you mean the White House? In Washington? What's that got to do with—"

"The white mansion," Ethan repeated. "Not the White House. I think it might be a real place, and I think I need to go there."

"Really? Well, I think I need to go to the freakin' *moon*. Are you crazy, kid? Is that it? You're out of your mind?"

Ethan stared into the glow of the oil lamp. Who was he, really? Where had he come from? He didn't know the answers to those questions, but he knew some truths and he decided to speak them. "I think I *have* to go there. I think something wants me to go. It's important, but I don't know why. This place...the apartments...it's no good. No one can stay here. The next time they attack...it's going to be all over for those who stay. But I believe the white mansion is a real place...and I think...I *believe*...something is telling me to go there." He looked steadily into Dave's eyes. "That name came to me in a dream. I keep thinking about it. Can you find out for me if it's a real place, and where it is?"

"Oh, you're having revelations in dreams now? What's next? Water into wine? Make it whiskey, and I'm sold."

"I'd settle for lemonade," Ethan answered, his face solemn. "I'm telling you what you already know about Panther Ridge. *Sir*," he said, so as not to sound disrespectful. "Can you please help me find out about the white mansion? Ask if anybody else has ever heard of it, and where it might be?"

"Oh, sure! We'll check the Net, how about that?" Dave stood up. He put on his baseball cap, still damp with oily rain. He had no idea why he'd come here to ask the boy these questions, but there were no answers that suited him. Maybe he'd *wanted* there to be...something... some answer he could grasp and hold onto. Instead...the boy had to be crazy, and that was that.

Ethan got out of bed and followed Dave from the room. In the hospital, a few people were sitting in chairs either waiting for treatment or being treated. As in Dave's apartment, pipes and wires dangled from the crooked ceiling. JayDee was busy applying a cast to the left arm of a weary-looking middle-aged man in a dirty white t-shirt and jeans, and the two nurses were tending to other patients.

"You okay to go?" JayDee asked Ethan as he worked on the man's cast, and Ethan nodded. Dave was almost to the door, which like the one in Olivia's apartment would not close in its damaged frame. "Be careful," JayDee told Ethan. "Raining pretty hard out—"

"Hey! Just a minute! You...*son!*"

The man with the injured arm had spoken. He was staring at Ethan. "*Wait.* I know you from somewhere. Don't I?"

Dave stopped just short of the door and looked back. Outside, the rain was slamming down.

Ethan didn't recognize the man, who had curly gray hair, brown eyes and the patch of a bandage across his bruised forehead. "I don't... think so." A little spark jumped in his heart. "Do you *know* me?"

"From somewhere. I came in a few days ago, with my wife. It seems like I've seen you before. Damn, that's hurting!" he protested to JayDee, and then he returned his attention to the boy. "I think I've seen you, but I can't remember from where. Wait a minute...wait a minute...you had on...different clothes. A shirt...a dark red shirt, with one sleeve torn off."

"That's right." Dave came back to stand nearer. "That's what he was wearing when he was brought in yesterday. So where'd you see him?"

The man started to speak and then seemed to stop himself. He wore an expression of dismay.

"Go ahead, tell us," JayDee urged, pausing in his wrapping of the plaster bandages.

"I remember," the man said. "We were with another group. In a strip mall. Maybe six or seven miles from here. The place was wrecked. We were trying to find a new place to hide, because our other place was torn up. *They* were fighting up over us...and we were trying to find somewhere to crawl into. Then..." He looked from Ethan to Dave and back again, and once more he seemed not to know what to say. "The aliens must've just gone through. We came to a place where there were bodies. People dead maybe a few hours...lying in the bricks where the walls had been blown apart. And...*you. You* were lying there, too. That's where I saw you. Only...you were dead. Like the others. Six people, all dead. Lying in those bricks, and that's where you were."

"Bullshit!" Dave snapped, with rising anger. "If it *was* him lying there, you can see he's not dead!"

"Yeah, but…he *was* dead. It looked like an explosion had thrown them around the room and blasted the walls out, but…his face…he looked like he was just sleeping, and Kay said for me to check him and make sure…because he was only a boy and we shouldn't leave him. So…I checked his heartbeat and his pulse, and there was nothing." His gaze found the floor. "I did check. I did. There was—"

"You were *wrong*," Dave interrupted. His face had reddened. "Damned wrong! Maybe his heart and pulse were slow, but…look at him! Does he look *dead* to you?" And then Dave caught JayDee staring at him, and Dave remembered he and the doc standing in the Secure Room looking at the ugly black bruises on Ethan's chest and back, and JayDee saying *I think he's suffered a very violent concussive event. An explosion of some kind. Might have been caught in a shockwave.* "Wrong," Dave repeated to the man with the broken arm, and then he turned away and walked out because questions led to questions and there were no answers and even in a madhouse world like this had become a dead boy did not rise from the dead. He kept walking, faster and faster, out into the driving rain that felt like small lead weights striking his skull, back and shoulders.

The white mansion, he thought as he strode up the hill. It was crazy. Made no sense. Nothing did anymore. *The white mansion, my ass*, he thought.

But he also thought how resolute the boy's voice had been, when Ethan had said *I think I have to go there.*

And more unsettling…*I believe something is telling me to go there.*

Dave looked back and saw Ethan following, a slim figure almost obscured by the rain. He started to pause and wait for the boy, but he kept going. He didn't know if he thought Ethan was crazy, or…

…something else?

Nobody could *make* an earthquake, Dave thought as he walked through the downpour. And that weirdness about the swimming pool, and the white mansion, and now the boy lying dead in the bricks of a destroyed strip mall, wearing the one-sleeved dark red shirt he'd had on yesterday.

But still…the boy, saying *I believe something is telling me to go there.*

Go where? And why? And how would anybody even figure out what the damned place was, and *where* it was?

Would be nice, Dave thought, *for this so-called voice that Ethan is hearing to tell him the whole story and not just bits and pieces.*

For all his toughness, for all his hardness and bitterness about what this world and his life—all their lives—had turned into, Dave McKane was suddenly overcome.

He felt himself stagger. He felt his knees buckle. He felt the hard rain beating on his back, driving him down. He had the crazed feeling that he was coming apart at the seams, himself becoming a Gray Man in this poisoned land, and once a certain threshold was crossed in that change he could never return to what he'd been.

Suddenly he was on his knees on the roadway, and he pressed his hands to his mouth to contain a cry for mercy, not just for himself but for all of them, all who had suffered and lost loved ones and become prisoners here waiting to die. He felt tears burning his eyes, but they were quickly washed away. He thought that if he let himself cry he would go over the edge, and all his pretend strength would fly away and be gone, baby, gone.

So he just knelt there in the pouring rain, and he hung on to whatever he had left.

"You need some help?"

Dave looked up. Ethan was standing over him. The boy offered a hand.

Dave wanted to believe in something. Anything, to get him to tomorrow. He asked himself if it was wrong to believe—at least in this moment—that Ethan Gaines *could* make the earth quake, that he *had* felt the movement of a spring beneath the pool's concrete and earth's rock, that he *had* been dead and brought back to life by some force unknown, and that he *was* being directed to go to a place called the white mansion?

Was it wrong, in this moment?

He didn't know, but at least in this moment with aliens battling across the world and nightmare creatures being spawned from their energies and poisons, he did believe. Just a little, just enough to get him to tomorrow.

But even so, he rejected the hand and stood up on his own.

He began walking again up the hillside to his crumbling apartment, more slowly now, with the labor of intense deliberation, and after a moment meant to give Dave McKane his space, the boy followed nearly in his footsteps.

SEVEN.

Near midnight, Dave spoke the words he'd been trying to get out for awhile but they hadn't come. They were ready now.

"What if there's a real place called the white mansion?"

"Surely there *is*," John Douglas answered. "A town somewhere. Or used to be a town. Could be in another country." He placed his tiles upon the Scrabble board to spell the word *oasis*, and then he took five more tiles followed by a long drink from his full cup of fresh water. "But just because Ethan heard it supposedly spoken to him in a dream…that doesn't mean very much. Does it?" He peered across the board at Dave. Two oil lamps and a candle lantern burned in the doctor's apartment, number 108, which had sustained shattered windows and a half-dozen fissures down the walls. The door had been reshaped with a handsaw to fit the warped frame. In any other cirmcumstance, the entire apartment complex would have been evacuated and yellow-taped off as a condemned property, but the beggars here could not be choosers.

Olivia Quintero studied the board on the scarred table between them. A rifle leaned against the chair at her side. The Gray Men had not come tonight, in the pouring rain. They might yet attack before dawn, but for now they were quiet. She needed to go to sleep, but Dave had asked her to join him and the doctor here, and it was at least a way to relax a little. The best she could do was add an E and a L to the word *bow*. She chose two more tiles, a T and a blank. "What do you think about the story?" Her question was directed to JayDee. "About Ethan lying dead?"

"I think the man was in a mental state and he missed the heartbeat and pulse."

"Maybe so. But after what you told me in my office…about the bruises. You were thinking the boy was caught in a shockwave and he ought to be dead. Isn't that right?"

"I didn't put it exactly like that."

"You didn't have to." She watched as Dave put an R in front of *oar*. "That was your meaning. As I recall, you were amazed he didn't at least have major internal injuries, and he could still walk." She leaned back in her chair, the better to judge the expressions of both men. "Dave, what are you thinking?"

Dave took his time. He watched JayDee add *with* before the word *draw*. Then he said, without looking at Olivia, "I'm not sure Ethan is what he seems to be. I don't know *what* the hell he is, but I'd say…if he really did cause those quakes…somehow…by using some force we don't—"

"Impossible!" scoffed the doctor.

"Is it?" Dave took a drink from his own cup of water. "Look, what do we know about anything anymore? What can we be *sure* of? All this the last two years…it defies everything humans ever believed in. And the Gray Men…mutating so fast. Who would have ever thought it was possible? And it wouldn't have been possible, without the aliens. Without whatever it is they've infected the world with. Okay…" He turned his chair to more directly face the doctor. "What *if*…Ethan is something different. Maybe an experiment the Cyphers or Gorgons made—"

"His blood didn't fry," JayDee reminded him.

"That's right, but still…something different. Something more advanced."

"Not human?" Olivia asked. "He looks like a boy, but he's not?"

"I don't know. I'm just trying to—"

"Talk yourself into believing Ethan Gaines has come to Panther Ridge to save us?" JayDee's white eyebrows went up. "To deliver the mighty earthquakes to keep the Gray Men from eating us alive? If that's so, even Ethan has to understand that one more tremor like that, and Panther Ridge is a pile of rubble."

"It's a pile of rubble already," Dave shot back. He took down another swallow of water and imagined it tasting like Beam, but it was plenty good enough as it was. "More than that. It's a graveyard."

Neither JayDee nor Olivia spoke. The doctor shifted uncomfortably in his chair, and Olivia regarded her little rack of letter tiles as if she actually was concentrating on the game and not just trying to avoid thinking too much about the onrushing future.

"We're all going to die here," Dave went on. "We can't hold out. That's what's impossible." He fired a quick dark glance at JayDee. "I've been asking around, if anybody has ever heard of 'the white mansion.' So far, nothing. I've asked if anybody's got a road atlas, but again…no. Maybe somebody'll come up with something, maybe not. In the meantime, I know there's a library at the high school." From the high school is where much of JayDee's medical supplies had come, and some of the canned food, but Dave's last trip there had been months ago. "I'm taking a horse over there in the morning, and I'm going to see if I can find anything…some maps, maybe…anything that could help."

Olivia said, "You can't go out alone. You shouldn't have gone out alone after Ethan. It was foolish. And you know you shouldn't go out at all, unless you're looking for food and ammo."

"Yeah, but I'm going anyway. I won't ask anybody to go with me, I can handle it."

Olivia paused, examining her tiles again. She decided to save her blank and placed *dart* on the board, then she chose three more tiles, one a dreaded Z. "You believe in this?" she asked quietly, as the oil lamps made soft guttering sounds. "That Ethan is wanting to go to a real place? That he's feeling…what would the word be…*summoned*? And that this white mansion place isn't halfway around the world?"

"*Summoned*?" JayDee managed a crooked smile but it quickly slipped away. "Summoned by what? A voice in a dream? That's what you have to go on?" The question was aimed at Dave.

"I have to go on what the boy tells me," Dave replied firmly. "Sure, that's all I've got...but I do know I saw the earthquakes. Felt 'em, too. I believe he knew the spring was there before it came up. I think he sensed it. Don't ask me, I can't explain." He leaned forward slightly, looking from John Douglas to Olivia and back again. "He's asked me to help him find this place. He thinks it's real enough, and he says it's pulling at him. Can it be found?" Dave shrugged. "Is it fifty miles away? A hundred? A thousand? Don't know. I have to get to that library tomorrow and try to find some maps. That's the best I can do. And John...you know what those bruises looked like on his chest and back. You said it yourself...you were surprised his lungs hadn't burst and he was still breathing."

"True, I did," JayDee answered, but there was a note of pity in his voice. "I *am* amazed he's alive. But Dave...that doesn't mean he died and has risen from the dead."

Dave was silent for awhile. The rain thrashed harder against the crooked roofs and broken walls of the Panther Ridge Apartments, whose glory was a distant memory.

Dave looked directly into JayDee's eyes. He said in a low, restrained voice, "But what if it *does*?"

JayDee slapped the edge of the table with both hands, upsetting all the little tiles of all the little words. He stood up, a frown etched across his face. "I'm not listening to this. Thank you for the company. I'm getting some sleep now, goodnight to you both." He motioned toward the door. "Push hard, it sticks."

Dave and Olivia said goodnight to JayDee. Dave picked his Uzi in its holster up from the floor beside his chair and Olivia hefted her rifle. Dave did have to push hard against the door. In the outside corridor, they walked together toward the stairs.

"It seems to me," Olivia said, breaking their silence, "that you want to believe in something very badly."

"Yeah, that's probably right. Sad, huh?"

"Not sad. I have to say...I wonder about Ethan myself. John does too, only he doesn't want to say so directly. It's hard to believe in very much anymore. That there's a purpose to anything." She stopped walking, and so did Dave. "So you believe that Ethan *has* a purpose? And it's beneficial to us, somehow? What might that be?"

"No idea. But the things he's done so far *have* helped us. I don't know what he is or why he's here, but I say…if he *can* help us…then I need to help him do what he's asking. If that means following a direction he heard in a dream, to the best of my ability…yeah, I'm for it. You should be too. We all should be. Otherwise, we're just waiting to fill up the graveyard, and I don't want to wait for that anymore."

"Hm," said Olivia, and she pondered that before she spoke again. Rain was pouring off the roof to their right. Lightning flickered across the troubled darkness. "I suppose…maybe I'm afraid to believe. That would mean opening yourself up again, wouldn't it? I guess it's safer to sit in a room with a picture of your dead husband and think…not too much longer now, and we'll be together."

"Don't give up," Dave said.

"Trust in a boy who has no memory? Trust in three words from a dream? That's hanging on with your fingernails, I think."

"Sure it is. But it *is* hanging on."

Olivia nodded and smiled faintly. There was so much pain behind the smile that Dave had to lower his head and look away. "I'll go with you tomorrow," she told him.

"You don't have to. No need for two of us to ride out."

"Maybe I also want to hang on a little longer. Besides, they're *my* horses." The herd had come from the ranch she'd owned with Vincent. Watching them being slaughtered and eaten, one after the other, had been at first devastating, and now a matter of survival.

"Okay." Dave put a hand on her shoulder. "Meet at the corral at eight?"

"I'll be there."

Dave had no doubt she would be. Shielding themselves as best they could from the downpour, they parted ways at the bottom of the steps. Dave returned to his apartment and his sleeping bag on the gray sofa. Olivia went to her apartment, touched a match to the wick of a lamp and sat at her desk, and there she picked up the Magic Eight Ball Vincent had given her. She turned it between her hands, remembering the day this had come to her wrapped in red paper with a silver ribbon. It had been, it seemed, a lifetime ago.

And now, against all logic and reason, she had to ask a question. It was whispered, as if into Vincent's listening ear.

"*Should I believe?*"

She shook the ball and then turned it over.

The little white plastic die emerged from its inky soup.

Maybe it was Vincent answering her, maybe it was Fate, maybe it was only happenstance, which she certainly thought was the most likely.

But the answer was: *You may rely on it.*

She took the lamp with her, and she went into the next room and undressed. She slid into her bed where good dreams and belief in miracles did not come easily, but that always had a pistol tucked under the pillow.

EIGHT.

A BROODING YELLOW SKY STRETCHED OVERHEAD. THERE WAS NO wind, but the air smelled burnt. The horses were skittish, nervous to the touch. Dave rode alongside Olivia as they went through the metal-plated door that had been opened for them. As soon as they were descending the road, the door was closed and locked again, according to Olivia's orders. At each corner of the wall that had been rebuilt and fortified around the Panther Ridge Apartments the machine gunners sat behind their weapons, scanning both the silent sky and the ominous earth.

The two riders headed toward the high school down in the valley below. Occasionally on the hillside they passed a hand, arm, or head of a nightmarish creature, caught like strange flowers in fissures in the ground. The vultures were busy; Dave thought that they didn't care what meat they ate, and so even those things were likely to be corrupted and turned into...*what*?

He had his Uzi in his shoulder holster and in a holster at his belt, a Smith & Wesson .357 Magnum revolver that had belonged to Mitch Vandervere. Mitch's apartment had yielded four boxes of bullets, twenty each, and the gun held five rounds. That was the way of things. When someone fell, you drew straws or cards with whoever else was on the burial detail and took the departed's weapons and ammo, no fighting or squabbling allowed, and Dave had won high card over Mitch's headless corpse. So in Dave's possession were 80 Magnum rounds and five clips of thirty-two slugs each for the Uzi, and that was it for now. Olivia had her rifle slung across her shoulder, along with a small black leather bag holding thirty more bullets.

They didn't speak as they rode. They had not talked about their mission before they'd left. A few men had offered to ride with them, as extra protection, but the offerings had been half-hearted, and Olivia had said no, they'd manage this by themselves.

They crossed open ground scarred by craters with edges seared crusted and black by the alien weapons. The road's asphalt was cracked and also cratered, and Olivia thought the Earth was being transformed into a planet the Cyphers and Gorgons perhaps better understood: a ruined charnel house of war that in another year or two would no longer be suitable for human life. Everything would be contaminated, if it wasn't already. And now she had to stop these thoughts before they overwhelmed her, and she had tears in her eyes and a deep, sick sadness in her heart and that old ticking time bomb in her mind that said it would be so easy and so right to join Vincent. Her spirit was so near to being extinguished. Her life force, tattered and destroyed. She could feel it leaving her, day by day. When she and Dave got back behind the walls, she knew two or three more people would probably have shot themselves. They were losing more and more, and it was getting faster now.

The white mansion, she thought as they neared the high school. Ethan's name right up there on the weather-beaten sign. The building itself a wreckage. And in the parking lot…what was *that*? Three huge… *things*…lying there covered with vultures like dark rippling skins…the thick, hideous bodies burned to crisps and seeping black fluids like scorched engine oil. And here and there the outlines of where smaller bodies had been lying, only now they were reduced to a residue of shiny ebony material like shreds of rubber. She knew what those were, she'd seen them before. The remnants of Cypher soldiers, bubbling and melting away to nothingness. But those creatures…those *monsters*…

Olivia's mind had to fix on something else, and quickly. "Dave?" she said in a weak voice, "what happened to the cars? The ones that used to be here?"

"Don't ask," he said, because Hannah Grimes had told him what she'd seen through the binoculars and he'd informed Hannah—a tough old bird if there ever was one—to keep that pinned under her wig, for the sake of Christ. So far Hannah wasn't talking, but it was probably just a matter of time. Creating alien flesh out of earthly metal was a new one; when that got around Panther Ridge, Katie bar the fucking door.

The horses nickered and shivered and would not go into the parking lot. "Go on, go on," said Dave to his mount but the animal's eyes had gotten wild and it rumbled like an avalanche deep in its lungs, the message being *You may be a damned fool but I am not. No further, bucko.*

"What are *those*?" Olivia had finally made herself fix on the monsters, even as her horse began to back away as if fearful of stepping into a tarpit. "*Dave*?"

"Whatever they were, they're dead." He got down from the saddle and looked for a place to tie his horse. Last time he'd been here, a few months back, he'd used the front fender of a pickup truck. That same truck had recently walked away and might be lying over there plucked by vultures. He noted the impressions in the asphalt that might have been caused by the weight of those things. Flesh from metal. Life from an inanimate object. A good trick, if you could do it. He recalled something he'd read maybe in a book at his own high school, but it had stuck with him because he'd thought it had sounded cool. How did it go? Something like... "Any super-advanced technology seems like magic." Was that it? No, but close enough. Well, here was the super-advanced technology on full magical display.

Damn 'em, he thought. Their weapons were getting stranger and more deadly. *An arms race*, Ethan had said. "Yeah, and we're stuck right in the fuckin' middle," Dave said to that thought, which made Olivia ask, "What?" and he just shrugged and walked the horse to a STOP sign that stood near the entrance to the lot. It had been bent almost in half by possibly the same concussion that had blown out the school's windows. "You want to stay here, that's fine with me," he said. "I can find the library."

Olivia was already dismounting. She walked her jittery horse over and tied it up to the sign as well. Her eyes were fixed on Dave, but they wanted to slide over to look at the dead creatures again, and she knew she couldn't stay out here alone.

She unslung the rifle from her shoulder, a smooth move she was getting good at. Never in her life would she have believed she might become a warrior. But here she was, ready to fight if she had to.

"Let's go," she said. They followed a cracked concrete path up to stone stairs that entered the building. One door had been blown inward off its hinges, the other hung crookedly like a Saturday night drunk. Or, Dave mused, how Saturday night drunks *used* to hang. The light within was murky, stained yellow like the ugly sky. Glass crunched under their boots, a noise that seemed to Olivia to be terribly loud in this silent place.

But not quite silent. Water dripped from the ceiling in a hundred places. Wet papers had grown to the floor and turned the color of strong tea. The floor tiles gave a little as Dave and Olivia walked; the floor itself felt spongy, as if upheld by rotten beams just on the verge of collapse. They passed what had once been a trophy case, the pride of the high school's sports teams, now shattered and the trophies darkened by waterstains. A huge mural on one wall that had likely been painted by students depicted the world and figures surrounding it linked arm in arm. The mural was blotched by large brown scabs where the wall's plaster had fallen away, but the faded message "The Family Of Man" was still legible.

"That was the office," Dave said as they passed an open doorway. "Lunchroom is up this way. I found the medical supplies in a room a little further along. The library must be past that."

Olivia nodded. The falling water *tap...tap...tapped*. Puddles washed around discarded notebooks and debris that had spilled from open lockers in the students' panic to get home on that day in April. She could imagine the teachers and the principal trying to keep order, the intercom system crackling, the parents swarming these halls in search of their children while the newscasts showed the Gorgon ships destroying cities all over the world. Only ghosts remained here now, she thought. The ghosts of a way of life; the ghosts of not only the American Dream, but the dream of the Family of Man.

"You okay?" Dave asked.

She said, "Yes," but he knew she was not so he replied, "We won't be in here too long," and she said nothing else.

They kept moving forward into the yellowed gloom. A tarnished trumpet lay on the warped floor. *Gideon has left the building,* Olivia thought. That almost made her laugh, but there was too much sadness in this ruin, too much expectation and promise gone and lost. She dared not let herself think about what might have happened to many of the students, parents and teachers. Some of them might have been among the Gray Men...if not here, then somewhere else.

"This," Dave said, "must be the place."

He had stopped in the hallway just ahead of her. On either side of rows of lockers was a door marked LIBRARY with a cracked glass inset. "Let's take a look," Dave told her, but before he opened the door he slid the .357 Magnum revolver out of his belt holster and clicked off the safety.

Olivia followed him in, and left the door open behind them.

It was a pretty mess. A complete disaster. The windows were broken out and the rain and wind had swept in and all the standing shelves had gone over. Everything was scattered and drenched. Yellow and green mold grew in patches on the walls and the floor, and both the visitors knew not to touch that. There was a sickly-sweet odor in the air, a vile miasma of corruption. Part of the ceiling had collapsed and wires and pipes were hanging down. On the floor the books were everywhere, locked together by dampness and mold.

They stood looking at the room in silence.

"Jeez," Dave finally said. He frowned and wished he had a cigarette. "I guess none of the bastards like to read, huh?"

Now that *did* strike Olivia. She laughed, a pure and hearty laugh, and Dave liked the sound of it. He gave a tight, passing smile and shrugged. The light was bad in here. He didn't like the idea of getting on his knees in that muck and weird mold and hunting for road maps. The place looked like somebody had turned it upside down and shaken it a few times. He thought they needed a shovel to go through all this, or at least rubber gloves. He cursed himself for not thinking of that. But they were here now, so where to begin?

Good question.

He began to try to move books aside with his foot, and this worked okay at first but at the lower level things had turned gluey and were stuck to the floor. Some of the books looked to have nearly melted away, and there was no telling what they once had been. He saw nothing of maps or road atlases, and he asked himself how would he know any if he saw them in this wet mess?

"Would this do?" Olivia had placed her foot on a battered world globe that lay on the floor.

"I don't think so. I don't know." Dave heard a note of resignation in his voice. "Even if we found maps, I don't know what we'd be looking for. Christ…this didn't exactly turn out like I thought it would." He kicked some melted books aside. "Stupid, I guess."

"Not stupid," said Olivia. "Hopeful."

"Yeah. Well…maybe that's as stupid as you can get these days."

Olivia began moving the fragments and wet skeletons of books aside with her booted foot as well. So much for the ideas and intellect of men, she thought. She uncovered some blue-bound Hardy Boys mysteries, and at that she almost teared up again. *Stay strong*, she told herself. Easy to say, tough to do. "I've known you long enough," she said, "to know you're the kind of man who doesn't believe in…let's say…*miracles*. But this boy has changed your mind? Dave, if this is even a real place, it could be anywhere. And *why*? What's telling him to go there?"

"He's a weird kid," was all Dave could offer, as he continued to search through the sodden mess.

"Yes, I get that. But sometimes…you know…dreams are just dreams. I've had plenty of bad ones. Sure you have too."

"Yeah," Dave said. He looked at Olivia in the dim yellow light. "I know it's crazy. I know being *here*, doing *this*, is crazy. But still…you know

Ethan is right. JayDee does too. We can't hang on much longer. We're going to have to move...find some other place, if we want to stay alive."

"You think the White Mansion is that place?"

"Hell if I know, but Panther Ridge is about done." He took his dirty baseball cap off, wiped the small beads of sweat from his forehead and then put the cap back on. "Ethan is *different*, Olivia. Whether that's good or bad, I don't know. But he's helped us so far...I believe that. Call me stupid or crazy or whatever you like, but I'm *here*...that's all I know."

She had no answer for any of that. She saw the librarian's office and the check-out counter across the room. A rack of DVD movies had fallen over and plastic cracked under her feet as she approached the counter. In all this chaos a small metal statue of a football player stood upright on the countertop, holding a little paper American flag in one fist and a football cradled in the other arm like a beloved child.

With Olivia's next forward step, the floor beneath her suddenly sagged. There was a thick wet sound of something rotted giving way. She cried out as her right leg went through the floor. She thought she was going all the way through into the basement and she nearly let go of her rifle to grab at the tiles around her but then she stopped, just the one leg dangling down into darkness.

Dave was there at her side in an instant, helping her up. "Easy, easy," he said. "You okay? Hurt your leg?"

"Bumped my knee pretty good. That's about it. Watch the floor, it bites."

"Yeah, I see." Dave peered into the hole but could really see nothing but dark. Water dripped down there and from the basement rose an acrid, musty odor as if from a diseased garden of poison mushrooms. "Careful."

"You too. Hey," she said, having seen something of interest. "There's a file cabinet behind the counter. Worth opening up."

"Right. Come on, stay with me."

They went around behind the check-out counter to the file cabinet, which appeared to have survived undamaged through whatever storm had raged in here. Dave opened the top drawer to find what appeared to be a couple of years' worth of school newspapers, the *Gazette*. The second

89

drawer held boxes of supplies like pencils, pens, rubber bands, gem clips and the like. The third drawer was mostly empty except for a few pads of printer paper, and the fourth and last drawer held two mousetraps.

"More drawers behind the check-out counter," Olivia noted, and she found herself limping over there because she really had taken a hard shot to the knee. *Thing's going to swell up on me*, she thought. *Magnifico!* Just what she needed, to have to hobble around for a few days like an old grandmother.

She opened the top drawer behind the counter and found another supply of pens, notepads, paper clips and someone's stash of several flavors of Orbit gum. The next drawer held a thick red-and-gold yearbook *The Mountaineer* from the past year, a couple of old cell phones that must have been confiscated on The Day, and…nearly hidden under the yearbook was something else. She lifted *The Mountaineer* out and saw the cover of a highway twisting through a pine forest. It was a *Rand-McNally United States Road Atlas*, three years old. A dead roach had been smashed flat between *The Mountaineer* and McNally. "Here!" Olivia said, as she took the road atlas out. A librarian's stern command was written across the cover in red Sharpie: *Not To Leave This Room.*

"Got what you need," she told Dave, with not just a little measure of triumph.

Dave came over to see. *"Yes!"* He was aware he hadn't sounded excited in a very long time, and this note in his voice surprised him. "Okay, then. Good! It's a start, at least." He rolled the atlas up and stuck it into the waistband of his jeans. "I don't know what we'll be looking for, but—"

The floor cracked. Just a quiet noise, but an ominous one.

"I think we should—" *get out of here*, Olivia was going to say, but she didn't have the chance.

Something was crawling up from the hole in the library floor.

It came up, swaying like a cobra. It was thin and gray-fleshed and had been a woman at one time, for the sagging exposed breasts and the scraggly patches of long, white hair. The sunken eyes in the skull-like face darted here and there, seeking either the sources of the human voices or where the smell of the fresh meat was coming from. The claw-like hands scrabbled to pull the body completely free but something seemed to be obstructing it, and the thing's mouth twisted with frustration and a little rattling noise came from the dry throat. Olivia started to cry out but checked herself. No time for that. Grim-lipped, she swung her rifle up to fire instead.

The library's floor rippled and heaved like a dirty ocean wave. The wet tiles burst open as clawed hands pushed their way free. Dave thought at first that he and Olivia had stumbled across a sleeping nest of Gray Men, and this was partly true…but in the next few seconds, as the floor continued to split apart and the glistening gray flesh slid out he realized with another start of horror that something very different had been incubating in the basement of the Ethan Gaines High School.

Dave had worked as a teenager on a crew demolishing old houses and hauling the timbers and bricks away. *Hey, hey!* the foreman had called one hot August afternoon. *Looky over here!*

And so Dave had seen, caught within a wall that had just been broken open, the sight of a dozen or more rats squealing and scrambling in their attempt to escape, but they had been joined and nearly knotted tail-to-tail in a circle and could not go in any one direction, and a few had died and begun to rot while the living ones continued to thrash wildly, their teeth bared, eyes glittering and breath rasping in their desperation.

It's a Rat King, the foreman had said. *Seen only one of 'em before, my whole life. They got stuck in a little space, peed on each other, and their tails growed together. Nasty!*

The foreman had lifted his shovel and gone to work smashing the Rat King, which died in a bloody and chittering mess. To Dave had gone the honor of throwing the remains into a garbage can.

Now, many years later in this nightmare world, Dave McKane was watching a Rat King made up of Gray Men crawling from the broken floor.

Their legs had grown together into something resembling long, thin tentacles not unlike rat tails. Some of the bodies had been engulfed by

other bodies so that they had nearly disappeared one into the other, can-
nibalized or absorbed, and maybe there were twenty or more of them
in this Rat King circle, what had been men, women, and children, and
heads and arms were not always where they were supposed to be. What
remained of their clothes were sodden, dark-stained rags. Scabrous gray
flesh pulled itself up from the basement. The ruined faces and misshapen
heads strained on their necks. In some of the gaping mouths glinted teeth
like little razor blades, and in others showed rows of sharklike rippers.

Dave realized at once that there were two problems.

This Rat King circle shared a common purpose and a direction, and
the writhing monster lay between him, Olivia, and the way out.

Her face a rictus of terror, Olivia had backed up and was pressed
against him. The thing struggled to get free from the basement, with wet
books and moldy pages plastered upon its flesh. The Rat King of Gray
Men made no noise but a hissing and a slithering, and now it appeared
to be gathering its tentacles beneath itself in an effort to stand. Dave
thought that if they were going to get out of here they had to go *now*.

He opened fire with his Magnum, which was incredibly loud and
bright with its bloom of flame. Two shots, and two of the nightmarish faces were blasted away. Then Olivia's rifle spoke, drilling a hole
through the white-haired head of the female creature that had first
begun to climb out. Black fluid spurted from the wound. Dave grasped
Olivia's shoulder, shouted, "Let's *move!*" in the strongest voice he could
summon and pulled her with him around the counter. The mass of
melded-together Gray Men moved faster; it reached for them with
serpentine arms. A gray mallet of a hand with seven fingers grasped
Olivia's right ankle and she would've fallen into the midst of them had
Dave not held onto her with all his strength. Olivia sent a bullet into
what might have once been a human shoulder, and she pulled free with
the resolve that if she didn't, she was dead. Dave fired again into one of
the faces. Gray flesh and dark matter spattered the library walls. A low
moaning like a chorus of the damned rose from the creature. The thing
was hauling itself forward on elbows and gray bellies, the broken heads
lolling. The tentacled appendages pushed at the floor. The bared teeth

of the remaining heads snapped at Olivia and Dave, and a gray forest of arms reached out for bloody sustenance. The two humans in the room opened fire once more at a range of no further than four or five feet. Dave's revolver went empty and he drew the Uzi from its holster, spraying the thing's body with 9mm bullets.

With a high, eerie cry that came from each mouth at the same time, the mutated horror suddenly began to retreat, pulling itself back to its cavern beneath the floor. There was room enough to get past. Dave shoved Olivia toward the door, mindful of her knee but mindful also of keeping them both alive. He fired his last bullet of the clip into the gray body and saw what looked to be a child's distorted face in its depths, either grown into or consumed by the others. The eyes were open and the mouth, which had no lower jaw, gaped wide as if in perpetual hunger or torment. Then Dave was out the door. They ran for daylight, Olivia damning her hurt knee and moving as fast as she could. Dave stayed beside her, giving her a shoulder to lean on. He thought that if either one of them dared to look back, it would prove their sanity had been permanently checked out in the Ethan Gaines library.

Neither one looked back, but Olivia was sobbing when she untied her horse and swung herself up. Dave was too tough to cry, but his stomach betrayed him. His breakfast of a pair of biscuits and a few spoonfuls of Spam came up. His horse smelled the mutated flesh on him and tried to run before he could get himself firmly in the saddle.

No one had to say *Ride* or *Go* or *Let's get the hell out of here.*

They rode. Behind them, as the horses galloped toward the uncertain safety of Panther Ridge, the vultures were disturbed by the commotion. Some flew up off the burned carcasses they were consuming, but after a few moments they settled down again over the dead monsters in the parking lot like a black shroud and fought for their places at the feast.

NINE.

KIDNEYS, STOMACH. LARGE INTESTINE, SMALL INTESTINE, PANCREAS. Liver, spleen, lungs. Brain, heart. Ethan was sitting in a chair in his apartment. The chair was made of scuffed brown leather and used to be a recliner but the mechanism was jammed. A candle lantern burned on a small table beside him. The table was crooked because the floor was crooked. The first sickly light of morning had begun to creep through the duct-taped windows. Ethan wore his dark green p.j. bottoms and a gray t-shirt. He had slept a little during the night, maybe a couple of hours straight. Even asleep, he'd been listening for the siren that meant the Gray Men were coming back, but it had been four nights since he'd found out he could make earthquakes. He felt like a raw nerve and a twisted muscle. When he'd gotten out of bed the first time he'd gone into the bathroom with the candle lantern, lifted his t-shirt and inspected his chest in the mirror. Then as much of his back as he could see.

The doc was right.

He didn't think he ought to be alive.

John Douglas had wanted him to come down to the hospital yesterday afternoon for another checkup. He didn't want to because he knew what he looked like, but he did anyway. They did the shot of saline solution while a man with a shotgun stood nearby. *Just a precaution,* JayDee had said. *Not that I don't trust you.*

Ethan's blood pressure was checked. No problem. Then when JayDee asked Ethan to take off his shirt to check the heartbeat was when the doc made a noise between a choke and a gasp and it seemed for a minute that he was going to press his hand against his mouth to stop any more sounds from coming out, but then JayDee got his bearings back and he said in a tight voice, "You've seen yourself, I'm guessing."

"Yes sir."

"Turn around, if you please."

"Same on my back," Ethan said.

"Let's take a look."

Ethan obeyed. The bruises were worse. They were still as black as a midnight funeral and now they had converged. There was no area of unbruised flesh on his chest, stomach or back down to the bottom of his spine. His sides were mottled with purple and green, the tendrils of one huge bruise reaching around to connect with the other.

"*Damn,*" said the man with the shotgun, whose name Ethan thought was Lester.

JayDee approached Ethan with caution. "I'm going to listen to your heart," he said, as if asking permission, and Ethan nodded. "Okay," JayDee said when he'd finished that, but he still had the stethoscope plugged into his ears. "Now...I want to listen to your lungs. Just take a deep breath when I ask you, and let it out slowly. Right?"

"You're the doctor," Ethan said.

JayDee began his work. "*Breathe.* That hurt you any?"

"A little."

He moved around to Ethan's back. "*Breathe.* Coughing up anymore blood?"

"No sir."

"Another deep breath, please." When JayDee was finished he came back around to look into Ethan's face. "Les," he said quietly as he took off the stethoscope and put it aside, "you can leave us now."

"Sure?"

"Yes, I'm sure. Go ahead." He waited for Les to shut the warped door behind him, as much as it would shut. Cracks from the earthquake riddled the walls. JayDee said, "You can put your shirt back on," and Ethan did. "Have a seat." JayDee motioned toward a chair, but Ethan said, "I'm okay standing."

"Well, *I'm* sitting down then." JayDee eased himself into the chair. Something creaked; either the chair or his weary bones. The doc stretched his legs out before him and, staring at Ethan, rubbed his clean-shaven chin.

"You know what I'm going to say," JayDee ventured.

Ethan shrugged, but he knew.

"At a time like this, a man needs a good stout drink of rye whiskey," JayDee said. "That was my drink of choice. In the quiet of the evening, before a nice fire in the hearth...a little Frank Sinatra on the stereo...*way* before your time, I know...and all was right with the world. Deborah... my wife, bless her soul...would sit with me and listen to the music or read. Oh, maybe that sounds *boring* to you. Does it?" This time his white eyebrows did not go up; it was a question that did not expect an answer. "Well, it was a life," he went on. "A damned *good* life." He gave a sad, crooked smile. "What I wouldn't give for that again, and as boring as you please. For two years now...Hell has visited earth. In many forms, too terrible to recount." His smile that was not really a smile faded and the expression in his eyes sharpened. "Tell me about the white mansion," he said. "I mean...Dave's already told me. But *you* tell me. All right? Wait... before you say anything...I'll tell you that a couple of days ago Dave and Olivia went down to the high school's library to find maps to help figure out where this white mansion might be. Dave's thinking it might be the name of a town. *Somewhere.*" He added a little sarcasm to that word. "They did find a road atlas. They won't talk about what happened over there, but Olivia hurt her knee a little bit. While she was in here she started shaking and crying, and she was about to go to pieces. I gave her a sedative, the best I could do. Dave won't talk about it either. So I want you to know, Ethan...that something terrible happened to them down there...while they were...let's say...acting on your behalf. It had to be

97

bad…because I saw how bad it was in Dave's face. And when you can read that in his face…brother, it was a whole big bag of *bad*."

Ethan nodded. He didn't know what to say. The best he could manage was, "I didn't ask them to do that."

"No, you didn't. But…you see…it's this white mansion thing. *And* the earthquake you said you caused. *And* that Dave believes that somehow you knew the spring was there under the swimming pool. Those things. Kinda hard for a rational person to swallow, isn't it?"

"I guess."

"But," JayDee went on, his brow furrowed, "Dave has a point. What's rational anymore? What makes sense? I've seen what looks like a man explode into something covered with black spikes, right in that secure room you were locked up in when you first got here. Seen a teenaged girl's face implode, and suddenly it was a mouth filled with greedy little teeth that tried to bite my head off, until Dave shot the thing to pieces. Does that make sense? Well…maybe it does if you're a Gorgon or a Cypher. See, I think they're making weapons out of what used to be human beings. Experimenting on them. On *us*. They've got a real slam-bang weapons program going on, they're wanting to see what works and what doesn't. Maybe they're just doing it because they can, and that's their way. What do you think, Ethan? You brought that up about the Gorgons and Cyphers fighting over the *border*. That's what you said, right?"

"Yes," said Ethan quietly.

"Why did you say that? What information do you have that I, Dave, Olivia and everyone else here doesn't have?"

Ethan didn't answer for a moment. Then he said, just as quietly, "I know it's true. It's what they're fighting over. The border between their—"

"What *are* you?" JayDee suddenly asked, and he drew his legs back as if they might be in danger of black spikes or a mouthful of little daggers. "You and I both know…those injuries you have…they should've killed you. And the bruises are worse, aren't they? Yet your blood pressure is fine, your lungs are in good shape, and your heart's just ticking along. And let me tell you…your lungs ought to be so clogged full of blood you couldn't draw a breath, and I still don't know how you're walking. God, if I only had an X-ray machine and some power to run it! So...young man who doesn't know his name or remember anything about his life before he suddenly *woke up* running across a field...what exactly *are* you, because I don't think you're human."

The statement tainted the air. Ethan felt a spark of anger grow into a flame. "You think I'm something *they* made? Like...a secret weapon? That I'm supposed to explode or grow two heads or something? Is that it?"

"I'd say somebody who can create an earthquake just by *wanting* to make it happen already has got a little secret weapon in him. My question is, what else is in there you don't know about?"

Ethan stared at JayDee. Did a little heat ripple in the air between them? Ethan said, "Kidneys, stomach. Large intestine, small intestine, pancreas. Liver, spleen, lungs. Brain, heart. Those are things I know I have. I *am* human, sir. And I'm remembering something, too. It's getting clearer and the details are filling in. I'm in a room, sitting at a desk under a green desk lamp, and I'm putting together a model of the Visible Man. You know what that is?"

"I had one. Every kid who ever grew up to be a doctor probably put that thing together."

"Okay. I'm looking at my desk, and that's what I see lying there. The parts. Kidneys, stomach, large intestine, small intestine, pancreas, liver, spleen, lungs, brain, and heart. I've got them arranged in that order, to be painted. My jars of paint are sitting there. The brand is Testors. A woman with dark hair comes into the room...and she starts to speak, but I can't hear what she says." Sadness pierced him like a blade; not only sadness, but a deep sense of desperation. Tears burned his eyes. "I *want* to hear, but I can't. And...what I want most of all...*most* of all...is for her to speak my name, because I think she's my mother, but...if she does say it, I can't hear it. Or maybe I just can't recognize it anymore." He wiped his eyes and stared at the floor. A shiver passed through him, quick and then gone. "I'm human. I know I am." And then he looked up into the careful eyes of John Douglas, and Ethan said what he was really thinking: "I've *got* to be."

It was another moment before JayDee spoke. "You have no idea what the white mansion is? You just believe it's a place you have to get to?"

Ethan nodded.

"Well," said JayDee, as thickly as if he had a mouthful of sand, "Dave believes it too. Maybe Olivia does. She's not saying much lately. But I know Dave's been going through that road atlas. There's no town in these United…in this *country*," he corrected himself, "bearing that name. Dave took my magnifying glass—the last one I have, incidentally—and he's been going through that atlas page by page. He must be nearly blind by now. I hear he's not sleeping very much either. I just wanted you to know."

"Okay," said Ethan, who thought he should respond in some way.

"You can go now, if you want to. Me, I'm just going to sit here for awhile and think…or maybe try *not* to think."

—◇◇◇—

Kidneys, stomach. Large intestine, small intestine, pancreas. Liver, spleen, lungs. Brain, heart.

Sitting in the broken recliner in the apartment of a dead man, with the thin sickly light of morning coming through the duct-taped windows, Ethan can see those plastic organs lying before him on the desktop. The dark-haired woman comes in. She is smiling, and Ethan thinks she is pretty, but her face is really just a blur. And what he wants to say is *Speak my name*, but he does not and she does not, and he returns his gaze to the shell of the Visible Man that he so desires to make complete.

He heard a tapping at the door, which like so many others had been sawed so that it closed firmly in the misshapen frame.

"Who is it?" he called.

The voice was a tired mumble. "Dave. Got something."

At once, Ethan was up and opening the door. Dave came in looking like he'd been on a three-day binge. He was wearing dirty jeans and a faded brown t-shirt that had so many holes in it a pitbull could have been using it as a chewrag. His hair was a touseled mess, and his eyes were weary, swollen maybe from deciphering too much small print. In his right hand was a page torn from the road atlas and in his left was the magnifying glass. "*Might* have something," he amended, holding up the page. "Want you to take a look." He came in as Ethan stepped aside. Dave went to the candle lantern. "Map of southeastern Utah," he said. "You probably won't need the magnifier, but I sure as hell did."

Ethan took the page as Dave offered it.

Dave touched the map with a forefinger. "*There.* About midway between the two towns of Monticello and Blanding. It's at the eastern edge of the Manti-La-Sal National Forest. See that?"

Ethan did. *White Mansion Mtn.*, it read. *10,961 ft.*

"It's over three hundred miles from here as the eagle flies. But we're not eagles." Dave rubbed his eyes. "That's what I found. Ring any bells?"

"No, nothing. But maybe that's it?"

Dave gave a short bark of a laugh. "Maybe? *Maybe?* You know what's it's like searching those maps with a magnifying glass, hour after hour?" Dave hadn't realized until he and Olivia had gotten back to Panther Ridge that the last few maps and the index had been ripped out. It had been close work, and hoping the White Mansion wasn't up in Canada because those were the missing maps. He had scoured everything remaining...all towns, military bases, lakes, bays, mountains, canyons, and at last had come to the name of the mountain in Utah.

"I don't know anything about that area," he said, "but I know to get there would be...like...a miracle. Going south to Denver, crossing the Rockies on I-70, with the Gray Men and the aliens everywhere. So, when you say *maybe that's it*...that doesn't make me feel too very confident."

"How am I supposed to know for sure?" was Ethan's next question, delivered flatly and as a matter-of-fact.

Dave looked down at the floor as if he were trying to control an outburst. It took him a moment to get himself stabilized; he was tired, hungry, and thirsty, and he figured he'd aged his eyes by about five years in the past two days. But when he lifted his gaze to Ethan again and spoke, his face was calm, and his voice as quiet as he could force it to be under the circumstances. "That's the only White Mansion I could find.

Either that's it or not. Either, like you say, something you don't under-stand is trying to guide you there, or it was just a bad dream and it meant absolutely fucking *nothing*. But I've decided to believe in you, Ethan. I've decided to *listen* to you. Got that?"

Ethan stared into Dave's eyes, his own face betraying no emotion. "Have you decided to *follow* me?" he asked. "If I go there, are you going with me? Is Olivia? Dr. Douglas? Anyone else?"

"You'll never make that by yourself. God only knows how *anybody* could make that trip."

"That's no answer. *Sir*," he added.

Dave took the map back from Ethan. He felt near collapse, near just lying down in a corner somewhere and peering into the Magnum's barrel until he gathered enough courage to pull the trigger. But still... *damn it*...the White Mansion. And this boy...this damned strange boy who JayDee had said ought to be lying six feet under by now. This boy... maybe an experiment by either Cyphers or Gorgons? So why was he here, and what was to be done with him?

"You ask too many questions," Dave said. "Right now I'm going back to my place and get some sleep. We'll talk about this later...when I can think straight." So saying, he turned away from Ethan and left the apartment, half-walking and half-staggering, with the map from the road atlas in one hand and the magnifying glass in the other.

The White Mansion, Ethan thought after Dave had gone.

Go there. It's important. Somehow...really important.

And he asked himself, that if he knew it was somehow really important, then how come he didn't know *why*? If his mind or whatever it was guiding him was only giving him bits and pieces, clues that right now made no sense...why wasn't it giving him the whole picture, so he could understand?

Over three hundred miles from here as the eagle flies, Dave had said. *But we're not eagles.*

It was a long way, to depend on a voice in a dream and a voice inside himself urging him to go. A long way, with all that out there, the Gray Men hungering for meat, and the Gorgons and Cyphers forever at war. And how were they supposed to get there? By walking? By the horses, which meant taking the last food from these people? And what would *they* do for food on the journey? *How could it be done?*

Ethan sat down and stared at the glow of the candle lantern. The morning's light was getting stronger, a yellowish hue. Ethan figured it was going to be what people used to call a "nice day", considering how screwed up the atmosphere was.

I should be dead, he thought. *But I'm human. I know I am. I remember a mother and a house and a room with a desk lamp and on the table, bottles of Testors paint and the plastic organs lined up. But I should be dead…and instead of that I am here staring at a candle and wondering…*

….who will go with me, when I go?

TEN.

WITH THE PASSAGE OF THREE MORE DAYS, LIFE AS SUCH WENT ON at Panther Ridge. Water was collected from the spring that had filled up the swimming pool. Another horse was slaughtered, and on that day Olivia Quintero did not emerge from her apartment. John Douglas talked a weeping young man out of killing himself, his wife, and little boy, but while he was doing that, a middle-aged woman who used to be a watercolor artist in Loveland blew her head off with a shotgun in the dark confines of Apartment 278. Work went on to strengthen the wall, as always. Up in the machine-gun towers the nightwatchmen saw the distant flickering of either lightning or two worlds at war over the border.

On that same night, Ethan Gaines walked the perimeter, lost in thought. The pull from the White Mansion was stronger now, and it was hard to sleep. The complex was quiet; it was about two in the morning, he figured. A few other people were up, walking alone or talking in small groups. He saw a woman sobbing with her head against a man's shoulder, and the man had a drawn, weary face and eyes that saw nothing. He saw a teen-aged girl lying on the ground staring up at the sky as if trying to pierce the mysteries there. She was hampered by that because she wore a black eyepatch over her left eye, but it was decorated with small stick-on rhinestones. She was about his age, he thought, and she had blonde hair and a pretty oval face with a small cleft in the chin. Maybe she was sixteen or seventeen, he decided. She didn't look at him as he passed by; her study was the stars that could be seen faintly through the drifting clouds. He saw a circle of a dozen people on their knees in the grass, heads bowed and eyes squeezed tightly shut as if that would speed their prayers; maybe they stayed there all night praying, he didn't know.

And that led to a question for him: where was God in all this?

Was the same God those people fervently prayed to the God who had created the Gorgons and Cyphers? Did God favor one civilization over the other, or were all left to the rolling of the celestial dice?

The White Mansion, he thought. It intruded upon him night and day, breaking in like an unwanted commercial in this ragged movie of his life. *I've got to get there, somehow.*

We're not eagles, Dave had said. And Dave was not speaking to him lately, had not spoken to him since that early morning revelation. There was no plan, there was just the waiting. And Ethan saw very clearly, as he walked with the weight of the unknown burdening his shoulders, that these people were waiting to die. Their hope was running out like the sand in the hourglass. Everyone had their limit; when that limit was reached...*blammo,* off to meet the Maker.

This is shit, Ethan thought as he looked at the broken-down, crooked and messed-up apartment buildings. *No one can stay here. If they want to live, they have to move because movement is life. Going somewhere is life. But here behind these stone walls that are worked on day and night...they are just waiting to find the limit of their hope, and it comes to everybody.*

Even if you died on the road to somewhere, he thought...*at least you tried.*

"*Hola,*" someone said. "Can't sleep?"

Ethan stopped. He'd almost walked right into Olivia, who was on her own circuit of the perimeter. She was carrying a lantern and was wearing faded jeans and a blue-patterned blouse. She had on a pair of sneakers the color of a bright yellow tennis ball, but dirtier. The candle-light showed a dazed look in her eyes. Ethan thought she was just barely holding herself together, but she was not too far gone to forget to wear her pistol in its holster around her waist.

"Oh," Ethan said. "Hi. Yeah. I mean...no, I can't sleep."

"Me neither. Not lately. I'm out of sleeping pills. Been thinking of hitting myself in the head with a hammer, but I'm not ready for anything that drastic."

Ethan gave her a guarded smile that did not hold very long, because there were important things to say. "Dave showed me the map. Did he tell you?"

"He did. White Mansion Mountain in southeastern Utah, a *long* way from here."

"A pretty long way," Ethan agreed.

"Maybe you and your parents visited that place once. Maybe that's why you want to go there, because you're remembering."

"I don't think so. There's no father," he said.

"*What?*"

"In the house I'm starting to remember, where I'm sitting at the desk putting together my Visible Man. Did JayDee tell you about that?"

"Yes."

"I thought he would. Well...there's a dark-haired woman who I think is my mother, but I don't think I have a father. There's just...not a *presence* there. I mean, I *did* have a father, but I think he left when I was a little boy."

Olivia lifted the lantern to view his face as if she'd never really stud-ied it before. Ethan's sharp blue eyes glinted; his jaw was set. He looked ready for something, but she didn't know what. He looked *expectant*. He shifted his weight from foot to foot, and seemed as uneasy as a horse sensing the killing blade. "Walk with me," she said, and started off. She was still limping a little and her knee was taped up under the jeans, but otherwise she was okay if one didn't consider the nightmares that had interrupted her sleep since that morning in the library. More than once she'd awakened in a cold sweat as a wave of mutated flesh and biting teeth had rolled up at her from a broken floor, and in those nightmares there was no Dave McKane to help her.

Ethan walked with her, noting the limp. "JayDee said you hurt your knee."

"It's nothing. Need to walk to keep the blood moving."

They had gone only a few paces more when something glowing bright blue streaked across the sky above Panther Ridge. It was maybe four or five hundred feet up, and it moved in a blur but soundlessly. Ethan and Olivia watched it disappear into the clouds beyond. In about three seconds there was a faint hum that became louder and louder still until it became a high-pitched shriek that would have left no one in the complex asleep, and suddenly a red and pulsing sphere with a fiery halo around it came out of the clouds and darted after the blue object. It, too, was quickly lost from sight.

"They're active tonight," Olivia said tonelessly. She saw candles and oil lamps going on in what remained of windows across the complex. There would be no more sleeping this night. Many times they had seen the battling lights in the night sky, seen and heard distant explosions and the otherworldly sounds of alien weapons at work, but how could anyone get used to it? "Come on, let's keep walking," she told Ethan, since both of them had stopped to watch the quick and deadly spectacle. "Okay," she said after a moment more. "About the White Mansion."

"I have to get there." In his voice there was no hesitation. "Soon."

"All right." Olivia wondered if the glint of his eyes meant he was feverish. "How do you figure on getting there? Walking?"

"It would take too long." What he said next just came to him, like a memory, or like another voice speaking through him. "I have to get there soon or the chance might be lost."

"*Chance?*" She frowned, a little unnerved by this word. "What chance do you mean?"

He opened his mouth, about to speak but not knowing exactly what he was going to say. He had no choice but to trust in whatever was guiding him, whatever was trying to pull—or push—him on this dangerous

108

and maybe crazy journey. He opened his mouth, but before any words could come out a sizzling white-hot thing shot across the sky above Panther Ridge and then another and another and suddenly dozens of them, sounding like bacon fat in a skillet, until the sky was crisscrossed with them and they left trails that burned the eyeballs. Up in the clouds there was thunder and lightning and then lightning and thunder but the lightning was red and blue and the thunder was the deep boom of ocean waves crashing against a jagged shore…harder and harder, louder and louder.

"*Jesus,*" Olivia whispered, her eyes on the heavens. Beside her, Ethan's muscles had tensed and his heart was pounding. His lungs did hurt, he thought. Have to tell the doc about that…but in the next instant he thought *too late…too late…*

"*Too late,*" he heard himself say, as if from a vast and unfathomable distance.

"What?" she asked him, a frantic note in her voice. And again, when he didn't answer: "*What?*"

From the clouds descended a monster.

Ethan figured it was nearly twice as big as the Gorgon ship he'd seen destroyed over the muddy field. It was the same triangular shape with the same prehistoric monster markings of brown, yellow, and black, but yet not wholly the same because each craft was different. It was razor-thin, had no openings nor ports and six of the eight electric-blue orbs that pulsed at its belly had gone dead black. Dozens of spheres of white-hot energy were attacking it from all sides, and the orbs tried to explode as many as they could but the ones getting through were burning red-edged holes in the reptilian hide. There was an electric smell in the air and the smell of charred meat that had been placed on a grill when it was already three days rotten. It was a swampy smell, the odor of fire-bombed rattlesnakes that had been left to decay under a hot August sun. There came the high-pitched, fingernail-on-blackboard and viper hiss of agony. The Gorgon ship was coming down upon the Panther Ridge Apartments. Olivia realized it a few seconds after Ethan, because her brain was stunned. It had seized up, run out of the lubrication of reality. Others realized what was about to happen too, for a sudden screaming and wailing arose from the apartment complex like voices of the doomed from the very center of Hell.

The tremendous bulk of the Gorgon ship shivered. Around it now could be seen maybe a hundred or more of the small black craft of the Cyphers, each hardly big enough to carry a human-sized pilot, with swept-back, vibrating wings, and a sharply pointed nosecone. Their skins glistened wetly, as they darted in and out and the white spheres of flame shot from the wings six at a time. They moved fast and silently, stopping to hover for a second or jink to one side or another like flying insects. Occasionally one was hit by a blue spark of energy and exploded into flying tatters, but there were too many.

Still screaming, the Gorgon ship had lost its equilibrium. It began to tilt to the left, and as it did some of the Cypher craft became blurs of incredible speed and speared themselves into the belly of the beast. They then exploded in white fireballs that scorched the eyes and burned more holes into the ship, and now from the craft's belly came bursts of dark liquid that spattered down upon the bones of the vulture-plucked Gray Men still reaching from their graves in the earth.

One of the men in a machine-gun tower began to fire at the descending ship, which was like throwing wads of paper at concrete. Ethan's mind was racing, putting together speeds and trajectories of which he had no knowledge of learning; he realized the ship was going to clear the wall but that the apartment complex was doomed. Even as he thought this and the Gorgon craft continued on in its death drop, he was aware of figures emerging through the stones of the wall like ghosts, then becoming solid again. The Cypher soldiers had arrived. There were dozens of them, skeleton-thin and seven feet tall. Their black featureless non-faces looked to neither right nor left. Their black fleshy weapons with two barrels connected to their bodies by fluid-carrying veins were held at the ready, as they likely always were. Some of them blurred onward toward the apartments, while others stalked forward at a more cautious pace. Now pistol and rifle shots were ringing out as the inhabitants of Panther Ridge tried to defend themselves, but the bullets—if any hit their targets—had no effect.

Olivia cringed down and held a scream behind her teeth as the Gorgon craft hissed overhead and plowed into the ground just short of the first level of apartments. Its mass and speed dug a plume of concrete and earth before it as it continued up the hillside, crossing the tennis courts and the swimming pool and slamming nearly dead center into the first building, which crumpled before it as if made of the cheapest cardboard. Both Ethan and Olivia realized the hospital and JayDee's apartment had just been destroyed. The dying Gorgon ship cleaved completely through the first level and smashed into the second building. Ethan knew his own apartment—and Dave's and Olivia's too—had just been reduced to kindling. The dust of ages swirled up into the air. The Gorgon craft stopped just short of the third building, which like the fourth was unoccupied. The damage had been done. Now the Cypher soldiers were closing in to make sure there were no Gorgon survivors.

Something had caught fire in the crushed midsection of the second level. Red flames were starting to curl upward. Screams came from the shattered buildings, along with more gunshots. The Gorgon ship lay still, its life liquid pouring from burned holes in the skin and steam rising up around it.

Someone had opened the metal-plated door and people who could still move were running and hobbling out to escape the battleground. "*Oh*," Ethan heard Olivia gasp, and she held onto his shoulders as if fearful of being flung off the world. "Oh no…oh no…"

"Come on!" he said, and took her hand to lead her toward the open door. Cypher soldiers were still coming in, blurring their way through the wall and then reforming. They moved past the terrified people trying to get out, and someone fired a pistol point-blank at one of them but it vibrated out to invisibility an instant before the slug could connect.

Olivia pulled free. Her face was drawn as tightly as a mask; her eyes wore the shine of near-madness and tears had run down to her chin. "No," she said, her voice low and strained. "I'm not…not going."

"Yes you are!" Ethan grabbed at her hand again but once more she pulled free.

"I have to...find something," she told him, and she began to walk not toward the way out but toward the crumpled and burning apartments. In her mind Vincent was in Apartment 227, and he was holding for her something he wanted her to have, and she would have it and then go, after everyone else had left. She would take from him the Magic Eight Ball, that joke gift, the gift that had laughter and love attached to it, because she realized even in her fugue that she could survive no longer without love and laughter, and she must have that gift from him or she would this night perish of a doubly broken heart.

"Olivia!" Ethan cried out. "Don't go back there!"

But if she heard him she did not respond; she was as much a determined wraith as the Cypher soldiers who blurred past her through the billowing yellow dust. She kept going, step after step, her eyes swollen with both desperate sadness and the rage she had pushed down and pushed down and pushed down and did not know what to do with for she could not fight these creatures from other worlds. She kept going with the smell of fire and the dead-snake smell of the Gorgon ship in her nostrils and in her lungs, and she kept going unaware that Ethan Gaines walked at her side, silent also in his anger, his blue eyes glinting like the edges of blades in a strong light.

Bloodied and staggering survivors passed them, struggling on toward the wall. A few stopped and tried to turn Olivia away from the wreckage, but they gave it up when they saw her sightless eyes. Through the dust and the smoke, she continued on with Ethan beside her, and they walked alongside the downed Gorgon ship with its mortal wounds of burnt holes and within them a glimpse of raw red meat formed into hexagonal-shaped corridors, wet and gleaming with unknown fluids. The way ahead was blocked by rubble. Olivia chose another way, and still Ethan followed. What had been a balcony was on fire. Glass crunched underfoot. A mass of timbers and a stainless steel kitchen sink lay ahead. A railing was twisted like a piece of melted licorice. In the smoky gloom the shadows of Cypher soldiers moved about as flames chewed on broken chairs and coffee tables.

"We can't get through!" Ethan said. "There's no way!"

But there *was* a way. Olivia knew there must be. Vincent was waiting for her, and he was all right, so there must be a way. She walked past the remnant of a standing wall on which still hung a metallic-looking plastic Horn Of Plenty. Ethan saw there was nothing but rubble, smoke, dust, and destruction ahead of them. Beside them loomed the dead Gorgon craft, and they passed a gaping hole from which the dark red liquid had poured to make a swamp of alien blood around the mangled belongings of men.

A Cypher soldier was standing in front of them, its weapon trained and ready.

"Go away," Ethan said, his voice weak but carrying enough strength to be heard over the crackling of flames. The soldier did not move for a few seconds, and then it stalked off into the ruins. Ethan knew it hadn't understood him, but what was working behind that faceless mask was the belief that the inhabitants of this world were not worth the waste of energy.

"We have to go back," Ethan told the woman, who had begun to sob and stumble as her resolve collapsed. He reached out for her hand, caught it and held her. "Olivia. Please. We have to go back…get out of here."

"Not yet," she answered, weeping. "Not yet…I've got to…find… Vincent. Vincent?" she called, into the dark cavern of despair. And louder: "*Vincent?*"

And that was when Ethan saw it coming, behind Olivia.

Through the smoke and dust, through the bloody swamp, through the tangle of timbers and broken walls…

…and it was not Olivia's Vincent.

It was crawling at first…slithering…and then it began to rise up from the wreckage, and it was not a Cypher soldier either. It moved with what might have been a serpentine grace, a strange kind of fascinating beauty, yet as it came closer a cold terror gripped Ethan's heart and his face contorted, and though he could not fully see the thing he could see enough to know that such a creature was so alien to men that it caused fear to freeze the body and the soul, that the guts drew tight and the stomach lurched, and he wanted to run from this transfixing horror but he could not leave Olivia and she had not seen yet…she had not seen but she saw his face and she was just about to turn and see what should not be seen by human eyes lest they be burned blind.

"NO!" the boy shouted.

And his free hand came up, palm outward, just as Olivia was turning, and to save the last of her sanity he wanted the Gorgon pilot to disappear, to be wiped from the face of this earth, and just in that instant his brain seemed to catch fire and the fire whipped down along his arm and into his hand. His palm burned as if it had been splashed with a bucketful of boiling oil. Did the air between himself and the creature contort? Did it change shape, become solid like a battering ram? Did it sparkle with flames that shot between himself and the alien like a thousand burning bullets?

Maybe all those.

Because in the next second the creature blew to pieces and Ethan was thrown backward, as if slammed by the recoil of an elephant gun. He had the sense to release Olivia's hand before he broke her arm. He went down into the debris, felt a nail go through his jeans into the back of his right thigh, felt the breath *whoosh* out of his lungs and his burning brain throb as if it were about to explode.

Olivia's arm had been nearly jerked out of its socket and would have been had Ethan not let go. She was full up with pain and yet she knew something had been there that was no longer there. She blinked into the gloom as the tears ran from her eyes and her mouth drooled threads of saliva. "What is it?" she asked, clenching a hand to her shoulder. "What is it? *What is it?*"

She dared not take another step forward, because something terrible had been there and now it was in pieces she did not want to see.

Ethan got himself loose from the nail, struggled up and fell again to his knees. His head was pounding, he felt sick to his stomach and in his mouth was the taste of bitter ashes. With a true force of will he commanded himself to stand, and he did. Olivia stared at him, wide-eyed; she shivered and wavered on her feet, as if about to pass out. Beyond her, just at the edge of recognition, Ethan saw something else slither away

114

through the debris. He tried to speak, could not find his voice, tried again, and said, "We have to go now."

"Go," Olivia repeated dully. Then: "Yes. We have to go."

Ethan looked at the palm of his hand that had seemingly been on fire. He expected to see it either covered with blisters or as one huge blister. Was the flesh a shade or two more red and maybe swollen a little? He couldn't tell for sure. The burning sensation was gone from his hand, arm and shoulder. He was tired, and his brain ached. He didn't look over at the thing that had been blown to bits; he just wanted to take Olivia's hand and guide her out of here. He realized he had the alien blood—the ship's blood—on his clothes. It smelled of the dead snake, and he wanted to be sick but there was no time for that because maybe the Cypher soldiers could smell it on him. They might swarm after him, and no insignificant humanity could save him.

He grasped Olivia's hand and started them back the way they'd come, and now there were other figures walking near them but they were not Cyphers or Gorgons, they were bloodied and ragged survivors picking their way out of the debris. Ethan couldn't recognize anyone. A man carried a little boy, and a woman staggered alongside, and all of them were battered and nearly nude for the clothes had been torn off them in the storm of destruction. An older man wearing a blood-covered shirt suddenly stopped walking and just sat down in a wicker chair as if waiting for the next bus to come along.

Olivia stared straight ahead, her crying now done, her face drawn and waxy. "We'll be all right," he told her, but he heard his voice tremble, and it sounded like the most stupid thing that had ever been said in the world. Where was Dave? What had happened to JayDee? What about Roger Pell, Kathy Mattson, Gary Roosa, Joel Schuster, and three or four other people he had at least spoken with? He doubted very many had lived through this…but…*he* was alive, and so was Olivia Quintero.

He thought that if the Gray Men came now, alerted by the noise and maybe the smell of blood, everything would be over. As it was…the Panther Ridge Apartments were finished as a refuge. The survivors were going to have to move, whether they wanted to or not.

The White Mansion, he thought.

Refuge or not, it was pulling at him harder than ever. He had to get there. *Had* to…but how? Who would help him on that journey, which seemed impossible? And he didn't know what he would find there, but…

I just blew up a Gorgon, he thought. *With my mind. Because I wanted to.*

And he remembered John Douglas, in the hospital, sitting in that chair and asking *What exactly are you, because I don't think you're human.*

"I am," said the boy, to no one, and Olivia was listening only to distant screams and cries for help and realizing she had come to her end as the leader of this sad fortress. "I am," he said, and again with more force, "*I am.*"

But at the same time he knew.

No human could cause earthquakes by wanting them to happen. No human could destroy a horror as he had just done, by *willing* it hard enough.

Ethan began to cry, silently. He was lost, even as he guided Olivia onward. He was lost, and somehow…someway…

…he must find out who and what he was, or die trying.

TWO.

THE
ANT FARM

ELEVEN.

EVEN THOUGH THEY SLEPT IN SEPERATE BEDS, SHE KNEW WHEN HE got up. She knew why, without looking at the clock. She heard him draw a long, shuddering breath that spoke volumes. She kept her eyes closed, because she did not want to look at him, did not want him to know she was awake. She hated him. He was on his own.

The man who was known as Jefferson Jericho walked into the bathroom and closed the door before he turned on the light. His wife, Regina, remained exactly where she was. Maybe she squeezed her eyes shut a little tighter. She was remembering that morning in April, two years ago, when she decided she could take no more of it, not a minute more. He was out sitting in his blue Adirondack chair on the lawn, under the big oak, with his mug of coffee that had GOD IS A HIGH ROLLER imprinted upon it. He drank his coffee black, with a half-spoonful of sugar. As always, he was sitting in that same place where the shadows cooled the Tennessee pasture. Horses pranced for him beyond the fence. She watched him stretch his legs out and grin at the sun and she thought *I can't take this anymore, not a minute, not a second.*

So she left the porch that wound around the big English-styled manor of a house and she went to his office and opened the drawer where he kept his Smith & Wesson .38. She had watched him at his target practice, and she knew where the safety was and how to load the cylinder. She had been born on a farm, had come up the hard way into these riches that now tormented her, and by Christ she could fire a pistol if she had to.

And now Regina figured she had to.

With the gun loaded and ready and her yellow silk nightgown flagging around her in the morning's sweet breeze, she walked off the porch and along the flagstone path that led past the decorative well and the gazebo. She dimly remembered that it was the third day of April and she had some dry cleaning to pick up, but fuck that.

Today was the day she was going to kill the preacherman.

The liar. The bastard. The twister of truth until you thought yourself a liar, and that your eyes and ears were no more than broken tools. She hated the way he grinned, hated the way he won everything, hated his luck and his handsomeness and his hand always outstretched to make some wayward young girl into a better Christian. And if she was pretty enough and pliable enough he could show her a glimpse of Heaven, but she had to be a High Roller, just like himself. Had to be a Dreamer and a Dare Taker and all those other buzzing buzz words and names and phrases meant to make people feel more important so they could be controlled just that much more easily.

Preacherman, Regina thought, and realized she was maybe crazy and maybe a little drunk still from the bourbon binge last night, *my loyal husband and lover, companion and fiend of the night…it's time for you to pack that fucking grin away.*

But most of all she was disappointed and destroyed, and she could not live like this or let him live another day. It was right, maybe, that they went together. The sixteen-year-old girl, the one who had the meth problem and had committed suicide, was the worst. That sad tear-stained piece of notebook paper Regina had found when she'd been gathering his suits for the dry cleaning. Had he *wanted* her to find that? Had he placed it there in the inner pocket so she would find it and realize how little she meant to him, and that she had better keep her mouth shut or all these High Roller riches would turn into smoke and ashes? And to find out he had been looting those girls and women, the ones who came to him burdened and life-beaten and begging his help? The ones from the drug program, and the unwed mothers, and the abused girls with the bruised eyes and the bleeding hearts that needed love?

Regina had known that girls who had trouble with their fathers were always looking for love, wherever they could find it. They were starved for it, and they needed to be filled. She knew, because she was one of them. And there grinning at the morning and all he surveyed from his favorite blue Adirondack chair sat the oh-so-handsome and oh-so-holy and oh-how-fucking-fatherly Jefferson Jericho, whose walls were about to fall because his farmgirl wife—older now, in her late thirties, ridden hard and put to bed wet—had suddenly found religion.

These walls were diseased. They were tainted and ugly, they were riddled with cracks and infested with vile creeping things.

A bullet would clean things right up. And then Regina would go back into the house, sit at the master's desk and write the story of why she had done this and every dirty thing the detective agency had told her after their investigation, and at the end she would write down Jefferson's real name so the world would know how the sins of Leon Kushman had taken him to a slab in the morgue.

She walked barefoot across the emerald Bermuda grass and came up silently behind him. She saw the vista he was seeing: below the hillock on which the Jericho house sat and beyond the pasture where the horses played was the town. *His* town, the one he'd envisioned and built. It was bathed this morning in sunlight and its copper-accented roofs glowed like heavenly gold. The town was named—appropriately for the woman who was about to cast the man out—New Eden. It was built to resemble an American town of the 1950s, though hardly anyone remembered what they had looked like anymore; it was a fantasy state of mind, if anything. The houses came in several different styles and sedate colors. They sat on small but expensive lots on streets that made radials all leading to the central, largest and most elaborate building, the Church of the High Rollers. From here, it seemed to Regina that the building was made not of milk-white stone but of milk-white wax, and to her it was worth about as much as a puddle of goo.

New Eden sat on what had been rolling hills and farmland thirty-six miles south of Nashville, Tennessee. Occasionally an entertainer who had been paid big bucks to embrace the High Roller doctrine came to give a concert on the equally big stage. That usually pulled in more of the artist's fans. There was a waiting list to get into New Eden as long as a country road. There was even a waiting list to be hired as part of the groundskeeping service or the security patrols. Everybody, it seemed, wanted in through the gilded gates.

Today, Regina thought, there would be a vacancy in a very high place.

She started to speak, to say something like *You greedy bastard*, or *I know everything*, or *I'm not letting you do this any longer*, but she decided to let the gun do the talking. As soon as the shot was heard down below, the security men in their golden Segway chariots would be racing up the long curving drive. So she wouldn't have a lot of time to write her letter and finish herself off. It was time. Time time time...way past time.

She aimed the revolver at the top of Leon Kushman's head of thick mink-brown hair and her finger started to squeeze the trigger. Her heart was beating very hard. She wondered if she should shield her face with her other hand, because she didn't want any of his brains on her. No, no, she decided; she needed both hands to steady the gun.

Do it, she told herself.

Yes.

Now.

But just as Regina Jericho, the former Regina Clanton, began to put some strength into the trigger pull the sky blew up.

The noise was not the solemn voice of God speaking out to save the life of Jefferson Jericho. It was more like the ear-splitting blast of a thousand demonic voices shouting at once in harsh and unknown tongues, an explosion at the zenith of a Tower of Babel in Hell, and then it turned into the low dark mutterings of a madman in a basement, speaking in riddles.

Jefferson had fallen out of his chair. The entire chair had gone over. The noise had made Regina whirl around in time to see a fiery red flash in the sky to the west, maybe twelve thousand feet up over the green fields and rolling pastures. And from the center of this flash, as if making itself whole as it slid out of nothingness, was a huge triangular monster mottled with yellow, black, and brown. Staring at it, transfixed by this scene that froze her with a horror she had never known, not even when her father in his Baptist rages locked her in a dark closet while he beat his wife—her mother—with the buckle end of a belt, Regina felt the gun fall from her fingers into the yielding Bermuda grass.

And Jefferson's voice rose up, the voice that thousands upon thousands depended on for wisdom, sustenance and wealth. Except now he spoke in what was almost a whimper. He said, "God save us." Then he first looked into Regina's face and next saw the gun on the ground. He reached for it with a shaky hand, and when he picked it up he gave her an expression that made her think of a closet door shutting in her face. And *click* went the lock.

Now, in her bed in that same English manor house overlooking the same yet terribly changed New Eden, Regina Jericho pressed her hand against her mouth because she wanted to scream. It would be daylight soon; the new gods would make it daylight, except it would be like the light Jefferson had just switched on in the bathroom. It would be a little too bright and a little too blue, and it would offer no real comfort or warmth. But the citizens of New Eden were alive, and they were well taken care of. They were accepted, in the new order of things. And now Regina heard the water running in the bathroom sink, and she knew also that the water was different; it was clean and clear, yes, but it left an oily texture on the skin that could not be towelled or wiped or scrubbed away. The water was running, and Jefferson was splashing his face before he shaved with his electric razor.

He had told Regina, in one of his hollow-eyed confessions of the thing, that *she* liked him to be clean-shaven when he arrived. After *she* called him, and that little tingling began at the back of his neck. Of course no one had any of those fancy razors with four or five blades anymore. Not even a razor with a single blade. There were knives in the kitchen, yes; but when Regina had tried to cut her throat with one last December, it had turned to something as soft as rubber and couldn't have cut a chunk of melting ice cream. Then it had turned back to a sharp blade again when she'd returned it to the drawer.

They're watching us, Jefferson had told her. *Always watching. They won't let us hurt ourselves.*

But why? she'd asked, in one of her panic states. *Why? What do they want with us?*

They like us, Jefferson had answered. She *likes us.*

And then he'd given the grin that might be a ghost of itself because his soulful dark brown eyes were so haunted, but it was still the grin of a High Roller who wanted always to be on the winning side, and he'd said quietly *She likes* me. *And everything and everyone else is like...a child with an ant farm, I guess. Just watch the ants and see what they do. The ants go round and round and think they're going somewhere. Think they have* freedom. *Or whatever that means to an ant. Baby, I think I'm going crazy.*

No, Regina had said, with the fire of hatred and disgust in her eyes. *I am not your baby anymore.*

She kept her eyes closed and lay as still as death. It was the only way to keep on living, if this was really life. The citizens of New Eden had no choice. They were all ants, and the ant farm was in its own little box somewhere far away from all that had been known before. Somewhere that made the mind want to stop thinking, because there was no answer to the question of *where.*

She heard Jefferson suddenly choke and throw up into the toilet. After a minute or so he flushed it and the fouled artificial water went to...where? He was afraid, she knew. Deathly afraid. If she reached over and touched his bed, she would feel the dampness of the sweat that had leaped from his pores as soon as he had heard—*felt*—the call. But he would go, because if he did not the pain would start at the back of his neck until it felt as if his skull might shatter. He'd told her this, as if she cared.

Go on, get dressed, she told him mentally. *Get dressed and get the fuck out of here and go to the arms of your ultimate mistress...*

She assumed the thing had arms. She had never asked, and Jefferson had never said. But when he got back—and that might be days, because

124

he said time was *messed up* in that place beyond knowing—he would be sick again and cry like a little boy curled up in a corner, a little boy in a big man's skin and suit. Regina would have no sympathy for him. Not an iota, because the real God of this Universe had decided to bring down the house on the High Rollers, and all of New Eden had been cast from the garden in the shadow of the snake.

Just let me sleep, she thought. *Please...God...let me sleep.*

But Regina would not sleep until her husband had emerged from the bathroom, had gotten himself dressed in a dark blue suit, white shirt, and tastefully-patterned tie—which he had a hell of a lot of trouble tying, as usual—and then left the room to go downstairs. He walked heavily in his shiny black wingtips, as if on the way to his own hanging.

Go to hell, she thought. *You deserve it.*

Then he was gone, and she did go back to sleep after a few long minutes of silent weeping, because the ant farm was a cruel, cruel place.

Jefferson Jericho opened the glass doors that led out to the rear terrace. He walked out upon the terrace and then down the stone steps to the backyard, which seemed to go on forever. Looking up into the dark, he saw no stars. There were never any stars. He continued to walk out further and further across the lawn, his heart racing, his mouth dry, his boyishly handsome face drawn into a tight mask and his teeth gritted so hard they might crack under the pressure. Several already had. His front teeth had broken into jagged edges, but in a few days they were just fine again.

He kept walking, and waiting for it to happen.

Then, with a single step, he walked into another world.

One second he was in the darkness of his own backyard, and the next...

Tonight it was a bedroom from what might have been a French mansion. It was maybe from around the year 1890 or so, he thought. But he was no student of historical furnishings; it just looked like something from a movie set…French mansion, 1890, white candles of many sizes burning all around, heavy purple drapes at the window, an opulent canopied bed also purple, on the wall a large tapestry of a woman offering an apple to a unicorn, about eight feet above his head a chandelier with a dozen more lighted candles in it. Under his shiny shoes, a thick, red rug, had been thrown down upon a hardwood floor. The walls were made of polished wood and across the room was a single door.

The summons at the back of his neck was still throbbing a little. His body felt as if it had been stretched and then compressed. His bones ached. His clothes smelled faintly burnt, as did his flesh. At the pit of his stomach was the same queasiness, and he was sweating again. He looked at the drapes that hid the window and wondered what he would see if he moved them aside. The last time, the room had been all-white, futuristic, with pulsing rays of light crisscrossing the ceiling. He wondered if they had somehow captured old movies and were watching them for ideas, or if they were reading minds or if…whatever they were doing, they were very good at creating these elaborate fantasies.

Jefferson Jericho stood waiting. He decided to take a backward step, to see if he would return from whence he came. He took the step but no, he did not return. God was punishing him big time, he thought. Big time for putting New Eden together in a series of Ponzi schemes. Big time for his calculations and deceptions and desires. If he saw something—or someone—he wanted, he took it. That was his way. And if God had wanted to punish him for that, he thought, then why had God given him the tongue and personality to talk anyone into doing anything he wanted, and why had God given him the will to find an outlet for his raging sexual fevers at every opportunity, and why had God given him this firm body and handsome face that could cause investors to open their wallets without question and teenage virgins to open their legs as if hypnotized by his glowing male persona?

The thing was, he was *good*. Good at every damned thing he did. Good at planning, at money management, at public speaking, at persuasion, at sex. Very good at *that*. Very inventive, and always wanting to experiment on new flesh. And if God was punishing him for all this, then why had God made so many frustrated women who were looking for the kind of thrills he enjoyed giving? Why had God made so many gullible people who listened, but did not hear, and so gave Jefferson Jericho just the challenge he desired to pick their pockets clean?

And everything had been so *easy*. Since the rainy Monday fourteen years ago at the car lot in Little Rock, Arkansas, when the shimmering rainbow had come out and the thirty-year-old Number One Salesman Of The Month Leon Kushman had stared at it from the window in his cramped little office and had a revelation.

To Hell with selling cars. If a man wants to make himself some real money, he gives the people rainbows.

What he does is...he creates a religion.

He rolls the dice for high stakes, and he gets people to believe in the words that flow from his mouth like a torrent of sweet wine.

I can do that, Leon Kushman decided. *Me, the son of a failed furniture salesman who wrecked our family and went out feet first on a week-long alcohol binge in a cheap little motel.*

By God, I can rise above. I can give them rainbows...I can make them high rollers, masters of their own destinies. Well...let's say they will think of themselves in that way...but isn't that what a good leader does?

Yes. Yes. Regina will go for it, and she might have some good ideas too. Yes!

The door across the room slowly opened, like a tease.

Jefferson Jericho felt the sweat bead on his forehead. He felt a cold shiver travel the length of his spine. He couldn't help it; his six-foot-two-inch, husky body trembled with fear.

She had come to play with her toy.

TWELVE.

SHE CAME INTO THE ROOM ELEGANTLY, DRESSED IN A GOWN OF black and gold. Tonight she was a brunette...long black hair in curly ringlets, her eyes pale blue under arched brows, her full, lush lips wet with a promising smile. She had been blonde last time, except she had had Asiatic almond-shaped brown eyes and heavy breasts. The time before that...brown hair in a ponytail, tawny flesh, petite, something between a Brazilian beach girl and a California Gidget. He understood that she was trying on different skins just as he might try on different clothes to match his mood. But surely they were watching movies, in some strange theater in the sky, and their inspiration came from the world's shadowplays.

"My *Jefferson*," she said, and maybe he imagined a slight hiss in that name, or maybe not. She approached him in what was nearly a gliding motion. Suddenly she was standing before him as if frames had been removed from the scene. She was as tall as he tonight, and nearly too slim. Her eyelashes were very thick. He wondered if they were also reading the fashion magazines of the 1970s and storing the images away for later use.

She was beautiful, in this disguise. Yet Jefferson knew that sometimes the disguises slipped, and when that happened he felt the fear curdle within himself and something abhorrent stir in the most primitive part of his being. As he looked into her face he thought that her eyes were too pale. They were almost white, and the pupils were more catlike than round. As soon as he thought this, the color of her eyes became more warmly blue and the slits of the pupils rounded.

"Is that more pleasing?" she asked, in a voice that mixed a husky taunt with a little girl's high, soft register.

Sometimes, also, she couldn't get the voice right at first.

He thought he said *yes*. He didn't know for sure, because this was all dreamlike to him and blurred around the edges and very often he only heard himself speak as if in an echo from an unfathomable distance.

"You are looking much pleasing yourself," she told him. She fingered the knot of his necktie. Her fingers were maybe a little bit too long and the nails looked like white plastic. "Much pleasing for me to look upon." The face came closer to his and the intense blue eyes peered deeply, as if choosing a starting point for dissection. "My *Jefferson*, come to play with his harlot." Her mouth gave a twitch. "I mean to say...*starlet*."

Yes, he thought he answered. *Starlet*.

Her hands—had the fingers corrected themselves?—fluttered to his face and slowly ran over his cheeks and down to his jawline. Her smile never changed, but it was a cunningly human smile, with cunningly perfect human teeth behind the lips. What most unnerved him was that she never blinked. Never. And maybe she couldn't, because even though he sometimes thought *Please blink...please blink* in a kind of panic-edged plea, she did not, and she didn't mention it though he knew she was always reading his mind.

He could feel her in there, exploring. Always curious. Lifting up the rocks of his life and observing what scuttled from beneath. She knew everything about him, had likely known from their very first meeting. When was that? Time was rubbery, a foreign object. Two months after that day with Regina and the pistol? When he, Alex Smith, Doug Hammerfield and Andy Warren had taken one of the pickup trucks out of New Eden to try to find gasoline somewhere. That night in late June, when the sky was streaked with blue lightning and after a few miles heading south Doug said nervously from the backseat, "Jeff...we'd better turn around. We've gone too far. Don't you think?"

Everything was dark except for flashes in the sky. They had containers in the back and hoses to siphon gas with if they found any. The regular stations around New Eden had long before gone dry and shut down. And the problem was, the men from New Eden were using up too much gasoline in the search for more, having to go further and further away from their refuge. Everything was dark in the world but for the cones of the headlights, and one of those was growing dim.

"Let's go back," Alex had said. "There's nothing out here."

"Try again tomorrow," Doug added. "When we can see something."

"Yeah," Jefferson agreed. "Yeah, okay."

He steered the truck onto a dirt road to back up and turn around, and suddenly there in front of them, standing in the glare of the dim-eyed headlights, was a group of twelve faceless, black-garbed Cypher soldiers. The creatures were staring up at the tortured sky, their weapons also upraised.

"Oh *shit*!" Andy shouted, and Doug shouted frantically *Shut up, shut up*. Jefferson tried to slam the truck into reverse and peel Firestones, but something slipped, and the gears ground together with a noise to wake the Confederate dead in their moss-covered graves. Several of the Cyphers took note of this, and turned their faceplates and their weapons upon the shuddering truck.

"They're gonna kill us!" Alex yelled, nearly in Jefferson's ear.

Jefferson saw no way out but the way he had always known: plow forward and damn it all. He found first gear and sank his foot to the floorboard. The truck crashed into some of the Cyphers even as others were blurring away, into whatever zone or dimension they were able to enter. Brown liquid splattered across the windshield. The dim headlight blew out. "Go, go, go!" Alex shouted. They were speeding along a dirt road at over seventy miles an hour, hitting every bump between here and the lap of Jesus.

Looking back through the swirl of dust, Doug gave a strangled moan.

Jefferson saw in the sideview mirror a rush of white-hot flame coming at the truck, like a floodwater of fire. In an instant it was upon them, too fast for him to avoid; there was no outrunning the speed of that flame, no way to escape it. The fire ate the back of the truck and melted the tires and exploded the gas tank, and as it turned the interior into a blast furnace Jefferson Jericho...

...found himself sitting on a terrace overlooking a green-shadowed garden. At the center of the garden was a silvery pond. Yellow and red fruit that resembled apples, but were strangely shaped, hung from the trees. The air smelled of air conditioning, a little metallic. He realized he was wearing a white robe of some kind of silky material, and on his feet were white sandals that might have been rubber. He looked at his unburnt hands and ran a hand through his unburnt hair, and he gasped aloud at the idea that indeed—in spite of all of his sins—he had been admitted to Heaven. He nearly wept.

And that was when *she* glided out onto the terrace, wearing a gown that sparkled with a million colors under the artificial sun, and she smiled at him with a mouth that still needed some work, and she said in a voice that was like listening to a dozen voices in a dozen registers at once, "I have been reading. It is written...the enemy of my enemy is my friend. Is that not correct, Leon Kush Man? Or prefer you do Jeffer Son Jericho?"

As Jefferson tried to stand up and, off-balance, fell to the glistening stones that floored the terrace, she stood over him with a blinding white glare at her back, and she lifted her too-long arms toward him and said, "No fear of me. I have saved you. Do I speak well?"

Yes...yes...you speak well...yes.

"I am learned. Learn *ing*," she corrected herself. "So much to..." She cast about for the right word. "*Absorb*," she said. "I am a..." Again there was a pause while she gathered her words. "...lowly student," she went on, her voices rising and falling while Jefferson Jericho thought he had not entered Heaven but had been pulled into Hell. "Ah!" she said, with a faint smile below the unblinking red-tinged eyes. "You must explain to me that concept."

Somewhere in that time, he slept. When he awakened he was sitting in his blue Adirondack chair overlooking New Eden in the morning light, dressed in the same clothes he'd been wearing when he and the three other men had left the night before, and there was a little irritation—like a Tennessee mosquito bite—at the back of his neck. He felt woozy and weak; what was wrong with the sunlight? Where was the sun? The light had a blue cast, and the sky was white and featureless. And the clothes he had on…the same, but not the same. The material of his shirt…the same gray-on-white stripes, but…the fabric had a faintly oily feel, as did the khaki trousers, as if they'd been manufactured from an unknown synthetic.

"Regina!" he called as he stood up and stumbled toward the house. "Regina…*baby*!"

He learned he'd been gone for two days. Doug Hammerfield, Alex Smith and Andy Warren had not returned. And something had changed about New Eden. It was soon discovered that trying to drive, walk, or bike out of New Eden brought you right back to New Eden. There was no way out. It was an eternal circle, one for Dante's appreciation. And the damnedest thing was, you were just turned around without realizing it, and there you were…home again, in the realm of the High Rollers.

At six o'clock in the morning, twelve noon and six o'clock in the evening white squares of what appeared to be chunks of tofu appeared on the dinner tables, along with smooth metal receptacles of a chalky milk-like substance. No one could stand and watch the items appear; they were just there, between breaths and eyeblinks. No one could likewise watch the receptacles disappear and yet they did, even put in a box and locked away in a cupboard. They could not be dented or crushed. The food and drink had a slightly bitter taste, yet they filled the stomach and even became habit-forming. Some said they believed this food gave them the most beautiful dreams, and they began to sleep their lives away.

There was no rain, no storms, no change of weather. It was always a blue-tinged sunny day with a featureless white sky. The light bloomed in the morning and faded in the evening. The grass stopped growing but remained green, like artificial turf. The leaves on the trees never changed, and never fell. The Fourth of July was Halloween was Thanksgiving was Christmas was New Year's Day was Valentine's Day, no difference. New Eden had running water and electricity. Bulbs never burned out. Toilets never stopped up or overflowed. Nothing needed painting, unless you wanted to paint. Nothing in the houses—dishwashers, garage doors, clocks, DVD players, washing machines—ever broke down. When the garbage was taken out, it was removed from the green bins by unseen and unheard maintenance crews.

New Eden had become the most perfect place not of this earth, for Jefferson Jericho and the others had come to grasp the truth through many late night council sessions. Their dream town now existed in some other dimension, some other slice of space and time, protected by the Gorgons from the war that ravaged the real world.

Protected, as well, from the Cyphers. From all pressures and worries of the tormented earth. Food and drink were supplied, and all the essentials of human life down to soap and dishwashing detergent. Even the toilet paper never ran out, but was on a continuous roll that replenished itself when necessary. Some found the paper to be very thin, and smelling somewhat like the disinfectant of a hospital room.

No woman had become pregnant, in the time since New Eden had been transported. No one had died, not human nor pet. Marianne Dawson's cervical cancer had simply vanished, and Glenn O'Hara's emphysema had gone away. Though eighty-four-year-old Will Donneridge still walked with a cane due to his hip implant, he was doing fine and walked the streets almost every day.

Many people walked the streets, almost every day.

And some, sleepless, also walked at night. Sometimes the dogs howled at night too, but it was a noise one had to get used to.

Our ant farm, Jefferson thought as he looked upon the creature in her elegant gown of black and gold, with her long black hair and her pale blue eyes that, unblinking, saw and knew everything. *Here is our creator.*

Whether she was one entity or many in one flesh, he did not know. Whether she was truly female or not, he dared not guess. And what she really looked like, without the disguise…he dreaded the thought and had to banish it as best he could.

Because here she was, his harlot starlet from the stars, and as she stroked his cheeks and played with the heroic-looking cleft in his strong and noble chin, she also began to feed him the mind-pictures that were his undoing. She knew all of his past deeds and misdeeds; she knew the face, aroma, and touch of every MILF and every drug- or pain-addled teenaged girl in every motel room he had ever paid for with his hidden account Visa card. She now offered them up to him, the ferrago of fleshly feasts that had over time become the central obsession of his life, and so potent were these pictures of his passionate past that—alien creature or not, female or not—Jefferson Jericho was responding to these mental images, and this was the true power he had come to know because it was not so much about the sinning as it was about the winning.

You know I compel to disrobe you.

Had she spoken with words, or with her mind? Her mouth had not moved; her understanding of the human language was still fractured, but her understanding of her toy was perfection itself.

Her fingers were working at his tie. He knew she enjoyed undressing him; it seemed almost an ecstatic ritual to her, for as she let his Ben Silver tie drop, took off his coat, and began to unbutton his Brooks Brothers shirt, her eyes were aflame like meteors in the night. As she unbuckled his belt and unzipped his trousers, her face in her ecstasy seemed to suddenly become like soft wax and shift on its bones, and Jefferson had to quickly look away lest he lose his hard-on…but she sensed this in an instant, and flooded his mind so thoroughly with memories of past conquests, moans, and orgasmic shivers from a legion of females who had fallen under his spell, that he quite simply was himself spellbound.

My Jefferson. Take my hand.

He held up his trousers with one hand and with the other took hers. It was, as always, almost the feel of human flesh but not quite. She led him to the bed, where he sat down to allow her to remove his polished shoes and his socks, which she did slowly…again, almost as an ecstatic ritual. Then she—slowly, slowly—pulled off his trousers and his blue-checked boxers, and she commanded him mentally to lie on his back upon the bed while she slid down beside him. Once in position, she began to play with that large part of him that she seemed to find as fascinating as any female who had never flown between the stars.

When Jefferson's mind began to betray him, the Gorgon mistress injected him with fresh memories. She made the dalliances of twenty years ago as real as the moment, and all he could do was drift in a territory of heated sexual dreams while she pulled and stretched and twisted him between her hands as if testing the strength of the material he was made of. Then suddenly the frames skipped once more and she was undressed, and her not-quite-human-flesh was pressed hard against him. When he dared to look into her face in the yellow candlelight he saw unwanted shadows there and he quickly looked away, but all the time she was feeding him his own past, the parade of images from a life of lustful debauchery, scenes contained within the walls of countless motels and apartments and the occasional back room of a strip club. She gave him back the world he had made for himself, and he was proud of his accomplishments, proud of his power to move at his whim any female object, proud of his abilities and attributes and gifts from God, proud of his silver tongue and golden persona, proud proud proud until he was nearly bursting aflame with pride.

The flame lit him up. She was trying to kiss him but she didn't know how to kiss, it was all open mouth that belonged to a hollow mask but he couldn't think that, couldn't go there that this creature mounting him was not human and *oh oh* back to a steamy shower in a Motel Six with a German exchange student named Jana who had come in wanting a good deal on a used Jeep Wrangler, and the wetness and softness and murmuring enveloped him and stole him away.

He was inside her now, pounding her as he would have any human female, a mindless rhythm that built to an explosive release. She was damp within, and it passed through his feverish mind that this was false too, part of the disguise, some kind of artificial lubricant developed in an alien lab...and then he was plunged back into a memory, examining a birthmark in the shape of a cat's paw on the left breast of a blonde woman named Georgia May who used to work at his bank in Little Rock.

As he turned her over on the bed or she turned him over, which was difficult to say who did what because the frames were skipping, Jefferson plunged deeply inside her and heard her give a soft hissing noise. He kept driving into her with all his strength and with all his past amours tumbling through his mind. He had endurance, he could keep this up until he decided they both had had enough; it had never been love, with anyone, it had always been the winning of something or someone, the praise, the attention, the admiration that had kept him going from one to the next to the next. And so too, did he perversely enjoy this admiration from his starlet harlot.

Then, as sometimes happened, as Jefferson plunged into his Gorgon mistress, a hot fleshy thing clamped upon him, there in her wet depths, and held him fast. He felt a shiver of panic, of terror, that passed away in the wiry embrace of a small-boned Asian stripper named Kitten who always smelled to him of burning leaves. And then, as sometimes happened in the heat of their encounters, small tentacle-like things began to slide around the backs of his thighs to hold him more firmly still, and here he squeezed his eyes shut and gave himself up fully to the memories she offered, for even in the bedrooms of the past, Jefferson Jericho could feel her coming apart at her seams, and things slithering out of her false body to snake-grip his own.

No memory she offered up, however lush, was enough to overcome this part of it. But she tried, and as she pumped his mind full of decadent opiates of his own making, a tentacle wound around the base of his balls and tightened there while another flicked and played with them, and deep inside her the fleshy thing clamped hard once…twice…a third time and he came to the tune of a blonde vagabond named Marigold sitting on a bed naked playing "Greensleeves" on a beat-up acoustic guitar.

The thing inside his Gorgon mistress—as strong as another hand— milked him. The tentacles writhed and whipped. He had never seen these things, but he knew what they must be. She was gracious enough to put them away when she was done with him. When she had wrung him out the fleshy clamp released him, and in a dazed and drifting dream-state he wondered if they were using his seed to make hybrids of human and... what? But it was no matter to him now, for though he feared this creature, and when she called him by that device planted in the back of his neck, he had to go into the bathroom and throw up, he was so afraid...he had to admit in the long-lingering afterglow that she was one great lay.

He had screwed women who needed to have bags over their heads. At least this one—this pretend woman—was beautiful and changed her skin and hair and eyes and always made him come like a champ. She liked him. What was so bad about that?

He would think that way until she sent him back, and then the reality would hit him and he would go into his ant farm house, throw up in his ant farm toilet, strip off the clothes that always smelled a little burnt and crawl into a corner. He would stay there, hollow-eyed and shivering as if from the most terrible nightmare, until Regina said *Get up, you pig.* Or something worse.

"My Jefferson?"

He was lying naked on his back on the rumpled bed. His eyes had been closed. Now he opened them to the dim candlelight. She was standing beside the bed, dressed again in her elegant gown of gold and black. Her face was a pool of shadows, but he could see her eyes glinting. Maybe he imagined it, but the pupils seemed to be blood-red. He thought that her disguise was beginning to melt.

"For you we have a task," she said.

He lay still, listening, yet too weak and drained to move.

"There has been..." She paused, rapidly searching through what she knew of his language. "An incident," she went on. "Four of your hours ago."

Was she taller than before? Larger? A looming presence that was as hard and cold as the darkness of the universe? All those, it seemed. And her voice...many voices in one, many registers and echoes, many ghosts upon ghosts.

"We require you," she said, "to help us." When he didn't respond, the voices asked sharply, "Hearing us?"

"Yes," he answered, newly unnerved. And again, so she—it—knew he was paying attention, though he did not want to look at her. "Yes, I am."

"What you would call a *boy* has…disturbed us. He has aided our enemy. We wish to know more about this boy. You will find him and bring him back to us."

"*What?*" Jefferson sat up, still groggy but clear-headed enough to process what she was saying. Her eyes with their red pupils—slit-shaped, now—seemed to hang in the dark over a large and strangely misshapen body in a gown that had changed dimensions to fit the form, and he felt the stirrings of dread and terror in the roots of his guts. He had started sweating; he had to look away again. "A *boy*? What boy?"

"Our questions must be answered," came the reply, in many octaves. "He is with others of your kind. They protect him. You are a…" Again, there was a pause while she searched. "*Persuader,*" she said. "Grow their trust."

Gain their trust, he thought.

"Yes," she said. "Exactly that."

"I don't…I don't know…what you're—"

"You *do* know. Penetrate their protection. Reach this boy. Put your hands upon him and bring him back to us."

"I…can't…listen…*listen*…why can't you do it, if he's so important?"

"This needs," she replied, "the human touch. We would be…how would you say…exposed. My Jefferson, you are very good at what you do. You are very…" A pause of a few seconds, searching. "*Skilled.* Put your hands upon him, flesh to flesh. Then you will bring him back to us."

"Bring him *back* to you? How can I do that?"

"We will manage the journey. My Jefferson, how you tremble! Be not feared, we will watch over you."

"*How?*" He shook his head, defying the hurtful device buried in the back of his neck. "I can't do this! You're saying…you want to send me out *there*? Out in that *war*?"

Did she sigh, as if with human exasperation? Her voices were cold when she replied. "We require the boy. We require you to bring him to us. You will have protection. One of our own, and one of yours. This male has been…" Once more the search of language. "*Modified.* He will

139

react to a certain level of threat. You need not worry yourself over this. Am I not speaking well?"

"Yes," he said, as he always did when she asked this question. He could not look at her; he was too afraid of seeing some part of what she might truly be under the disguise.

"The boy," she continued, "is in a place called Col O Raydo. Do you know this place?"

"Colorado," he corrected her. "Listen...no...please, I can't—"

"You can and you will. We have given you much, my Jefferson. *Much*. And much given can be much taken away. You will be removed from this place and sent to find the boy. It will be up to you to carry out our command." She was silent for a moment, and then the voices said, "Our *wish*. Once this is done, you may go home and all will be well."

Jefferson almost laughed at that one, but what came out was more of a choked gasp. "All will *never* be well," he managed to say.

"We intend to win this conflict." The Gorgon's face was shadowed in the candlelight, her voices rising and falling. "We will be beneficent rulers. But now...we need the boy, and you must sleep for a time."

Jefferson was aware that the thing at the nape of his neck had begun a soft throbbing. It was like having his neck and shoulders rubbed by warm hands, and the sensation began to move down his back and along his arms, down his spine, into his hips and his legs.

"Sleep," said the Gorgon. And Jefferson darted a glance up into where the face must be but saw only a black hole above the shimmering gown. "*Sleep*," urged a thousand voices. The comforting warmth of the implant soothed him, lulled him, filled his head with the memory of the beauty this female creature had been a short while ago. He felt sleep coming upon him and he couldn't fight it; he didn't want to fight it. He lay down upon the bed of this fictitious French mansion room again, stretched himself out and closed his eyes, and breathing deeply and steadily the last thing he heard her say—and maybe this was spoken in his mind directly from hers—was:

You will know the boy when you find him, my Jefferson. Now sleep in peace. You have earned it.

THIRTEEN.

"O*H,*" OLIVIA WHISPERED, AND IN THAT SOFT, TERRIBLE SOUND was the noise of a world falling to pieces.

The smoky light of a weak sunrise revealed all. It was disaster upon disaster. It was fire and dust and death. It was a massive dead reptile in the living room, and no one could take it out to the garbage. As the wounded continued to stumble out and the dead were carried out, Olivia sat down on the cracked parking lot pavement almost in the shadow of the crashed Gorgon craft, and she put her hands to her face and wanted to cry, wanted to let everything go, but Ethan was still with her and so she did not because she was still the leader of this wreckage. Ethan had not left her side, and he was standing nearby watching bloody and dust-covered figures emerge from the murk.

Ethan had seen a few Cypher soldiers still moving about. He knew there was another Gorgon up in the complex somewhere, probably hidden low in the ruins, and the Cyphers were not going to leave until they'd destroyed the creature. He was dusty and tired and his damp clothes smelled of Gorgon-reek. Already the craft was losing its markings, the colors fading into a grim, grayish cast. In a few days, the odor of rot would be unbearable. Even so, tonight the Gray Men might come looking for meat and even a dead alien ship might do for a feast. He shuddered at the thought of that, and at the memory of what his brief glimpse of the Gorgon had been.

He had blown the thing up. Completely destroyed it, just by wanting it to happen. His hand was back to normal, his arm, his brain, everything. Back to normal. But he was thinking that *normal* for him was far different than for anyone else who had survived that crash. He thought he remembered seeing what looked like fiery wasps or burning bullets striking the Gorgon and tearing the thing to shreds. And that recoil, knocking him down as if he'd actually fired a wickedly powerful rifle. He examined the palm of his right hand again, as he had several times already. Nothing there but the lines of fate.

And then Ethan let himself think it, and let it sink deep.

I am not just a boy. JayDee is right. I'm something different.

Something…but not totally human anymore.

Survivors were still emerging from the ruins. A few of them, bloodied and battered, stood around Olivia waiting for her to speak, to take control, to make Panther Ridge a secure fortress again, but she could not, and so they passed on. The wooden door covered with metal plates was opened, and people began to leave. Some refused, even as they were urged on by friends or loved ones; dazed and hopeless, they sat down on the ground and could not be moved. An occasional shot was fired up in the remaining apartments, but whether someone was shooting at Cypher soldiers or the slithering Gorgon or taking their own lives was unknown.

"Oh my God! Olivia!" A figure wearing a blood-spattered white t-shirt and khaki trousers came hobbling toward Olivia and Ethan. John Douglas had found a rusted length of rebar and was maintaining a precarious balance on a sprained right ankle. He had a few bumps and bruises, but otherwise he was all right. The blood on his shirt had come from others he'd helped out of the ruins. He had escaped death by going out his front door to watch the show of alien fireworks, had seen the ship coming down, and with a shout of warning to anyone who could hear, he'd thought to get into the hospital for whatever he could grab. The door was chained and padlocked, as usual after dark. The ship seemed to be coming right at him. There was no time to get the key. Other people were already running past him. A collision with Paul Edson had twisted his ankle, but Paul had helped him get clear of the crash. "Jesus," he said to Olivia, his voice hoarse and harsh. "I thought you were likely dead!" His swollen eyes went to Ethan. "*You*," he said, and maybe there was a hint of accusation in it. But then he took a long breath to regain his composure and his focus, and he asked, "You all right?"

"Yes sir," Ethan answered. The nail-puncture wound at the back of his thigh was nothing, not compared to the wounds he'd seen on people coming out of the ruins…and there were eleven dead bodies covered with bloody sheets and blankets lying about twenty feet away.

"John!" said Olivia, as if she'd just recognized him. "I was trying to find Vincent. He was calling for me. I heard him calling…but I couldn't find him. Did you hear him?"

JayDee glanced quickly at Ethan and then back to the woman. "No, Olivia, I didn't."

"Ethan was with me," she explained, her voice steady and earnest but her eyes sunken and wild. "He took care of me. I think…there was something bad up in there. Something…" She struggled to find meaning. "*Bad*," she repeated. "I think Ethan…kept it away from me."

"A Gorgon from the ship," Ethan told the doctor. "Up in the ruins."

"You kept it *away* from her? *How*?"

It was time to tell the truth, no matter how incredible it might sound. When Ethan spoke, he stared directly into the doctor's eyes, and he spoke like a man instead of a boy. "I killed it. I tore it to pieces." He followed that up with, "I wanted it to be destroyed, and it was. But there's another one up there somewhere. The Cyphers are looking for it. I wouldn't want to see one of those again."

JayDee gave no reply. His face was pallid except for a purple bruise on his chin where someone's elbow had hit him in the confusion of escape. "Well," he managed to say, "I've never seen one, and I sure as hell don't want to. Spare me any more details, won't you?"

Ethan nodded, and that seemed to close the subject.

Someone suddenly moved past Ethan and sat down beside Olivia, hugging her and then beginning to sob. It was the young blonde girl with the eyepatch that Ethan had seen lying on the ground, studying the stars last night. He saw now that the stick-on rhinestones formed a star on her eyepatch. It was, he thought, an effort at making the best of a bad thing. An eyepatch as a fashion statement, or a statement of attitude. Her long blonde hair and her face were dirty with dust and smoke. She was wearing jeans, a dark red blouse and blue Nikes that were all the worse for wear but maybe as clean as any clothes Ethan had seen on anyone so far. As the girl hugged Olivia and continued to cry, Olivia sobbed a little bit too and then she got herself under control; she put her arms around the girl and asked in a voice that was nearly strong, "Nikki, are you hurt?"

The girl shook her head, her face buried against Olivia's shoulder.

"All right," Olivia said. "That's good." She gently stroked the girl's hair, her own eyes reddened by tears. "We're going to get out of this," she said. "We're not done yet."

Ethan took stock of the apartment complex, while JayDee hobbled over to give whatever aid he could to a bloodied Hispanic couple who was being helped along the road toward them. A little boy about seven or eight was holding onto his mother's hand. The father had suffered a gash across his face, his hair whitened by dust. Ethan said quietly, "We have to leave here. We have to get out before dark."

"Just *where* are we going to go?"

It had been spoken by the girl with the eyepatch. She was staring up at Ethan as if she thought he was insane. "Who are *you?*" she asked sharply. Then: "Wait...wait. You're the boy they brought in a few days ago. Your name is...Ethan?"

"Yeah. Ethan Gaines. Well..." He shrugged. "It's a made-up name. I can't remember my real one." He tried to find the semblance of a smile, but could not.

"I was a sophomore at the high school," she replied. "How'd you pick that name?"

"Just did. Saw the sign, I guess. As good as any. You're Nikki...what?"

"Stanwick." Her good eye, though bloodshot from dust and smoke, was chocolate brown.

"Where are your folks?"

"Both dead," she answered, without emotion. Ethan figured it had happened in the early days. "My older sister, too."

"I'm sorry."

"Me too. How about yours?" It was asked matter-of-factly, as if they were discussing brands of sneakers. It had become a hard world, Ethan thought, and those who survived had seen and endured much. If they weren't hard by now, they would have already died.

"I can't remember that, either." Ethan noted a scar just above her eyepatch and several small scars on her cheeks. A deeper scar on her chin ran up to just beneath her lower lip.

"Nikki's been with us a long time," Olivia said. "She came in that first summer. I need to stand up. Can you help me?"

Both Ethan and Nikki helped Olivia to her feet. Olivia wavered a little bit, and Ethan was ready if she fell, but she held herself steady. "Thank you," the woman said. She saw a group of six people walking down the road in their direction, two of them nearly carrying a third. She recognized among them Joel Schuster, Hannah Grimes, Gary Roosa, and…

"Dear God," she said, her voice choked with emotion. "There's Dave!"

Ethan's heart gave a jump. Dave McKane was one of those supporting a thin elderly man with a white beard and long white hair braided into a ponytail. Dave was dusty and dishevelled but he looked like he'd come through the catastrophe intact; he was wearing his jeans, a black t-shirt torn almost to tatters and his usual dark blue baseball cap. His brown beard edged with gray was made more gray by dust. He had his Uzi in its holster at his side and, around his waist, the holster with the .357 Magnum in it. His face was grim and there was a bloody cut across the bridge of his nose. He saw Olivia, Ethan, Nikki Stanwick, and JayDee and nothing about his face changed; he gave them a nod of recognition and said in a husky voice, "Let's set Billy down here. JayDee, I think his right leg's broken. How about you?"

"Twisted ankle. Nothing much." JayDee shrugged, but in truth his ankle hurt like blazes. "Billy, how're *you* feeling?"

"Like shit on a cracker," the old man said through gritted teeth. "Fellas with broke legs usually don't feel so good. Don't need a doc to know *that*. Ow, Jesus...be careful with my old ass!"

Olivia hugged Dave and wound up squeezing him so hard he gave a grunt of pain. Dust puffed off him in the embrace. "Oh my God, I thought you were dead!"

"I might've been," he said, returning the hug but not so firmly in respect of her bones. "I was sitting on my balcony, thinking. I saw the spheres, and then I heard that thing plowing in and getting louder and louder. I had time to get my guns and then I jumped. After that, I don't know what happened. I do remember running like a jack rabbit." His eyes found Ethan. He would not tell Ethan that he'd jumped not from his own balcony but from Ethan's after he'd kicked the door open to try to get the boy out. He stared darkly at the row of bodies under the sheets and blankets. "Any idea how many?"

"No idea yet," she said. "But *many*."

"Shit! Shit! Shit!" Billy Bancroft had been lowered to the grass and was fuming as the fingers of a gnarled hand felt along his injured leg. "Seventy-six years old and I never had a fuckin' broken bone in my life!" His eyes, bright blue, turned upon the row of corpses. He was silent for awhile, and then he said, speaking to everyone and no one in particular, "Jake Keller in there anywhere? Joel, take a look for me, will you?"

"I'll do it," Dave offered. He went about the task quickly and efficiently. The third body was particularly bad, and the fifth was worse. The ninth body was..."Jake's here."

"Damn it." Billy's voice was tight. "Little bastard got away owin' me fifty dollars from our last poker game. Well," he said, "rest in peace. *Cheater*."

"We can't stay here," Ethan said, and was surprised at the power of his own voice; again, it carried the strength of a man's. He fixed his attention on Dave. "*You* know we can't. We don't even have time to bring all the bodies out and—"

"*Where* are we going to go?" Nikki sounded on the edge of panic. "Out *there*? This is our home...our protection...we can't...we can't..."

146

And then she looked at the huge Gorgon craft sitting at the center of the destruction, and her remaining eye went glassy. Her knees buckled. Before she fell, Ethan reached her first and then Joel Schuster, and together they lowered her gently to the ground as she moaned and put her hands to her face. She began to cry again, and once more Olivia sat down beside her to stroke her hair and soothe her.

"She lived a few miles away, in a regular neighborhood," Olivia said, speaking mostly to Ethan. "Westview Avenue, she told me. She said the whole area caught fire one night. The houses started blowing up. When she walked in, she was in rags, in shock, and badly injured. So...this *was* her home. At least her *shelter*, for whatever it was worth."

"Ethan's right."

Dave had not spoken, though he'd been about to.

John Douglas limped forward on his makeshift crutch. "That thing... that *smell*...of dead meat. It's going to bring the Gray Men tonight. We've got to get out while we can. Find some other place. We won't have time to bury the bodies or do much more searching through the wreckage." He frowned. "All these wounded people can't be left behind. Damn if I know how they're going to travel, though. And myself included in that." He looked up at the top of the hill, where the seven horses grazed. They were jumpy, and when two brushed each other one kicked and galloped away. Seven horses...but no magnificent seven in this bunch.

Everyone was silent. Then Ethan knew what he should say, and he said it. "We've got to find a truck. Something big enough to carry...I don't know...fifty or sixty people, I guess."

"You mean a *semi*?" Dave asked. "With a trailer big enough? Yeah, *right*! Like we're going to find one..." He was about to say *sitting around out there*, but he stopped himself. It *might* be possible to find a tractor-trailer truck at a loading dock or parked near a warehouse. An industrial area wasn't but about three miles away. And as for fuel...

"Diesel," he said. "I'll bet there's still diesel left in some of the gas stations' tanks. Or maybe at the truck terminals. If we can find a barrel pump somewhere we can get fuel from a diesel tank. Have to find ten to twelve feet of hose. *Maybe* there's a hardware store that hasn't been

cleaned out. Have to be careful, though. There are other people hiding in
their holes and they're armed and scared. Crazed, too. You remember."
He directed this to Olivia, referring to a time last August when he'd
gone out with Cal Norris searching for food and water, and Cal had
been shot in the neck from the window of a house and bled to death on
West Skyway.

"We don't necessarily need a truck," Olivia said. Her face had taken
on a firmness once more and there was life in her eyes. "We can use a
school bus or a metro bus. Whatever we can find that maybe still has
some gas in it, and a battery that works."

"Right." *A battery that works*, he thought. That was going to be
a trick. But he couldn't let it throw him, not yet. "Hold on. *We?* No,
ma'am, you're not going out on this one. Joel, can you ride a horse?"

"Haven't since I was a kid, but I'm game."

"I can ride," Nikki said. She had wiped her face and no longer
needed to lean on Olivia. "I *had* a horse before all this."

"I need somebody with a gun." He had already noted the .45 in Joel's
belt holster. "I'd like a third rider, though. Gary, you're elected."

"Okay, but I hate horses and they hate me."

"I'll go," the wizened older woman named Hannah Grimes said.
Her hair was white and wild, as if perpetually blown by a tempest. She
held up a pistol that looked as big as her head, locked in a hand full of
blue veins. "This elect me, Mr. President?"

"By a landslide." Or *earthquake*, Dave thought. He looked at Ethan
and could almost see the gears turning in the boy's mind. *White Mansion
mountain. Got to get there, somehow.* "Finding a hand crank pump is
going to be a tough one right there. Then we find a truck. The battery's
going to be long dead, but pray we can find a spare," he said, and found
himself speaking only to Ethan. "If we can find a truck that's already got
some gas in it, enough to get to a station with some diesel left, all the better." *Tall orders*, he thought. Little wonder they hadn't tried this before.
But *before*, there was no Gorgon ship sitting on top of them. "After that,"
he went on doggedly, "we find medical supplies in a hospital, a phar-
macy, or a Doc-in-the-Box. We may have to head south. Got that?"

"Got it," said Ethan, who understood exactly what Dave was talking about.

"Have to get all this done before dark," Dave said to Olivia. "Better gather up all the food, water, and weapons we can find. Anything else of use." He cast a doubtful eye toward the smoky ruins and the huge rotting carcass of the Gorgon ship. A storm of vultures was beginning to gather overhead. "Don't let anybody go too far in, though," he told Olivia, who quickly nodded agreement. He added, "There's been enough people dead for one day."

He hoped.

FOURTEEN.

JEFFERSON JERICHO, PAST MASTER OF NEW EDEN, AWAKENED ON A park bench in an unknown city, under a sick yellow sun and a leprous gray sky. He sat bolt upright, catching from skin and clothes the burnt smell that he was so familiar with. Only he realized that maybe the smell was not just coming from whatever transformative power the Gorgons possessed, for around him were the black, twisted skeletons of burned trees and, further on, a mass of ashes and broken structures that might once have been a neighborhood.

As soon as he stood up, he threw up…but there was nothing in his stomach, so nothing came up. Then, wiping the saliva from his mouth, he realized he had a beard…not a large one, but scraggly…maybe two weeks' worth. Had he been "out" that long, or was the beard something the Gorgons could force from his pores just as *she* forced him to take that last step into the realm of the unknown? And his clothes…

"Jesus!" he said, in utter amazement. He was wearing a sweat-stained brown t-shirt and a pair of dirty jeans. On his feet were sneakers with holes in them. He was wearing no socks. He looked at his hands and arms. The fingernails were caked with dirt and his arms were grimy. When he looked at his palms he saw the lines there were like filthy roads leading across the plains. He had never been so dirty in all his life. He was sure that if he had a mirror he would see the rest of the disguise the Gorgons had given him; he probably still looked like himself under the beard, but they had made him appear to be a homeless survivor of the cosmic war. The clothes felt slippery somehow…the fabric was not quite right. He had the feeling that he was trapped in snakeskin, and terror leaped up within him. Nearly whimpering, he started to pull the offending t-shirt off and over his head.

There was a noise, and Jefferson stopped with the t-shirt halfway off because something had just happened that he knew he and his hammering heart would not like.

It was hard to say what the noise was. Maybe it was a soft whistling, like the displacement of air. Maybe it was a whirring sound, like a little machine in motion. Whatever it was, it came from behind him—very close—and Jefferson pulled the t-shirt back down off his eyes so he could see, and he turned to face his future.

A man was there, standing beside the skeleton of a burned tree. He was a large man, square-built and broad-shouldered, though his face had taken on the appearance of someone in need of food; his cheekbones and eyes were beginning to hollow out. He had a flat-nosed boxer's face, a tangle of shoulder-length black hair, and two months' growth of black beard. His dark blue t-shirt, gray trousers, and black sneakers were just as filthy as Jefferson's clothes, if not more so. The eyes in the hungry face were small and dark, like chips of flint. He wore a backpack, an olive green one, likely from an Army surplus store.

The man just stared at him impassively, and he did not blink.

"Who are *you*?" Jefferson's voice was far from the strong baritone bell that tolled for the congregation of the High Rollers, that had been caught and carried on the GHR network to a hundred and fifty-six markets. God's High Rollers. That seemed like an age ago…him on the podium with the dozen-screened light show going on behind him, his inspired grin casting further illumination, his arms outspread, and the message delivered as only a salesman as himself could deliver it… *The secret to being rich—just tearing that ol' stock market up—is a code in the Bible that I have deciphered…*

"Vope," said the man.

"*Vope*? What kind of name is that?"

"It is the one," came the answer, "you can pronounce."

"You're a Gorgon? Sent to protect me?"

"I am a creation," Vope said. "What I am does concern you *not*. But...yes, I am here to protect and guide you." The small flinty eyes scanned the sky. "There are no enemies in this sector, in this frame of time. We can move freely."

"To where? Where are we going?"

"Follow," said Vope, and he began striding quickly and purposefully across the destroyed park, past an overturned swing set and a group of seesaws turned black by alien fire. Jefferson followed. They crossed a street and went past burned and wrecked houses and crossed another street, the same. Jefferson knew they were walking in the direction of a metropolitan area because he could see larger buildings. A couple of them had been sheared off as if by a gigantic and very sharp blade.

"Where are we? What town?"

"Fort Col lins," Vope answered, putting a pause where there should be none. "Col O Raydo."

"What do you know about this boy I'm supposed to find?" He was having to hurry to keep up, and—enemies in the sector or not—he kept scanning the sky and the ground around them. "I'm a *salesman*," he said, before Vope could reply. "I shouldn't be out here. I'm not a soldier!" Vope didn't respond. "I *sell* things," Jefferson went on, sounding desperate even to himself. "Do you even know what that means?"

Vope was silent. *Doesn't give a shit,* Jefferson thought. They were going through another neighborhood that had survived total destruction; only a few houses here and there were demolished. Some were boarded up, or *had* been boarded up. The boards had been broken into. To Jefferson, most of the houses looked like coffins. Like so many others, this was a town of the dead.

"Stop," Vope suddenly said, and immediately Jefferson halted.

They were standing in front of a wood-framed house with six steps leading up to a porch. On the porch was a single rocking chair. The address was 1439. The windows were broken out, and the darkness was very deep within.

"It will happen here," Vope announced.

"What will happen?"

There was no answer from the Gorgon in its disguise of human flesh.

A moment slipped past. In the distance Jefferson heard dogs barking and then howling, and he thought that wild dogs could kill a person just as easily as a death ray.

The rocking chair moved, just a fraction. It *creaked*. And as Jefferson Jericho watched, a form began to materialize in the chair. It began first as a barely discernible whorl, as if the air itself was becoming solid and an invisible finger had stirred it. There was that soft hissing or whispering or metallic sound that Jefferson had heard in the park. *This is Star Trek shit*, he thought...but within three seconds—and in total silence—a body came into being in the chair, first as a ghostly, paled-out form outlined by what might have been flickers of blue energy, and then fully realized and solid. The rocking chair creaked back and forth, and the man in it stared at both Jefferson and Vope with huge frightened eyes under a bald dome that sparkled with sweat.

"Lemme alone!" he croaked. "Please...Jesus...lemme alone!" Looking about himself and getting some idea of where he was, his hairy hands gripped hold of the chair's arms and locked his body there.

"Come with us," Vope commanded.

"Listen...*listen*...I don't know where I am. Okay? I don't know who *you* are. I'm stayin' right where I am, I ain't movin'."

"You will move," said Vope.

"No," the new arrival protested, and instantly he winced and grasped at the back of his neck. "Please...please lemme alone," he begged, as tears bloomed in his eyes. "Don't hurt me anymore."

"You will move," Vope repeated, with a robotic tone in his—its?—voice.

The man gritted his teeth. He frantically rubbed the back of his neck, as if that would cancel the pain spreading through him from the implanted device. But Jefferson knew it would not. Two more heartbeats, and the man stood up and gasped, "Okay! Yeah...make it stop!" He came down the steps, breathing hard and wheezing just a bit. "Christ... oh my God...what a world," he said, as his terrified brown eyes surveyed the scene. He was a short man, maybe five-foot-seven, and he had been fat at one time because he had heavy-hanging jowls that quivered as he spoke. Under his dirty white shirt and black pants, the man's flesh seemed to be loose and hanging off him. He, too, was in need of food. Or...maybe, Jefferson thought, the Gorgons wanted him to look that way. He had a grizzled gray beard and was probably in his late forties. He had spoken with a Brooklyn accent, or at least that's what it sounded like to Jefferson. On the man's feet were black loafers, scuffed all to hell and back, that probably at one time had been expensive.

"Nice shoes," Jefferson said. "Used to be, I mean. You need some sneakers. More comfortable."

"Yeah, right." The man narrowed his eyes, taking Jefferson in. "Who are *you*? You human?"

"Jeff," came the answer. "From Nashville, Tennessee," he decided to say. "I'm human." *Don't ask Regina that question,* he thought. *Don't ask Amy Vickson, either.* But Amy was dead, killed herself "but left my undying love," the note had said. Lucky little bitch, is what she was.

"Burt Ratcoff," said the man. "From Queens, New York." Burt's gaze moved to Vope. "Yeah, you're one of *them*. Where you from? Fuckin' Mars?"

"You make no sense," said the Gorgon. "You will call me Vope. From this point on, both of you will do as I command." The flinty eyes were lifeless, and horrible in their unblinking fixation on his subjects. "To fail to obey is to receive pain. Follow me." He turned and began walking toward the metropolitan area again, and Jefferson and Ratcoff obeyed.

"How'd they get *you*?" Ratcoff asked.

"It's a long story."

"They got me when my apartment buildin' was shot to hell. They lifted me out of it, as it was fallin' down around my head. I woke up..." He stopped speaking and shook his head. "They did things to me. You know you used to hear when people got abducted and all that, they got needles put in their bellies and metal rods up their asses? Well...I remember a table. Freezin' cold. Maybe metal, but different. But...it was like the table was alive...'cause it moved underneath me. Like it... *shifted*. It *rippled*, like flesh. I was on that table and there was nothin' holdin' me down but I couldn't move. And...the figures around me. More like shadows than real. They didn't *walk*...they just...like...I don't know...it was like bein' in a room with snakes that could stand up...or slither, or glide, or whatever the hell. But they did things to me, Jeff...can I call you Jeff?"

"Yes."

"They did things. They opened me up. I think...I remember seein' somethin' pullin' my insides out...like ropes. Bloody. I think they hollowed me out...and put somethin' else inside me."

"I've got that implant at the back of my neck too."

"No...*no*. More than that. *More*," Ratcoff said forcefully. And then, quietly, "That kind of thing could drive a man crazy. You know?"

"I know," Jefferson answered.

"Silence," Vope said. "Your chatter urinates me."

"You'd better get your language straight," Jefferson dared to say. "You want to pass as a human, you need some more lessons." And those unblinking eyes...a dead giveaway. So the Gorgons weren't as smart as they thought they were, at least not in the area of disguise.

For this remark, there was a little twinge of pain at the back of Jefferson's neck, just a pinch and a quick burning of nerves to let him know who was the master and who was the slave.

They were nearly halfway along the next street when a door banged open. Two thin, bearded, and dirtied men with rifles emerged from a dilapidated house. "Hold it, hold it!" the taller of the two said. "Not a step more, mister!"

Vope did understand this much English. He stopped, and so did Jefferson and Ratcoff.

"Inside," the man said, motioning quickly with his weapon. "Come on, *move* it!"

"Sir," Jefferson began, "we don't—"

"Shut up! Get your asses inside that house! *Go!*"

"You are interfering," said Vope. "That is not permitted."

"Hell, I'll shoot you all down right here! Who's first?" The rifle swung toward Ratcoff. Jefferson could tell the little man wanted to run for it, and he said in his most golden salesman's tone, "I don't believe that would be wise, Burt. Vope, I personally do *not* want to be shot down in the street today. We should do what they say. You *need* us."

Vope stared at him for what seemed an eternity. Jefferson thought the rifles were going to go off at any damned second. Then Vope said, "Correct." They entered the house, with Vope leading the way. In the dingy little front room, empty food cans and other trash littered the floor. A third man was in there, brandishing a revolver. He had a burn scar across the left side of his face, and his sunken eyes were either wild or crazy. A skinny woman also occupied the dismal room, with its faded and peeling wallpaper the color of dust; it was hard to tell her age or anything about her because her lank brown hair hung in her face and she held her arms around herself. Every so often she shivered as if at a memory of winter.

"Where'd you come from?" The leader's rifle went up under Vope's throat.

"A distance."

"Where *from*, idjit?"

"Fuck that," said the man with the revolver. He held the gun against Vope's head. "You got food? Take off that backpack and let's have a look."

"Hey, I'm from Queens, New York," said Ratcoff, holding his hands up. The sweat glistened on his head. "I don't want—"

"*Shut up!*" the second man with the rifle snapped. He was gray-haired, long-jawed, and wore glasses held together with duct tape. The right lens was cracked. "Did you hear what Jimmy told you? Take off the *backpack*!"

"There is food," Vope said. "For you, not."

"The hell you say! We're starvin' in here! Take it off now or we'll kill you where you stand!"

"No," Vope answered.

"How come he don't blink?" the woman suddenly spoke up, in a thin, high, and possibly also crazed voice. "His eyes...he don't blink."

The leader lowered his rifle, grasped Vope's backpack and started to wrench it off him. Vope stood motionlessly, unblinking, with Jimmy's pistol against the right side of his head.

"I wouldn't do that," said Jefferson gently, but he could not sell them on this. They were too desperate, and they couldn't eat words. The manufactured framework of Vope's face seemed to shift and change for the briefest of seconds; it looked to Jefferson as if the mask was beginning to slip and what was underneath it was trying to push its way out. Jefferson felt some kind of power coiling in the room, something getting ready to strike, and he began to hunch his shoulders forward in an effort to brace himself against it.

Suddenly a boy came into the room from a hallway. He was about fourteen, Jefferson judged, and he had shoulder-length blonde hair. There was a dirty bandage on his jaw and his left arm was in an equally dirty sling. His eyes were dazed and dark-circled, and he went to the woman and put his good arm around her.

Jefferson asked, "Is *he* the boy?"

Vope didn't answer. The backpack was being pulled off him. His face had stopped moving. His eyes staring at nothing.

"Is *he* the boy?" Jefferson asked again, louder.

Vope's right arm changed. It became a mottled, scaly yellow thing striped with black and brown. Where the hand was there was no longer a hand but a yellow spike that erupted with small black spikes, and those smaller spikes were barbed and writhing as if each one was a separate living weapon. The arm that was no longer an arm punched forward with ferocious power and the spiked thing that was no longer a hand ripped into Jimmy's guts and on through his body to come out the other side in an explosion of gore that spattered the dusty wallpaper with bits of lungs, kidney, stomach, and all the makings of man. The vertebrae broke with a noise like a broomstick, and as Jimmy collapsed his finger spasmed on the trigger and the revolver fired into the side of Vope's face. What looked like human blood ran from the wound, but still the Gorgon did not blink nor did it register pain.

Vope's appendage picked Jimmy up off his feet and, as the leader and the others fell back in stupefied horror, Vope threw Jimmy's body so hard against the opposite wall that the broken young man smashed through it.

The leader had his back to another wall and raised his rifle. Vope's left arm, also transfigured into a killing machine with the yellow, black and brown markings, struck out like a snake and lengthened by at least four feet. The hand of this arm had become a black reptilian head with slitted red pupils and fangs that gleamed like metal. The teeth caught the man's rifle, wrenched it from his grip in a heartbeat, and destroyed his face with one tremendous blow from the rifle's butt, at the same time the spiked weapon of the right arm whipped out to pierce the other rifle-man's chest and on out his back like a twisting buzzsaw. Again, Vope threw the body aside like a piece of bloody garbage.

As Jefferson and Ratcoff watched in frozen terror, Vope's snake-hand closed on the woman's head as she turned to run with the boy. The jaws crushed her skull and facial bones with obscene ease. The brains ran out onto the floor as she fell, her face compressed to a knotty bleeding lump.

The boy was running, trying to get into the hallway. He was whimpering. Jefferson thought it was the worst sound he'd ever heard. Something went dark inside his mind as if to turn off the lights to spare him any more.

Because he knew Vope was not done.

The spiked arm lengthened, a scaly mottled python sliding out of Vope's shoulder, going after the boy, and so fast it was nearly a blur the spike drove through the boy's back, through his chest, and impaled him. His legs were kicking, and his body twitched as the Gorgon lifted him up, and then—almost gracefully, with a smooth show of power—the boy was thrown through the next wall, which Jefferson did not fail to notice was decorated with a faded portrait of Jesus in prayer. The impact caused the portrait to fall and the dusty glass to shatter.

The man with the destroyed face was lying on his back, moaning through a distorted mouth that had neither lips nor teeth.

Vope's left arm drew itself back in and began to return to counterfeit flesh. The black reptilian head with the metallic teeth became a fist, which Vope opened and closed several times as if to test its elasticity.

The right arm drew itself back into the shoulder. The spiked murder weapon began to change to something that resembled a forceps, still mottled with the color of what was maybe the true Gorgon flesh. The forceps entered the wound in Vope's head and searched there. Vope's face did not change, and registered nothing. In another moment the forceps emerged with a slug. Vope examined this with interest. Then he walked to the ex-leader on the floor. His small eyes stared down at the man on the floor as someone would consider a roach about to be crushed.

With incredible speed and power, the forceps-hand whipped forward and sent the used slug into the man's forehead with easily the velocity of a gun, if not many more times so. The man shivered once, and moved no more.

Vope's right arm and hand returned themselves to what passed for normality in a matter of seconds. Then Vope drooled slimy spittle into the cup of his right hand and began to rub the liquid into the bullet wound. It took him a few drools and the hand rubbed in maybe two dozen circles, but when he was done the wound was no longer there, just the remnant of Gorgon blood that had leaked down his neck and onto his t-shirt.

"Now we go," Vope said to Jefferson of Tennessee and Ratcoff of New York, who had pressed themselves against the far wall as if to push their own bodies through the wallpaper and plaster. "And...no," he told Jefferson as he straightened his backpack like any day hiker would, "that was the boy, *not.*"

FIFTEEN.

THE BOY IN QUESTION WAS WAITING. HE STOOD UP ON A GUARD tower with Gary Roosa, watching the road that led from town to the ruins of Panther Ridge. Dave, Joel, and Hannah had been gone almost eight hours. The yellow sunlight had gotten hotter. There was a sticky, otherworldly dampness in the air. Somewhere in the distance, thunder echoed in the low gray sky. Ethan's eyes ticked in the direction of the noise. *Just thunder,* he thought. *Presently no enemies in this sector.*

He caught himself.

What?

I don't talk like that, he thought. *I don't* think *like that. But how come I know it was just thunder and not the sounds of their war?*

He just knew.

A memory came upon him…or a dream of a memory. It came upon him so fast he was left nearly breathless.

He was in a classroom. The sun—bright sun in an unblighted blue sky—shone through the windows. He was sitting at his desk. The girl in front of him had red hair. Her name was…that was lost. At the front of the classroom was the teacher's desk, and at it sat a man wearing a white shirt and a dark blue bowtie with gold stripes. The man's name was…

Think hard.

161

The man was slim, had a sharp chin, and wore horn-rimmed glasses. He had brown hair with a lock of white at the very front, as if a finger dusted in flour had touched there. His name was…Nova-something? Novak?

Science teacher.

Yes, Ethan thought. A science teacher, at…what was the school? And where was the school? Lost…all lost. But on the desk before Ethan was his Visible Man, ready for the demonstration. All the organs painted, the veins painted, everything ready. In a few minutes, he would stand up and take his Visible Man to the front of the class, where he would remove the organs and explain their function one by one as he rebuilt his human…wouldn't he? Wasn't that right? Or was this a tainted dream, and it had never happened?

Up at the front already, casting a shadow in the golden sunlight, was a boy wearing a black jersey with something in silver written across it. The boy was Hispanic and had long black hair and thick eyebrows. Written on the jersey was…

Remember…remember…please remember…

And there it was, as if through a dark glass: *Jaguars.*

The boy was talking, and gesturing over a model of…the universe? No…not the universe as it is…but the universe as someone in ancient Rome had envisioned it. The earth was the center of the universe. The boy had rigged an electric motor to his model, and turning on a little switch showed how the painted Styrofoam balls of planets revolved around the earth on their wires. A *geocentric universe*, it was called. Ethan remembered that. Somebody named Claudius something had come up with it. Ethan thought that the Hispanic boy—no name, no name—had done a pretty good job, and this would be a hard act to follow and he needed at least a B for his presentation. Ethan's eye followed the shadow of a gesturing hand, and it fell upon a calendar page that read *April 3*. He would be going up soon, the presentation of the geocentric universe was almost done.

Ethan—not his name, his name was something else—looked at the clock and saw it was four minutes after ten. Ethan would be the second up; they were going in alphabetical order.

Alphabetical order, he remembered. It was the first day of science project presentations.

The Hispanic boy's name was…what?

Last name… 'A'?

It came to him like a blow to the stomach. *Allendes.* First name… no, that was lost. But Ethan realized his real last name must end in either an 'A' or a 'B', because there were twenty-six other students in the class and—

"Can I come up?"

Both Gary and Ethan turned around to see Nikki Stanwick hanging onto the ladder that led up. She was just a couple of rungs shy of pulling herself onto the platform.

"Come on," Gary said, and he went over to help her.

She came up smoothly and spent a moment brushing the dust off the knees of her jeans. Then she walked over beside Ethan and looked along the road, the rhinestones of the star in her eyepatch glittering with a fragment of captured light.

"They've been gone a long time," she said.

Ethan nodded. The wounded were being cared for as best as possible, but there were some like Billy Bancroft who just couldn't walk. There were a few dying ones, and a number who'd passed away since they'd been found in the wreckage. Ethan figured there were maybe sixty people left and half of those were wounded in some way, about ten in really bad shape. Seventeen people, including Roger Pell, Roger's wife, and their surviving child had started off on their own with their guns and remaining ammunition, a few plastic jugs of water and some of the last of the canned food. They had taken, as well, the rest of the horses. No one had tried to stop them. They were going cross-country, heading east toward… they knew not what, but they didn't put much faith in the search team finding a vehicle or any fuel, and they didn't want to wait any longer.

"I hear that if they find a truck, we're going to Denver." Nikki was speaking to Ethan.

"Who told you that?"

"Olivia."

163

"Hm," Ethan said. He remembered what Dave had told him after finding White Mansion Mountain in the road atlas: *Going south to Denver, crossing the Rockies on I-70, with the Gray Men and the aliens everywhere.* Did that mean Olivia and Dave were going to take him there? That they believed, as he believed, that he *must* find this place?

"Denver is gone. They started fighting over Denver and tore it up about three months after the war started. Don't you know that?"

"I don't know much of anything."

"That's what people who got out of Denver said. Some survivors who came here. You can ask Mrs. Niega. She saw the buildings fall. There's nothing left, so why do we want to go to Denver?"

The gateway to I-70, Ethan thought. "Where would you like to go?" he asked her.

"Out of this *nightmare.* Home again. With everything like it was. My Mom and Dad, and my sister. All of them alive again." Nikki's voice was getting strained and her face had flushed. "I'd like my eye back. So, I guess I'd like to go to the one place nobody *can* go."

Ethan waited without speaking.

"The *past,*" she said. "But that's gone, isn't it?"

"Yeah," Ethan agreed. "It's gone."

"Hey, something's coming," Gary said. "Look there!" He gave over his binoculars to Ethan.

—✖—

Nearly eight hours before, a rifle bullet struck the left side of Hannah Grimes' horse and a follow-up whined off the pavement of Windom Street, about two miles from Panther Ridge. Hannah jumped clear as her mount fell. The sniper was in a boarded-up house among rows of boarded-up or abandoned homes, but exactly where the slug had come from was impossible to tell. Hannah braved another attack to put the horse down with a shot to the head, then she took Dave's hand and pulled herself up behind him, and they went on, and that was how things were these days. After another twenty minutes, they came across four tractor-trailer trucks parked at a lumber company at the intersection of South College Avenue and Carpenter Road, but no keys were in the ignitions, and the facility's main office was locked. A brick through a pane of smoked glass cleared that obstacle, but a search still turned up no keys and there were too many locked desk drawers to tackle.

"Listen," Hannah said, "I wanted to come along because Olivia said we could use a school bus. I drove one for a couple of years as a volunteer. I know where the depot is, and I know there's a diesel tank. Got a workshop there too, and I figure they may have some kind of pump we can use. It's a ways from here, but I think that's our best bet."

"Hell, yes!" Dave answered, and so they started off under Hannah's direction north toward the school bus depot on LaPorte Avenue. They were getting into areas that had been ripped apart by alien weapons, whole neighborhoods burned to ashes, cars melted into shapeless hunks of metal, shopping malls and stores gutted and merchandise spilled out over the flame-scorched parking lots, a few larger buildings chopped in half as if by surgical lasers and debris blocking the streets. They passed three abandoned metro buses, the first lying on its side, the second with three flat tires and a shattered windshield, and a third with most of the two upper floors of the First National Bank covering it. The downtown Ace Hardware store on South College Avenue was crushed as if by a gigantic boot, ending Dave's hopes of finding a barrel pump before they reached the depot.

"We've got another mile to go," Hannah announced, and nothing more needed to be said.

Though in an area of burned buildings, charred trees, and more wreckage, the depot had escaped the flames of war. There were twelve buses in the lot, rusted by the rain and parked haphazardly by their rattled drivers. Four of them were sitting on flats, so those were out. Either someone had already gone at the gates with a chain-cutter, or the gates had been left unlocked on what had seemed like the last day of the world.

First problem: finding the keys to these vehicles. Were there any in the ignitions or up under the sun visors? No, there were not. But the door to the office had been broken open, likely in a search for firearms. Hannah went to a metal cabinet on the wall and tried to open that but the lock was secure. "Keys are in there on hooks with numbers that go with the numbers of the buses." She'd drawn her six-shooter. "Seen this done in the movies plenty of times, but in real life I figure you can blow your own head off if you're not careful. Both of you step back."

It was a wise move. It took two bullets to do the job, and even then the lock was more mangled than agreeable and the whole thing had to be nearly torn off the wall. But there were the keys, and the numbers, and the buses outside. It didn't take long for another problem to assert itself as they'd started opening up the hoods and looking at the engines: the two large, heavy-duty batteries in every bus was gunked up with yellow sulphur deposits and likely stone-cold dead.

"Damn it!" Dave fumed, as reality bit deep. "We're not going anywhere in one of these!"

"Okay, son," Hannah said, a little caustically. "You think there's never been dead batteries in this lot before? Think nobody's ever screwed up and left batteries in a school bus over a Christmas holiday or a spring break? How about all *summer*? Yeah, it's happened. They keep spare batteries in the workshop." She motioned toward a long flat-roofed red brick building with closed-up garage bays. There were no windows. A green-painted metal door was closed at the top of a set of cement stairs. Dave figured that if all these entrances were locked, it was going to be a bitch to break into. Alongside the building were two diesel fuel pumps, and in the oil-stained concrete, a yellow fill cap that indicated the underground tank. "You want to stop wastin' time, get in there, and see what's what?" Hannah asked.

"Yeah. Have you got any explosives on you?" Dave looked at Joel. "You got any ideas?"

"We can try the door," Joel answered with a shrug. "If it's locked, try to blow it open, the Hannah Grimes way."

"Or maybe," Hannah said, "we can walk around to the other side of the building. There's one window in this place, and it's in the shop manager's office. Used to overlook a flower garden."

"How do you know all this?" Dave asked.

She smiled, the deep lines crinkling up around her eyes. The smile was of a memory, and Dave thought it softened her hard face enough to reveal someone who had once been almost pretty. Almost. "Kenny Ray was my honey for awhile," she said. "I planted the flowers so he'd have somethin' nice to look at when I wasn't around."

"So that's why you volunteered to begin with, I'm figuring?" Joel asked.

"Maybe. Never know who you'll meet at your neighborhood bar. Time's movin', friends."

The window was positioned just above Dave's head and was broken out. The flower garden had long gone to the corrosive rain and the twists of time. Dave figured that if someone had broken in this way, they'd probably come out through the door but had closed it behind them. A scavenger with a sense of order, in a mad, disordered world.

"Let's try the door," he said.

As he went up the steps, Dave felt like asking God for a favor. He wasn't religious, was far from it, and if he'd been at all religious before the death of his family, that terrible event had wiped the visions of Heaven out of his head. He knew Hell existed, though. No doubt about that. It was everywhere now, burst from its realm of space and time. *God,* Dave thought as he reached the top of the stairs, *if there's anything to you, how about giving us a break? How about manning up and helping us?*

They needed so much to get one of those buses moving. They needed luck and about eight feet of hose, a hand crank pump of some kind, and two new batteries. They needed a probe to find out if there was already fuel in any of the buses, tanks so they wouldn't be wasting their time on a dry hole. They needed so much, and there were so many people depending on them.

But right now they needed for that door to open.

Dave reached out for the handle.

He felt his face tighten in preparation for disappointment. *But even if this damned door is locked*, he thought, *we've got the broken window.* Old Kenny Ray's window, looking out at the flowers of love.

Help us, he thought, and tears stung his eyes. *Please.*

He grasped the door's handle and pulled.

—⊗—

Through the binoculars, Ethan saw what was coming.

It had once been a yellow school bus, but the rain had done its damage. The top of the bus was rusted brown, and brown streaks of rust had dripped down the sides. *Poudre School District* was imprinted on the bus in faded letters, and the number 712. The bus was going slow, in allowance for the two horses whose reins were tied to the rear bumper.

"They found a school bus!" Gary shouted to the people who waited below. There was a stir of activity as even some of the severely wounded managed to haul themselves to their feet. JayDee, Olivia, and and a few of the others had been trying to give them comfort, as much as could be done without medical supplies. Gary took the binoculars from Ethan once more and watched the bus approach. "Christ, I *never* thought they'd find anything!"

Ethan said, "I believe in Dave."

In another moment, the bus pulled into the open entranceway, came up the quake-cracked road, and stopped where the survivors had gathered near the swimming pool, in the shadow of the dead Gorgon ship.

The doors opened, and Joel was the first one off, followed by Dave and then Hannah. All of them were dirtier than before, if that was possible. They looked wrecked. Dave staggered and had to catch hold of Joel's shoulder to keep from falling. As those who could walk crowded around, Dave caught sight of Ethan standing up on the tower with Gary and Nikki, and he gave a slight nod that said, *I haven't forgotten.*

"Let's get these people on board," Dave said to Olivia, who came up to him with a plastic jug of water. He took a swig and passed it to Hannah. "Sorry, we lost one of your horses."

"We lost the rest to a group who decided to go on. No matter, we can't keep them." Her eyes looked bruised, but her voice was steady. "I'm going to untie those two."

Dave nodded. The important thing now was getting everyone out of here. Bus 712 had had a little more than a quarter tank of fuel already in it before Dave had used the pry bar, rubber hose, and metal containers he'd found to siphon diesel out of the underground tank. There had been four boxed-up heavy-duty batteries in the workshop; now two were in the bus and two were still in their boxes at the back of the bus. While they were at it, they'd put new oil in the engine, and though the thing still ran rough after being awakened from its long sleep, it did run, the wheels turned, it had an uncracked windshield, and six pretty good tires, and Dave thanked God for the Blue Bird bus company. He thanked God also for Hannah, who had gotten them around a lot of debris without tearing up the tires.

"Couldn't get to Poudre Valley North. Every way we tried was blocked," he told JayDee as he helped get people aboard. "We went to Poudre Valley South, but every drug in the storeroom was gone. Hell, I wouldn't know what to get if there'd been anything there but empty shelves. We stopped at a CVS and two Walgreen's, both cleared out. Figure we might do better down the road." Billy Bancroft was still cursing as he was carried on, but Dave knew it was to mask a lot of pain. A small number of canned goods had been recovered, as well as a few pistols, rifles, and some ammunition. Four oil lamps and two bottles of fuel made the cut. A dozen plastic jugs of water were put aboard. There was not going to be room in the bus for the heavy machine guns, and the ammunition was almost gone for those, so Dave and Olivia made the tough decision to leave them.

Ethan, Nikki, and Gary stood up on the tower as the bus was being loaded, and finally Gary gave a sigh and said, "I'm not going to say I'll miss this place, but it kept us alive." He put a hand out to stroke the machine gun on its swivel. "I'd take this, if I had *my* way. Just hope we don't wish we had it, wherever we're going." He cast one more look around at the sorry fate of the Panther Ridge Apartments, and then he went down the ladder.

Ethan was alone with Nikki.

She was staring at him, and her silence was making him nervous. "We'd better go," he said. He started for the ladder.

"I've heard things about you," she said, and he stopped. "I've heard somebody say you think you caused the quakes that night."

He shrugged, but he didn't look at her. "Who told you that?"

"Somebody who heard it from somebody who heard it from somebody else. People think you must be...like...whacko."

169

"Good word," he said. "Maybe that fits." He remembered he had said *I think I caused the earthquakes* in front of a roomful of people. No, more than that. He'd said *I know I caused them.*

"People say you're spooky," Nikki went on, her single eye fixed on him.

"Yeah, another good word." He turned to face her, and he pulled up a smile and gave it to her. "If I'm so whacko and spooky, why did you climb up here to see me?"

She said nothing for a moment. Then she blinked, and it was her turn to shrug. "Maybe...I like whacko and spooky. 'Cause maybe *I* am, too." She rubbed at an imaginary spot on the boards with the toe of a dirty blue Nike. "My folks said I was. After I got my third tattoo. They're like... skulls and vines and stuff, on my back. You know, a little freaky. A friend of mine was studying to be a tat artist, so he did 'em for free. But I *don't* have a tramp stamp," she said quickly. "That would be a little much."

"I guess so," Ethan agreed.

"You got any?"

"Tattoos? No."

She approached him. "You've got a bad bruise...right there." She could see the dark purple of it just above the neck of his t-shirt, and she touched her own neck. "I mean...it looks *real* bad. What happened?"

"I'm not sure. That's something I can't remember." *Or don't want to remember*, he thought.

"Does it hurt?" Maybe impulsively, Nikki reached out with her right hand and the index finger touched the bruise. Then, immediately, she gasped and stepped back. Her hand went to her mouth. "Oh...*wow*," she said. "I mean...*look* at that!"

He tried to, but he couldn't see it. He didn't like the tremor in her voice. "*What is it?*" His own voice had climbed.

"Where I touched...my finger...the place turned *silver*. It's starting to fade now. *Wow*," she repeated. Her eye was wide. "Pull up your shirt."

Ethan did. Exposed was the ebony bruise that covered his chest.

"Can I touch you again?" she asked.

"Go ahead, it doesn't hurt," he answered, but he was scared, and his heart was pounding.

Nikki reached out again, slowly, spread her fingers, and touched them to Ethan's chest. Ethan felt nothing but her touch, though it appeared that the flesh seemed to shimmer around her fingertips. When she pulled her hand away, the fingermarks remained there in silver.

Quickly, they began to fade. Ethan saw the look of wonder on Nikki's face abruptly change. She stepped back from him in fear, as if she were about to leap from the tower, and he said in an outpouring, "I'm human. I *am*. It's just...there's something different about me that I don't understand. I'm okay, I'm not going to hurt you." He pressed a thumb into his chest and watched the silver mark it left melt back into the darkness of the bruise. "Listen," he told her, "I'm *not* an alien. Like... one of their experiments. I'm *not*."

Her voice was very quiet when she spoke. "If you don't know who you are or where you came from...how do you know *what* you are?"

That was a question Ethan couldn't answer. He lowered his shirt. "Please don't tell anybody about this. Not *yet*. Okay?"

She didn't reply; she had backed away and was almost to the platform's edge.

"*Please*," he said, and didn't care that he was begging. "I feel like there's someplace I have to go, and something I have to do. It's so strong in me, I can hardly sleep. The place is White Mansion Mountain, and it's in Utah. Dave found out where it is for me. I have *got* to get there. Nikki...I think maybe...there's something that wants me to go, because there can be an *end* to this."

"An end? An *end* to what?"

"Their war. I'm just saying...I feel like if I can get to that mountain, and find out why I'm being called to go there...there can be an *end* to it. Do you understand?"

"*No*," she said, very quickly.

"Ethan!" It was Dave, calling for him from below. "We're loading up! Come on!"

"Okay, I don't either," he told the girl, "but please...*please*...don't say anything about this."

171

"Maybe you're turning into a Gray Man," Nikki answered. "Maybe that's what's happening to you, and I ought to go down there right now and tell them, and they'll take care of you before we pull out."

"You mean *shoot* me? Listen...Dave trusts me. So does Olivia...and I think Dr. Douglas kind of does. I'm telling you...I have *got* to get to that mountain, and if I do...*when* I do...I think something important is there for me. Either to have, or to *know*."

"What, you think you're Jesus or somebody? Like you're supposed to lead your believers out of this...this *shit*...somehow?"

"I'm not Jesus," Ethan said. *And I'm not really Ethan either*, he thought. "Just give me a chance, okay? You tell people about this, and it'll scare them. I don't need that. Nobody does."

"Maybe we should all be scared of you."

He was done. He could go no further with her. He said grimly, "Do what you want to do. Either tell them, or not. But I'm saying...I feel like I have a purpose. A reason to be here. Maybe we all do, but we don't know yet what it is. The only things I want to hurt are the Cyphers and the Gorgons. I want them *gone* off this earth."

"We all want that."

"Yeah, I know." Ethan had to look away from her frightened and accusing eye. "I'm going down to the bus," he told her, in as calm a voice as he could manage. "Whatever you want to do...do it."

She didn't wait for him. She was down the ladder so fast she nearly blurred out like a Cypher. *I've freaked out the freak*, he thought. He climbed down, expecting...he didn't know what to expect. But the last group of people were being helped or herded into the bus, and Nikki Stanwick was among them. She didn't look back at Ethan or speak to Dave as she went past him and Olivia.

"Let's go," Dave said to Ethan as he approached. "Squeeze in back there." Seats had been removed starting from about the middle of the bus back to the rear, thanks to the toolkit Darnell Macombe had saved from destruction, but still the bus was packed. The badly wounded were lying down or being supported by other people. The hardest part of this was the fact that JayDee had pronounced three wounded too severely torn up or bone-crushed to travel, and that their deaths were imminent. *No other way,* JayDee had said as he held himself up on his crutch. *They may pass in an hour or two, or they may hold on for another five or six hours, but they don't know where they are. It's reality. There's nothing I can do for them but suggest mercy.*

And just who's going to do that, Doc? Dave had asked. *Who's going to pull the trigger three times and live with* that?

They shouldn't be left alive here, JayDee had answered. *In the dark, alone.*

Shit, Dave had said. *Is there absolutely nothing you can do?*

I can't even give them any pain pills. Only thing I've got is one bottle of hydrogen peroxide. I can't fix Neal's punctured lungs, and I can't fix Dina's broken back and her shattered legs, and I can't give Asa a new brain to fix the one inside his crushed skull. I've got too many others that I can at least help…but…I guess what I should do…is…give out the medicine of mercy, because we don't want any of our friends left behind—alive—if the Gray Men come tonight. So I'm going to take a pistol, and I'm going to walk over there where they're lying, and I'm going to do what a doctor is sometimes called upon to do…play God. An imperfect, tortured, and feeble God… but someone has to do this. Now excuse me, Dave, while I finish my rounds.

Inside the cramped bus with the last residents of Panther Ridge, Ethan heard three shots. No one spoke about them, and no one asked any questions of JayDee when Dave helped him up into the bus. Last on was Olivia, who eyes were bloodshot and who looked as if twenty years of heartache and despair had been burdened on her overnight, which Ethan thought was probably true. He stood up so others could sit. He caught a glimpse of Nikki, standing further at the back and staring a hole through him, but he quickly looked away.

The terrible thing was…he knew he was changing. He was becoming something unknown…some kind of nightmare creature…and if he was anything human at all, he was in defiance of the Visible Man, because he figured he had died in the shockblast of a strip mall, and his bruises told the story, but he was not yet dead—as humans used to know death to be—and now his injuries were beginning to speak to him in another language, with a tongue of silver.

"Everybody hold on to somethin' or someone," said Hannah as she slid behind the wheel. She turned the lever that closed the door, as she must've done a thousand times. She started the engine and heard it knock and complain, but then the wheels started turning, and they were moving away from Panther Ridge, moving out through the wall and the metal-plated door, out into the violent world of cosmic war, out upon the road that led south to Denver and hopefully to pharmacies or hospitals that had not yet been fully looted. And hopefully, then, to some kind of refuge from the madhouse that had claimed the earth, and some kind of safety, wherever that might be. JayDee, sitting with his injured knee outstretched, stared into empty space, and Ethan noted that his blue eyes were moist, and where they had been very clear, they were now dimmed and clouded.

They passed within sight of a neighborhood burned black, everything looking like a firestorm had whirled through. Ethan saw Nikki staring out at it, and he figured her house used to be out there and now there were only ashes and bones, like the rest of the world.

"Looky here, looky here," said Hannah. She was speaking to Olivia and Dave, who stood near her as the bus rumbled and jounced along. "Three fellas walking our way in the road. One of 'em's waving us down. Want to stop, or go right on through 'em?"

Both Dave and Olivia could see the three figures ahead, walking in the middle of the road. The one at the center was waving his arms. On one side was a stocky man with long black hair and a beard and on the other a short bald-headed gent in a white shirt who might have been a banker out for his afternoon stroll, except he was filthy and staggering.

"Run 'em down?" Hannah asked. "Take no chances?" She was keeping her foot on the accelerator.

It came to both Olivia and Dave that three people had just been executed—and call it mercy if you want to, but that didn't make it any easier. Three friends of theirs who had pulled the weight just like everyone else and at the end had been crushed by it. The bus hardly had room for one more person, let alone three...and there was always the chance that these were only counterfeit humans.

But there they were, right in front of the bus, and they weren't getting off the road and Hannah wasn't slowing down, and the decision had to be made in a matter of seconds.

Olivia took a deep breath to clear her head, and she made it.

They were not animals yet, and certainly not killers of human beings who could be helped. They had a dozen loaded guns if they needed to use them. They had accepted plenty of wanderers into Panther Ridge. What was the difference now?

"Stop for them," Olivia said. "Let's see what the story is. But," she added, "let's keep our guns ready."

Hannah let up on the gas and mashed the brake pedal. The bus neared the three figures and began to slow down. Toward the back of the bus, Ethan was standing in the aisle with people packed all around him, and he could see nothing, but someone passed the word back that there were three men on the road. As the bus stopped with a squeal of protest, Hannah opened the door and pointed her big-ass pistol at the doorway. She called out matter-of-factly, "Any trouble and the first bullet comes from my cannon!"

The three men were talking and made no effort to approach the bus. Olivia said, "Dave, let's find out what they want," and they went out, cautiously, with Dave's Uzi drawn and a .45 Colt automatic in Olivia's right hand. Her finger was on the trigger, and her mind was set that they could spend only a few minutes here, and whatever these three wanted, they'd better have a good salesman among them.

SIXTEEN.

"I USED TO BE...LIKE THEY SAY...PRETTY WELL FIXED," SAID BURT Ratcoff, as he and Jefferson Jericho followed Vope on the long road that led through destroyed suburbs where no lawnmower would ever growl again and no summer lemonade would ever be poured. "My wife left me six years ago, but I learned to live with it. Kept in touch with our son. Lives in Glendale, California, he's an insurance adjuster. That one with the talkin' gecko." Ratcoff nodded. "Yeah. I bet he's okay. Him, Jenny, and the girls. They're okay, I bet. They found someplace to hide, they're gonna make it. Hey, spaceman! You're killin' my legs, I can't keep up with you! Can you slow down a little...*shit*!" he said, wincing, and touched the back of his neck.

"I wouldn't get him angry," Jefferson said, but he too was short of breath, and his legs were starting to cramp. Had they walked across this entire damned city? It seemed like it. Vope had picked up the pace in the last half hour, as if eager to get to a certain place at a certain time. "Vope!" Jefferson called. "We're going to have to rest awhile." There was no response, and the pace did not falter. Jefferson said, "Vope, we're only human. We're not...as *strong* as you are. Our bodies give out, because we're weak. Will you have some pity on us and let us rest for a few minutes?"

Vope suddenly stopped and turned toward them, and on the disguised face there was a second's fleeting expression of haughty disdain. "You *are* weak," he answered. "You do not deserve a world you are unable to *hold*. Even…" He paused, searching for a word from his inner dictionary of their language "…*slaves* are stronger than you."

"I bow before you knowing I am weaker than a slave," said Jefferson, keeping his voice light and easy. "But may I ask if we can rest? We'll be useless to you if our fragile bodies are worn out."

Vope's small dark eyes slid toward Ratcoff.

"What *he* said," was the New Yorker's comment.

"Rest, then," said Vope. "Eat." He shrugged off his backpack, opened it and brought out two small cubes of the white tofu-like substance that Jefferson knew so well. He held them out to his captives.

"*That* shit again?" Ratcoff moaned. "What is this, your kind of dog food?"

"Take it and eat it," Jefferson advised. "I don't know what it is, but it'll keep your energy up." He took one and Ratcoff took the other, and they stood eating the manufactured nutrients under the low yellow sky in the land of the dead. The sun, a faint glow in the humid murk, was on its descent. Jefferson could feel darkness coming, and he didn't care to be out here with a Gorgon—even one who was supposed to be his protector but had taken the role of master—when night fell.

"Vope," he said as he ate the alien fodder, "who's this boy you're after? Why's he so important?"

"What boy?" Ratcoff asked. Obviously he knew nothing about the parameters of this mission.

"*They*," Jefferson said with emphasis, "want me to bring a certain boy back to them. He's supposed to be *here,* somewhere." He cast his gaze around at the desolation. "So who *is* he, Vope? And if you can do what you did back at that house…then why don't you find the boy and take him yourself?"

"My orders stand," said the Gorgon.

"I don't care how many humans are protecting him," Jefferson went on. "You could destroy them all, if you wanted to. Why do you need *me*?"

Vope didn't reply, and Jefferson thought he was going to remain silent, but after a few seconds the alien spoke. "He would resist force."

"So? Maybe he would, but..." And then it struck Jefferson Jericho, quite clearly. "Oh my God," he said. "You—she—whatever you are... you're *afraid* of him, aren't you?"

Vope's face turned away, his gaze directed to the distance.

"You're afraid," Jefferson continued. "And that must mean...is he a Cypher in disguise?"

"No sense is made of that."

"Your *enemy*. Whatever you call it. Is he the enemy, in disguise? He must've done something really—" *Awesome*, he was about to say, "—*bad*, to get you—her, it—so bound to lay your hands on him. *My* hands, I mean. What did he do? Kill a couple dozen of—"

"Refrain your curiosity," the Gorgon interrupted, "or I will give you pain. We are moving now." He began to stride away, and Jefferson and Ratcoff felt little sharp tinglings at the backs of their necks and so were compelled to follow.

Jefferson thought he would never survive this. If the boy was a Cypher in disguise he must be like a special forces soldier, and if the Gorgons were afraid of him...no telling what destructive powers this so-called 'boy' was capable of. Lay hands on a Cypher commando and expect to whisk him back to Gorgon-land for a little torture session? *Right.* The first thing that would happen is, an ex-car salesman named Leon Kushman was going to be blasted out of this world as quickly as if he'd taken a gunshot to the back of the head.

"They keep me in a place that looks like a suburb with little houses like from the fifties," Ratcoff said as he struggled to walk alongside Jefferson. Ratcoff's head was wet with sweat and sweat stained the front of his shirt and his armpits. Jefferson knew the man was terrified and had the need to talk, so he just listened as best he could with his own death sentence hanging over his head. "There're seventy-eight people in that place, brought from all over the States. We call it—"

"The Ant Farm?" Jefferson asked.

"Huh? No. We call it Microscope Meadows. Know why?"

179

"Because you always feel you're being watched from above?"

"Yeah, that's right. But we've got everything we need to live. Electricity, water, cars that don't need gasoline or oil anymore, that white shit they feed us with and some other weird stuff you drink...and the weather never changes. It's like...always early summer. But know somethin' *really* weird?"

You can never leave, Jefferson thought.

"You can't get out," Ratcoff said. "You can drive and drive, and pretend you're goin' somewhere...but all of a sudden you turn a corner and you're right back where you started from. Weird, huh?"

"Yes," said Jefferson. The Ant Farm, Microscope Meadows...he wondered what the Japanese, the Russians, the Norwegians and Brazilians called their prisons. The Gorgons were students of humans, just as some scientists were students of insects. He wondered also what they had done to Ratcoff when they'd taken him apart, and what they'd added to make him so valuable to this little jaunt. He hoped he wouldn't have to find out.

"I miss the stars," Ratcoff said, in a quietly reverential voice. "My Dad and me...long time back...used to camp out in our backyard, in Jersey. Used to put up a tent. I was a Boy Scout, believe that or not. So after we cooked our hotdogs and had our Indian blood—that's what my Dad used to call mixing up grape juice, Pepsi, and root beer—we would say goodnight to Mom when she came out to the back porch, and then we'd go to sleep. Us guys. You know?"

"Sure," said Jefferson, whose memory of his father involved breath that smelled like cheap whiskey, a crooked grin on a slack-jawed face and a salesman's empty promise that tomorrow would be a better day.

"But...long after midnight," Ratcoff went on, "I always crawled out of that tent and lay on my back looking up to count the stars. And where we lived...you could see a lot of 'em. Just shining and shining, like rivers of light. I thought I was the luckiest kid in the world, to be where I was. Only now...when I go out to my backyard and lie down in the dark...I can't see any stars. Not one, in all that dark. My Dad died a few years back and my Mom had a condo in Sarasota. I called her that first day, to make sure she was okay. I wanted to fly down there, but you know all the airplanes were grounded. I told her to get to one of the shelters the National Guard was setting up. That was the last I heard from her. I hope she made it. You think maybe she made it, Jeff?"

Jefferson Jericho heard the pleading. He was many things in this life—a manipulator, a con man, a man who always put his needs and desires first, a man who disdained the weaknesses of others and played upon them, a money-hungry and power-hungry and sex-hungry 'fiend of the night', as Regina would have said—but at this moment, in this fearful world with a Gorgon leading him onward to what was possibly his death and at his side another human being wounded in heart and soul—he found something in himself he did not recognize, and it was so foreign to him he could not name what it was.

He said, "*Sure* she made it, Burt. No doubt. The National Guard... those guys knew what they were doing. They got people to safety. Lots of people. And your mom too, no doubt."

"Yeah," said Ratcoff, with a quick smile. "That's what I think too."

Jefferson Jericho was always amazed at how easily people could be led. How when they *wanted* to believe, the job was halfway done. It was even easier if they *needed* to believe. Sometimes you met a rock who refused to be turned, but mostly it was like this, especially when he wore his minister's suit. And that scam about finding and deciphering verses in the Bible that told an investor what stocks to buy and sell...well, it was helpful to have inside traders working for you, and maybe when the info was faulty and money was lost by the High Rollers, Jefferson could say it was the will of God, the teaching of humility and above all patience, and that even he—Jefferson Jericho—was being taught a lesson too. But mostly things went as planned, and when the High Rollers paid the Jericho Foundation the voluntary yearly fifteen percent commission off their God-given and Bible-verse-directed earnings, as well as whatever they wished to give from the heart, the used-to-be Leon Kushman looked at the stained-glass window in his office and regarded the rainbow depicted there.

The last he'd heard, those shelters the Guard had set up had first been pits of panic that descended into chaos and violence among the human kind. It was likely some had been destroyed in the battles between Cypher and Gorgon. It was very likely Burt Ratcoff's mother had perished in the first few months, if not the first few weeks, and like hundreds of thousands—millions?—of others around the world, the bones and ashes would be found only when the war was over and the human survivors crawled out of whatever hole they'd been hiding in. To be what? Slaves for the victors? Experiments in human genetics and mutations? The creation of new weapons for new wars on more worlds?

My brothers and sisters, Jefferson thought, *there are no rainbows in this window. We are caught in the middle of two power-mad forces, and no matter who wins we are screwed.*

"Yes," said the preacherman, "I'm sure your mom is just fine."

And then he saw something on the road ahead, approaching.

He thought he was seeing things. A mirage, maybe. But…*a yellow school bus?*

Vope halted. His head seemed to vibrate so fast that for two seconds he was headless.

"We will stop that vehicle," he said.

"The boy's in it?" Jefferson asked.

"Yes," came the answer. And again: "We will stop that vehicle."

To Jefferson it didn't look at if the driver of that bus intended to stop. Vope began striding forward again, with Jefferson beside him and just behind, and on the other side Ratcoff winced and staggered along on his blistered feet and aching legs. Jefferson lifted his arms and waved them back and forth as the bus drew nearer.

"They're not stoppin'," said Ratcoff. "We better get off this road."

But Jefferson continued to wave and suddenly the bus began to slow down. He heard the shriek of old brakes engaging.

Vope said, "Hear me. Do as you're instructed. If there is any…" He paused, searching for the word. "*Difficulty,*" he continued, "I will kill every one of your kind in that vehicle."

"It may not be that easy," Jefferson answered.

"We will take the boy," Vope repeated. "If there is any difficulty I will kill—"

"No, you will *not*," said the preacherman, and the alien turned toward him with a blank face but Jefferson knew what was going on behind it. The pain couldn't be delivered as Vope would like, or the humans in that bus would see him fall to his knees. "I'm supposed to put my hands on him, isn't that right?" The bus was stopping a dozen yards in front of them. "Then we'll be teleported or whatever back to...wherever? If I'm supposed to get past whoever is protecting him, you have to leave it to me. You want that boy delivered alive. Yes?"

"Yes."

"Then don't set off any alarms. Do you know what that means? It means you stand back and let me do what I *do*."

Vope seemed to be thinking about this; Jefferson could tell the alien gears were turning.

The bus's door was opening. A woman's rough voice called out, "Any trouble and the first bullet comes from my cannon!"

"They have weapons," Jefferson said. "Primitive to you, deadly to me and Burt. You don't have to worry about being shot in the head, but *we* do. You're going to let *me* take charge of this if you want it to be successful. Hear me?"

Vope said nothing, but neither did his arms grow to be snakelike monsters nor did any pain clench the back of Jefferson's neck.

"Do you understand that a human being blinks his eyes every few seconds?" Jefferson asked. He saw a man and woman coming out of the bus; the man had a submachine gun and the woman carried a .45 automatic. "You don't blink, they're going to know you're not human real quick. So do it, keep *quiet*, and let me talk."

Then he turned his full attention to the man and the woman, and he said with a great exhalation of relief, "Thank *God* we've found somebody who's not totally insane! We've been wandering all day, trying to—"

"What are you doing out here?" Dave asked sharply, keeping the Uzi's barrel pointed at the ground between himself and Olivia and the three men.

"Well," said Jefferson, "we're not walking for our *health*, sir. We've been trying to find safe shelter before nightfall."

"Is that so? And where the hell have you *come* from?"

Jefferson realized this rough-edged man in his torn black t-shirt, his faded jeans and a dirty dark blue baseball cap would rather shoot them all than spend any more time jawing. The man had a crust of blood from a cut across the bridge of his nose, and he might be a rock that refused to be turned. "We have come *from* Hell," Jefferson answered, in a voice as grim as the grave. He kept his eyes fixed on the man's. "A few days ago there were ten of us. We're what's left, after..." He lifted his chin just a fraction, as if in defiance of the world and this man's Uzi. "After we were attacked on the road from Denver. I guess you know there are gangs of men driven insane out there. They fell on us and they shot our friends to pieces. We got away with one backpack, but we lost the rest of our supplies, our clothes, everything." He made a point of eyeing the Uzi and the automatic. "I wish we'd had more guns, we could've fought back."

"You don't have guns? Why not?"

"I *did* have a gun," Jefferson offered. "A Smith & Wesson .38. A nice piece." He let his gaze slip toward the tall, slim woman, who was Hispanic and probably in her fifties. She had short-cut white hair and her face was tense, but Jefferson thought she'd been very attractive in the life that used to be. "When I ran out of bullets and couldn't find any more, I traded my gun for a few cans of vegetables and some canned soup to keep my wife and daughter alive. That was in Kansas, four months ago." The lies came so easily when one had a story-line. He gave the woman a sad and bitter smile. "I wish I could say my wife and daughter had made it out of Kansas with us, but..."

"What happened to them? *Exactly*," growled the man, who still looked as if he wanted to shoot first and ask questions later.

Jefferson decided to go for the high roll, a shocker quickly conceived to back the bastard off. "Regina was raped and murdered in a basement by a madman who hit me over the head with a shovel and tried to bury me alive," he said, his gaze steady. "When I crawled out of there and got to my gun, I used my last bullets on him. Amy wasted away. After her mother died, she lost the will to live. You want more details, sir?" He turned his full and intense power on the woman, who he perceived to be more malleable than the hard-ass. "My name is Jeff Kushman. This is Burt Ratcoff, and…" *Don't pause*, he told himself. "Jack Vope."

He had not earned his place in the world by being slow of mind or timid at launching tales to suit his purpose, and with two guns pointed in his direction his mind was going a hundred miles a second. He intended to stay alive as long as possible. He looked at Vope and launched not a tale but a searing thought that reached out like a slap to the face: *Blink, idiot!*

Vope returned the gaze. Something must have clicked, because suddenly Vope started blinking as if he had eyes full of gnats or the worst facial tic ever recorded. *Slow down*, Jefferson thought. *Once every seven or eight seconds!* He hoped the Gorgons were smart enough to understand Earth time, but maybe not.

"What's wrong with *him*?" Dave asked. He'd seen the black-haired man start blinking like his eyes were on fire. Otherwise, the guy's face was emotionless.

"Jack's still in shock," Jefferson said quickly. "He's lost his family too."

The blinking was still out of control. Dave thought the guy was about to have a fit. "Can't he talk?"

"He needs some time. He'll be all right. Settle down, Jack, you're among friends."

"*Friends?*" Dave asked. "How do you figure that?"

Jefferson brought up an expression that was partly quizzical and partly hurt. He asked the woman, "You *are* going to help us, aren't you? Please say you're not going to just *leave* us."

"Yeah," Ratcoff spoke up, finding his nerve and realizing he had to follow Jeff's lead to get on that bus and do whatever it was the Gorgons demanded. Then at least he could get back to Microscope Meadows. "Don't leave us, okay?"

Olivia looked from one man to the other. Jack Vope had stopped his rapid-fire blinking and he seemed to be controlling that better but still… his face was devoid of any expression, like a painted mask. She said, "Dave, let's talk," and she motioned him over nearer the bus.

Dave didn't care to turn his back on these three so he retreated toward Olivia, all the time keeping watchful and ready for anything.

Olivia said quietly, "We can't leave them. We have to—"

"Take them with us?" Dave interrupted. "Why? We don't know them, why should we care?"

"Because they're human beings and they're in *need*, that's why. We never turned anyone away from Panther Ridge."

"Sure we did. We killed the ones who weren't really human. How do we know these three are? And how about that Vope guy? Gives me the creeps. He looks like he might go nuts any minute." Dave shook his head. "Olivia, we can't test them with the saline. There's no *way* we can know if they're really human or not."

Jefferson had seen the man shake his head. The rock was holding steady. Jefferson said, "Can I ask where you're going?"

"To Denver," Olivia answered. "We've got a lot of wounded people on board and we're trying to find medical supplies."

"Maybe I can help," said the salesman, who had already decided his pitch when he heard the word *wounded*. "I'm a doctor." He decided to give the lie more texture. "I was a cardiologist in Little Rock."

"I've been to Arkansas," Dave said, which was his own lie. "Who's the President who was governor there?"

"William Jefferson Clinton," said Leon Kushman, who had taken the name 'Jefferson' from that very person, after getting an autographed picture of himself as a seventeen-year-old, grinning political volunteer standing between Bill and Hillary at a fund-raising banquet. He would always remember what Clinton had said to him: *You're a comet with your tail on fire, aren't you?* That was the same weekend he'd wound up at a party smoking weed and discussing porn films with a law student named Andy Beale, who had become a Missouri senator and now—or was—President of these Used To Be United States. "Otherwise known as 'Bubba' or 'Slick Willie'," Jefferson went on. He frowned. "Is this a test?"

This joker was a human, Dave thought. Had to be. Still…he had a bad feeling about this. The weird guy blinked a few more times in rapid succession. The short bald guy was moving from foot to foot as if standing on a hot griddle. "*Damn*," Dave said under his breath. They had to get moving, the sun was going down.

"We've got to go." Olivia had read the situation just as he had. "All right, get aboard," she told the three.

"But you'll stand at the *front*," Dave added. "Where I can watch you."

"Thank you," Jefferson said. He gave more texture to the spin: "I don't really care to go back to Denver, but I guess there's not too much ahead, is there?"

"Just get on the bus and keep quiet. And watch your buddy there, I don't want him freaking out and hurting anybody. Any trouble from him and you're all off."

"As you say." *If you only knew*, Jefferson thought. *Idiot*.

"I'm Olivia Quintero and he's Dave McKane," Olivia said as they walked to the bus. "We've been holed up in an apartment complex. Early this morning a Gorgon ship crashed into it." She shuddered inwardly, with a memory of something half-seen and totally repulsive. She asked, "You men have your own food and water in the backpack?"

"Food, yes," Jefferson said. "Water, no."

"I'll get you some. I guess you need it."

"We sure do!" Ratcoff gasped. "I'm parched!"

They got aboard. Hannah gave the three newcomers the evil eye and when Olivia nodded she put her pistol away and closed the door. "We're movin'!" she called to everyone, and then she started them forward again on the long road that in a few miles curved to a ramp onto I-25 south to Denver.

Olivia passed the word back to send up a plastic jug of water. Dave stood right behind the three men and he kept his Uzi in hand just in case. "Where'd you stay last night?" he asked, directing the question to Ratcoff.

"A farmhouse," Jefferson said. "But—"

"I asked *him*. You shut up until I tell you to talk."

"*Look*." Jefferson turned toward Dave. Their faces were only inches apart. The preacherman glanced down at the submachine gun that was aimed somewhere south of his navel, into God's country. "What's your point, Dave? Can I call you Dave?"

187

"You can call me Mister *Careful*. We've seen things that try to pass themselves off as human, and they ain't *pretty*. They're things either the Gorgons or the Cyphers have made in their Frankenstein labs. So that's why this gun is still out and it's staying out."

"I hope you have the safety on. You could make a real mess when we hit the next bump, Dave."

"Ratcoff, where'd you stay last night?" Dave persisted.

To his credit, Ratcoff hesitated only a few seconds. "Like Jeff said…a farmhouse. I don't know how many miles away it was, but we walked a long time. My feet are killin' me."

"Why didn't you stay there?"

Ratcoff shrugged, still keeping his composure. "The place was half burned down. We were tryin' to find people. Not crazy ones. And…you know…just us three alone…how long were we gonna make it?"

Good man, Jefferson thought. *Listen and learn from the master.*

Vope was immobile at his side. That was good too, Jefferson decided. Let everybody think the idiot was in shock and couldn't talk. The Gorgons didn't understand contractions, and everything Vope said came out as stiff as a high schooler trying to speak Shakespeare's English. At least he had the blinking part taken care of, mostly. So just let him keep his mouth shut. When the plastic jug of water arrived, Jefferson took a drink and also took the opportunity to look around. The bus was so crowded it was hard to see beyond the people standing behind McKane and the woman. He saw a young blonde-haired kid who was maybe nineteen or so, with a bloody rag wrapped around his head, his eyes bleary, but that wasn't who they were seeking. He remembered his starlet harlot saying *You will know the boy when you find him, my Jefferson* as he drifted into a dreamless narcotic sleep in the room that was not a room in the false French mansion. He wondered if in that sleep they had added some sensor device to him along with the pain stimulator in his neck, because he was absolutely sure the young man with the injured head was not *the boy*. He could see no one else who might be *the boy*, so *the boy* must be further at the back. The kid was here, though; if he wasn't, Vope wouldn't have wanted to stop the bus. Oh yeah, he was here. When the chance to take him came, Jefferson would know that too. Only he hoped the Gorgons would teleport them out of range of that Uzi before McKane could get the safety off.

"One drink and pass it on," Dave said.

"Sure." Jefferson gave the jug to Ratcoff, who drank noisily. Then came the moment when Ratcoff put the red cap back on the jug and offered it to Vope, and the Gorgon just stood there looking at it like it was a half-gallon of Cypher piss.

"Don't you want a drink, Jack?" Jefferson asked, his voice full of concern for a brother of the road who had lost his mental bearings. "Here, let me open it." He was aware that not only McKane and the woman were watching, but others were too. He removed the red cap and said as if to a pitiful imbecile, "Open your mouth, Jack."

Vope's hands came up. He took the jug. There might have been a little angry spark deep in the black eyes.

"I know what to do," Vope said. *"Idiot."*

The Gorgon tipped the jug into his open mouth, as he'd seen the two humans do. Only Jefferson saw the creature flinch just a fraction, as if the liquid tasted vile. A small amount was taken and then allowed to slowly dribble from the sides of the mouth down into the black beard.

Vope gave the jug back to Jefferson, who recapped it and returned it to Olivia. "Thank you kindly," he said, giving her just a glimpse of his Southern charm but not enough to fire anyone's jets. The bus was moving on, curving toward the I-25 ramp. Jefferson noted that McKane's gun had moved away from his proud parts. "I imagine you people have been through a lot," he said to Olivia. "Like we have. Like everyone has."

She nodded. "We're glad you came along. You can help JayDee with some of these people when we find supplies. He's our doctor."

"Oh." His blink was maybe a little too slow. "Right."

About fifteen feet away from Jefferson Jericho, standing amid other survivors who hung onto whatever handhold they could find as the bus turned onto I-25, Ethan couldn't see the three new arrivals for the crush of bodies around him, but his heartbeat had picked up and the flesh of his chest and back had begun tingling. The bruised parts, he thought.

It came to him very clearly.

An alarm had been set off.

Why? he wondered.

He had not seen the three men, but he thought that they were not who—or what—they appeared to be. His first impulse was to pass it forward that he needed to talk to Dave, but in another moment he decided against it. Dave likely couldn't get back to him, and he would have to leave Olivia, and whatever the "men" were, they might have alarms too. If those went off, they might…what? Tear the bus apart and kill everyone?

No, Ethan thought. *They're not here to do that.*

He was certain they were here for an unknown reason, but destroying the bus was not it.

Best to wait, he told himself. *Give it time, get a look at these three and try to figure them out.*

His heartbeat began to slow and the tingling went away, which was good because he was just about to start scratching himself and he could hardly move amid the others packed around him. He wondered what would happen if he lifted up his shirt and played tic-tac-toe in silver on the blackboard of his chest.

Nikki was still watching him from where she stood behind him. He could feel her eye on him, drilling into his head for an answer. He knew she was still not comfortable with keeping to herself what she'd seen. She might yet crack and start shouting that in their midst there was a freak, a danger to them all, a creature that had to be thrown off the bus and shot down on the side of the road…

…an alien among them.

Ethan steadied himself. They passed a few wrecked cars and a bread truck that had turned onto its side. Something crunched under the tires, and Ethan wondered if Hannah had just run them over a skeleton or two the Gray Men had left behind.

Denver lay ahead. So also did White Mansion Mountain. The boy who had been raised from the dead and was no longer fully human felt the pull of that place on him, never ceasing and growing more urgent.

An answer was there, he thought. But it was not *the* answer. And why he knew this to be so he had no idea, but there it was like a flash of light in his mind. An answer was at White Mansion Mountain, but there too, were more questions.

But first Denver, as dark began to fall and somewhere out there the Gray Men stirred, hungry for the meat of pilgrims searching for a place of peace.

Hannah turned on the headlights. The one on the left side failed to illuminate.

"Figures," she muttered.

The bus went on into the falling dark, tires occasionally crushing bones that lay scattered on the cracked pavement like ancient runes pointing the way to the heart of the mystery.

THREE.

LIFE DURING
WARTIME

SEVENTEEN.

STEERING THE ONE-EYED BUS THROUGH THE DEBRIS SCATTERED along I-25 was no easy task, even for a driver who'd once gotten a wad of bubble gum pushed into her hair while at the wheel and another time had a kid throw oatmeal up in her lap on a rainy Monday morning. Beyond the reach of the single headlight was dark upon dark. Occasionally the shape of a wrecked and burned car loomed up, and there were many skeletons or parts of skeletons, but Hannah Grimes kept her nerves steady and the bus moving forward at about ten miles an hour. The slow speed saved their lives when the light fell upon a black-edged crater burned into the pavement. Hannah said "Shit," under her breath and deftly got them onto the median and past the danger. She had switched on the interior safety lights, which cast a yellow glow upon her passengers.

Dave McKane was standing watch over the three new arrivals. He didn't like the smell of them. He didn't like the cardiologist who talked like a car salesman, having a smooth and quick answer for every question. He didn't like the little bald Ratcoff, who was sweating and nervous and looked to be in utter torment, and he didn't like Jack Dope, who stood like a statue and stared ahead into the darkness with that weird double-and-triple blinking he was doing. That guy looked to Dave to be a basket case in the offering, somebody who might go berserk and start flailing at the people around him. Dave almost hoped he would so he could cold-cock the freak into the next century. But that wouldn't happen, because he was so tired he was near collapse.

"We ought to be seeing Denver by now," Hannah announced. "If there were any lights, I mean."

Ahead lay only the night and on the pavement in front of the bus a ribcage and a skull that Hannah could not avoid. It popped like a gunshot under the right front tire.

Jefferson Jericho had not prepared himself for this. All these human remains that littered the highway…most of them not complete skeletons, but scattered by…*what*? Animals that came out of their lairs to feast on the fallen? Yes, that had to be it. He stared ahead into the dark where the city of Denver should be, and he fully realized now what the Gorgons had shielded him and the residents of New Eden from. This hideous reality was nearly more than the human spirit could bear, it buckled the knees with its brutality and hopelessness. He found himself wanting to get back to New Eden, to the running water and the electricity and the false sun and everything else that might be false but was at least a comfort and a shelter. Even back to Regina's hatred, because he thought that someday—after this war had ended—she would come around again, and understand that he was only using the gifts God had given him.

He remembered what his harlot starlet had said in that false French bedroom: *We have given you much, my Jefferson.* Much. *And much given can be much taken away.*

He shivered. *Dear Jesus*, he thought as the bus moved on into the endless night. *I couldn't survive out here in this world.*

So the boy must be taken. Whatever the boy was and whatever power he possessed, he must be taken and the sooner the better.

Jefferson realized Vope had turned his head slightly to gaze upon him, reading the thoughts as they crashed between the walls of a fearful mind. Was there the hint of an arrogant smile upon the Gorgon's mouth, or was it Jefferson's imagination? Did Vope even *know* how to smile?

Whatever. It was gone now, and Vope looked away from him.

Behind Dave and Olivia, in the middle of the crowded bus, Ethan had come to the conclusion that he had to do *something*. He could not wait for the three men to strike, because that was the feeling he was getting: a poisonous snake about to strike from the depth of shadows. And just like that he knew: *one of them is a Gorgon, hiding in human form.*

Everyone in the bus was in danger. He had to do something, and he had to do it now.

He started pushing his way forward. "Sorry," he said. "Excuse me. Can I get past, please? Sorry...sorry..."

And on between the survivors of Panther Ridge until he reached Dave and Olivia, and then he saw the three men standing at the front of the bus facing toward the blacked-out city, and slowly one of the men turned his head and a pair of small dark eyes like pieces of flint above a black beard caught and held him, and Ethan knew the enemy on sight.

"Dave?" Ethan said.

"What is it?" Dave asked, a note of tension in his voice because he could hear the tension in the boy's.

The Gorgon stared at him, and suddenly one of the other men turned to also take Ethan in. This man had unruly brown hair and a growth of brown beard, and he was dirty and haggard-looking, but Ethan thought there was something about his face that was too soft, too handsome, to have fully known the hardships of life during wartime. He looked like he, too, was cloaked in a disguise. But this man was human...as was the third man, with the bald and sweating head...and yet...

"What's wrong?" Olivia asked, when Ethan didn't reply to Dave's question.

The human with the brown beard had a look of recognition in his eyes. His face was frozen for a few seconds, and then he smiled like the parting of clouds before the sun. "Hi there," he said. "What's *your* name?"

"Big effing crater ahead," Hannah announced loudly. "I'm dodgin' it. Everybody hang on!"

The bus veered to the right. The light revealed a UPS tractor-trailer truck that had crashed through the railing on the right lane, and as Hannah gritted her teeth and steered for safety the bus scraped along the rear of the UPS trailer with a ragged shriek of distressed metal. A few people cried out in alarm, if they had the energy to do so, and Hannah called back, "Hush up, you babies!"

"You want to come up front?" Jefferson Jericho asked Ethan. Here is *the boy*, he knew. Nothing particularly special about him...or was there? "Come on, then!" He beckoned with the fingers of an upraised hand, though the hand trembled just a bit with frightened anticipation of what might happen.

"Don't talk to him," Dave told the man. "He doesn't know you, and you don't know him. Just *don't.*"

"I thought he might want to come up here where he can breathe better. It looks mighty tight back there."

"He can breathe fine. What do you want, Ethan?"

Ethan, Jefferson thought. His eyes narrowed. *Come on, Ethan, let me get my hands on you.*

The Gorgon was staring at Ethan again. The creature blinked rapidly...one two three...and again...one two three. Ethan felt a shock... something like cold fingers reaching into his brain and trying to rummage through it as a burglar might rummage through drawers in a search for valuables.

I won't let you go there, he thought, and instantly something like a metallic wall of tight bricks appeared in his mind, and though he could still feel the fingers scrabbling at the bricks, trying to find a weak place, the Gorgon was unable to reach in and pluck out what he wanted.

Ethan found he could give his attention to Dave, formulate thoughts, and the wall of bricks remained solid. The fingers were getting more insistent, and stronger and stronger, but they could not break through.

He was about to say *The man with the black beard is a Gorgon* but he checked himself. Instead he envisioned his own hand, but the hand he saw glowed silver, was long-fingered and more slender than the one at the end of his own arm. He envisioned the silver-glowing hand reaching out like a coil of mist past Dave and Olivia, and the long slim fingers probing into the head of the creature that wore a black beard, and then piercing through the alien-constructed skull of some unknown material he saw—

—a landscape of swamp with yellow and brown tree-like growths protruding up through a soup of wet fog, their forms tortured into shapes more like cactus and having skins across which rippled spikes rose and fell as if the vegetation breathed the miasmic air. Birds of prey with gray flesh and long beaks studded with teeth roamed the clouds, swooping down upon things that resembled crabs and eels sliding through the red-tinged liquid, which shimmered not like water but like quicksilver. There was a change of scene…the skipping of frames as if a movie had suddenly sped up…and there stood under double moons a massive city with thousands of low-slung buildings like sculpted adobe mud-dwellings, but engineered by an alien eye and created by alien tools. Blue globes of light moved back and forth across the city, illuminating figures half-walking, half-slithering through narrow alleys. Another skipping of frames and change of scene…and there a darkness, a cavity, a place where machines thrummed and creations strange and fearful to the eyes of an earthman took shape. Ethan had the sensation that it was deep underground, in what might have been a nest, now becoming a place of shadows and flickering blue light, a place of explorations into the imaginations of warriors ever-seeking new and more powerful weapons of destruction, a place of power unknown to the human mind where the walls breathed with artificial life and were mottled with the colors of their warships.

In the nerve center of pulsing machines and the flicker of blue energy stood a form that seemed to be beckoning him with a scaly, five-clawed hand, a figure draped in leathery black robes. Above the robes was a dark, dimly seen head and face that brought sweat out upon Ethan's flesh even as he knew he was only probing the memory pictures of a Gorgon, and in that face was a pair of narrow eyes with hypnotic, red-slitted pupils that, unblinking, bade him mentally to come closer and closer, until he was drawn in so near he saw a cobra-like grin that exposed sharp, wet fangs and felt a freezing terror that might well have turned a human to stone.

He could take no more. He got out but it was not easy, as if having to pull the silver hand out of a mass of clinging mud.

He felt a tremendous power coiled within the Gorgon who stood only a few feet away from him, with Dave and Olivia between them. He felt a destruction that could savage everyone in the bus, that could destroy the bus itself as completely as if it were a child's playtoy. But as their eyes held, Ethan had a sudden strange thought that broke through his fear, and almost without his bidding the thought seeped through the metallic wall and on toward the Gorgon's mind, and that thought was: *I can destroy you*.

The Gorgon blinked blinked blinked.

"Hey!" Hannah said suddenly. "I think I see a *light*! There's a glow in the sky over—" Something hit the right side of the bus with a jarring *thump*.

"What the *hell*...?" she said, interrupted in her directions. She weaved the bus back and forth a little. "What'd we hit?"

A small, spindly figure crawled up the side of the bus and stuck to one of the windows about midway back. There was a stunned silence from the passengers. The creature's fingers and toes had flattened into suction cups. The thing looked to be a nine- or ten-year-old boy, dressed in tattered rags and with a completely bald and mallet-shaped head, its eyes sunken so deeply into the face they could not be seen. The creature was as gray as the ash from an all-consuming fire, and looking through the window into the bus the thing suddenly grinned as if delighted to see all the traveling meat, and then its head struck forward and shattered the window to pieces.

The screaming began.

"Holy Christ!" Ratcoff yelled, and Jefferson Jericho's infamous member peed into his jeans. Ethan saw the Gray Man—Gray Child, in this instance—climbing through the window, still grinning to show sharp little rows of serrated teeth.

"Somebody shoot it!" Dave shouted. He drew his Uzi but there were too many people in the way. "*Shoot it!*" he shouted again, as the thing reached out and grabbed Carmen Niega by the hair.

A .45 automatic cracked twice and the Gray Child shuddered, two holes in its chest, but still it drew Carmen, screaming, towards its open mouth. Then a piece of rusted rebar smashed the thing across the face and Joel Schuster followed JayDee up by shooting the creature a third time in its bony head at point-blank distance. The Gray Child fell backward through the window, hissing, and took a handful of Carmen's hair with it.

Something hit the back of the bus with a force that bent the emergency exit inward and cracked the middle of the three rear windows like another gunshot. Hannah yelled, "Shit!" and stomped the gas pedal, no matter what obstacles lay ahead.

The gnarled hands of another Gray Man gripped the bottom of the window broken out by the child and pulled the body up. This one was a stocky, muscular beast with curved red spikes growing out of its head, naked shoulders and chest. It made a low, rasping noise and flung itself into the bus even as Joel and Paul Edson shot it, and as the jammed-in passengers tried to get away from it the thing leaped upon Gary Roosa, impaling him on its chest spikes. A savage set of fangs ripped Gary's throat open and began to chew through his neck until a Hispanic man with a white-streaked beard put a shotgun to the side of the monster's head and gave it both barrels.

Another creature, thin and wiry with a grotesque and misshapen face that was nearly all mouth with an eye just off the center of its forehead and the second on its right cheek, was clambering in through the window. Clinging to its back was a gray-haired female with a face like an axeblade and another female head growing out of her left shoulder. The passengers were trying to get away but there was nowhere to go. Those without weapons were crushing themselves up against the far side of the bus. Handguns and rifles were firing, combined with the screams a tremendous noise, but before these horrors were killed another man's arm was nearly chewed off at the elbow and a young woman's face gnawed to bloody tatters by the Gray Woman and her ingrown sister.

Hannah swerved the bus wildly back and forth. Dave was trying to get back to the broken window and Ethan had gotten out of his way. Olivia stood beside Ethan, her back to the three new arrivals. Suddenly the handsome man with the brown beard gritted his teeth and started forward, his hands reaching out as if to grasp Ethan's forearms, and in that moment Ethan looked into his eyes and saw behind them what he could only describe as a whirlpool of terror.

"*Jesus Christ!*" Hannah shouted. She hit the brakes.

Jefferson Jericho stumbled past Ethan, who had dodged aside and grabbed the back of the seat nearest him. One of the preacherman's hands grazed the boy's left arm and the other closed on empty air. He crashed into Olivia and fell to his knees in the aisle. The single headlight showed Hannah dozens of Gray Men swarming toward the bus, a tide of monstrosities flooding across the highway...not dozens, she realized in another moment, but hundreds. They ran and crawled and hobbled, some with jellied and hanging skin and others mutated into killing machines with clawed hands and flesh like spiny plate armor.

In a matter of seconds they were all over the front of the bus and climbing up toward the windshield. Ratcoff had fallen to the floorboard, whimpering, while Vope stared impassively at the onrushing mass of inhuman humanity.

"*Go!*" Olivia shouted at Hannah, as she saw the bus's yellow snout being covered over by gray bodies.

Hannah floored the thing. Bus number 712 backfired a blast of black smoke and lunged forward like a whipped horse. Gray Men tumbled off the front of the bus and the wheels jubbled as if running over a dozen speedbumps. The bumper and front grill slammed into more and more bodies and the tires slipped over their slime, but ahead there was a solid wall of horrors. Two of the larger and stronger Gray Men had kept their holds on edges of metal and one of them crawled up to slam a knotty fist against the windshield. The fist came through in a shower of glass and Burt Ratcoff screamed like a woman.

"*Get off my bus!*" Hannah shouted. She followed that demand with two booming shots from her six-gun that pierced the windshield and sent the mutant flying backward off the hood. She shot the other Gray Man in the head before it could use its fists, but the bullet left a hole almost in front of her face and cracks snaked across the windshield.

Olivia realized there were too many, just as Ethan did. The things were running at the bus from all directions, and it seemed that hundreds of them were directly ahead.

"Keep going! Keep going!" Dave yelled as he pushed his way up front. Jefferson Jericho had crawled out of the aisle on his knees, curling up on the floorboard to seek some kind of safety among the other bodies, but there was still enough of him exposed for Dave to step on the man's right hand as he passed. There was a crunch of knuckles breaking beneath a hard-soled workboot, and in the burning flare of pain that followed, the super salesman and fiend of the night realized he had just lost the use of all his fingers.

Hannah was trying to keep going, but the bus was jamming itself up on Gray Men beneath the wheels and the undercarriage. The engine shrieked as the tires lost traction over jellied flesh and crushed armor. More were climbing up over the hood, and one with hands like bludgeons and two stubby extra arms was coming up to finish the job on the windshield.

In the chaos, Ethan looked back to find one person.

He saw Nikki, crushed in with others who had gotten as far away as they could from that broken window and the still-twitching bodies of the Gray Men. At least she was all right, but this battle was far from—

A blinding white light flooded the bus.

It was followed almost immediately by the chatter of double machine guns, and first hit were the Gray Men on the hood. Red tracers zipped through the air in front of the windshield, and now Hannah did slam her foot on the brake pedal because those slugs were just too damned close. But whoever was shooting knew their business, because the Gray Men fell away and the one with the bludgeon-hands had its head half shot off, yet no bullet hit the glass or the hood. The machine guns kept firing, mowing down the Gray Men in rows. They began to turn and run, climbing over each other to get away, while the bullets continued to tear them to pieces.

Squinting into the harsh glare, Ethan was able to make out a vehicle coming up from the right, huge tires crunching over the guardrail.

"Good Christ!" Dave breathed. "An armored car!"

The vehicle's dazzling searchlight turned to follow a knot of ten or more Gray Men running for the cover of a burned-out Yellow Cab. The double-barreled machine guns, firing from an armored turret, caught eight of them but the others scurried into the shadows on the far side of the cab. There was a hollow-sounding *whump!* and about three seconds later the Yellow Cab blew up into a fireball and burning gray body parts were tossed into the air.

"Grenade launcher!" Dave said, his voice rough and ragged.

The armored car was painted steel-gray and had a massive front bumper-cage defended by iron spikes. The machine guns were still firing as the searchlight revealed more mutants running along the highway. A second grenade was launched and exploded about fifty yards away. Then the guns were silent and the armored car turned so it was directly in front of bus number 712, its heavy-duty ribbed tires crunching over malformed bones and heads and smashing hard armored flesh into paste. The searchlight swung over to illuminate the interior of the bus brighter than daylight had been for a long time.

A loudspeaker crackled.

"Nice night for a firefight." It was a woman's sarcastic voice. "Somebody come out and talk to us, but watch out for shit on your shoes."

Dave said to Olivia, "I'll go." He glanced quickly at a grim-faced Ethan, then took stock of the other passengers. Some were sobbing, but most were in shock. He saw JayDee, who was being helped by Joel Schuster and Diego Carvazos down to give aid to Gary Roosa, though it was obvious Gary had escaped this madhouse by a tough way to go, but escaped it nevertheless. A belt had been used as a tourniquet for Aaron Ramsey's chewed-up arm, and two women were tending to Lila Conti's face, but the wounds were severe.

Ethan saw that the Gorgon had not moved. Dave was going to have to pass him to get out of the bus. *Look at me*, he commanded.

The Gorgon did.

Touch this man and you'll die, Ethan said in his mind. How he would do that he didn't know...but he was sure beyond a doubt that he could wish this creature to an explosion just as he'd blown the Gorgon pilot to pieces, and to demonstrate it he sent an image of that moment into the Gorgon's head on its mist of silver fingers.

The creature remained still, nothing to be read on the hard, expressionless face.

204

Dave went past Jack Vope and out of the bus when Hannah cranked the door open.

The highway was a mess of gray bodies, some half-smashed and still trying to crawl away. "Put your weapon on the hood and stay in the light," the woman on the speaker said. He obeyed the first command, and the second one as he picked a path through a grisly landscape of gray arms, legs, torsos and heads.

A hatch opened next to the armored car's turret. A slim figure in Army camouflage and wearing an olive-green helmet with a headset microphone pulled itself out and then came down a series of foot-and-handgrips to the pavement. The searchlight shifted a few degrees, out of Dave's face, but the soldier switched on a small flashlight and kept that directed at him.

"Good shooting," Dave said. Inside, he felt like crumpling into a shivering ball at the soldier's boots, but he kept all fear out of his face and shakiness out of his voice, which was very hard to do after the last few minutes.

"That wasn't me at the guns," said the woman who'd addressed them over the loudspeaker. "I'll pass the compliment on to Juggy. Any casualties?"

"One dead. One man with nearly a severed arm and a woman with facial wounds. But we've got a lot of wounded on board, some very bad. Can you help us?"

"Copy that." She was speaking not to him, but into her headset. "Okay, what's your name?"

"Dave McKane."

"Follow us, Dave. We'll keep it slow and we'll keep the guns ready. There are *thousands* of those freakies in this city. What used to be a city. Mount up," she said, and as she turned toward the armored car something that pulsed bright blue shrieked across the sky about a mile high, followed by four red balls of flame that were spinning around and around each other like atoms in a molecule. The female soldier never looked up.

Welcome to Denver, Dave thought. He was so glad to see an American soldier with some firepower that he wanted to sob with relief, but that wouldn't do for anyone to witness, so as he picked his way back through the gray garden of death, he wiped the wet from his eyes with the back of a hand. He retrieved his Uzi from the bus's hood. Weary to his bones, but knowing he had to keep going a little longer, he mounted up.

EIGHTEEN.

There was indeed a glow in the sky. Beneath it had once been a large shopping mall. Now it was a fortress that dwarfed by many times the puny fort of Panther Ridge.

Tangles of concertina wire surrounded the place except for the road in. Beyond the wire were log barricades and beyond that a twenty-foot high wall of bricks, stones, pieces of jagged metal, broken bottles, and whatever else was strong, sharp, and nasty. The moldering corpses of a dozen or so Gray Men lay amid the concertina wire's razors. A few had been flattened into gray jelly on the road. Flat-roofed watchtowers with machine guns stood all along the walls. Generators were at work, powering two searchlights that followed the armored car and the school bus in their approach. A huge door covered with metal spikes was hauled upward on chains, like that of a medieval castle, for the vehicles to pass under and then allowed to settle back into place.

Part of the mall was lit up. There were many cars and several Army trucks in the parking lot, as well as a second armored car. As Hannah followed the first armored car toward what appeared to be the mall's main entrance, she—as well as Dave, Olivia, and Ethan—saw a welcoming committee of ten soldiers with automatic rifles waiting for them. There was a sobbing of relief from many in the bus, but Ethan was watching both the Gorgon and the man who it seemed had been trying to grab hold of him. The human was sitting in a seat nursing what looked to be an injured right hand, while the Gorgon had hardly moved during the journey from the highway to this refuge. The bald-headed man who remained huddled on the floorboard next to Hannah was also a human, Ethan thought, but he felt some kind of strange vibration from him and saw in the man's mind a terrified confusion of darkness and half-glimpsed, gliding shapes.

The man with the injured hand kept glancing at Ethan and then clasping his knuckles. Sweat was on his face. Broken fingers? Ethan wondered. He had sent the silver hand out to explore and discovered an impenetrable sphere that seemed to be protecting the man's thoughts: past, present, and future. The sphere was incandescent blue, and so bright it burned the mind's eye. He'd had to call the silver hand back, but he knew now...this man was for some reason helping the Gorgons and they were shielding his mind with immense power, because...*why*?

Because, Ethan thought as his gaze slid from the Gorgon's pawn to the Gorgon and back again, they didn't want someone like *him* seeing why the man was really here?

Something to do with me, Ethan decided. *The man had tried to grab hold of my arms. What would have happened if he had?*

He was so close to telling Dave. To saying it was probably better that all three of these creatures were dumped off the bus, or now turned over to whoever was running this place. But he thought that if he did, the Gorgon might not like it...and, for now, he had the Gorgon in control. They wanted something that must be very important, to have put on all these disguises of body and mind.

Me? he wondered.

And then: *Yeah. Me.*

The bus stopped. Hannah opened the door. Immediately two soldiers with their automatic rifles came up the steps to cover everyone. They were followed by a Hispanic man with a black goatee and a stubble of hair. He was wearing civilian clothes and had a pen in the pocket of his tan-colored shirt. "Who's in charge here?"

"I...guess I still am," said Olivia. "I'm Olivia Quintero."

"Okay. I'm Dr. Hernandez. Any other doctors here?"

"Right here. John Douglas," JayDee answered. "Sprained ankle and all."

Jefferson Jericho had no choice but to lift his injured hand. "And here. Jeff Kushman...with a few broken fingers, I think. Going to be a little tough for me to do anything for awhile." He cast a quick hard glance at Dave McKane, but inwardly he was thinking this had saved him from discovery...but how might it affect what he was supposed to do?

"We want to get the most severely wounded off first," Hernandez said. "Clear the aisle as best you can, let's get this done." He gave a grimace as he saw the dead Gray Men. "No...first get this *garbage* out of here."

The process continued. More soldiers were on hand to help with the wounded. Gary Roosa's body was taken off, and the injured Lila Conti and Aaron Ramsey. Billy Bancroft cursed like a drunken sailor when he was picked up, but he sailed on into the mall where Dr. Hernandez told Olivia a hospital was set up, with plenty of medical supplies. Then the female soldier who'd been in the armored car came aboard the bus, and removing her helmet, she showed a tangle of auburn-colored hair, like the last of the leaves to catch flame in autumn. She was about thirty-five and had a haggard but strong-jawed face with high cheekbones and dark blue eyes. Her uniform bore the name *Cpt. Walsh*.

Ethan saw that she was standing about three feet from the Gorgon, who blandly stared at her and blinked his eyes a few times. Ethan felt the power in the creature, but no immediate threat. Tell Dave or not? he asked himself. The Gorgon then turned his head slightly to stare at Ethan, and the boy who realized he was something more than a boy thought he would be quiet for now, and let this play out as it would. He could defend his friends if he had to...that was enough to know for now.

"I'm Captain Ellen Walsh," said the soldier. "I'm second-in-command here. Beautiful place to hole up for a year or two, if you like malls." There was no hint of a smile. "Or if you like safety. *Relative* safety," she amended, with a quick glance at Dave. "We've got about three hundred civilians here and forty-two soldiers. First thing: everybody on this bus gives up their firearm when they hit the pavement. It'll be numbered and tagged and it'll go into a plastic bin. You can pick it up when we say so. Second thing: everybody goes to an area where you strip down and you're inspected. We don't worry much about privacy here. Everybody's going to walk single-file to the entrance, and you'll be escorted by soldiers with guns who know how to use them *real* well. Where'd you come from?" The question was directed at Dave.

"Fort Collins."

"From the frying pan into the fire. We've got three infrared heat sensor cameras up on towers on the roof. We picked you up about a mile out. You people are lucky, Dave. Sometimes we don't get there quick enough. Okay, let's move."

Ratcoff and Vope were first and second off the bus. "You!" The captain, standing on the pavement, reached out to put a hand against Vope's chest. "Open the backpack and let's see what you've got."

Ratcoff stopped. He almost said *Nothin' special in there* but he figured that would only antagonize the woman. Vope hesitated only a few seconds. He removed the backpack and opened it, showing Captain Walsh three dirty shirts and two pairs of jeans. She patted the backpack's sides, feeling for a firearm this Silent Sam might be trying to sneak past, and found nothing. "Okay," she said, "pass on." Unconsciously, she wiped her hand on her fatigues.

Ethan was following Hannah out and wondered what was going to happen when the Gorgon was stripped down. He decided to stay away from Jeff Kushman, whose index and second finger of the right hand were discolored and swollen; he didn't want to be touched by the man, he thought there was a danger in that, but exactly what it was he did not know. The blue sphere was keeping it from him. It was powerful energy he could not crack…or, maybe, he wasn't strong enough yet to crack.

"Ethan?" Dave said when they were off the bus and he was giving up his Uzi to a couple of soldiers at a folding table to number, tag and then put into the plastic bin. "Hold up a minute. Captain, can I speak to you?"

"Speak."

"Where we can have some privacy."

"I said we don't worry much about that here."

Dave had one hand on Ethan's shoulder. He took the receipt tag that was given to him, and he looked into Ellen Walsh's eyes and said, "It's *important*. Something you'll want to know before we get inside."

She looked from Dave to the boy and back again. Her face was hard and her eyes had seen sights that had left burn scars on her brain. She figured she'd better listen. "Over here," she said, and motioned them both a few yards to the side.

"When this boy is stripped down," Dave began, "you're going to find something real different about him." He caught sight of JayDee, limping on his rebar cane toward the entrance, and he called, "John! Come over here, will you? Olivia? You too, please."

"What are we having?" Walsh asked. "A parking lot party?"

"Dr. Douglas can explain some things to you, maybe better than I can." He waited for JayDee and Olivia to join them, and then he said, "You want to lift your shirt and show her, Ethan?"

"I guess," Ethan answered, though he wasn't too thrilled about it, and he realized if he was touched he would display the silver element, but he did it anyway.

"What the hell is *that*...?" The captain's flashlight came on, directed at the area just above Ethan's heart.

"Christ!" Dave eyes had widened. "I wanted you to see the bruises, but that's *new*!"

"What is it?" Alarmed, Ethan looked down at the area touched by the captain's light.

There were what appeared to be upraised silver tattoos above his heart. The tattoos were not large, but they stood out clearly against the black bruise.

There were four of them, and they read: ✕↓↓丷.

JayDee dared to look closer. "Ethan, can I touch those?"

"Yes sir." The same question Nikki had asked. "Go ahead."

The doctor traced his finger over the symbols. They became slightly brighter with his touch. Ethan felt no pain, no sensation at all. A fifth symbol seemed to be coming up, a faint bit of silver rising from a dark pool, but it was impossible yet to make out its shape.

"We have a lot to tell you about this young man," Olivia said. She offered him a faint smile and then gave it also to the captain. "Our *hero*," she added.

Ethan dropped his shirt. He felt more like a freak than a hero. Now he could tell Nikki that he had tattoos too...but how they'd been delivered to him, he had no idea.

"Okay," the captain said. And repeated it: "Okay." She sounded shaken, which she was. "Let's go see the doc. I'll bring Major Fleming, and we'll hear the story. I've seen a lot of freakies out here, but this one... *okay*." She moved her flashlight to peer into Ethan's eyes. She held his gaze for a few seconds, the flashlight roaming over his face, and then she switched it off. "Gotta be careful, folks," she decided. "Juggy!" she called to one of the soldiers. "Come over here and bring your rifle. On the double!"

Dave nodded. He would've done the same. He gave a pat to Ethan's back.

Under guard, Ethan walked across the parking lot with his companions. *My protectors*, he thought. Or was he the one protecting them? A light rain began to fall, oily to the skin. In the distance, there was a red flash: a streak of light, going somewhere. At the center of his friends, Captain Walsh and the guards, Ethan entered the lit-up section of the mall into a crowd of curious onlookers—survivors all, thin and weary from the constant war—and knew now he was on a journey into the unknown that he must at all cost complete.

"I see it," said the major. He was studying a map in an atlas on the desk before him. He looked up at Ethan, Olivia, JayDee, Dave and Captain Walsh. The cut across the bridge of Dave's nose had been cleaned, an antiseptic applied, and then a bandage. JayDee's sprained ankle had been strengthened with a tight wrapping of gauze and the pain diminished with two Tylenol tablets. Major Fleming's office lamp, powered like the other lights by the mall's generators and some solar cells the troops had scavenged when they'd holed up in here after the Cyphers and Gorgons had destroyed most of Denver over a year ago, threw a pool of illumination upon Utah, but the major was far from illuminated.

He was a tall, square-shouldered man who'd been born for the United States Army. He had lost a lot of weight in the last year but the loss had just made him tougher, as it had all the men and women under his command. He was bald but meticulously shaven, had a pair of thick brown eyebrows and steel-gray eyes under his wire-rimmed glasses. He was forty-two years old, but the network of deep worry lines that cut across his face aged him by ten years.

"So you don't know what's there?" He directed this question to Ethan. "In fact, you don't know if *anything* is there, do you?"

"No sir." It was spoken quietly.

"What?" Ray Fleming had the habit of not liking to be spoken to quietly; he liked to hear and be heard.

"No sir, I don't," Ethan answered, "but I believe I have to go there. That's all I can say."

"You took a blood sample?" The major threw this at Dr. Hernandez, who stood in the corner.

"Yes sir. It's normal, type A positive. His lungs are fine, his heart's in good shape, his blood pressure is fine too. In all other ways he's a normal fourteen- or fifteen-year-old boy."

"Anybody fail their exam?"

"None."

Ethan gave a soft grunt that no one else heard. At last the Gorgons had perfected their disguise. They had created artificial blood and organs that could pass for human. They had made their own lifelike Visible Man, but visible only to him. He wondered how many humans had been laid open by Gorgon surgical tools before the right chemistry was achieved.

"If I had a better lab, I could do a better job," the doctor said, indicating maybe a persistent argument between the two. "I have to make do with—"

"What you have, yes," Fleming finished for him. The hard and careful eyes returned to Ethan. "You say you killed a Gorgon without weapons. Exactly how?"

"I wanted it gone. It blew up into pieces."

"Not enough. Let's hear an explanation that makes sense."

Dave suddenly reached over and pulled up the boy's t-shirt to expose the four strange symbols that had emerged from the darkness of the bruise. Fleming had already seen them, but Dave wanted to drive home a point. "Does this make sense? Does any of it? Like I say, he made an earthquake happen. So...killing a Gorgon without weapons...I believe that, yeah." He let Ethan's shirt fall back down again, which Ethan was grateful for because he still couldn't wrap his head around the freakishness of what was changing him. Though he was outwardly calm, a little place deep within himself was a crunched-up ball of terror.

"Do all of you believe that?" The major lifted his eyebrows and waited.

"I do," Olivia answered. "Yes, I *know* I do."

JayDee smiled thinly at the major. He leaned his weight on the rebar. "I think," he said, "that Ethan is not a Gorgon or a Cypher, nor anything created by them. I think he used to be a boy, but he's no longer *just* that. I think...what he is...what he's becoming...is something different."

"Explain."

"I wish I *could*, sir. Ethan's condition defied all medical sense when we *found* him. Now...with those symbols, which look to me like ancient runes...maybe Nordic, I don't know...I can't explain anything."

"Reassuring," said the major.

"I believe," JayDee went on, his voice stronger, "that Ethan is being called to go to that mountain. And I believe, sir, that we ought to trust whatever is calling him."

Again the major's penetrating gaze speared Ethan. "Do you have *any* idea why you would be..." He paused, deliberating before he went on. "Compelled to go to this place?"

"I do have an idea," Ethan replied. "I think it has something to do with stopping this war."

"Oh...*you* can stop the war?" Fleming gave Captain Walsh a quick sharp glance. "A kid can stop the war between aliens fighting over—"

"The border," said Ethan. "That's what they're fighting over. The border between what they believe they own. And I don't know if *I* can stop the war or not...but..." The next thing was hard to say, but it had been working on him since leaving Panther Ridge, and knowing the disguised Gorgon and the human Kushman were after him. "But," he went on, "maybe what I'm turning *into* can."

Fleming said nothing for awhile. He studied the map again, took another long appraisal of the boy, and then his eyes went back to the map. "That's a long way. Tough road up in those mountains, once you get off I-70. If there's much left of I-70." He balled up a fist and knocked gently at the mountain on the map, as if knocking at a secret door that only Ethan Gaines could open. "So you're wanting to continue your trip in that school bus, is that correct?"

"Yes," said Olivia.

"Who's going?"

"All of us," Dave said. "We've talked, and we've agreed."

"You too, Doc?" Fleming's eyes went to JayDee. "On a bad ankle?"

"Me too," John Douglas replied. "Bad ankle or not."

"Well," was the major's next comment. He took off his glasses and spent a moment polishing the lenses with a white cloth before he put them back on and spoke again. "I can't spare you any soldiers. We have responsibilities here. Your bus has taken some damage, yes?"

"A little bit," Dave said.

"We can fix that for you, maybe make some improvements. How are you doing for fuel? We're down pretty low ourselves, I don't know if I can give you any."

"We'll make do. Find diesel tanks at stations along the way and siphon it out."

"Got the tools you need? The containers?"

"I could use a longer hose, say about twelve feet."

The major nodded. "We can find one of those. Your bus is going to eat up a lot of fuel on those grades. You know that, right?"

"We know it," Dave said. "Look…Major…I'm going to have to get some sleep. We're all dog-tired. Can we bunk down somewhere?" They had already gone through the search procedure, and now the need for sleep was dragging Dave down. "Set us all up together?"

"We've got extra sleeping bags, but you ought to get some food before you crash."

"Sleep first," Dave said, and the others nodded agreement. Except for Ethan, who had business to tend to.

"Right. Captain Walsh, find these people a place to sack out. Mr. McKane, you don't mind that I post a guard over this young man for the rest of the night." It was a statement, and there was to be no argument.

"No problem."

Ethan said nothing; it was to be expected. "All right, then. At least get yourself some water. There's bread and soup in the food court if you change your minds." He checked his wristwatch. "It'll be open for about another hour. Captain, you're in charge of them now. Find someone to stand guard duty. You're all dismissed…except you, Carlos. Stick here a little longer."

When Captain Walsh had escorted the group out, the major steepled his fingers and peered through the desklamp's glow at Carlos Hernandez. "Honest answer. Am I crazy or are they?"

"Sir?"

"I want to believe," Fleming said. "Dear God…I *want* to believe." He gave a sigh that sounded to him like wind past a tomb, but maybe… *maybe*…there were seeds of hope in that wind, and they would be scattered and take root on fertile earth. *The border*, the kid had said. *That's what they're fighting over.* The thing was…that sounded right. Fleming did believe him. And only something from beyond this world would know that. "You've got patients to take care of," he said. "Long night ahead."

"Yes sir," the doctor answered, and left the office.

Fleming sat for awhile, staring at that particular landmark on the map of Utah. After a few more minutes he switched off the desklamp with a hand that no one ever saw tremble. It would be lights out in two hours, except for the hospital that was set up in what used to be a Gap store, and then the mall would be patrolled by soldiers with flashlights. He sat in the dark, thinking of what his hometown of Seattle used to be, and the wreckage of what it was now. He imagined that the rest of the world was like that, and how could it ever return to what it had been? Without comm to the outside, there was no way to know. Had all the nuclear plants been shut down by the book, or had a few of them been abandoned and melted down with no humans to control the cooling elements? And what about the hundreds of thousands—millions?—of "freakies," as Captain Walsh termed them, loose in the ruins of the cities? Even if the war was stopped, what about all that?

But did the fate of the earth depend on the boy who had been standing before him?

If so…if it was at all possible…Major Fleming would not be the one to stand in his way. There would be plenty of things eager and hungry to do that job.

NINETEEN.

Ethan found he couldn't go to the bathroom without the soldier following him. No water was running, so in the green-tiled bathroom between what had been an Abercrombie and an American Eagle aluminum cans stood in for urinals and black garbage bags for toilets. The smell was rank, but at least there was toilet paper. The soldier looked away while Ethan was doing his business, but when it was done the young trooper was all bird-dog again.

The lights were still on in this section of the mall where the generators were working. A mass of people occupied tents, cots and sleeping bags. Some were playing cards or dominoes, some were reading, talking or praying, others just lying and staring blankly at the walls or the ceiling. Children played with toys taken from the Learning Center or the Disney Store. As it had been at Panther Ridge, there were all ages and seemingly all races: a true melting pot, in this Land That Had Been Plenty. It appeared that the mall had been ransacked in the early days of the war, because some of the windows were broken out and all the clothing and shoe stores were empty holes, even the mannequins picked clean.

Ethan slowed his pace. The soldier was right behind him. "Just a minute," he said, as he saw who he was looking for. He went past the dry fountain and stood before the Gorgon, Jeff Kushman, and the short bald man. Kushman had popsicle-stick splints and tape wrapped around the two broken fingers; he had already staked out his area and was sliding into his sleeping bag. The Gorgon stood with a rolled-up sleeping bag as if he intended to stand there all night, and the bald man was sitting on the floor with his shoes off, rubbing his feet and grimacing.

Of course the soldier followed Ethan's footsteps, but he knew that would happen. Kushman, eyes heavy, looked up at him from the sleeping bag. The Gorgon's head turned, and the flinty black eyes took him in. The bald man paid him no attention, so intent was he on his own two problems.

"You men all right?" Ethan asked. Before anyone could answer, he spoke to the Gorgon: "Don't you know how to use a sleeping bag?"

"Sure he does," Kushman said. "Just put it down anywhere, Jack. Right over here would be fine."

The Gorgon obeyed, moving slowly and stiffly as if the lubrication of his joints was drying out.

"*Jack?*" Ethan repeated. "That's funny, he doesn't look like a 'Jack'."

"Shouldn't you be getting some sleep, Ethan?" Jefferson Jericho offered a smile that didn't have a lot of wattage behind it. "Is that *your* real name?"

"Real enough. Dave told me you three came from Denver. Right?"

"That's right, son."

"How'd you make it past all the Gray Men?"

"We were lucky." Jefferson had already asked Joel Schuster what those horrors had been. There were none of those monsters in New Eden, and being so close to the things gave him extra incentive, if any more was needed. "We never saw any."

"Captain Walsh said there are thousands here. You *must've* been lucky."

"Yeah." Jefferson watched Vope figuring out how to unroll and unzip the sleeping bag. He wondered if the Gorgon even needed sleep. One thing, they could mimic human habits pretty quickly.

"So everybody passed the blood test," Ethan continued. He tried to probe Kushman's mind with the silver hand, but again the bright blue sphere would not be pierced. "That's a good thing. I wouldn't want to think we were traveling with any aliens in human skin."

"Me neither. That would be very disturbing, wouldn't it? Listen… Ethan…I'm really tired, okay? Let's talk tomorrow, I've got to get some sleep." Jefferson saw that, to Vope's credit, there had been no reaction and no reaction from Ratcoff either. But he thought: *Ethan knows.* The question being: *if the boy knows, why hasn't he done anything about it?* He zipped up his sleeping bag as best he could, one-handed. "Goodnight," he said as he settled in, and he gratefully closed his eyes against the overhead lights though there was still more than an hour before lights out. He would get another chance at the boy later, he thought, but at the moment the pain pills were putting him under.

"Night, Mr. Kushman," Ethan said, and with the soldier at his back he walked toward the area where Olivia, Dave, and JayDee were sacked out. Dave had already been asleep when Ethan announced his bathroom trip to the trooper, and Olivia had been drifting that way. He was almost to them when someone touched his right arm.

He turned to face Nikki. The soldier stopped also, and being a sensible guy he backed up a few paces to give them a little more of that precious privacy.

"Hi," Ethan said.

"Hi." The overheads made the rhinestone star on her eyepatch glitter. "You found a place?"

"Yeah, I'm over there. You?"

"Over that way. Not far."

He nodded. "Good to be in a safe place tonight."

"Yeah. You get some food?"

"Somebody brought me a couple of pieces of bread and a can of Sprite. That's all I need right now." The *somebody* being a runner for Captain Walsh.

Nikki didn't say anything for awhile. They both looked around at the people getting themselves and their children ready for a night's rest. Then Nikki said, "It was bad…what happened to Mr. Roosa. I was standing right there almost beside him. He was a pretty good guy. It was bad, wasn't it?"

"Yes," said Ethan. "Real bad."

"Do you think they'll come here tonight?"

He heard the fear in her voice. She looked pale and shaken, and maybe she was just hanging on. "I don't think so," Ethan answered. "No, probably not."

"I don't think so either." She seemed to relax a little, at the confidence in Ethan's voice. "Seems like if anybody would know, *you* would."

He didn't care to follow up that comment, which for sure dealt with his being—in her eye, at least—part alien. He had a sudden thought, though, and it involved a need to know. He said, "Would you come with me for just a minute? Let's get away from some of these people?"

"Why?"

"I want to show you something and I want to ask you something. It'll just take a minute. Okay?"

Nikki hesitated. She looked from him to the trooper and back again. "I don't know, Ethan. Where would we go?"

"One of the bathrooms. I just need a minute."

"No way," the trooper said. "You had your bathroom time."

Ethan had had enough. He gave the young soldier a look that might've melted iron. "Listen, I know you're doing your job, but I need to ask this girl something in as private a place as there is around here. You can come in and stand there, if you want to, but I'm doing this. Shoot me if you need to." His anger welled up. "I don't give a fuck," he said. And he took the girl's elbow and began steering her back toward the bathroom. Amazingly for Ethan, Nikki let him guide her. The soldier started to say something else but closed his mouth and followed along right at their heels.

In the less-than-fragrant bathroom, with the soldier standing back a distance to give them the privacy Ethan had requested, Ethan said to Nikki, "Get ready. Okay?"

"Ready for what?"

"This." Ethan lifted his t-shirt to show her the four upraised silver symbols. She gave a quiet gasp and stepped back a couple of paces, and for a few seconds she stared at the markings without speaking.

Then she said, with sort of a dazed but true admiration, *"Cool."*

"They just happened," he explained. "I was itching on the bus, maybe they came up then. But what I want to ask you...you said your friend was studying to be a tattoo artist, right?"

"Yeah."

"So I guess you saw some of his tattoo books and stuff? Have you ever seen anything like this?"

"Well...*maybe*. I remember him showing me...like...way old lettering. Like ancient, I'm saying. But something like that *exactly*, I don't remember. That one there...it looks like an 'R'."

The soldier was trying to edge closer to take a peek. Ethan let his t-shirt fall back into place. "They don't hurt," he said. "But they're upraised, almost like they were burned on." He felt a place within himself start to crack and break, and he feared that if it happened he would fall to pieces in front of Nikki and the guard. All he could do was stare at the floor until he could shake the feeling off and get control again. "I'm *some* kind of big time freak now, huh?" he said, not without bitterness.

"I guess Olivia and the others know about this? That's why you've got the guard on you?"

"Uh-huh."

"I'm sorry," she said. "I wish I could help you more."

"It's okay." Ethan shrugged. "I mean...it is what it is, right? That's what my mom used to tell me, whenever I was feeling down about anything." He had a sudden start, because he remembered that...his mother's voice, speaking to him. *It is what it is*. And did she speak his name when she said that? Yes, she did. It was so close...so close...yet still so far away. "Nikki," he said, quietly choked, "I don't know what I'm turning into but I swear to you—I *swear*—I used to be just a regular guy. I *am* human. *Was* human, I mean. Now...what am I?" Pain leaped from him, and he felt it enter her.

Nikki took a step forward.

She put a finger to his lips.

She said, "You'll figure it out. Don't let it knock you down, Ethan. One thing I do believe...whatever you are, you're on *our* side."

He nodded. When Nikki withdrew her finger, he could feel the burn of it across his mouth.

"Meeting done?" the trooper asked.

"Done," Ethan answered, though he would've wished to talk to Nikki longer, to get to know her...really know her...but he thought black bruises and silver tattoos and general weirdness was not going to endear him to anyone.

"Out of here, then," came the command.

They obeyed. Out in the mall, Ethan walked with Nikki back to where her sleeping bag was. He said goodnight and then returned to his own place. Dave and Olivia were both gone to the world. JayDee was staring up at the ceiling, lost in thought, but his eyelids were drooping. Ethan crawled into his sleeping bag with a final glance toward the area where the Gorgon, Kushman, and the short bald dude were sacked out. The guard took a position nearby, leaning against a wall and cradling his rifle. He had a flashlight on his belt, which he would use many times during the night to check on his charge.

Rain began to hammer on the roof, the noise thrumming through the mall. It sounded as if they were all trapped within a gigantic bass drum. Ethan's eyes were starting to close, but before he gave himself up fully to sleep some mechanism within him was triggered and also went on guard-duty, so he would know instantly if while he was in a sleep-state any threat got too near.

He was slipping away. Again he asked himself...why not tell Dave or Olivia or JayDee or Captain Walsh or Major Fleming what he knew to be true about the Gorgon, and about the blue sphere that protected Kushman's mind? It wasn't that they wouldn't believe him. So...why not?

He knew.

If they had come to find him, then they had some idea of what he was, or what he might be. If he revealed them to anyone, his chance to know might be lost. And, also, people might be injured by the powerful serpentine presence he felt coiled within Jack the Gorgon. He thought that he shouldn't tell what he knew just yet, for the sake of the safety of others. But he could handle the Gorgon; he was sure he could. He didn't fear the thing, and he understood that Jack the Gorgon knew it.

So…wait. Just wait, and see what happens tomorrow.

The rain beat down. Ethan's eyes closed. After awhile someone on a loudspeaker announced lights out, and the mall's overheads went dark. The flashlights of patrolling soldiers played back and forth over the sleeping survivors of many days and nights of alien war, and like the survivors of any war some cried out and moaned and wept in their restless slumber while the earth turned toward another morning.

—⊗—

It was barely the dawn of a stormy day when Ethan felt his alarms going off. His body tingled and his brain said *wake up and defend*. He came fully awake almost instantly, and it seemed he recalled for just a few seconds a boy who liked to curl up in his bed and sleep late on a Saturday morning until his mother coaxed him out with breakfast of a waffle and bacon.

That boy was nearly gone.

The rain was still pouring down on the roof. Thunder boomed— real thunder, not alien weapons. Yet Ethan knew the alien presence was very close, and this sensation of alarm was not coming from the black-bearded Gorgon, Jeff Kushman, or the short bald guy. Other people were waking up, but not with Ethan's sense of urgency. His guard was sitting cross-legged on the floor against the wall with his rifle beside him. The man was awake, either had just awakened—improbable—or had been watching Ethan and occasionally checking the boy with his flashlight all night, which was likely the case.

Ethan heard the crackle of walkie-talkies and several other soldiers rushed past, heading for the mall's main entrance. This flurry of activity caused a stir of unease among others who had awakened, and they in turn awakened their family members or friends around them. One soldier came running along the pathway that was kept clear of sleeping bags and tents on the far side of the corridor; he was talking on his walkie-talkie in a voice that though unintelligible was charged with tension. Ethan's guard stood up; he seemed torn between his duty here and his desire to go find out what was happening. He clicked on his own walkie-talkie, which had been hooked to his belt. "Chris, you there? What's going on?"

Dave was waking up. He unzipped his sleeping bag and stretched so hard his joints cracked. Then he was aware of the commotion and he looked dazedly around, his need for sleep still not fully supplied. Olivia, too, had begun to stir. "What's up?" Dave asked Ethan, who shook his head.

The soldier listened to his friend, and then he said to Ethan, "I'm off guard duty now. Something's going on outside."

"What is it?" Dave asked, reaching for his cap. His hair was a mass of cowlicks.

"Don't know yet. You folks just stay here." With that, the soldier was striding away.

"Hell if *I'll* stay here." Dave put his cap and his workboots on and stood up. Other people were moving toward the entrance, drawn by the unknown. Olivia was getting out of her sleeping bag and JayDee said in a voice still husky with sleep, "What's wrong? What's happening?"

"I'm going to find out."

Ethan saw Kushman, Jack the Gorgon, and the short bald dude joining the throng of people who moved past. Kushman gave him a quick glance, as if to note his position, and then walked on. Ethan sat watching the procession of humanity. He saw mothers holding children, teenagers so burdened they had aged prematurely far beyond their years, men who had likely lost their entire families, women bedraggled and thin with hunger and sorrow, elderly people struggling onward. An old woman on a walker was being helped by a man about her age, and a young boy about sixteen or so was helping both of them. Here was a middle-aged man on crutches, missing his left leg from the knee down. There a man with long gray hair and beard and the look of a suffering saint. A wizened woman who was likely only in her early thirties held the hand of a little girl and clutched a baby to her chest. A black man with a bandage covering half his face staggered past, his hand gripped in the hand of a skinny white man who urged him along in a quiet, patient voice.

The survivors, Ethan thought. And what made them want to live a day or an hour or a minute longer? Why had they not left this earth already by their own hands, as so many had at Panther Ridge? What did they believe in that made them struggle on, as painfully as that might be? Many had given up, faced with what they believed to be hopeless odds, but many had stayed too, holding onto some measure of hope, however fantastic it might be.

He respected these people. These humans, struggling on in the darkest of hours. They wanted to live, and they were fighting for whatever scrap of life they could claw from this battle of ancient foes. They deserved the chance to live without the shadows of Cyphers and Gorgons oppressing them, he thought. They had been through much and suffered much, just as humanity all across this world had suffered, and now they deserved freedom.

He stood up.

"Going with you," said JayDee as he steadied himself with his rebar cane, and both Ethan and Dave helped him to his feet. Olivia still looked dazed from an uneasy sleep, dark circles under her eyes, and Ethan went to her side to make sure she didn't fall because she looked so frail and unsteady, but she said, "I'm all right. Just hold my hand, okay?"

"I will," he promised.

They made their way through the growing crowd to the mall's entrance, where soldiers were trying to maintain some kind of order and failing miserably. Ethan saw people looking and pointing through the glass at something that seemed to be up in the dark, rainswept sky. He let go of Olivia's hand and pushed his way toward the front, avoiding Kushman and the other two who stood nearby also peering through the glass. Captain Walsh was there, communicating with another soldier on her walkie-talkie, and Ethan was about to ask what was going on when he saw it himself.

A sphere of glowing red flames about five feet in diameter was hanging over the parking lot. As Ethan watched, what appeared to be red lightning bolts crackled out from it in all directions a distance of ten or twelve feet. Though the rain was still pouring down, the sphere was unaffected.

"You have any idea what that is?" the captain asked Ethan, pausing in her use of the walkie-talkie.

"I know it's from the Cyphers."

"How?"

"Red and blue. The Cyphers' weapons put out red flames, the Gorgons' blue. It's different forms of energy."

"Thing's been sitting right there for the last fifteen minutes." She levelled her gaze at him. "Any more ideas? The major's out there with a recon team. He'd be real interested."

He did have an idea, but how it came to him was another mystery. He just knew. "Recon," he said, as he watched the sphere, "is right. That's what it's here for. It's found something and it's reporting back to wherever their command center is."

"Found what? *Us?*" She didn't hesitate, but shouted at another couple of soldiers, "Move these people back! Get them away from this glass!"

"You heard the captain! Come on, everybody move back! Let's *go!*"

"Not us," said Ethan, who was aware that Dave was coming up beside him.

"What?"

"They doesn't care about us. They've found a—" *Gorgon*, he almost said. But he knew it was the truth. The Cyphers had sent out their own form of reconnaisance, searching the ruins of Denver for the enemy, and in this mall they had found one in human disguise who called himself Jack.

"Found what?" the captain asked. Suddenly dark shapes appeared out of the rain and Major Fleming came through the doors with four other soldiers, all of them wearing hooded ponchos and all dripping wet.

"Get these civilians back from here!" Fleming, his face strained and pallid, had nearly shouted it at Captain Walsh. "Away from this glass, *now!*"

"Back! Move back everybody!" another of the soldiers was yelling. He was using his rifle, held sideways, as a tool to push several people away from the doors but the crush was too thick.

Dave took hold of Ethan's elbow. "Come on," he said, "let's move—"

Ethan saw something coming through the rain. His guts knotted up, because though it was moving very fast he thought he recognized what it was.

"It's here," he heard himself say, and Major Fleming spun around to look toward the parking lot, his eyes narrowed against the sphere's glare.

A thin black missile about twenty feet long plowed into the parking lot just to the left of the sphere. Chunks of concrete flew up into the air. A second missile came in and hit about ten feet to the left of that one, digging itself a small ragged-edged crater. A third and fourth missile sped in, hitting the parking lot so close to the doors that pieces of concrete cracked the glass and caused the crowd to fall back trailing shouts and screams.

"Shit!" the major cried out. "What the—"

He never got to finish that sentence, because in the next instant four thin-legged, glistening black spider-shapes, each as big as a pickup truck, scrabbled out of the rain pursued by machine-gun bullets from the watchtowers. They crashed through the doors and sent them flying, even as the crowd retreated and then turned to run. Dave pulled Ethan with him, almost picking the boy up under his arm. The major and the captain had their pistols out and the soldiers were backpedalling but firing their rifles as fast as they could. The Cypher spiders were unharmed by bullets. The claws at the ends of their legs left grooves in the tiles, and the multiple rows of sharp teeth in the crimson slashes of their mouths were searching for meat, if not Gorgon then human, for all now were at the mercy of the Cyphers.

Which, Ethan realized as Dave pulled him away, was no mercy at all.

"Let me go!" he said, and just that quickly he wrenched loose from Dave, found his footing, and stood before the spiders as they scuttled forward.

"Come on! Don't be a fool!" Dave shouted, still pulling at him, but Ethan would not be moved. The soldiers were still firing, using up clip after clip, and Ethan noted that before the slugs could hit little sparks

229

of red jumped out of the creatures and seemed to either incinerate or evaporate the bullets. The Cypher spiders carried their own force fields with them.

Two of the things were almost upon him, as the crowd and the soldiers drew back. Dave tried to pick Ethan up, but the boy fought free, and now Dave had to retreat too because it was certain death to stay where he was. Ethan remembered these things eating the Gorgon ship, and he recalled thinking that the claws and fangs could likely tear through concrete and metal. He heard Olivia screaming his name, and suddenly Major Fleming was beside him firing a .45, and Captain Walsh was on his other side firing a pistol, but the red sparks flared and jumped and there was no stopping these monsters.

Ethan braced himself and thrust his right hand out, his palm aimed at the closest spider. He was his own weapon, his own force of destruction, and now in needing to destroy these things he felt the awesome power move and build within him from its secret place, only a matter of seconds, until he thought he himself would explode into flaming, bloody pieces.

The air between them rippled, as with tremendous heat. A swarm of a thousand burning hornets shot out between his hand, and the spider he had targeted, and maybe no one else could see it, but to Ethan the thrust of deadly energy was clear.

Every hornet was incinerated by the thing's force field before any one of them could penetrate, and suddenly Ethan realized he was not yet strong enough to kill these things.

They were upon him. The major had the back of his t-shirt and was pulling him away as Fleming emptied his clip, and Captain Walsh continued to fire as she scrambled back.

In the crowd behind them, Burt Ratcoff felt a tremendous pain that began in his midsection and coursed through his arms and legs. He cried out in agony, a pain that made the tears burst from his eyes. He had a sudden vision of himself striding down Fifth Avenue in his life that used to be, happy to be alive, with his wife beside him and their son healthy and well and studying to be an insurance adjuster, and just that quickly the human being who had been Burt Ratcoff was gone and in its place stood a Gorgon-engineered weapon.

The body burst into blue flame. The body elongated, the blue-burning clothes flying away as the people around him screamed and tried to put distance between them and a thin figure that was growing to be seven…eight…nine…ten feet tall.

The burning, featureless giant strode forward as Ethan, Major Fleming and Captain Walsh retreated, and standing to one side of them it began to fling from its flaming hands blue spheres that exploded against the Cypher spiders' force fields, sending blue and red sparks of energy spinning into the air. One of the spiders was overwhelmed and caught blue flame, and as it sizzled it began to turn in a tight circle of what might have been agony and panic, around and around, as the three others scrabbled past it.

Ethan stood his ground, shaking off the major's hand clasped to his shoulder. He tried again, summoning up power from a well he knew was full but that terrified him with its fearful depths. It was there when he needed it, and he needed it *now*. Sweat broke out on his face in an instant. He felt the surge of storms within him. From his fingers or from the palm of his hand—possibly from his entire body, he wasn't sure—came thousands of the small, flaming bullet-shaped projectiles and what looked like jagged silver bolts of lightning. The force field around the spider he had targeted sparked a thousand times in two seconds and then was breached. As the creature advanced across the tiles between the remnants of a Brookstone and a Foot Locker, it blew apart into black fragments that smashed into the walls oozing ebony fluids.

The burning blue giant had grown to twelve feet tall, as thin as a shadow, and was throwing fiery spheres past Ethan at the remaining two spider-shapes. Ethan felt no heat from them, but as they zipped past him with their soundless power, he felt the flesh crawl on his bones. One missed its spider target and punctured a hole with melting, dripping edges in the concrete wall next to the Build-A-Bear Workshop, a seccond, third, and fourth sizzled out in the creature's force field, but the fifth got through and lit the thing up in blue fire. The first spider that had been hit was collapsing in a black puddle, making a *tock...tock...tock* noise like a machine running down.

The fourth spider scrabbled toward Ethan; at the same time Cypher soldiers began to materialize through the walls.

"Back! Get back!" Major Fleming was shouting to his own men. He didn't need to issue the order twice. Captain Walsh was down on one knee emptying another pistol clip at the Cypher spider, but again the bullets were quickly incinerated. Ethan willed loose another burst of concentrated energy, which once more might have issued from the center of his body but was being directed to its target by his hand; he was aware of his runaway heartbeat, what seemed like a stream of heat flowing out of him to warp the air between himself and the spider-shape, and thousands more burning bullets and silver spears of lightning flew into the creature's force-field. At the same time, one of the blue giant's spheres penetrated and a dozen or more of Ethan's flaming projectiles got through, and as the red maw opened to consume Ethan's head, the monster burst into blue fire and then exploded into pieces.

Eight faceless Cypher soldiers had emerged from the walls. As one they fired their fleshy black weapons at the blue giant that had once been a human being. Fourteen orbs of white-hot flame hit the thin twelve-foot-tall figure at the same time, two missing the target and whirling over the heads of the Army soldiers, the civilians and Jack the Gorgon to blast holes through the mall's ceiling.

Ethan had little time to think, just to act. A swarm of the little fiery bullets and the silver bolts of energy crackled out to blow one, two, three and four Cypher soldiers to smoking shreds that smelled of grasshopper juice. Two of the white-hot orbs hissed over Ethan as he threw himself to the floor, and just that quickly he took aim with the weapon of mass destruction that his hand had become and destroyed the fifth, sixth, and seventh Cypher in spinning, burning fragments. The eighth turned, disappeared into a wall, and was gone.

The blue giant staggered. Its flame was going out. Ethan saw the last of the blue fire flicker and go dark. Exposed there was a tall thin figure made of gray ash. With a sound like a quiet sigh, the ash collapsed into a pile, and that was the end of whoever and whatever the short bald dude had been.

Back in the stunned crowd, among those who had crouched down on the floor to find whatever cover they could, Jefferson Jericho looked up at Vope, who had remained standing during this confrontation. Only Jefferson had seen the prickling of small black spikes and a yellow discoloration on Vope's hands, as if the Gorgon wanted to join the fight but was constrained by his mission. Then the spikes were gone and the false flesh color returned, and Vope looked down at Jefferson Jericho with a faint sneer of derision at the earthman's puny lack of courage.

Ethan felt a wave of exhaustion pass over him. He sank to his knees. He heard behind him the confusion and terror of the crowd. A hand grasped his shoulder and helped him up, but his knees were weak, and he nearly toppled again.

Olivia had come to help him. Behind her were Dave and a little further back Nikki. JayDee was limping forward on his rebar cane, and following close behind him was Hannah Grimes. The second burning Cypher spider was still, its body crisping away. The mall smelled of acrid burnt plastic and grasshopper juice. Major Fleming was approaching Ethan. Captain Walsh and three other soldiers were standing over the pile of ashes that had once been a human being.

Olivia looked into Ethan's face and suddenly drew back, her own face tightening, but to the credit of her courage she kept her hand fixed to his shoulder.

"What is it?" he asked her, because he sensed that something about himself had further changed.

She said, as matter-of-factly as she could, "Your left eye has turned silver."

TWENTY.

I N THE HOLOCAUST THAT THE WORLD HAD BECOME, IN THE BATTLE
between star-faring races that had begun before memory and might
last into eternity, the city of Chicago had been reduced to ruins nearly
two years ago but the battle lines were always shifting, and it was not
ruins that the warring races fought over but territory. They had burned
Chicago and most of its suburbs to ash and melted wreckage, the great
buildings fallen, the streets pocked with blackened craters and covered
with the stones and shattered glass of man's creations, now lost to the
constant warfare. It was the same all over this world, one of many that
lay on the line of dispute. It would so forever be, the ravaging of planet
after planet, some populated by higher forms of life and others just awakening to life in whatever bizarre form it might take to crawl from the
slime of beginnings.

The wreckage of Chicago lay under pouring rain from a low sky
of ugly yellow, and on this grim morning the Gorgon and the Cypher
ships battled in the turbulent air and their soldiers fought amid the
fallen buildings, crushed cars, human skeletons, and the few remaining
mutants hiding in their holes. Whatever there was to burn had already
burned, in this city that had long ago known the tragedy of fire, and yet
now the flames were red and blue and created by alien minds devoted to

the study of destruction. Hundreds of Cypher soldiers moved through the gloom firing their fleshy blasters at furtive, sliding shapes, and then hundreds of small blue spheres emitting piercing shrieks came flying from an unknown source and with flaming whips tore the Cyphers into pieces that gushed brown fluid and oozed black intestines streaked with yellow and red. Above the battlefield, explosions flashed in the clouds. Burning Cypher ships came crashing down, some to explode themselves in the rubble and others to sink, hissing with heat, into the fetid, lifeless water of Lake Michigan.

After one of the shrieking spheres had passed, five Cypher soldiers climbed from a crater near where the Willis Tower had stood before it was blasted to pieces by a Gorgon energy beam on the first day of their arrival. They drifted through the rain-swept ruins, ghosting in and out, their black and featureless heads swiveling back and forth in search of the quick reptilian movements of the enemy. The human kind could not understand the communication signals sent to these soldiers, or from where, or what these creatures truly were; it was beyond human knowledge, and thus as much magic as it was technology far advanced.

The five soldiers were identified by a small red glyph on the lower right slope of their faceplates: ⋗

It was a symbol of great honor and equally great prowess in battle, and though no human could fully understand its meaning the closest human language could decipher it would be First Born Of The Blessed Machine. The soldier who led them had one more addition to its glyph, a second crescent beneath the first, and the nearest meaning in the human language would be: Bringer Of Ignoble Death.

Neither male nor female, neither truly born nor wholly constructed in the weapon pods, the First Born moved through the wet rubble with the careful stealth of ancient warriors. Behind their faceplates worked calculations, soundlessly and rapidly, in no mathematics that could be fathomed on Earth. Distant sensors sparked pinpoints of light on floating grids, marking the proximity of kindred forces and the despised enemy of all that was correct and true. Above them a huge battleship of that enemy emerged from the clouds and began to fire its destructive beams at another target on the ground. Explosions, dust, and debris plumed into the dirty air some leagues distant. The First Born moved on, seeking enemy contact and fully aware that their foes were masters of camouflage, had learned the art of becoming one with any surface that afforded a hiding place, and that this foe had also learned to trick the spatial sensors by projecting a multitude of false images.

Through the rubble they went, silently calculating in their alien mathematics built on the geometrics of the tenth dimension. The First Born entered the dark hulk of a fallen building, where sheets of gold-colored glass had shattered on the stones. Human bones, skulls and ribcages lay scattered about, some bearing teeth marks. The First Born recognized them as the interior foundations of the denizens of this world. They did not know they were walking in what used to be an international bank, and underfoot were hundreds of pieces of paper currency from many nations of the world, now moldering in puddles of diseased rain.

Deathbringer suddenly stood still. The creature was receiving a message from the high command. The other First Born stopped as well, standing motionless on a floor of broken tiles.

The language was also mathematics. Behind the faceplate it pieced together an image of a burning blue giant throwing spheres of enemy fire at crawler weapons as seen through the viewpoint of a podmate…and then a denizen of this world attacking other podmates and destroying them with what seemed impossible ease.

The orders came. The nearest proximation of human understanding would have been: *Capture this specimen. High altitude tracker on station. Begin immediate deployment.*

This was surely a task to heighten the honor of the First Born of the Blessed Machine.

Deathbringer's faceplate grid showed a concentration of enemies at a measure of what would have been two hundred yards in human distance. The count of enemy soldiers might have had different root structures, but there appeared to be twenty of them.

Therefore when the monsters erupted from the cracked gray walls all around the First Born, exposing themselves as having been disguised by the stonework, Deathbringer was not caught unaware because this creature had seen the pulsing, wet red oval of the camouflage organ in many field dissections. It was a mystery yet to be conquered.

They knew no fear, neither First Born nor the reptilian attackers with their scaly flesh of yellow banded with black or brown, or black banded with yellow and red, or brown banded with black and yellow, no two exactly alike. To an inhabitant of the earth this would have been a hypnotic beauty, as God might have created the serpent before cursing it to crawl on its belly after the Fall of Man. Yet their quick and slithering movements and the visage that was too close to that of a king cobra was terror beyond terror, and to be caught by the slitted red pupils in narrow eyes that never blinked was more than enough to paralyze a human being.

The weapons of these soldiers were simple. They had been bred for this war. Beyond the claws, fangs, and speed to tear their enemy apart at close range, at long range some could spit spears of acid that would eat through any earthly material short of tungsten steel. Six of the twenty had been bred as creations that could extend their upper appendages a length of seven feet in human distance, and their claws would transmutate into any number of deadly implements according to the creature's braincore.

Instantly the First Born pressed back-to-back. They began to fire their double-barreled weapons as they spun in a rapid wheeling motion. They turned so fast they were ghostly imprints, nothing solid about them but the white-hot gouts of energy streaking out across what used to be a refined lobby of commerce, now a battleground where reptilian forms exploded into burning pieces.

Still the enemy darted forward, diminished now by half their force. The spears of acid came sizzling through the air at the First Born. They blurred out almost as one, and yet acid hit a faceplate before all had displaced themselves. The one struck lost its distortion and vibrated back into focus, its faceplate being melted away and beneath it a sparking of red schematics. An elongated yellow-and-black arm with a spinning yellow spearhead for a hand pierced the chest and a black-and-brown-banded arm that ended in a dozen crimson spikes drove into the lower body and tore loose a slide of glistening black intestines. As the dying creature crumpled to its knees, its acid-burned head was ripped from the neck by the brute strength of a reptilian commander with a growth of three thorny spikes on each shoulder. The remaining four First Born blurred back in across the chamber behind their enemy. Their weapons cut apart another six of the hated foe. Four enemy soldiers were left, among them their commander. There was no retreat; all knew this was a battle to the death.

A stream of acid spittle came at one of the First Born, who vibrated out and left the viscous slime burning into the concrete wall. The four reptilians streaked forward with incredible speed upon the other three First Born. The energy blasters fired, missed, and blew the far wall to pieces as their targets went into slither mode across the floor. An elongated arm with a barb-covered mallet at the end of it swung within inches of Deathbringer's faceplate. Deathbringer's weapon destroyed the offending enemy. The fourth First Born ghosted back in a few feet away and blasted a second enemy into burning pieces. The reptilian commander sent a spear of acid flying at Deathbringer, who went to one knee the liquid passed over its left shoulder. Deathbringer fired but missed as the commander snaked aside. Then, as another First Born's energy bolts blew the third reptilian apart, the commander camouflaged itself amid the rubble and vanished, leaving not a blip on the faceplate search grids.

The orders must be obeyed. *Capture this specimen. High altitude tracker on station. Begin immediate deployment.*

A shift of Deathbringer's search grid showed their destination. It was a distance from where the four First Born of the Blessed Machine stood, but what was such a distance to an interstellar traveller who could enter and leave the fourth dimension at will? A mathematical picture of the specimen could be brought up, but that information was already burned into Deathbringer's numeric code and the codes of the other soldiers. If the specimen moved during the time it would take to reach this destination, the tracker would maintain contact if it was not destroyed by enemy action, for the skycraft battleships fought even at the edge of this world's atmosphere.

Deathbringer transmitted the coordinates and the path to the other soldiers. They took no notice of the headless body lying nearby, for that one had become a negative. They began to ghost out, one after the other. As Deathbringer began to vibrate into distortion a claw attached to a scaly and sinewy arm with a shoulder adorned by three spikes reached from the gray stones on the floor. It seized the ankle of Deathbringer's left boot. Then the rest of the reptilian commander began to restore itself from the state of camouflage and rise up from the rubble, its facial hood flaring wide to show the same violent scarlet as the slitted pupils, its mouth opening to spew acid into the black faceplate.

Deathbringer knew two things that might be termed emotions: loyalty to the Blessed Machine and hatred of the enemy. In its complex mathematics, there was no room for anything else. Except, perhaps, an integer's sliver of cruelty. Deathbringer fired its weapon at point-blank range, a single energy orb, and severed the left arm at the shoulder, thrusting the commander backward to the floor as a spool of acid flew into the air. The right arm was burned away by the next single burst. The legs were burned off one after the other, and the flesh of the reptilian commander's scorched and squirming torso changed back and forth from the gray of the rubble stones to its yellow-and-black banding, the camouflage organ overcome with the chemicals of agony.

The black faceplate with its small red glyph of glory angled down at the tortured commander and drew in a numerical picture of the scene. Then, satisfied with its work, Deathbringer did not bring death but instead ghosted out.

A specimen had to be captured for the honor of the First Born, and for the triumph of the Blessed Machine.

TWENTY-ONE.

"Let's hear it," said Major Fleming, his jaw set like a chunk of granite. "The truth."

The mall's maintenance room bristled with guns: automatic rifles, machine guns and pistols. The ashen-faced soldiers who held these weapons aimed them at two figures seated on metal folding chairs: Jefferson Jericho and Jack Vope. Ropes had been lashed around the prisoners, tying them together back-to-back under a harsh incandescent light. Standing out of the line of fire were Dave, Olivia, and Ethan, who had one blue eye and one silver with no discernible pupil. JayDee had come down on the elevator and stood leaning on his cane behind Olivia.

After the chaos was over, Ethan had gone into the bathroom to check out his silver eye in the mirror. He'd thought he would've been afraid to see it, but he was no longer afraid. Instead, he was simply fascinated. The feeling of power that had flowed through him during that encounter had been incredible...impossible for the part of him that was still a human boy to understand, but for the other part of him... whatever that was, and was going to be...an immense satisfaction at having been able to save human lives. There in the bathroom, with an armed guard still at his back, he had lifted up his t-shirt and seen that a new figure had appeared in the silver tattoo just above his heart. Now it read ᚷᚡᛥᛝ, with another symbol just beginning to come up from the dark slate.

He'd had no choice but to go to the major and tell him.

The Cyphers sent a recon probe and those weapons, because there's a Gorgon here disguised as a man. I haven't said anything because I can handle him. Do you believe that?

And the hard-assed major who thought he'd seen everything in this nightmarish war had said, *Yes I do.*

I'm sorry for not telling you, but I wanted to watch him. The man with him…Kushman…is a human, but he's being protected by the Gorgons. I don't know why, but I need to know. When you take these two men, I'll need to be with you. The Gorgon is afraid of me, and so is the man.

Hell, the major had said, *I'm afraid of you too.*

You don't have to be. My task is somewhere else, but as long as that Gorgon is here this place is in danger from the Cyphers. I should've expected that, but I'm thankful no one was hurt.

Except that…man who got burned up, said the major. *What was that?*

A Gorgon-engineered weapon. We should be glad for that, because those spiders were nearly too much for me.

Okay. Right. Well…how old did you say you were?

And here was the question, because Ethan knew whatever was in him was *old.* Whatever was in him, growing stronger and taking control of everything, was so ancient these runes on his chest might have been its most recent communication with the inhabitants of this world. Whatever it was, it knew the cosmic dust and dark matter that blew between the stars to seed the lifeless spheres of raw planets into new life; it knew how cold and remote could be the outer reaches of space whose distances and dimensions defied the minds of men to imagine, and it knew how ruthless these two enemies were, and how military men and women of Earth might wish to stop this war but it was the only entity who could, and it was not from around here.

I'm fifteen, going on way more than you can count, Ethan said, and the major asked no more questions.

"Waiting to hear something that makes sense," Fleming said to the two figures tied together on chairs in the maintenance room. "Kushman? You want to say anything?"

"Sir?" said one of the soldiers. He was young and lean and had a Southern accent. "Pardon, sir...but I think I've seen this man before. I mean...not here, but somewhere else."

"How would that be, Private?"

"I don't know, sir. He just looks real familiar. Like...somebody I remember from television. My mom used to watch him, back in Birmingham...or who he looks like."

"I doubt this bastard was ever a television star," Fleming answered, and then he returned to his business by pulling back the bolt of his .45 automatic and levelling the barrel at the man's head. "I'll kill you, friend. And if your Gorgon buddy moves, I'm leaving that up to Ethan. So let's hear it."

"Major," said Jefferson Jericho, his eyes wide and set with an expression of puzzlement and pleading, "this is a big mistake. I hardly knew either of these men. I just met them on the road. Hey, I'm from the South too," he told the young Southern soldier. "I used to live in—"

"Shut it," Fleming interrupted. "Ethan knows the Gorgons are protecting you. Why do you need protection?"

"Protecting *me*?" Jefferson brought up a crooked smile. "If that's so, they haven't done a very good job, have they?"

Dave was watching Vope, who blinked...blinked...blinked.

"Major," Dave said, "I think you ought to go ahead and put that sonofabitch there out of our misery. I'll do it, if you like. Glad to."

"*No*," Ethan said. "Besides, you wouldn't know how."

"Would *you*?"

"Yes," Ethan answered, sure in that knowledge, and looking into the silver eye made Dave go silent.

"I have let you restrain me," Jack the Gorgon suddenly said. "I have allowed this indignity, but I could easily break loose from these bonds. The boy could destroy me, but not before you, called Major, are dead."

"This guy's crazy," Jefferson spoke up. "*Mental*. But how does that mean he's a Gorgon?"

"You want to tell him what you've told me?" Fleming asked the boy with the silver eye.

Ethan stared for a moment at Jeff Kushman. Looking into the man's face, at the softness that seemed only lately to have been touched by this brutal war, he had the feeling that there was something wrong with the name…that it was an alias to an alias, that this man was a walking lie but he was good at lying, he was very skilled at it, and he may have been able to convince and persuade someone who could not see the hard blue sphere that shielded the images in his mind. Ethan said, "I can read the Gorgon's mind. I can see *things* in there." He decided to try his luck at persuasion. "I can read yours too, Mr. Kushman…but that's not the name you really use, is it?"

Jefferson's face flushed; he looked around for help and found only hard faces and accusing eyes. "Listen to me," he said, speaking to everyone, "I'm *human*! I'm one of you! Look at this boy and tell me what *he* is! You're not going to trust a…an *alien* over a human, are you?"

"I know who and what you are," Ethan said. "Denying it just makes you smaller."

"This isn't a boy!" Jefferson had almost shouted it. His eyes were shiny with fear. "I don't know what he is, but he's not one of us! Listen, listen…okay?" He directed this to Major Fleming, and specifically to the hand that held the pistol. "I didn't want to get involved in this, I was somewhere else! It's not me that wants him!" He felt the ropes tighten as the Gorgon shifted in his chair. He looked to Dave and Olivia. "I swear to God, I don't want to hurt him! I don't care, I just want to get back to where I *was*! Back to my people! You know?" It was all pouring out of him, he felt that his dam had broken and he couldn't hold back the floodwaters but he thought that he could be killed three ways now: by this weird boy, by the Gorgon he was roped to, or by the major's pistol. "I was pushed into this!" he said. "I was forced to do it, I didn't want to be here!"

"Forced to do *what*?" the major asked, and he looked as if he were *so* ready to use that gun.

"I was forced to—"

244

"I will speak," said the Gorgon.

Everyone was silent. Jefferson Jericho looked at the floor, his heart pounding and his mind racing.

Vope couldn't turn his head enough to look at anyone directly, so he stared impassively at the far wall. "The boy is a curiosity to us. How he kills without weapons. He is something that should not be, yet he *is*. We wish to know his internals and systems. You would do the same, Major, if you were fighting an enemy such as we are."

"We *are* fighting your enemy," Fleming answered. "And we're fighting *you*, too."

"You have lost both those wars long ago. The only chance your kind has for survival is to nest with us. Release us from these bonds, Major. We will take the boy and consider him an offering."

"Like *hell*!" Dave growled. "Nobody's taking Ethan!"

Vope was silent. Then his head cocked slightly to one side and he said, "Your refusal has been noted. You ask for an attack that will burn you all to the ground. In the end, we shall have what we want."

"Then maybe I should blow your damn head off right now," said Fleming, who stepped closer to press the pistol's barrel against Vope's temple.

"Good luck with *that*," Jefferson said bitterly. He tensed himself for what he feared was to come, the sweat running down his sides under his shirt.

"Yes," said the Gorgon, as if in agreement with that last statement. Jefferson Jericho couldn't see what happened next, but the others could. The Gorgon's body shimmered and began to lose its substance. There was a sound like a soft whistling, as if air was being displaced. Maybe it was a whirring sound, like a little machine in motion. As Vope faded out and the ropes that had bound him fell slack, the black-bearded and dark-eyed face angled to look up at Major Fleming, and it seemed to the major that something behind that face was struggling to get out, to cast off its disguise, because the face was as distorted as if made of melting wax, or like an empty rubber mask seen in a funhouse mirror. There came the harsh, otherworldly echo of the Gorgon's final word to him: *Idiot.*

Then the body was gone, but perhaps there remained for a second or two the faintest impression of a dark aura where the body had been… and that too passed away, and the barrel of Fleming's automatic was aimed at empty air.

"*Jesus!*" Jefferson Jericho shouted, as he realized the ropes had fallen from him and Vope had been teleported from the room. "Don't leave me here!" Jefferson stood up from his chair, causing all the guns in the room to train on him. "Don't leave me!" he called into the air, with a voice like that of a broken child. There was no reply to his plea, not even the merest pinch of pain from the device buried in the back of his neck.

"I can't live out here! I can't *survive* it!" he babbled to the major, as tears of terror burned his eyes. "This is all wrong! I've got to get back to where I was!" He turned his agonized appeal upon Ethan, Dave, Olivia and JayDee. "Please…you've got to help me get back!"

"I'll help you into a fucking grave, if that suits you," Dave said.

Ethan sent out the silver hand again—it was easy now, so easy, as if he'd been doing it all his life—to probe into the head of the man who called himself Jeff Kushman, but the incandescent blue sphere still protected the man's memories. Whatever the Gorgons had done to him, they were still shielding him. It was a strong force. Ethan's force couldn't remain in there very long without feeling that it was sapping his strength; he had to pull out, and he brought the silver hand back to rest within himself. From beginning to end it had taken less than three seconds.

"What are you *talking* about?" Olivia asked the frantic Kushman. "Help you get back to *where?*"

Jefferson Jericho decided the time had come. Even with all these guns trained on him, even if it meant his death in the next thirty seconds. He had to get back to Her protection, back to the Ant Farm, and there was only one way to do that…broken fingers or not.

Flesh to flesh, She had said. He figured that must trigger the process of transportation or whatever the hell it was that would get him out of here.

He stepped out of the ropes and with the courage of desperation lunged past Major Fleming before the man could stop him.

He grabbed hold of Ethan's forearms, flesh to flesh except for the splints around his broken fingers. *Now!* he thought as he peered into the depths of the boy's silver eye, though he was calling mentally to Her, Queen of the Gorgons. *Get me out of here NOW!*

Ethan clearly heard that call, as if the man was speaking it to him. The room began to fade. He was aware of Dave reaching for him, but it was too late. It was as if the light was simply going out, the walls dissolving, and Ethan knew it was his own body—and Kushman's too—that was leaving the room, bound for an unknown destination.

Ethan had the impression of a figure standing behind Jeff Kushman—a large, leathery shape with a dark and dimly seen face, and set there were the fearsome, hypnotic eyes of the Gorgon, commanding him to *obey* but that was the last thing he wanted to do, and as he felt the Other Realm beginning to close in upon him he thought *no, I will not be taken…I will not be taken, I'm going back to where I was.* He didn't know how he did it. He just knew he needed to fight, and he was not going to be removed from his friends and the task he had to do. He felt a tremendous pressure, pulling at him as if drawing him into a whirlpool, or over a waterfall to dash him to pieces on the rocks below. But he thought *no, no…you're not taking me…*and his strength of will—the strength of will worlds beyond that of the human boy he used to be—was enough to break the power of what was transporting them; it was enough to scramble the signal or block the portal or do whatever was needed to be done, for the figure of the Gorgon behind Jeff Kushman faded away and the presence of the Other Realm was gone, and quite suddenly they were standing in the maintenance room of the mall again, with the light shining down upon all those guns in the hands of the soldiers.

It had happened so quickly that Dave was still moving. It had appeared to Dave and everyone else in the room that the bodies of Ethan and Jeff Kushman had faded almost to shadows and then had come back into focus in the space of time it took for two anxious heartbeats. Dave wrenched Ethan out of the man's grip, and pushing Ethan aside he laid a right hook into Jefferson Jericho's jaw with every bit of wiry muscle a tough-assed ex-bouncer, brickmason, and general owner of a bad attitude could throw.

The Tennessee stallion went down so hard most of the people in the room, including John Douglas, thought he was dead.

But the dead man returned to life after a few seconds with a spitting of blood and a moan that seemed to emanate from the center of a tortured soul, and Dave McKane stood over him with fists clenched and shouted, "Stay down, you sonofabitch! Just stay down!" all the while wishing the bastard would at least try to get to his knees.

"We'll take it from here," the major said. "You all right?" he asked the boy, who nodded. It was all Fleming could do not to ask Ethan where he had gone—or almost gone—but he didn't want to know.

Olivia pulled Ethan to her and hugged him. Then it came out of her. Everything...the loss of Vincent, the loss of her world, the tragedy and senselessness of this war, the hardship and struggle, the deaths of so many people she had known and cared for, and though she knew she hugged in her arms a boy who harbored a presence in him that was not of this earth, she didn't care because she needed someone to love and protect, and just that fast she broke. She began to sob, to weep for the dead and for the living, for those who had long ago given up hope and for those who still hung on to what tomorrow might bring, for those who had lost everything and for those who had kept their families intact only by good luck or the determination of the damned. She wept for those who, like her, kept their loved ones alive by a treasured picture or a memory held like a candle on the darkest night or some kind of Magic Eight Ball to ease their loss. It seemed in that moment that she wept for the young students of Ethan Gaines High School, who had painted a mural upon a wall proclaiming the dream of the Family of Man that had been torn to pieces by the terrible, arrogant power of red and blue fire.

And she wept also for the boy who knew no name but Ethan Gaines, who had once been alive and in the care of a mother who loved him, but was now embraced and guided by an alien force, raised from the dead to carry out a task only that force could understand. He could never go back to what he'd been, before. Never. And neither could anyone else, because even if the war was ended tomorrow...the world was not a computer, and it could not be rebooted.

JayDee put an arm around her shoulders. He leaned his head against hers. He wished he could find something to say, but there were no words. He wished he could weep himself, could get rid of the pain of having to put those three poor souls out of their misery back at Panther Ridge. He looked at Dave, who was rubbing the knuckles of the fist that had almost knocked Jefferson Jericho out of this world.

"We need to get Ethan to the White Mansion," JayDee said. "The sooner the better, I think."

"Yeah," Dave agreed. "How about it, Major? When can we leave?"

"I told you we'd make some improvements to your bus. You'll need 'em. If you'll give me the rest of today and tonight, you can head off in the morning."

Ethan gently pulled away from Olivia. "That would be good," he said. "Thank you." He felt weary and a little lightheaded. The joints of his body ached. He knew he was paying a price for the force that was using him. He wondered when it would happen that the part of him that was still human would be completely gone, and the alien within him took total control. He figured he was halfway there already. Would he even know when it happened? Would it be like going to sleep, or dying, or would it be like being a bystander in his own super-charged body?

He didn't want to think about these things too much, because they scared him. "I think I need to get something to eat and then lie down and rest for awhile," he said, running a hand across his forehead. "Someplace quiet."

"What about *me*?" asked the man on the floor. Still groggy, he crawled away to put more distance between himself and Dave McKane's fist. His tongue found two loose teeth and tasted blood. "What's going to happen to me?"

"We'll find a place to lock you up nice and tight," Fleming said. "If I'm understanding all this, you've been aiding and abetting the enemy. The Gorgons wanted the boy and they got you to help? Save your speech, I don't care to hear it," he said, before Kushman could speak again. "In my Army, that's reason enough for an execution."

"*Kill* me? Just like that?"

"Execute you," said the major. "Just like that."

"Ethan, listen to me!" Jefferson Jericho started to struggle to his feet, but he saw that McKane wanted to hit him again so he stayed where he was. "I was *forced* to do this! I didn't want to! Who would want to help the Gorgons or the Cyphers unless they *had* to?" He probed his teeth again; one was so loose it was just about to come out. "I can't…I can't explain it all to you, but they were protecting me and my people. They were keeping us out of the war. So…it was either find you and take you back—and I don't know how they do that, that's way beyond me—or lose our protection. Do you understand?"

"Why'd they choose *you*?" Dave asked.

"They chose me because they thought a real human could get to him easier. Just like Vope said, they want to study him. But they're afraid of him, too." Jefferson tensed, ready for pain to be delivered to him at any second for his failure and his betrayal, but no pain came. He realized he had truly been abandoned, She had turned Her back on him, and probably everybody in New Eden had been destroyed like ants beneath a crushing boot, the Ant Farm whirled away into space or some other dimension and burned into nothingness. "I thought…he must be a Cypher weapon or something, but…what he did out there…killing those soldiers…he can't be one of them."

"Ethan is something different," said Olivia, who had regained her composure. "*Becoming* something different," she corrected herself.

"A third kind of alien," JayDee said, and surprised himself by voicing the thought. "He believes he can stop this war. I say, give him the chance."

"Right." Jefferson nodded strenuously. "A chance. Yes. Absolutely. But…listen…nobody can stay *here*. Vope says they'll be coming to burn this place to the ground. They can do it. They *will* do it."

"I'll know when they're coming," said Ethan.

"*How* will you know? ESP or something?"

"You can call it that. I'll just know when they get close enough." Ethan turned his attention to the major. "If I'm gone, there's no need for them to attack this place. They may do it just because they *can*, but like JayDee said…the sooner we get on the road, the better."

"Okay, but give us time to work tonight. If I were you I wouldn't want to head off after dark, anyway. It's too risky."

"It's a risk to stay here," Ethan said, but he knew that night travel was pushing even his powers of survival and certainly they didn't want to run into any more armies of Gray Men.

"I'm not staying here!" Jefferson Jericho stood up and staggered but held himself upright. "Hell, no! I didn't ask for any of this! You want to lock me up with the Gorgons coming to kill everybody? And execute me, for trying to save the lives of my people? How was I supposed to know that the boy wasn't a Cypher weapon? I didn't know he was a human!" He glanced at Ethan and the boy's silver eye, which sent a shiver up his spine. "If you can call *that* human!"

"Before we go," Dave said to Major Fleming, "I'd like the job of putting a bullet through this scumbag's head."

"What do you mean, your *people*?" Olivia asked, disregarding Dave's remark. "What people? And where?"

"In Tennessee. I…had a housing development, near Nashville." Jefferson decided not to reveal too much about himself, in case the Southern soldier's mother had lost her bankroll betting on the book and DVD of God's High Rollers' System For Riches And Happiness, forty-nine dollars and ninety-nine cents but for a few dollars more could be delivered overnight by Federal Express. "The whole development… everything…was scooped up by the Gorgons. Put somewhere so they could study us. I was taken by one of them…she looked like a woman, she could change her face and her shape…and she told me if I didn't bring the boy back, our protection would be gone. That's why I did it. For my people, like I said. And I swear to God I thought he was a Cypher weapon. I thought that's why they wanted him." He turned his agonized eyes upon Ethan and figured if he ever needed an iota of salesmanship he needed a ton of it now. First, the build-up: "I know you've got a fantastic power…I've never seen anything like that…what you did out there. You saved everybody." He brought upon his face the expression of a desperate supplicant, which was closer to reality than he cared to admit. "Can you stop this war?"

Ethan probed the man's mind and found that, not surprisingly, the blue sphere was gone. His Gorgon keeper had left him to his own resources in penalty for failure. The silver hand of Ethan's curiosity roamed through a landscape of scenes from the man's past that in some places were hard to view; he found bits and scraps that told him the real name was Leon Kushman but the man went by another—Jefferson Jericho—and there were scenes of adoring crowds and stacks of money being counted and women, many women, who—

Ethan had the complete picture of Jefferson Jericho in the time it took between the words *Can* and *war*. He saw the Gorgon creature in its many guises and knew all. He saw a rainbow through a window and knew the sudden elation of a car salesman with a grand idea to make himself rich. He saw Jericho's wife—her name Ramona? No...Regina— with a pistol, and knew how close this man had come to paying for his many sins with a bullet to the head...but saved by the Gorgon ship blast- ing into view over the Tennessee pastures.

"You were lucky that day she was going to shoot you," Ethan said, and saw the blood drain from the man's face. "Or maybe not, because here you are with us."

Jefferson touched his right temple, as if he could feel Ethan moving around in there but the silver hand had already gone. "You know what I'm telling you is true, don't you?" He heard a little begging in his voice, but that was all right; the boy might respond to it.

"*That* part is true. Some of the rest of it, not so much. And to answer your other question: I'll know more about that when we get where we're going, White Mansion Mountain in Utah."

"Are you done bulling the shit?" Dave asked, speaking to Jefferson. "Time you got locked up or put down with a bullet." He looked again to the major. "I'll do it, if nobody else will."

"This man has done some bad things," Ethan agreed, "but he doesn't deserve to be killed for this one. His real name is Jefferson Jericho, and he was a—"

"God dog it!" said the Southern soldier. "I knew he was familiar! My momma watched him, nine o'clock every Sunday night, bought his book too! I should've known from his *voice*!"

"A preacher, of a kind," Ethan went on. "He sold dreams. Some turned out good and some went wrong. There's no point in locking him up, either. His Gorgon protection is gone. He has nowhere left to go."

"That," said Jefferson, "is unfortunately correct." He maintained eye contact with the boy, as difficult as that was for him. "By this time, my people and my town are gone, too." His tongue finally worked the loose tooth out and he spat it to the floor along with a spatter of blood. "You know what we called my town?"

"New Eden," Ethan said.

"Why did I even have to ask?" Jefferson worked up a tight smile. "Well, the snake got in it."

"You mean *another* snake got in it?"

"Yeah. That's what I mean." The preacherman should've felt trapped, backed into a corner, but instead he felt strangely free and strangely strong. With this boy able to read his mind, there was no longer any reason to pretend, to put on a show, to hide behind any façade. It was almost, in a way, a relief. "I didn't ask to be here. So do whatever you want with me. Like you say, I have nowhere else to go. A rifle bullet now or blown to pieces by the Gorgons later…what's the difference?"

"None," said Dave. "So I say the rifle bullet."

"You give up very easily," Ethan said, "to be such a good talker."

"What?" This had come almost simultaneously from Dave and Jefferson.

"Your skill is talking people into doing things. Sometimes things they don't really want to do, but you make them believe. That's what your life has been, hasn't it?"

"Some might say."

"I say, because I know." Ethan was getting a feeling he couldn't shake. It was true that the man was a user of other people, that he had crushed others down for his own needs and left many impoverished, but many enriched as well. He did have a gift of persuasion, though it was

no match for the silver hand that uncovered all truths. He had talked his way onto the bus over Dave's objections, and he had hidden a Gorgon and a Gorgon-engineered human under their noses, and he might have spirited Ethan away to the Gorgon realm if the alien presence hadn't been so powerful. Ethan had no idea what was waiting at their destination, but this feeling he could not shake made him look at Dave and say in a voice that was direct and forceful and far older than the years he portrayed, "We might need this man."

"*What*?" Dave repeated. "Why in hell would we need *him*?"

"I'm not sure yet," Ethan answered, "but I might not be enough."

"Enough for what?" Olivia asked, as puzzled as both Dave, JayDee, and even Jefferson Jericho.

"For the task. What that is, I don't know yet, but this man..." Ethan paused, trying to read this feeling but unable yet to decipher it. "He's too valuable to leave behind. He's seen a creature who might be the Gorgon queen...if she really is a female. He's been favored by her," he said. No need to go into the other details he had uncovered, he decided. "I believe he should go with us, no matter what else he's done."

There was a moment of silence. Jefferson couldn't decide if going to this mountain Ethan was talking about was any safer than staying here, but he did know one thing: as long as he was with this boy, he would be more protected than by the soldiers with all their useless guns. On the other hand, Ethan was a target for the Gorgons, and they weren't giving up; they would find him, wherever he was. And out there were the Gray Men, too. Thousands of those things...

Still...what was the tradeoff?

"I'll tell you everything I know," Jefferson said, speaking to Dave because the rock needed to be turned. It wouldn't take much; the boy was in command here. He turned his focus on the woman. "Things about Vope and Ratcoff you'd probably want to know too. I can make myself useful, I promise you that."

Dave's eyes were dark and dangerous. "You make a move toward Ethan again and I'll kill you," he said, "and that's my promise to *you*, scumbag."

"Fair enough," said the preacherman, with a slight bow of his head. Maybe it did register in him that he might still have a chance to seize Ethan and be transported to the Gorgon queen, might still have a chance to save his people and his town and himself, but he felt the boy's eyes on him, imagined he felt the boy's alien power taking his brain apart and examining those thoughts one by one to test their weight, and so he let them fly away.

"I'll know," Ethan said. That was enough for Jefferson Jericho to hear.

I'll be a good boy, Jefferson thought, and Ethan answered, "I'll count on that."

Major Fleming and the other soldiers had work to do. Dave vowed to keep himself between Ethan and Jefferson Jericho at all times. Olivia took JayDee's hand and helped him to the service elevator. There were supplies to be gathered for the trip, and Hannah Grimes had to be approached about driving the bus because Dave didn't think he could handle a rig that size, not on the roads they would face when they left I-70 in Utah. The interstate itself might be a cratered challenge; who knew what was out there, in those mountains that must be crossed?

But something was out there that Ethan had to find. No one doubted it. They would be leaving as soon as the work was done on the bus, out into the world again, out into the war.

Jefferson Jericho realized everything he had ever built was likely destroyed. Regina, also destroyed. Or maybe New Eden was returned to its original plot on the Earth and left for the ravages of the war or the Gray Men to tear it to pieces. Which did he think was the better fate? He didn't want to think, but he figured he would never see the place again. He was throwing in his lot with this boy and the others, and maybe Dave McKane would kill him before they got to this mountain that seemed for some reason to be so special, or the Gorgon queen would transport him out of here and kill him in retribution, or something was waiting on the road that could overcome even the boy's power and kill them all. But at least he was alive today. He was not going to be locked up or executed.

The boy might have a use for him. That made him a little nervous, but for now Jefferson counted that as a victory. And for now, it was the best payoff a High Roller could hope for.

TWENTY-TWO.

ETHAN WAS PREPARED FOR WHAT AWAITED HIM IN THE MALL. A BOY with a silver eye who could blow apart Cypher spiders and soldiers by the power of a mind-weapon was going to find people cringing from him as if he carried a plague. They would be terrified of him, and who could blame them? He would be terrified of himself, if he wasn't in this suit of skin. Dave went to find Hannah Grimes and took Jefferson Jericho with him. Ethan, Olivia, and JayDee went to the food court to get something to eat. The people who were already there left in a hurry, and that included a few nervous soldiers. The three survivors of Panther Ridge, alone in the food court, served themselves bowls of thin vegetable soup from a big metal pot and cups of water from plastic jugs and then sat down at one of the bright orange tables.

They hadn't been there very long when Olivia motioned to her right and said, "We have company."

Ethan saw Nikki approaching. She, at least, seemed to have no fear of him anymore. She came up to the table. For a moment she looked with true wonder into the silver eye that had no pupil and then she asked, "Does it hurt?"

"No. It's not any different from the other one."

"That is…so *freaky*," she said, and she gave a quick little laugh that she tried to stop with a hand over her mouth, but too late. "I mean… it looks kind of cool. It doesn't make you have…like…X-ray vision or something?"

"Not that I can tell." *Worrying about if I can see through her clothes?* he wondered, but he didn't care to violate her privacy by wandering around in her mind.

"Get yourself something to eat, sit down and join us," JayDee said, nodding toward the fourth chair. "Looks like we've scared everybody else away."

"Thank you," Nikki told him, "but I just need to speak to Ethan for a few minutes."

"Is that our cue to disappear?" JayDee asked, with a spoonful of soup halfway to his mouth.

"No sir," said Ethan, "we'll move to another table." He took his soup bowl and his cup of water and followed Nikki to a table across the food court, because though he didn't want to peer into her mind, he knew this was something she needed to speak to him alone about. When they were settled, sitting across from each other, Nikki looked from one eye to the next as if trying to figure out which one to talk to.

"I can see through both of them," he explained. "One's just…like you said, *freaky*."

"How did that happen? Did you *feel* it happen?"

"No, I didn't." Just more evidence, he thought, of the change he was going through. Whatever the alien force was inside him, it was asserting itself more and more. "I didn't feel anything. I was too *busy*."

"Wow," she said. She pushed a drift of blonde hair off her forehead. "That was like crazy *amazing*! But…do you mind if I ask you something?"

What does it feel like? she was going to ask, but he nodded and let her ask it anyway.

"It feels…like all I have to do is concentrate on something, and I can do it. It's getting easier, but I wouldn't say it's really easy. I just have to *want* to do it…in a way I can't explain. Like…life or death. You know?"

"I guess."

"Let me ask you a question. When I killed those spider things, and the Cypher soldiers, did you see anything come out of me? Like come out of my hand, I mean. Where it was aimed at those things. Did you see anything?"

"No, there was nothing."

"To me it looked like bolts of lightning or...I don't know...burning bullets is how I would describe them, I guess. Thousands of them. They just come out of me when I need them. And the air does something funny too. It seems like it twists between me and what I'm aiming at. It's like my whole body's a gun, or an energy weapon...and everything comes out here." He showed her his right palm, which looked like the ordinary palm of any teenaged boy. "I'm thinking I'm the only one who can see that?"

"I couldn't see it," she said. "I was right there, and I couldn't."

Ethan figured what he was seeing might be beyond the range of normal human vision. Maybe that had something to do with the change in his eye, and his visual spectrum was also changing. "That dude who caught fire and started flinging it," he said. "If he hadn't done that...I'm not sure I would've been able to handle them all. His name was Ratcoff. I just found that out. He was a human—mostly—but the Gorgons got to him and made him like that." Ethan took a sip of water and put the cup aside. He looked into her good eye. He asked quietly, "How come you're not afraid of me? Really." He thought her eye was the color of a chocolate brownie, which made him hungry for something sweet. "Everybody else is, except for my friends. How come you're not?"

Because I'm your friend, she said.

But Ethan did not reply until Nikki actually spoke it: "Because I'm your friend."

I am, right?

"Sure you are," he said, before the words came out. "It's just...you know...how I'm changing. It's way beyond weird. And now, with this eye..."

He knew what she was getting ready to say, the words were there in her mind, and he made himself focus just on her face and her mouth because it wasn't right to be there in her head, but he couldn't help it, it was too easy, it was becoming so natural for him…

"You want to see mine?" she asked, in a small voice.

He knew she wanted him to, so he answered, "Yes."

She took a long deep breath of courage, and then she started to lift up her eyepatch, but then she stopped and there was a lopsided grin on her mouth but a terrible sadness in her good eye, and she said…

"I'm sure," Ethan told her.

"It's not very pretty," Nikki said.

He shrugged. "Do you think *mine* is pretty? When I went to the bathroom and looked in the mirror I almost fell down. Hey, I don't even know how I can *see* through it!"

She nearly laughed at his inflection of helplessness, but a laugh was hard to come by. She still felt dazed by what had happened in the mall, and by the attack of the Gray Men and Gary Roosa's death last night, and sometimes she thought she had to go numb to deal with all the horrors of life now, and with all the bad and sad memories, all the people she knew who had died. But what happened when you went too numb, and you lost all your feeling, and you couldn't find your way back from that dark and empty place?

She wanted him to see what the eyepatch hid, because she needed a connection with someone. She needed someone to know the pain she had gone through…not that it was any worse than what most had experienced…but she needed Ethan to see it, maybe as a way to keep the numbness from taking over more and more of her until she was just a mindless, soulless cinder on this burned and wrecked earth. She needed a human touch, from this boy who was no longer truly human…or maybe, more human than most because he had an aim and a purpose, and she needed that too.

"Go ahead," he told her.

She lifted the eyepatch and showed him the crimped socket where the destroyed orb had been removed by Dr. Douglas before infection set in. The scar began just below the socket and continued up almost to her eyebrow. "A piece of glass got me, is what the doctor says. I don't remember that. I just remember fire and houses blowing up on Westview Avenue.

"It was at night and they were fighting in the sky. I was cut up pretty bad in other places—my face a little bit—but most of the worst are under my clothes. Some of my hair was burned off, they told me, but it grew back. I guess I was lucky, huh? Not to be all burned up."

"Yeah," Ethan said.

Nikki let the eyepatch down again. The little rhinestone star sparkled. "Some people came in to the apartments, early on, who were really burned. They didn't last very long. A family came in with two little boys who were twins, and they were both burned really bad on their arms and legs. One died during the day, and the other one died almost exactly twelve hours later. I heard Olivia and Dr. Douglas talking about it. It was like…when one twin died, the other one quit wanting to live. The mother and father didn't live very long after that, either. A lot of people killed themselves. I almost did, too, but Olivia stopped me. Twice."

"I'm glad she did," said Ethan.

"Hm," the girl answered, in a way that told Ethan she wasn't sure if she was glad or not. "Olivia brought these rhinestones for me, for my patch. Know who had them? The mother of those twins. Where she got them from, I don't know. A Dollar General, maybe. Just picked up a pack of something she thought was pretty. People do crazy things when they need to hold on to something, I guess."

Ethan nodded. It was the truth, and what was there to say? He knew what Nikki needed: a listener, and so he waited for her to go on without reading the scenes of her story before she could tell them.

"My sister's name was Nina," Nikki said. "She was a year older. Wow, could she ride a horse! Well, we both could…but she was way better than me. She was a junior at the high school. Was going to go to Colorado State and major in fun, is what she told me. But she really wanted to be a vet and work with horses. Maybe she would've gotten there, she was good at math and chemistry and stuff. I was a dud at those things, 'cause I was the real partier." Nikki stared off into space for a moment, and Ethan let her take her time.

"Sometimes," Nikki said, "I see my sister in my dreams. She's always pretty and smiling and happy...not burned up or hurt at all, and she says, *Nikki-tick, you can make it out of this. You're not one to be wanting to give up, so tell Olivia about those sleeping pills you found after Mr. and Mrs. Estevez passed on. And tell her about the knife with the serrated blade in the bottom drawer of your dresser, under the red blanket.* And I say back, *Quit bossin' me, you always liked to do that and who made you the queen of me?* But she just grins a big queenly grin and she answers, *Put a cork in it, 'cause you're the last of our family...the Stanwick family of 1733 Westview Avenue, and Dad always said he didn't raise quitters. So,* she says, *find your way.* And I didn't know what she meant, until now."

Ethan was silent; he allowed himself not a peek into her thoughts, but he had an idea of where she was headed.

"If a person doesn't have hope," she said, "they die. Inside, first. If they don't find a way, they're finished." Her chocolate-brown eye focused on him. "I don't want to stay here and wait to die, Ethan. If I'm going out, I want to go trying to find my way. I know you need to get to this mountain in Utah. I know it's important." She paused, maybe readying herself if he denied her this path. "Will you let me go with you?"

He had no hesitation. He said, "I *want* you to go."

"You do? Really?" It was spoken with an outrush of breath. "I know it won't be safe, but—"

"No place is safe," he reminded her. "No place will ever be safe while this goes on."

She nodded. "Do you know what's on the mountain?"

"No. I don't think I'll know until we get there, and it reveals itself." *It reveals itself?* He realized his thinking was changing too, and the way he spoke...it wasn't how a human boy thought or spoke...it was the alien thinking and speaking, becoming more and more dominant. "I may be really different soon," he told her, and offered a faint smile. "Like I'm not *already.* But I may not be Ethan Gaines much longer. That part of me may just go away, or go to sleep...I don't know. But I don't want you to sit here and wait to die, either. Your sister is right. We've got to find our way, so...I'm glad you want to come with us." He

262

motioned toward the unattended pot of soup. "You'd better get something to eat while you can."

"I will, thanks."

Ethan was weary and needed to find a place to rest. The battle against the spider-shapes and the Cypher soldiers had depleted him. There was some part of him now that was always on alert, and he trusted that to let him know if the Gorgons or the Cyphers were anywhere near. For the moment, he felt they were not. He wound up taking his sleeping bag into the empty storeroom of the Brookstone and stretching out on the floor there, and he was asleep within a few minutes.

But something within him did not sleep, did not need the solace of rest in this realm of misery, and it spoke to Ethan with four words: *This is my world.*

Ethan saw in the eye of his mind a rugged gray landscape strewn with boulders and cut by wide crevasses. The sky was milky white, shot through with streaks of vivid purple lightning, and just visible through the stormy atmosphere was a massive, clouded planet encompassed by three shimmering rings of debris and dust. Ethan had the sensation of standing on a mountaintop with a fierce, dry wind that smelled of alkali blowing into his face, and looking out across a wide valley, he could see a huge silver obelisk, thin but thousands of feet tall, with a spire that was slowly and silently rotating. Ethan had the sense that it was a watchtower of a kind, or a lighthouse sending out not beams of light but energy and messages that were far beyond his understanding. Messages were also coming in to this particular way station, and why he thought of the tower as a way station between worlds or dimensions he did not know, but he was sure there were others of its kind on more planets. It was a lonely place. He was struck by its loneliness and desolation, and he knew that the keeper here was an ancient creature who had either been chosen or had chosen itself to give up another kind of life for this duty it carried out. It was a double-edged sword: an honor to be a soldier in this service, but a lifelong responsibility. Time here was not Earthtime, nor Life governed by the laws of Earth. Ethan was unsure that the creature who was hosting him, and who he hosted, was capable of a physical body or not.

The creature might be the construct of pure energy and intelligence, and though this part of its origin and nature was not allowed to be known, Ethan was sure that it did possess two things that made it akin to the human kind: what would be termed *compassion*, and a sense of justice. Those seemed to be its driving forces, as well as an innate curiosity about the workings of the universe that even it was not allowed to be fully understood by the wisdom of a higher power.

The spire rotated. The wind blew and purple lightning streaked across the milky sky, but the image was fading. When that vision of another world vanished entirely, the human part of Ethan fell deeper into a dreamless sleep, yet the alien being within him remained silently and tirelessly vigilant, for that was the only way it had ever known.

FOUR.

WESTWARD

TWENTY-THREE.

"I**S THIS REALLY NECESSARY?**" JEFFERSON JERICHO ASKED AS DAVE McKane fastened the black plastic zipcuffs to his wrists, basically tying the man's hands together. Dave didn't answer. He pushed Jefferson up the steps into the bus and wished the bastard would fall down and break his beak.

Hannah Grimes was sitting behind the wheel. She had decided that driving this bus to their destination in Utah might be the last driving she would ever do, but there was not much else on her social calendar that seemed important, and Dave had convinced her that this indeed was an important trip. So she was in it, for better or for worse; she figured Dave would've driven the bus off the road at the first hairy curve, anyway. The meager light of a rainy dawn had begun to crawl across the horizon. Already aboard were JayDee and Olivia, and they were waiting now for Ethan and Nikki. Major Fleming had returned their guns, canned food, and jugs of water to them and told them he wished he could do more, that he could spare some soldiers and one of the armored cars as an escort but he couldn't abandon the people here. He'd decided to top off the bus's tank from their own dwindling supply. Otherwise the most he could do was give them a longer hose to help siphon fuel along the way, scavenge a headlight from one of the trucks and make repairs and improvements to the bus.

A work team had labored all night under the glare of generator-powered arc lamps. They'd replaced the shattered windshield with a piece of metal that had a rectangular glass inset through which the driver could see the road. Nothing could be done about the window the Gray Child had broken through, except for a sheet of plastic duct-taped over the aperture. Other windows bore bullet holes from all the firing that had gone on, but again nothing could be done for those. The main work had been the construction and welding of a cowcatcher-like cage attached to the front of the bus and studded with iron spikes. All the metal was going to make the bus heavier and so use more fuel, the major had told Dave, but if they ran into any more Gray Men this might help them get through without the cavalry coming to their rescue…which, out there in the Rockies on I-70, was definitely not happening. He said if they'd had time and ammunition to spare he would've put a machine-gun turret up top, but again there was the weight to consider, and they needed the ammo and every available M240 at the watchtowers. A wiper blade had been fixed to keep the glass inset clear, and the last thing the major and his troops could do was clean the interior of the bus of all bloodstains and fleshy parts, both human and gray. *Sorry we don't have any air freshener, Fleming had said, but maybe you can find a pine strip when you stop for gas.*

What the major had not told any of them, and they'd only seen this on their way to the bus from the mall, was that every soldier had signed his or her name on the sides of the bus in black or red spray paint, and maybe every soldier didn't fully understand the importance of this journey, but both Fleming and Captain Walsh did and they had been the first to sign. From the major also had come the wrist zipcuffs, a pair of shears, and a suggestion to keep Jefferson Jericho bound up for awhile, just in case.

"Sit there," Dave said, pushing the preacherman into a seat on the left side of the bus a few rows behind Hannah. Olivia and JayDee had taken seats on the right side, and Dave sat down behind Jefferson Jericho, so he could slap the dude on the back of the head if he needed to, or just wanted to. His Uzi felt good in its shoulder-holster, and in his belt holster was the .357 Magnum revolver that had helped save him and Olivia from the Gray Men in the high school library. He figured these weapons might not stop a Cypher or a Gorgon, but they would do the job on anything else and…if he really wanted to be truthful about it… they would save their owner from capture by the aliens if they came in numbers too many for Ethan to hold back, and they would save Ethan, Olivia, and the rest of them too if it came to that.

He reached forward and slapped Jefferson across the back of the head. "Shut up!"

"Ow, *Jesus*! Did I say anything?"

"No, but you're thinking of talking. So shut up."

Olivia's .45 automatic had been returned, along with a supply of two packs of ammo given up by Joel Schuster, who had the same make and model of weapon. John Douglas got an Army-issue M9 Beretta that had not been his, since his weapons were lost at Panther Ridge, but Captain Walsh had given the gun to him as well as four extra clips. A couple of rifles and boxes of bullets had been "confiscated" by the soldiers and left aboard, along with two high-powered flashlights. Hannah Grimes had her hogleg revolver and a few cylinder loads. A machine-gun turret would've been a nice extra, Dave thought, but they had to go with what they had. At the back of the bus were plastic containers, a hand pump and a twelve-foot hose for siphoning fuel, along with the prybar Dave had used to crack the underground diesel tank's fill cap.

In a few minutes Ethan came across the parking lot from the mall, followed by Nikki and Major Fleming. The major was carrying a small olive-green drawstring bag.

"Okay," Fleming said, as Ethan and Nikki took seats behind Olivia and JayDee. "Good luck to you." He focused on the boy, who still scared the shit out of him, but his rock-solid demeanor would never show it. "I hope you find whatever you need to find." He gave the bag to Dave. "Four fragmentation grenades in there, model M67. Just pull the pin and throw, like in the movies. You can throw 'em about forty meters, but get in cover because the pieces can travel more than two hundred meters. Don't blow yourselves up, save 'em for the enemy."

"Thanks," Dave said.

"We appreciate everything," Olivia told him. "Especially the work on the bus, and the fuel."

"Did what we could. Ethan, take care of these people if you can."

"I will, sir," Ethan answered. He was feeling the Cypher presence, had felt it since long before dawn and their breakfast of bread and canned pork'n beans, but he knew what it was and there was no point in mentioning it until they got on the road west. It was not a forthcoming attack, it was something different.

"Right," said Major Fleming. "Wish us luck, too. We're going to hold out here until somebody says otherwise." He gave them a quick salute. "Good-bye, folks," he said, and when he left the bus Hannah closed the door and started the engine. It fussed and rumbled, just like Hannah had when she'd been awakened around four o'clock, but like her, it was ready to go.

The metal-spiked entrance doorway to the fortress was hauled upward on its chains and the yellow school bus with the names of forty-two soldiers and a captain and a major on its sides passed underneath and along the road lined with concertina wire. Vultures were picking at the half-eaten Gray Men corpses splayed amid the coils. The sun shot crimson rays through holes in malignant-looking black clouds. The broken towers of Denver lay to the south, and so also did the ramp onto I-70.

The fortress doorway was lowered. Hannah said, "We're on our own now, kiddies."

Ethan could still feel the Cypher presence. It was like a prickling of his skin, a shadow in his mind, and he knew what it was because the alien within him knew.

"We're being followed," he said. "It's a Cypher tracking device. High altitude."

"Christ!" Jefferson swivelled around to face the boy as best he could. "Are they coming after us?"

"Just following, for now. But it's sending out signals, so...they'll be along, sooner or later."

"The Cyphers want you too?"

"Yes," said Ethan. "The one that got away probably communicated with its central command. They want me just like the Gorgons do." He offered the man the semblance of a smile. "They don't know what I am, and they're trying to figure me out. But...it's good to know that they're *afraid* of me."

"They're not stupid," said Jefferson. "But do *you* even know what you are?"

"Not everything. I think I—what's in me—must be a soldier, too." Ethan tapped the symbols over his heart. "I think I'm growing my own uniform, and this is my designation. I'm—*it*—is getting stronger by the day. Maybe by the hour. Which means...when they come after me, they're going to send their best."

"Yeah, and the *worst* for us!" Jefferson was beginning to think he would've been better off staying at the mall, getting a gun or two and putting his back into a corner, but Ethan said, "I'm going to need you before this is done. I don't know how, but you're going to have a chance to help me. To help *us*. Do you believe that?"

"I don't know what to believe. But why bring the girl?" He directed his attention to Nikki. "What's your story?"

"I want to be with Ethan. I trust him. That's all."

"No, I mean your eye. What happened?"

"Shut your mouth now, Jericho," Dave said, leaning forward, "or I'll shut it for you. How many more teeth would you like to lose?"

"The war happened," said Nikki, with queenly dignity. "I'm lucky to be alive."

"Lucky," Jefferson repeated, and he gave a bitter laugh. "Yeah, we're all really lucky, aren't we?"

"We're alive and we have a chance to do something important," said JayDee. "I trust Ethan too. Now maybe you'd be better off if you did shut up for awhile."

"Good thing, so I can concentrate through this damned viewslit," Hannah told them. "We've got a mess of wrecked and abandoned cars in front of us. Gonna have to slow down and ease our way through, so everybody just sit tight."

271

It was a torturous route. Fifty or so cars, SUVs and trucks jammed this stretch of Federal Boulevard. A few had caught fire and burned into unrecognizable masses of metal. A thirty-foot-wide crater near the intersection of Federal and West 80th Avenue told the story of damage done by either Gorgon or Cypher weapons that had heightened the panic and caused people to leave their vehicles. Buildings had been burned out on either side of the boulevard and some had collapsed into piles of melted black rubble. Hannah had to thread the needle several times, scraping the bus between cars, erasing some of the names on the paint. "Come on baby, come on baby," Hannah urged Number 712, as she had no choice but to guide the bus over dangerous shoals of broken glass and pieces of metal. It occurred not only to her but to everyone else on the bus that this could be a very short trip if a couple of tires blew.

"Hang on, this one's nasty," Hannah said, as Number 712 slowly scraped between a burned metro bus and an overturned Hormel meats truck. She got hung up on something, and she had to back up and try the approach again. The sound of rending metal made Jefferson Jericho lean his head forward and squeeze his eyes shut in a vain attempt to escape the noise. Nikki clutched Ethan's hand in a grip that he thought could crush a Jaguars linebacker's hand at—

"D'Evelyn High School," he said suddenly, with a flash of recognition. "Right here in Denver. That's where I went to school."

"*What?*" Olivia asked.

"I remember," Ethan said. "The science class was at D'Evelyn High School. Where I was going to show my Visible Man." Was he babbling now? He didn't know. "The teacher's name was Mr...." It was close, but still not there. "My mom's name was..." That, too, was not there. But *something* was there. "I'm from Lakewood," he said. "I lived at...it was a number with two eights in it. My house—" He was trying hard to remember, while the scraping sound of metal went on and on and the school bus shuddered as Hannah pushed their way through. "There was a park down the street. A huge park, with a lake in it. I think it was called...Belmar Park." He nodded, as the name came back to him.

"Kountze Lake. I remember that. I used to go fishing there." He looked into Nikki's face and felt the return of a small amount of joy. "I can remember a *little* bit!" he said, almost tearfully. "I know where I'm from!"

The horrendous sound of metal against metal ceased. Hannah let loose a whoosh of breath. "We're through! Damned if this road's not a mess. Dave, I'm seeing signs to I-70 West but everything's blocked up pretty bad."

"Figured it would be. Just do the best you can."

While Ethan tried to struggle to recall more of the life he used to know, he was also aware that the alien part of him was alert and questing for the presence of enemies. It was like he was a highly sophisticated radar, searching for many miles in all directions for approaching blips on a mental screen. He could envision the Cypher tracker: a glowing red triangular shape about half the size of the bus, slowly rotating around and around near the edge of the atmosphere, its crimson eye of energy directed down upon him and a multitude of calculations going out across the Cypher network. They would have already sent a team after him. They would strike at their own time, at the place they felt held the most advantage, but for the moment he couldn't feel them anywhere near. Neither were the Gorgons anywhere near, but neither would they give up trying to capture him. It helped that they feared him, for sure, and they weren't going to blunder into the range of his weapons without calculating the odds of success. They were coming, though; it was only a matter of time. And if they could figure out what he was and what he was trying to do...they weren't going to slink quietly away, they would try to destroy him with everything they had.

"Ramp's blocked," Hannah announced after awhile longer of weaving in and out of tight places. "Maybe we can get up the next one."

"You can't levitate the bus out of here, can you?" Dave asked Ethan, only half jokingly.

Ethan thought about it. Could he? The answer was quick in coming. "No, sorry. I can't do that. I can't move us by any kind of mental transportation, either. Hannah's in charge of this trip."

"Thanks, Spacekid," she replied.

"So let me ask you a question or two, Ethan," Jefferson said. "If *you* don't mind?" He had asked this of Dave, who shrugged his shoulders in such a way that told the preacherman to go ahead but to be careful with his mouth. "We're going to this mountain that you feel you need to get to, but you don't know why. You started out a human boy but now you and everybody knows there's a…a *thing* in you that's not Gorgon or Cypher, and they're afraid of you because you…this thing in you…has the power to destroy them and they don't understand it. Am I right so far?"

"Yes."

"Okay. You say this thing in you is a soldier. How do you know that?"

"It's just what I feel. What it lets me understand, if that's the right way to put it. Only…maybe…it's not a soldier in the way we would think of."

"I think of a tough-assed bastard who's trained to fight and to win a war. What other kind of soldier is there?"

"There's another kind," said JayDee, who'd been thinking about this ever since Ethan had used the word. "There's a *peacekeeper*. Like the soldiers who wear the blue helmets for the United Nations. They have to be tough too, but they don't fight to win wars…if they have to fight, their purpose is to *end* a conflict." He nodded toward Ethan. "If Ethan…if the being that's keeping Ethan going, when he should've by all rights been dead a long time ago, is trying to stop this war, I'd say he…it…whatever…is like a universal peacekeeper. A galactic United Nations soldier, I guess I'm trying to say." JayDee shrugged. "Maybe this war upsets the balance of things, on a cosmic scale. Maybe the Gorgons and Cyphers have been at this for hundreds or thousands of years, and this United Nations of the cosmos has decided it's gone far enough. So…why did the peacekeeper pick a young boy instead of a man? I don't know, and who can say? Maybe it was a good fit. Possibly there were things already in Ethan's personality that the soldier could use. Hey, I'm just from Earth…I don't know the answers to the mysteries and I'm not saying all this is fact, but…there it is: my opinion, and that only."

"God, this is crazy," Jefferson said. But he couldn't think it was too very crazy, because of what he'd experienced himself. The boy with the silver eye was staring at him, likely reading his mind again, tromping through the memory of all the rotten flowers in there. "So how did this thing get into you?" he asked. "How'd it get here? By flying saucer or what? And if it really wants to stop this war, why didn't it come with an army? And why doesn't it just tell you what it wants you to find, if it knows so much? Doesn't this thing *know* what we're supposed to be looking for? Why doesn't it just spell everything out for you?"

"Maybe it doesn't know everything," Olivia offered. She'd been thinking about this question too, and why Ethan seemed to be being fed by bits and pieces from the alien intelligence. "Maybe it has an *idea*, but doesn't know for sure. Maybe, too…it doesn't want to overload Ethan too much, because he's still got the mind of a boy. A limited mind, as any human mind would be. That's why it's been a gradual process, and the thing didn't take him over all at once."

"Didn't want to shellshock him," Dave said. "I get that."

Ethan said nothing. It was interesting, in a way, to be talked about like this, but disturbing too. There was so many questions; he doubted there would ever be answers to them all, because Olivia was right. The limited human mind could not fully understand this alien force, how it had arrived here and chosen him and how it was growing stronger, no more than he could understand how the power exploded out of him to create an earthquake or to blow Cyphers and Gorgons to pieces. It just was there when he—when the alien inside him—demanded it. He noted that this last encounter with the spider-shapes and the Cypher soldiers had left some pain and stiffness in his joints, like he was becoming an old man, so there was a price to be paid from the human flesh. He wondered if he could use his left hand too, as a double-barreled weapon. Anyway, it seemed to him that even though the alien power within him was incredibly strong, there was still a physical weakness inherent in the human body that was wearing him down. But if he was dead and the alien was keeping him alive…had taken control of this version of the Visible Man and was powering heart, lungs, blood pressure, digestion, and all the rest of the systems, he figured when the soldier had completed its mission—if that was possible—he was done for, and no doctor on Earth could change that. At last Ethan said, "I don't think it needs an army, but I do think it needs *us*."

"Needs us? How?" Jefferson asked.

"It needs us to..." Ethan paused, considering how to phrase this. "It needs us to give a damn," he went on. "As humans, I mean. I think...it wanted to know first if any of us even wanted to fight back. If we were strong enough to keep going. Dave, I think that's why it didn't tell me where the White Mansion was. It needed...it *needs*...to know that any of us care enough to stand up and fight, instead of waiting to die in a hole somewhere. So if you and Olivia hadn't gone out that day to find a map...if you'd said I was crazy and the earthquakes and finding the water were just things that happened, and I couldn't make you believe anything else...then maybe it would've figured we weren't worth helping. Maybe it would've just gone away, and I would've died and the Cyphers and Gorgons would keep on fighting until the whole world was destroyed, because nobody here cared anymore." He looked from Dave to Olivia, to JayDee, to Nikki and then back again to Dave. "That's what I think," he finished.

"This conversation is way over my wintry head, gents," Hannah said. "I'm just along for the ride. And I'm lettin' you know I'm lookin' at another on-ramp right now that's a jammed-up parkin' lot, no way are we gettin' up that." She wheeled the bus in another direction. "Well...no cops around, so let's try the off-ramp."

That was how Hannah got them up onto I-70 and westbound. The eastbound traffic during the incident that had caused all this chaos—likely the first battle that had devastated the central part of the city—had been virtually nil. There were a few wrecked cars and a big tractor-trailer truck that had slid into three other wrecks and caught fire, but Hannah was able to get them around the mangled blockage. She worried most about the glass and pieces of metal in the roadway, but the streetsweepers had been off-duty for a good long while and there wasn't a damned thing she could do but to grit her teeth and dance the bus along as best she could.

The interstate started a slow ascent. Mountains stood on both sides, and ahead were the looming giants of peaks—now partially obscured by an ugly yellow mist—that had been born eighty million years ago. Ethan wondered how old the being was inside him, what it had seen and where and how it had been born, if the Rockies had been specks in the eye of God when it had first come to life, and what Life meant to it. He had the feeling from what it had shown him that it was a lonely creature, one of a limited or dying race, but above all it clung to its duty. And here was its truth and its meaning of existence, as clear as if the alien was sitting at his side telling him these things: the futility of wars was known to all but never accepted by those who held power as their God. Pride, arrogance, and stupidity were not just the worst traits of the human kind but were spread across the span of galaxies as the price to be paid for the desire to be held in esteem, or recognized as better than any other civilization, or simply the appetite to conquer and control. Ethan felt a sadness and heaviness in what might have been the heart and mind of the alien—now becoming his heart and mind as well—in that it knew it fought a losing battle. Yet here, right here on the border—this young world that might not make much difference in the unfolding of a galaxy old beyond the meaning of Time—a stand must be made, and with that stand a message to be sent to the warlords of Now and Forever who assemble soldiers, weapons and ships for dispatch to destinations of destruction and misery.

That message might be futile, but it was the creature's duty to make it known: *I am the guardian of this sector. I was old before your civilization took root in swamp or was created by machine. If you reject peace and insist upon the satisfaction of horror, then prepare you to be satisfied in the horror of your own making.*

Ethan could feel the tracker following them, far above at the atmosphere's edge. Its Cypher eye was fixed directly upon him.

They would be coming soon. They would find their place and time to try to take him...but he knew it would be soon.

And the Gorgons?

They would be coming soon too. What the controllers could not control, they would attempt to contain or destroy.

He was not ending up on the dissection table of any reptile or robot, and neither were the people he knew to be his friends on this endangered planet.

277

I will be—

"Ready," said Ethan.

Nikki asked him what he had said, and he shrugged and explained that he was thinking out loud, and then he smiled at her and squeezed her hand and thought that nothing Cypher or Gorgon was going to harm these creatures that had been hurt so much already. A great battle was ahead...he could feel their forces of destruction massing, for they too would be ready.

The bus went on, westbound in the eastbound lanes, as I-70 steepened toward the gigantic mountains, and the boy with a silver eye now realized he was more alien than human, and so mused upon both the question of destiny and what his mother would think if she could see him now.

TWENTY-FOUR.

LIGHTNING STRUCK SO CLOSE IT FILLED THE BUS WITH DAZZLING blue light, and then the following crash of thunder made Number 712 shiver to its rusted bolts.

"Great night to be out on a drive," said Jefferson Jericho in a hollow voice. No one answered him. Hannah was concentrating on the highway ahead through her viewpane and the others were in their own worlds or else too tensed by this building storm to have any use for talking. Jefferson shrugged; he couldn't do a thing about his circumstances, and he figured he was better off here under Ethan's protection than at the mall. The device at the back of his neck was not filling him up with the flames of agony, he felt he was—for the moment at least—out of *Her* reach, and so what was a little thunderstorm? Still...Hannah was having a tough time, creeping along I-70 at about fifteen miles an hour because of the thickness of this yellow mist they'd run into up here at the high altitude with the jagged mountains all around. Beyond the guardrails were steep dropoffs that could swallow up earthmen and spacekids alike.

"Hey, Ethan!" he called back.

"Yes?" The boy had been mentally observing the Cypher tracker, which continued to pinpoint his location even as the large battlecraft of both sides fought each other at the threshold of space.

279

"This storm natural? Or is it *them*?"

"Natural," Ethan replied. "But their weapons have screwed up the atmosphere. So all storms will be many times amplified in violence."

Amplified in violence, Jefferson thought. That wasn't how a kid talked. That was the alien talking. How did it know English? Reading the boy's mind, he figured. An alien who could come to this world without a spaceship and enter a boy's dead body...that had to be *some* kind of weird. Well, no weirder than *Her*. Or the Ant Farm. Or Microscope Meadows. He had not allowed himself to think much about Burt Ratcoff. He remembered the guy saying *I think they hollowed me out and put somethin' else inside me*. Poor dumb bastard, Jefferson thought. But Ratcoff probably didn't know what hit him and he was out of this nightmare now, so...good for him.

Jefferson scratched his beard. His hands were free. A few hours ago, the conversation between he and Dave was: *Okay, I have to pee. Want me to go ahead and do it here, or can we pull the bus over for a minute?*

Good idea, Hannah had said. *I've gotta go too. Might as well pull over while we can, everybody take a break.*

So, Jefferson had asked Dave, *are you going to cut these things off my wrists or do you want to hold it for me?*

They had stopped at a lookout point with a view to the forest below, and one by one they all saw the wreckage of the crashed United States Air Force fighter jet amid the burned trees.

Jefferson flinched at the next strike of lightning, because it too had been close. Up here in the high mountains, the weather had gone berserk. He'd tried hard not to think too much about Regina or the people at the Ant Farm. There was nothing he could do for them. They might all be dead by now, swept away into space, or left on their unprotected own. Which would be the better fate? He wished he'd had a chance to smooth things with Regina, to make her understand that a special man like himself with special gifts could not be expected to live a normal life, constrained by a society of dumb sheep. No, he had to make his mark and take what he needed when he needed it; that was just how he'd been born, and who could change that? But...it was too late now with Regina. Maybe that day she'd nearly shot him in the back of the head would've been the best, he thought. Wouldn't be here right now, in this bus in a rising storm with a damned itchy beard and an alien boy, heading for God only knew what. He hoped Regina had died quickly. She was all right, she just hadn't recognized that the gifts he'd been given had to be used. He hoped she had died in one quick second of being cast off into airless space, because in his way he had loved her. Whether he could ever come to tears about her passing, he didn't know nor did he care to dwell on it very much longer; after all, if she was dead she—like Burt Ratcoff—was in a hell of a better place and he was still here in this shitmess.

No rainbows here, folks, not even after the hardest rain. Move along… nothing to see.

Sitting a few rows behind Jefferson Jericho, Ethan felt himself drifting away. It was like he was becoming a spectator to his own life. He realized his speech was changing, no way he talked or thought like an earthkid anymore. Maybe he hadn't, really, since all this had started. It was really weird now, though, because he knew the Big Change was happening. There was nothing he could do about it, it was for the best but…the Big Change was death for him, for the boy who'd called himself Ethan Gaines, and when the alien—the *peacekeeper*—had done what it needed to do, Ethan Gaines was finished. As the lightning flashed and the thunder crashed outside the bus, Ethan tried very hard to concentrate on that day at D'Evelyn High School—the third of April, the morning the first sonic booms had announced the coming of the Gorgons—when he had been waiting to take his Visible Man to the front of the class and make his presentation. The details of that had always been hazy; now they were becoming truly clouded, and more and more out of reach. He tried very hard to hold onto that morning and onto the memory of his dark-haired mother looking in on him in his room the night before, but it was all slipping away. His father…was there even a memory of him? The man had been gone a long time, it seemed. There were no memories of fights or shouting or anything that spelled out *divorce*. There was just the feeling that his father had left

281

many years ago, and his mother had not remarried. She had soldiered on and given the boy the best life she could. Who could ask for much more than that?

As the alien's powers strengthened and what had been the personality of a human boy continued to disappear, Ethan found himself trying to hang on, but knowing it was like being very tired and trying to stay awake after a very hard day. Sooner or later, he must give himself fully up to sleep; it would take him, no matter how hard he tried to fight it. And fighting it was not only useless, but wrong. The peacekeeper had a job to do. This body was just a vessel. The peacekeeper had raised him from the dead, had kept him alive so far, but the boy who called himself Ethan Gaines was a small grain of sand in the cosmos. He was a means to an end, and he understood this and accepted it. Not without sadness, though; he was still human enough to feel that, and he knew he would miss life no matter what it had become.

The alien presence within him gave him strange benefits. Not only could he clearly envision the Cypher tracker and sense the heat of its eye directed on him, or know how close or far away the Gorgon and Cypher armies and ships were, but he could feel the huddled humanity in a few of the small towns they'd passed, nestled up within the mountains on roads off I-70. He could see rooftops and a church steeple or two, and just in a matter of seconds he could know there were humans hiding there, always in some central location where community meant survival and isolation was death. The peacekeeper had great respect for these humans, who had held out so much longer than they should have against such overwhelming odds. The peacekeeper would have liked to have stopped and made sure these ragged and weary humans had enough food and water, but the larger picture was what needed attention. And Ethan was aware that there was a time factor involved...a need to get to the White Mansion as quickly as possible, though maybe even the peacekeeper itself did not fully understand why.

Most of the small towns they'd passed, and which could be seen from the interstate, felt to Ethan cold and lifeless. To him they gave off the rusted iron smell of violence, of human turned against human in the battle for food and shelter. Or they gave off the rotting flesh smell of Gray Men, hiding in the basements and in the dark damp places.

Beside Ethan, Nikki shifted uneasily in her seat in the aftermath of another close lightning strike. She couldn't see anything out there, darkness had claimed the world. Her hand found Ethan's again. She had been very afraid of him at one time, and so close to telling Olivia that she thought he should be put off the bus and left behind. Now she felt ashamed of that. She'd been so afraid that he was a Gorgon or a Cypher in disguise, and now she understood he was a human boy but not really, that he'd *been* a human boy, and he was now working for another alien who was trying to stop the war, but this was all so beyond her it spun her head. It was like looking up at the stars and trying to imagine how big the universe was. She longed for the simplicity of planning her next tattoo, hitting the Bowl-A-Rama on Saturday nights, flirting with hot guys, and sneaking a beer or a joint with her friends Kelly and Rita and Charmaine who were all probably very much dead. Or worse.

She missed her family. Who'd have ever thunk she would miss her mother's sharp-edged voice getting after her for whatever reason and her father in his recliner with a beer in his hand and his eyes glued to the football game on the fifty-two-inch flatscreen? Or her older sister's snitty ways of getting her in trouble with the Duke and Duchess of Denial, as they called their parents. But she missed them, because they were her blood and now they were all gone and nobody—*nobody*—deserved to die like that.

"No, they don't," said Ethan quietly, and Nikki did not answer. At first she thought she must've spoken aloud but then she realized she had not, and how long he'd been reading her mind she didn't know but now she—

"Not long," he told her. "Don't worry, I'm not in there all the time. It just happens."

She pulled her hand away and he let her. He understood. The mind was a sacred place, it should not be spied upon but it was one of the least of the peacekeeper's powers. *That's why you live alone,* he told the entity. *You scared everybody else away.*

And the answer came back to him, in his own voice but different, a little more adult, sadder and darker in that way: *I wish it were so simple as that.*

Rain suddenly began to pelt down. It was not a shower, it was a deluge.

Hannah turned the wiper on and found that the Army meant well but this was not their specialty. The motor sounded like a man moaning with a toothache and the wiper's action couldn't keep the glass clear. "I can't see a damned thing!" she growled. "We're gonna have to stop and wait it out!"

No one tried to second guess Hannah, who put on the brakes and eased the bus to a halt. She cut the engine, noting that with the bus's extra weight and the inclines they'd been climbing, they were getting about six miles to a gallon. "Light us up a couple of lamps, somebody," she said. "No need to run the battery down."

Dave got up, went to the back of the bus where some oil lamps were stored in a box, and used his Bic to light two of them. He brought them up front and set them where the glow would be a comfort, and Hannah turned off the interior safety lights. Rain was hammering down on the roof, a noise that further tested the nerves. Dave returned to his seat and stretched his legs out in the aisle. "I figure we're about seventy or so miles from the turnoff to Highway 191." That was the road in Utah that would take them south to the White Mansion. From I-70, the distance to their destination was about one hundred miles. "That what you figure?"

"Near it," said Hannah. She stood up and stretched her back. "We'll need to fuel up again real soon."

"Right." Dave had had no illusions that they'd be able to get to the White Mansion on a full tank of fifty gallons. "We're about a quarter tank now?"

"Little less."

"Okay." Dave looked out the window nearest him and saw only rainswept darkness; they were vulnerable here to whatever might be lurking in the night, but in this downpour they couldn't move. "You all right?" he asked Olivia.

"I've been better. But…yes, I'm all right."

"JayDee? How you holding up?"

John Douglas had known Dave was going to ask him this, and the truth was that he was not holding up well at all. His bones ached. His joints seemed to be on fire. It had begun early this morning as little jabs of knife-like pain here and there and had gotten worse through the day. He'd tried to let it go as his age or being worn out or whatever…but he was afraid it was much more than that. Pain was shooting up his right leg, and it was more than the sprained ankle. He said, "I don't think I'm doing so well. Would you bring one of those lamps a little closer?"

Dave did. JayDee caught Ethan watching him, and he thought *the boy knows. Just as I know, because I've seen it happen.* JayDee pulled up his pants leg to check his injured ankle.

There on the thin calf of his leg was a splotch of gray. It was about eight inches in length and four in width. It was upraised just a bit, like a keloid scar.

No one said anything.

JayDee stood up. "I'm going to take off my shirt," he said in a calm and quiet voice though his heart was pounding. "Let's check my chest and back."

His chest was clear. But when he turned around to let Olivia and Dave check his back he knew because he heard her catch her breath.

"Is it just one or many?" he asked.

It was a moment before anyone answered. Then Dave said, "Just one."

"How large?"

"I guess…twelve or thirteen inches across. About ten inches long. Almost right between your shoulder blades."

JayDee made a noise—a mumble of assent, a grunt, a muffled curse. Even he didn't know exactly what it was. The rain was a torrent and a torment. He felt light-headed but was keenly aware of all the pricklings of pain in his body. "I don't think there's any need to take my pants off," he said, trying for some levity that did not lift off. He put his shirt back on, buttoned it with hands that were remarkably steady, and tucked the shirttail neatly into his pants. He said, "Thank you, Dave. You can put the lamp down now."

"What is it?" Jefferson asked, his voice tense. "What's that thing on his back?"

"Shut up," Dave told him. "Nobody said you could talk."

"Yeah, well...I think I have a right to—"

"I said SHUT THE FUCK UP!" Dave roared, and was on Jefferson Jericho before anyone could stop him. Both Olivia and Hannah tried to get in the way, but Dave had hold of the man's dirty brown t-shirt and was shaking him like a mad dog with a bloody bone. For a moment it looked as if Dave might smash him in the face with the oil lamp he was holding. "Shut up shut up shut up!" Dave shouted, and Jefferson cringed down in his seat because he thought the guy had gone crazy, and both the women were pulling at Dave and over the noise of Dave's shouting and the rainfall crashing down JayDee said, "It's not his fault. It's not anyone's fault. Let him go, Dave. Come on, let him go."

Dave did not, though he stopped making the brain rattle in Jefferson's skull.

"Let him go," JayDee repeated, and this time it was spoken with a grim finality that made Dave remove his hand from the other man's shirt and step back.

"*Why?*" Dave asked. It was not a question directed to anyone on the bus, for no one could answer it. It was directed to God, or Fate, or whatever threw the dice in this insane game of Life. Ethan had seen the gray patches on JayDee's leg and back as clearly as anyone else, and he knew what that meant. It looked as if the blood had stopped circulating on those places and the flesh had begun to die. A new Gray Man was about to be born; this was just the beginning of the changes.

"*Well,*" said JayDee, and he couldn't look at anyone so he stared at the floor. He gave a quiet sigh of resignation. "My friends...I don't think I'll be finishing this trip with you."

"*Do something.*"

Dave had fired this command at Ethan, who stared blankly at him not knowing how to respond. "Yes," Dave said. "*You.* Master of the Universe or whatever the fuck you are." Dave's eyes were black and his mouth twisted with helpless anger. "Heal him. Fix him. Whatever. Don't let him be one of *them*."

All attention was concentrated on Ethan, who felt their nearly overwhelming pain. John Douglas was more than a friend to Dave, Olivia, Hannah and Nikki; he was as dear to them as the loved ones they had lost. He had been a journeyer with them over this landscape of despair, and he had been there when they needed him. They could not bear this moment, it crushed their hearts because they did love him, and they knew…they knew…

"He can't fix this," said JayDee, who lifted his gaze to Dave. "Don't put that on him."

"He's from *outer space*," came the answer, as if it was really an answer. "If he can make earthquakes and kill monsters with his mind…he can heal you. Can't you, Ethan?" The last three words had left the sound of begging in the bus, which might have been the supreme gesture from a man with the stony countenance of Dave McKane.

And Ethan's answer, the answer he was given when he asked himself if he could do this, was *No, you cannot*. He didn't have to speak it out loud, though, because John Douglas spoke it for him. "He can't do that, Dave. God…I wish he could. But if he *could* do that…he would've helped those three people I had to…" He stopped for a moment, steadying himself. Rain thrashed the bus and lightning streaked amid the mountains. "I had to leave behind," the doctor finished. "Don't ask him about this anymore. It's not what he's here to do."

Dave started to protest, to keep going like a bull the only way he knew how to go, but he looked back and forth to Ethan and JayDee and he saw that, no, the alien could do things that were miraculous, could come to this planet on a beam of light or through the door of a different dimension, could raise an earth boy from the dead or from near-death and keep him breathing and powered like a puppet on galactic strings for the task it had to carry out, could sense fresh water and cause the earth to quake and do other things that were so far beyond the human kind it made all the technological advances and scientific miracles of this planet seem pathethic and childlike in contrast, but—no—the alien could not save Dr.

John Douglas from becoming a Gray Man, and *don't ask him about this anymore*, said the doomed man, *because it's not what he's here to—*

"I want you to try," Dave said to Ethan. "I'm telling you to try. Heal him. Don't let him turn into one of those things."

Ethan didn't know what to say to this, so suddenly the peacekeeper spoke.

It was his voice, but different in its inflections and its knowledge, and Ethan was made an observer to the moment.

"I'm not sure how you become infected with this, but the doctor is right. Once it...takes hold, let's say...there's no stopping it. Or healing that can be done."

"What...you can destroy life, but you can't create it?" Dave was fully aware who he was speaking to now, and he gave the creature both barrels. "You're in the body of a dead boy! You raised it up, didn't you?"

"He was almost dead," said the peacekeeper. "His will to live, his youth, and strength of mind suited my purpose."

"Okay, whatever. Are you like a spirit or something? Is that it?"

"I am an entity you wouldn't comprehend. I needed flesh to work with, and I took the opportunity. I knew that our destination was close. More than that would be damaging to your mind to hear, because it's beyond your limits."

"I'll second that," said JayDee. "I figure we're not very intelligent as a species, compared to you."

"Olivia is also right," came the reply. "I don't know everything and I am not infallible. I know something of importance is on this mountain...*in* the mountain, actually, but I'm not sure what it is, and I'm not sure why it's so vital. But it is, and that's what I know."

"*In* the mountain?" Jefferson asked. "What does that mean?"

"Exactly what I say. It's something inside the mountain. It will only be revealed when we get there." The peacekeeper turned one blue eye and one silver eye upon John Douglas, and said with a depth of sadness, "I'm sorry, JayDee. I can't stop what's going to happen to you."

The doctor nodded. Thunder rumbled so heavily the bus vibrated with the bass boom of it. Rain was still thrashing against the roof and the windows. JayDee knew from seeing the progress of this—and he was aware that Dave and Olivia also knew—that by tomorrow morning he would be in agonizing pain as the changes in his bones and bodily structure progressed. Then the changes would speed up, as if the humanity had been conquered and the disease was in a rush of victory to distort the body into an alien horror show. Two or three days at most, and those spent in increasing torment. JayDee recalled watching the transformation happen to the first person at Panther Ridge, the twelve-year-old girl whose father had shot her when she began to grow a second head. He was having none of that. It was time to take a walk in the rain.

"Damn it," he said quietly. He had been through so much—they all had, of course—and he felt cheated at this last moment, of not being able to witness what the White Mansion held for the peacekeeper. He could hang on, maybe, as he lost his human structure, but it seemed to him that now he ought to get off this bus and go find Deborah while he could still walk like a man. *Limp* like a man, that is.

He said, "I'll trade you the Beretta for one of those grenades in the bag."

"You don't have to do anything right now," Olivia said. "No, JayDee. *Please.* Not right now."

"Hush," he told her, but gently. "I'm not sure there's ever a good time for this. But...my God...I took the lives of those three people back at Panther Ridge because there was nothing else I could do for them. I made the decision for them...now I need to make it for myself."

"Please," Olivia repeated, though she knew there was nothing else to say.

"Christ on a cracker!" said Hannah. "Why don't you at least wait until the rain stops, you old fool?"

JayDee had to smile at that and give a crippled little laugh. He was aware of the pain beginning to lance through his nerves and muscles. He recalled that the little girl had been unable to stand up after the first day, but he'd wanted to observe what was happening to her in a safe place and her father had agreed. They'd chained her up in the Secure Room and he had made notes as the changes progressed. Which seemed terribly cruel and medieval both then and now, but it had been important to give him a reference as to how these fractures and rearrangments of bones and growth of new and strange flesh happened.

He was aware also of fiery sensations and stitches of sharp pain on his back, on his left calf, and at the back of his left thigh. The gray tissue there was growing, leeching deep.

"Let me have a grenade," he said.

"What if I say no?"

"I'd answer that I'd do it with the gun, but you may need it and the grenade will do the job just fine. Also that…" He felt something close to breaking inside him—maybe his heart, but that had been broken so many times it must look like a specimen from Frankenstein's lab. He had to wait a moment to compose himself with decorum. "Also," he went on, "that I want to go out remembering all of you, and remembering who *I* am. I don't know when my memory would start going, or what my thought processes would be. I don't know what this does to the brain. It may be that when the changes really begin, the disease removes all thought but that of animal survival…so one of you would have to kill me, just as we've had to kill the others. Which one of you would do that very necessary job?"

"If you say one word," Dave told Jefferson, "I swear to God I will kill you and drag your body out on the road."

"I'm not saying anything! Did you hear me speak?"

Dave ignored him. "I'll do it when the time comes," he told JayDee. "The time is not now."

"Maybe it would be tomorrow, then?" JayDee gave up a sad smile. In the lamplight, he thought his old skinny, wan and worn-out self must already appear to be a ghost. "After eight o'clock and before noon?" He nodded toward the peacekeeper. "He'll get you where you're going, God willing. I'm getting off the bus *here*."

"Jesus," said Dave, but he could say nothing more.

"Give me a grenade. Dave, do I have to say *please*?"

Dave hesitated, but he knew the exchange had to be made. It was a mercy, really. The Beretta was given for the grenade. JayDee inspected it, making sure it was as simple a procedure as he hoped it would be. The rain was still falling hard; it was a hard rain everywhere these days.

"I'll walk with you," Dave said.

"No, you won't. There's no use in both of us getting out there."

"I will walk with you."

The peacekeeper had spoken in a voice that was decisive.

"All right," JayDee answered after a short pause of thought. Maybe it wouldn't do to be jumped by anything out in the dark before he could pull that pin. "Just a little ways, though. No need to drag this out."

Olivia had begun to weep. She put her arms around John Douglas and he hugged her, and he told her to stop crying, but she couldn't stop, and he told her that he was proud to have known her and proud to have known Dave and Hannah and Nikki too, and that she and Dave had been right about Ethan and good thing they hadn't listened to his scientific objections, because all this was far beyond any science he'd ever learned in school. And now, if the alien within the body of Ethan could stop this war, it would be a second chance for Earth given from the stars or from a realm unknown to the human mind. *So be it,* said JayDee. He reached out to shake Dave's hand, but Dave pulled him in and hugged him too, and Hannah and Nikki said their goodbyes, both tearfully, as Jefferson Jericho watched from his seat and figured one word from him would be his death sentence because the rock was ready to roll over him.

Then the peacekeeper was there at JayDee's side with a flashlight, and the boy who had been known as Ethan was looking out as if through a window edged with fog. He had had a moment of being afraid, as the alien took him over, but now…it was not fear he felt, but peace.

He remembered his mother's name. It was Nancy, otherwise known as Nan. And his own name?

He had a memory of the science class at D'Evelyn High School on that third day of April, just before a shaken Mrs. Bergeson from the office had come to Mr. Novotny's room to tell him that the "kids," as she put it, were going to be leaving school early. *Something is happening,* she'd told Mr. Novotny. *It's on all the news, everywhere. Something is happening, and the kids will be leaving school early.*

Which interrupted his demonstration of the Visible Man right as he was talking about the brain, and it pissed him off mightily but it scared him too, because Mrs. Bergeson's voice was trembling, and she looked very afraid.

"I'll open the door myself," JayDee told Hannah, and he did. Then he looked with watery eyes at the others and he said, "What we've been through...this is a walk in the park. Good luck and God bless and keep you." He gave them a tough old smile. "You are all my heroes," he said, and then he went down the steps on his rebar cane into the force of the driving downpour. The peacekeeper followed just behind him, directing the light so JayDee could see his way.

Somewhere on their walk into the turbulent darkness on the strip of I-70 that no car had traveled in a very long time, the boy who had called himself Ethan Gaines went off upon his own journey. It was a journey, like the one JayDee was about to take, that no human expected to return from. It was a voyage into mystery, but the peacekeeper told Ethan he was going to be all right, and there was nothing for him to fear anymore, nothing at all.

I thank you for your help, the entity told him. *You are a creature of strength and honor. There is a place where heroes rest, after their battles are done. Both you and the doctor will find comfort and peace there. I promise you.*

I'm okay, said the boy. *I'm a little afraid, but I'm okay.*

I am going to set you free now. What remains to be done, I have to do in full command of this form. Do you understand?

I do. But...don't I ever get to know about the White Mansion?

You'll know, the entity replied. *Both of you will. Again...my promise.*

The boy started to reply, to say he knew the promise would be kept, but at the same time, he knew he didn't have to say it...and then he went to sleep, just like in a warm bed on a cold winter's night, and knowing that when he awakened there would be someone there to love you and say good morning to the bright new day.

"I guess this is as far as I need to go," said the doctor, loudly against the storm.

"Yes."

"I wish I could know what you really are. What you *look* like, inside there."

"You would be surprised," said the entity.

"Will we be okay?" JayDee asked, steadying himself as the rain beat down. "Will we survive this?"

"That's my hope," was the answer.

"Mine too," said JayDee. "Protect them if you can."

"I can."

"Goodbye, then. Let me do this and get it over with before I drown."

The boy's hand clutched JayDee's arm for a moment as a reassurance.

"You have earned my greatest respect," said the peacekeeper. "Goodbye, my friend." Then there was nothing else to be said, and he turned and walked away.

JayDee stood strong, holding his balance against the forces that raged around him. He thought of Deborah, and their beautiful life together before all this had happened. He hoped that someway, somehow, they could pick up where they'd been interrupted.

He dropped the rebar. It made a clanging noise against the concrete that sounded to him like a church bell in the town of his childhood.

He held the grenade against his heart.

He took in a last breath of rain-thick air, of the earth that he was leaving.

The border, he thought. And was relieved, finally, to be about to cross another border to what he was certain beyond a doubt would be a better place than this.

JayDee pulled the pin.

TWENTY-FIVE.

THEY HEARD THE EXPLOSION AND SAW THE FLASH ABOUT A HUNDRED yards away.

Olivia had returned to her seat. She put her hands to her face and lowered her head, and she mourned John Douglas in agonized silence.

Hannah opened the door. Dripping wet, the alien in the form of a boy came up the steps, his head also lowered. Hannah closed the door behind him. When the creature looked at her she saw, as Dave and Jefferson and Nikki did by the lamplight and the flashlight's reflected glare, that both his eyes now glinted silver. The face of the earth boy was grim, something about it more gaunt yet more resolute.

"I want to know this," Dave said. "What do we call you?"

The alien replied, "Ethan. What else?"

"But you're not him anymore, are you? Is he gone?"

"Yes."

Olivia looked up then and saw his eyes, and she returned to her posture of silent bereavement. Ethan switched off the flashlight to save the batteries and started toward his seat.

"Your chest," Dave said, before Ethan could sit down. "Let's see it." He held a lamp up to take a look as Ethan lifted his t-shirt, and there against the dark-bruised flesh the upraised silver letters just above his heart were ᚷᚢᚾᚱᛗᛁᚾᛏ. It seemed to be finished, for no other letters were beginning to emerge from the depths. "What does that mean?" Dave asked.

"My designation," Ethan said. "I *am* a soldier."

"What are you? Like...special forces from outer space or something?" Jefferson asked, risking a fist to the teeth.

"Something like that," Ethan answered. He noted that the rain was beginning to ease up; he noted also a new sensation, which to him was the shimmer of an image in his mind. "We're being followed."

"Yeah," said Dave. "The Cyphers."

"Your name for them. Their species name is based on mathematics of a nature unknown to you. No...this is what you call the Gorgons."

"Following us?" That had set Jefferson's heart pounding like a ten-ton drum. "How close are they?"

"At a safe distance yet. It's a warship. Its tracker is focused on the device implanted in the back of your neck, Mr. Jericho."

"Shit!" Dave exploded. He reached out to grab Jefferson's shirt, but this time the preacherman got his hands up to ward off the punishment. Dave slapped them aside, bringing a cry of pain from Jefferson as two broken fingers took the impact. He took hold of the man's bearded chin. "You didn't tell us about that? Why not? Because you're still spying for them?"

"He's no longer a spy," Ethan said calmly. "The device was implanted when he was first taken. They were collecting humans as subjects for experiments."

"Yeah, I know all about those damned *experiments.*"

"For whatever reason," Ethan went on, "the Gorgon queen found our Jefferson very interesting." He knew the reason; it had to do with a curiosity about human anatomy and he didn't care to go there. "He was spared being turned into a weapon, but a control and monitoring device was implanted. It's likely small, the size of a pinhead in your experience, but it is powerful. He had no idea how else it could be used, except for giving him pain when he was disobedient."

"Listen to him...listen to him," Jefferson pleaded.

"Can we find a knife somewhere and let me cut it out of the bastard?"

"I don't think you'd ever locate it. If you...got lucky, I think is the expression?—touching it would probably cause instant death for both of you."

"You sure we need him? I swear I'd as soon take him out and shoot him."

"Let him go, Dave," Ethan said. "Whatever he *was*...he's on our side now."

"I always was. I swear, I—"

"Shut your hole," Dave told him, and he was tempted to loosen the preacherman's remaining teeth, but he released his grip and stepped back. "So what do we do?" he asked Ethan.

"We go on when we can. I believe the Gorgons are curious about where we're going. The queen probably would like to know, because she must understand we wouldn't be out in the open unless it was vital. And we have to find fuel soon, I think." Ethan put his hand on Olivia's shoulder, and when she looked into the strange silver eyes she saw not the coldness of space there, but the warmth of compassion. "I'm truly sorry about JayDee, and I'm sorry I couldn't help. It was what he wanted and needed to do, whether we agreed with it or not. We have to go on as soon as we're able."

"You mean when I can see shit through this glass," said Hannah. At least she had two headlights now, though the right one burned dimmer than the left.

"Yes, when you can see shit," Ethan replied. He went along the aisle to the seat he'd left, but before he got there Nikki stood up. She was afraid of him now, really afraid, because she understood he was not the Ethan who had left the bus with John Douglas. She knew he wouldn't hurt her—he saw that clearly—but still, there was the strangeness about him that she could not quite manage to handle anymore.

There was a tear in her eye.

"You took him away," she said, "and you didn't even let him say goodbye."

"It was time," he explained in a quiet voice. He watched the tear roll down her cheek to her chin, and the beating heart within him that kept the blood flowing and all the systems in operation felt heavy with grief, that this girl had held onto the human Ethan as long as she could and now she knew she had to let go. She had lost so much already. The images in her mind were horrific and tragic. He touched there only briefly and lightly, and then drew away, because his duty was clear.

"He understood that I'm ready," said the new Ethan.

"I don't. I never will. It was cruel not to let him live."

How could he make her see that without his power, the human Ethan would've been dead long ago? That this thing of great cosmic importance—call it cruelty, yes—must be done to bring the end of a war, and for a race to survive?

He couldn't. "From this point on I've got to be in total charge of the body and mind. The reflexes, the nervous system…everything. I can't share those with him, Nikki."

"Don't speak my name." She recoiled from him, even standing still. "You creep me out."

There was no possible reply to that. It was the plain truth, plainly and truthfully spoken.

"I'm going to sit over there," Nikki told him, and she turned away with what might be a shudder and went to sit directly behind Dave.

Ethan returned to his seat. Through his window, he saw that the rain was stopping. The storm had passed, but there would be others.

Hannah started the engine, turned on the headlights, and tried the wiper. The motor still made an ugly sound, but the blade was keeping the glass inset clear. She doubted it was going to hold up very long scraping across all that metal. "I guess we can move on. Everybody ready?"

No one answered.

"Giddyup," said Hannah, speaking to herself in a raspy whisper. At a slow crawl, she put distance between themselves and the body that lay over on the westbound lanes.

They had to find a gas station, and soon. The good thing about the interstate was that, even crossing the Rockies, there were many exits and many gas stations with diesel for the long-haul truckers. It wasn't but about another twenty minutes before the headlights made out an exit— an entrance ramp, really, since they were still traveling in the eastbound lanes—and when Hannah asked Dave if he wanted to try there he said, "Yeah, go ahead."

Hannah pulled the bus into a truck stop. There were still some abandoned rigs and cars in the lot, and who knew what had happened to their owners? It didn't take long for Dave's flashlight to find that both of the stop's diesel tanks had already been uncapped and emptied, so Hannah went on down the road to a Shell station. Again, the diesel tank had been drained. Dave recovered his hose and came back into the bus, and told Hannah to drive on.

On the other side of the interstate was a Phillips 66 station. Beyond it the headlights picked out the shapes of a few small houses in a little community, all dark. Ethan smelled the foul, sickly-sweet odors of rot and pestilence coming from one of the houses. It was something the others could not detect. "There are Gray Men here," he said.

"Don't stop, for God's sake!" said Jefferson, his eyes wide. "Let's get the hell out!"

"We're needy, gents," Hannah said. "Gas gauge is lookin' sorrowful. What do you want to do, Dave?"

"*Damn*," he answered. Hannah had pulled the bus to a halt under the station's roof that overhung the two diesel pumps. Dave felt the flesh at the back of his neck crawl; he had no doubt that if the alien said there were Gray Men here, it was a fact. "How many?"

"I can't tell. More than one, for sure."

"Jesus!" said the preacherman. "Why are we still here?"

"Your call, Dave," said Hannah. "We're burnin' fuel, just sittin' still."

"We shouldn't stay," Nikki said. Her voice quavered. "Really. We need to get out."

"Olivia?" Dave prompted. "What do you think?"

She shook her head, her face still drawn and downcast. "I don't know. I'm not thinking so well right now, but if we're stuck without gas further on...it'll be bad."

"Right." Dave was loading a fresh clip into his Uzi. His hand shook a little, but not too much. It had to be done. "I'm going to check first to see if the tank's empty or not. Ethan, will you come with me? I may need some protection."

"Yes."

"You're *crazy!*" The shine of fear sweat was already on Jefferson's face. "Those things will *smell* us! It'll be like the dinner bell ringing!"

"Just sit tight." Dave slid the loaded Uzi into its holster. "Back in a minute." Dave and Ethan took both flashlights out. Rainwater dripped from the roof, which slanted precariously to one side. It didn't take but fifteen seconds for their lights to fall upon the yellow cap of the underground diesel tank. It was still in place and looked to have been undisturbed.

"Cut the engine," Dave told Hannah when he and Ethan returned to the bus. "Jericho, I need your help."

"Not me, I'm not getting out there! I've got two broken fingers, thanks to you!"

"Listen up! The faster we get this done, the better! We don't have to fill the tank. Just get us enough to make it further along. Come on now, put your balls on."

"No way!"

"Hell, if he won't help you I will!" Hannah got up from behind the wheel. She already had her hogleg Colt in hand. "What do you need me to do, Dave?"

"I need you to stay right here and take a break. You're the driver, not the mule. Jefferson, get your mule-ass off that seat!"

"I'll do what needs to be done," said Ethan. He already knew. Dave needed somebody to cover him while he did the work of popping open the fill cap on the tank and using the hose and hand pump to bring fuel up into the containers. He just needed Jericho as the mule to help carry the stuff out there.

"Here." Dave loaded the Beretta and held it out to Jefferson. "Can you use one of these without shooting your pecker off?"

"God forbid," said the preacherman. He stood up, took the pistol with his left hand and hefted it to get used to the weight. "Yeah, I can handle this." Then he aimed the gun directly at Dave's chest. "You know, I don't like being treated like dirt."

"Lower your weapon," Ethan said, his voice quiet but sternly persuasive.

"Can you stop a bullet from this distance?" Jefferson asked him. "I'd like to see that trick."

"You're not going to shoot me." Dave turned his flashlight right into Jefferson's eyes. "Number one, Hannah would take you down in about half a second, because she's already got her gun pointed at you. Number two, you don't have a damned place to go and I really don't think you want to stay here. And…number three, we're the only friends you've got right now. So Mr. Jefferson Jericho the TV star, I'd say you ought to do as Ethan says. We've got to put gas in this bus, and we've got to do it fast. You're wasting time. Now come on, let's get the gear." Dave started walking toward the rear of the bus.

"*Please*," said Olivia, who looked to Ethan to be in a state of numbed shock. "Just do what he asks, all right?"

Jefferson hesitated for a few seconds. He glanced at Ethan and then lowered the pistol, which was aimed at empty air where Dave had been standing. "All right," he told Olivia, in a voice that was partly forlorn and partly belligerent. "Because you asked me *nicely*." He found the Beretta's safety, thumbed it on and slid the gun into the waistband of his dirty and pee-stained jeans.

They got the containers, the hose, and the hand pump out, and Dave used the prybar to crack open the tank's fill cap. While Dave cranked up diesel into one of the containers, Jefferson nervously watched the darkness where the houses lay, and Ethan stood nearby, his senses probing for any movement beyond. He was satisfied he could protect everyone from the Gray Men if need be; the question for him was, what could this physical body withstand? The heartbeat was good and the lungs were working, everything was all right for the moment, but Ethan knew that this body was not built for the strain of such combat even though the energy was only mental until it left the body, and then became a physical force on its way to a target. "You see anything?" Jefferson asked, as Dave continued to draw the fuel up.

"Nothing. Relax. I'll let you know if something's coming."

"*Relax*, he says. Right!" Jefferson had his pistol out and aimed toward the houses. "How'd you get here without a spaceship? Did you ride in on a beam of light or something?"

"A close proximation," Ethan answered. "There are dimensions you can't comprehend and methods of traveling that are also beyond you."

"Forgive us for being so backward and stupid."

"It's not that. It's just that you're a very young civilization. You're focused on issues that speak to your youth. You couldn't be expected to understand these things for...oh...a few hundred more years."

"If we last that long," said Jefferson.

"Yes," Ethan agreed. "Very true."

"Jericho, help me get this gas in the tank!" Dave said, and the preacherman left Ethan's side to oblige.

Ethan scanned the darkness, left to right and back again. He could smell the foulness of the Gray Men, he knew they were in those houses, but how many, he couldn't say.

"Hold it steady, don't spill it!" Dave told Jefferson.

Suddenly Ethan felt them in a prickling of the boy's flesh and maybe what was an electric charge up the spine.

It was a strange movement in the dark. Low to the ground. Not moving as a human being would. He picked out three shapes, running fast toward them. There was a glint of wet eyes that his flashlight caught... again, low to the ground.

They were very hungry.

"They're coming," he said, facing the attack. "Three. Not human-sized, though."

"What are they?" Jefferson asked, and as he tried to turn around he caused fuel to be spilled from the container down the side of the bus.

"Careful, damn it!" Dave said.

The shapes were almost upon them, but they were avoiding the cone of Ethan's light. They were circling around to attack from another angle.

"They're dogs," said Ethan. "What used to be, I mean."

Jefferson tried to draw his gun. Dave commanded, "Keep your mind on this!"

Ethan followed the arc of their movement. Three dogs, somebody's pets. Two were faster than the third, which seemed to be heavier and bulkier, likely burdened under plate armor. Ethan imagined that over the span of two years, humans in that community might have become Gray Men too, and the animals had eaten them and probably any other dogs there. In a matter of time, they would probably turn on each other. Ethan jabbed his light in the direction from which they were coming, and they veered away from contact with it. Again the wet eyes glistened...five of them. The third creature had not yet caught up with the first two.

"Let's go, let's go!" Jefferson urged, but the fuel into the tank would not be hurried.

"We need to draw up some more," Dave said. "Ethan, you got an eye on those things?"

"I'm watching them. Right now they're afraid of the light." Jefferson drew his pistol, thumbed the safety off and fired two shots in the direction Ethan's flashlight was aimed. A bullet ricocheted off concrete but there were no animal cries of pain.

"Let's move, the faster the better," Dave urged, and Ethan went with them back to the opening of the underground tank while more fuel was siphoned up.

The things began to growl, out just beyond the edge of the light. They'd been joined now by the third dog. Ethan couldn't see the bodies but he saw the shine of seven eyes. The growling was low and ragged, more like the sounds of cement mixers in action. Whatever kind of dogs they were, they were big.

"Come on, man!" Jefferson said, but Dave was doing the best he could. Another five gallons in each of the two containers and then in the bus's tank, and they'd be done.

Hannah came off the bus with her hogleg. She saw what the situation was and positioned herself beside Ethan, aiming her Colt toward the ominous noise of mutated beasts ravenous for fresh meat.

A shape ran through the light. It was gray and hairless and looked to have a row of spines protruding along its backbone. A second distorted and hairless gray shape came darting in, its teeth bared and drooling saliva. Its three eyes glinted red. Before Hannah could get off a shot, it turned back and sped away.

"I think that thing had two mouths," Hannah said, visibly shaken.

"It did," Ethan answered.

"Hurry it up, gents," Hannah advised quietly, as she held the Colt steady with both veiny hands.

The creatures were coming in from another direction. Ethan swivelled around to use his light as a weapon, but something was there at the edge of illumination even as he aimed the flashlight. It was the third beast, what might have been an Alaskan Husky at one time, now gray and hairless and wrinkled, its back and sides covered with interlocking scales of plate armor. The creature's face had distorted, the jaw underslung and showing rows of sharklike teeth, the eyes not exactly what they should have been, and an extra two legs growing from the armor of its left flank. As the thing rushed in toward Ethan and Hannah, its extra legs also moved as if in a dream of running.

Hannah made a choking noise and fired twice, the Colt spitting flame. One bullet whined off the concrete and the second went to parts unknown, and the creature was right there upon them, its underslung jaw opening and the teeth sliding out to take hold of Hannah's leg.

Ethan thrust his right hand forward. All the alien had to do was visualize the force necessary, and it was delivered. There was a heated shimmer of air between his palm and the mutated dog, and in the next instant the beast was hurled backward head over scabrous tail and into the darkness again.

"Thank you," Hannah managed to say.

"I think you should go back inside," Ethan told her, and she went.

As Dave was getting the second five-gallon container full, Jefferson poured gas from the first container into the bus's tank. Some spilled, but not much; Jefferson was fixed on the task as single-mindedly as he could be with the monsters—silent now in their hunger—roaming the dark.

Another one darted in, coming at Dave. This one was smaller but had the row of spines along its back. Its teeth snapped at the air in anticipation of a feast. Ethan extended his arm, saw the creature hurtling backward and it was done. He envisioned the beast blowing apart in midair; it was done so quickly, with a burst of energy from the alien's reserve of power, that the animal likely had no time to register pain. The pieces fell upon the concrete beyond the pumps, and the other two creatures fought each other for the scraps.

"Okay, last five gallons," Dave said, bringing the container. "Jericho, get the gear and put it aboard."

There was no argument.

The last of the gas went into the tank. Dave, Jefferson and Ethan went aboard the bus, the door was closed and the gear was stowed away at the back.

"Let's go," Dave said. He pulled his Uzi from its holster and pointed it at Jefferson's belly. "Hand the gun over."

"Okay, okay, take it easy." He gave the Beretta up without complaint, and Dave took a seat beside Olivia. Ethan heard Nikki let out the breath she'd caught.

Hannah had never been so glad to start an engine. The gas gauge did not show Full, but it was enough to make another hundred and forty miles, God willing.

She switched on the headlights and started pulling out, back toward I-70. Before they could get out of the station one of the Gray Dogs—the largest one, Ethan figured—threw itself at the side of the bus in a frenzy. There was a *whump* that shook everyone, but then Hannah was picking up speed and they were on their way again.

Jefferson Jericho came back along the aisle toward Ethan.

"Where do you think you're going?" Dave stood up to block his way. "Get in your seat."

"I'd like to speak to Ethan."

"Get in your seat," Dave repeated.

"I'm not going to hurt—"

"I won't tell you again." A hand went to the Uzi's grip.

"It's all right," Ethan spoke up. "He just wants to ask me a few questions."

"I don't want him near you," Dave said firmly.

"I can ask you from here," Jefferson decided. "But maybe you already know what I want to ask?"

"I do." It was simple now to read their minds, a matter of seconds. "Dave, he wants to know about my power. Where it comes from and how I control it. Jefferson has a keen interest in power."

"Damn straight I do," Jefferson said. "And that's exactly what I want to know. How do you do that?"

"Directed energy," Ethan answered. "I can modulate the intensity. The human hand is an efficient director of energy. It's a good aiming device. Both hands, in fact. I am a being of what you would think of as concentrated energy. I can inhabit various forms as need be. If I give a desire enough focus, it's done. The earthquake was difficult. The boy had to be convinced that he could do it, but I wasn't ready yet to take full control of the organism. Neither was he ready. So I led him along as best I could, and as gently as I could."

"*Organism*," Dave repeated, with a shade of bitterness. It was weird to be hearing these words come out of the mouth of what appeared to be a fifteen-year-old. "You make that sound so clinical. He was a human boy and a good person. He didn't ask for this."

"Should I regret my choice?" Ethan asked, and let the question hang.

"No," Olivia replied. Her voice was still soft and sad. "It seems so unfair, after all he went through, to throw him aside."

"As I told Nikki, there's no room for him here. He knew eventually I was going to have to take everything. He suited my purpose, and he did what I asked of him."

"Organism," Dave said again, like something nasty was caught in his mouth. "We're a hell of a lot more than bodies for the taking."

"I know you are, but sacrifice was required for the greater good. Surely you understand that."

Dave did, but damned if he was going to admit it. Anyway, he figured the alien already knew what he was thinking.

"Yes," said the peacekeeper.

"Were you born? Created? *How*?" Jefferson had to ask.

"Created, by a greater power. I know my duty and that I'm ancient in your measure of time, but more than that about myself I don't know."

"And you're alone out there?" Olivia asked. "For all that length of time?"

Ethan didn't reply for a moment. The silver eyes were downcast, the face solemn. "There are others like me, but distant. I receive information, process it, and send it on, and I know my duty," he repeated.

"Your power has to have a limit," Jefferson said. "It can't be infinite. *Can it?*"

"Infinite is a matter of definition. Whatever power I have is more limited in this body than in my original form, but I need the body as a means of communication."

"We're back on I-70, gents," Hannah announced. Her voice was a little shaky, after hearing these things spoken from the boy's mouth. "She thanks you for the gas, let's just hope our tires hold out."

"Is there a God?" Jefferson asked quietly, his gaze fixed on Ethan. "You know...I've traded on Him for years. I've done...some pretty bad things, in the name of God. I'm kind of surprised I haven't been struck dead by lightning or something before now, but I just kept going. And it's like...I was testing God, maybe, because He *let* me keep going. So tell me if you can...*is* there a God?"

Ethan didn't reply. How to explain to them that his knowledge was limited too, and there were things he was not allowed to know? They were waiting for an answer, and they thought he must've seen the face of the entity they called God, and maybe they believed he was what they called an 'angel,' in their understanding of the mysteries. He gathered his thoughts, and he said, "I can tell you that there is intelligence and direction in the cosmos. As I have seen, much is left to the will of the civilization...even to the individual, to rise or fall. Is your God the same as that known by the Cyphers and the Gorgons, or by any of the—can I tell you—*billions* of other civilizations 'out there,' as you put it? Each has its own mythology and meaning, its own structure of values. The entity you know as 'God' I would think would have as many names as there are languages, hearts, and minds. Understand me...I don't have all your answers. I would likely present to you *more* questions, and some might be beyond the scope of your intellect to grasp. No offense meant," he added.

"But," Ethan continued, "I am here. I was summoned here by a power I can barely grasp myself. I was created by that power. I was given a duty and directives. My intent—and the intent of my being summoned here—is to stop this war and save your world. I am not given precise instructions as to how to achieve that, but I am given what you might call a waypoint…White Mansion Mountain. It's up to me—and a test of your willingness to fight for survival—to reach that waypoint and proceed from there."

"A *test*?" Dave said. "You mean all this…the war and all of it…could have been just a test to see if we were worthy to keep on living or not? That doesn't sound much like God's love, does it? And even if you can stop the war…what about the world? *Our* world. It's fucked up, man! All the people that we knew and loved, dead! All those Gray Men out there, and who knows how many millions around the world! It'll never go back to what it was!"

Ethan nodded. His mouth was tight-lipped. The silver eyes fixed on Dave.

"One thing I've learned in my long existence," said the peacekeeper, "is patience. Trust that the intelligence that summoned me here and allowed the journey has a purpose. I do. If you believe *anything*, now is not the time to let it go." He directed his gaze to Jefferson. "This body and its systems need rest. Is there anything else?"

"No," Jefferson answered. "That's all." He returned to his seat and found himself staring at nothing, but thinking of the progress of his life and what it had meant. He couldn't crack up now, that was for sure, and weighing too much of the 'good' and the 'bad' in his past might crack him, so he would put those things aside, try to blank them out, and go on as any man must…from where he was.

Silence ruled on Number 712.

The bus went on into the fitful dark. Rain fell again, but not hard enough to overpower the wiper. Mile after mile, the distance rolled away.

Olivia slept, and dreamed of sitting with JayDee on the balcony of her apartment. JayDee took her hand, and he leaned his head close and said quietly *There's a way out of this, Olivia. There must be a way to fix things, to make things right.*

Do you believe that, John? her dream-self asked. *Do you really believe?* He squeezed her hand and smiled, and his blue eyes glinted with not a dirty yellow sky but one that was clear and clean, and something about his face seemed much younger than she remembered.

Oh my Olivia, he said gently, *you may rely on it.*

TWENTY-SIX.

THE SUN WAS COMING UP, A SLASH OF RED TO THE EAST BEYOND the Rockies.

Number 712 was sitting on the interstate at the exit to Utah State Highway 191 south. Hannah had pulled them over after another gas stop short of the Utah line. It had been an isolated station with an uncracked diesel tank, and unlike the last stop they'd had the luxury of time to fuel the bus to its capacity. Hannah had told Dave she was tired and needed sleep, and it would be best to continue on 191 at dawn. He didn't argue, because he needed sleep too, but he'd gotten very little of it. Ethan had awakened after about an hour and told Dave he could rest soundly, that the trackers weren't close enough to be alarmed and he'd let everyone know if that changed.

Olivia had slept, and so had Nikki and Jefferson. Dave had drowsed for awhile and then jerked himself awake as if he were about to fall into a bottomless pit. He figured another hundred miles, give or take, to the White Mansion. Then who knew if there was even a road up the thing. Highway 191 was a four-lane and looked totally deserted from where he sat, not a single abandoned car or truck on it as far as he could see. The morning light reddening the sky showed a vista of what used to be called a western paradise, a land of low scrub and crimson rocks, distant mesas

311

and mountains rising in the distance, arches and cathedrals of stone standing as they had for eons. It could be the surface of another planet, torn and shaped by ancient cataclysms. What a creation Earth was, Dave thought. He'd never stopped to think much about it before this war had begun, because making a living got in the way of philosophical appreciation, and he was never inclined to that, but Earth was an amazing world. From warm seas to frozen tundra, from lush grasslands and pine forests to the red rock mountains that rose from the plains along Highway 191, it was an incredibly diverse creation. And all the life it held…stunning, when you really considered it. Maybe when you lost something, Dave thought, it became that much more valuable. The life forms that would die or be malformed under this alien poison…probably in the thousands. So even if Ethan could stop the war, which Dave couldn't imagine even as powerful an entity as Ethan being able to do, what would be Earth's future? It looked to him like continued wrack and ruin. The world was never going to be able to recover from this.

He realized that Ethan was awake and was staring silently out a window. If the alien was reading his thoughts, there was no response.

He doesn't know either, Dave thought. *Do you?* he asked, but still there was no reply. *You may be a hell of a lot more powerful than us and know secrets of the universe and all kinds of shit that would knock us to our knees…but you're not sure of anything either, are you? You're just groping in the dark, like any ordinary human. Like this with the mountain…you don't know what's there because if this is a test for humanity you're being tested too. Is that what Life really is, Ethan? A test designed by some alien we think of as God? That would be a fine laugh on the race of mankind, wouldn't it? All the centuries of struggle and misery and everything people have had to go through, and at the end they find out whether the teacher gives them a passing grade or not?*

"Centuries also," Ethan suddenly said, "of invention, perserverance, and in many cases genius. Your race seems to always find a way to push through obstacles. That's why you're still here."

"What?" Jefferson had awakened and was squinting in the morning light. "What are you talking about?"

Ethan said, "Dave and I are having a conversation."

"Oh," said the preacherman, and he looked puzzled, but he didn't ask anything else.

The others began to awaken. This morning Ethan noted that Olivia was hollow-eyed and haggard. She was still mourning John Douglas, could not accept the fact that he was gone. She was also mourning the loss of the human boy known as Ethan Gaines, and maybe she'd let herself feel motherly and protective of him, so that loss was doubly painful. He could not pretend that any part of the boy was left in this shell. What could he say to soothe her that she would understand? Nothing, so she must be allowed to grieve her way to finality.

When everyone was awake, they took turns going outside the bus to relieve themselves, which Ethan had already of course observed through the boy. It was an interesting process, but in his experience all species had the need for elimination. Almost all: the half-flesh, half-robotic soldiers of what the humans called the Cyphers did not, they absorbed and recycled any wastes from the nutrition that fueled them, and he knew of three more civilizations that were machine-based, but on the whole all shared this need. He participated in it when his time came.

Afterward a jug of water was passed around, which Ethan in his true form did not need but knew it was vital to keep the body going. Dave opened up a couple of cans of pork 'n beans, a jar of peanut butter, and some stale crackers, and that was their breakfast.

The sun had climbed toward eight o'clock, but yellow-tinged clouds were closing in and the light was dimming. Ethan tried to speak to Nikki, to console her however he could, but she turned her face away from him, and he realized it was useless. She, too, had to work through her grief—what seemed in her mind to be a world of grief—and he was helpless to give her any comfort. He took his seat, knowing that everyone on the bus needed him and counted on him, but he was a strange intruder to them nonetheless and they were all, as Nikki had put it so truthfully, "creeped out."

At last Dave regarded the deserted stretch of Highway 191 again, and he said, "Hannah, let's move on."

She started the engine and guided the bus off I-70 onto the road to the White Mansion.

"Ethan?" Jefferson said. "The trackers still there?"

"The Cypher tracker is nearly overhead. The Gorgon ship is..." He paused to get a correct reading on it, calculating distances from its harmonic signature. "Seventy-two miles to the east, at an altitude of...I would say...between forty-seven and forty-eight thousand feet. It's keeping its distance, but also keeping its tracker on *you*."

Jefferson nodded but said nothing else. Ethan knew he was as worried about this as everyone else, but he detected a subtle change in an element of Jericho's thoughts. The man now was not entirely focused on himself, but had opened the cavern of his soul a little bit to allow in concern for the others and the mission ahead. Still...the man had known selfishness all his life, it was part of his being, and he used it as both sword and shield.

Number 712 rumbled on, across a landscape of surreal beauty with its red rock cliffs and formations of stone that seemed fashioned by an alien hand. Mesas and mountains loomed in the misty distance, across a plain of gray-stubbled vegetation. Ethan took it all in with as much interest as any tourist. He'd been aware of Dave's ruminations on the planet but had lingered there only briefly. If these people knew what he had observed of worlds across the cosmos, they would be amazed by the variety but also frightened, because the physics of this planet did not hold true on others. Some of the civilizations had evolved into pure cerebral energy, others were animalish and still fighting from the mud of their beginnings. Some had found their way to interstellar travel and use of the dimensional portals, others lived in caves. There were great cities and noble rulers, there were harsh prison-states, and males and females who existed as leeches on the societies they commanded. It was out there, a billionfold. And the languages and mathematics, clothing styles and entertainments, fields of study and commerce, rites of passage and customs, mythologies and rituals, sexual practices, births and deaths...beyond counting.

Yet for all this, he was alone.

He was rarely summoned to intervene, but always for a cause that involved the death of a world by conquest. Sometimes the greater power that had created him did not summon him, but the vast network of information that he was tuned to told him civilizations were being destroyed by others either greedy, envious, or in a religious fervor. He understood that he was not called to intervene in the politics and progress of a world, but rather to keep a world from being destroyed by an external force. The Gorgons and Cyphers, their real names impossible for the humans to speak or understand, had been at war over unpopulated planets for eons. They had fought each other across space, over dead pieces of rock and worlds of ice and flame, but in all that time this Earth was the first populated world they had contested. Their self-proclaimed border between what they considered their territories passed directly through the planet.

It could not be allowed, that this world should be destroyed. And why? Was it so important, in the view of the greater power that the peacekeeper obeyed? He had wondered about this but had received no answer. In its silence, the greater power could be very cryptic at times, and also unsettling even to Ethan's steady nature. He didn't understand it, but he was not expected to. The ways and plans of the greater power were unknown to him; he was a small part of a massive undertaking that left even his thought processes numbed. He did what he was called to do, though it was left to him to decide the course of action. A test, as Dave had put it? A test of both himself and the will of the inhabitants of this world? He couldn't say. There was some element of curiosity in the greater power as to how civilizations progressed, he knew that, but even to him, there were many mysteries that would never be revealed.

He kept watch on the trackers. The Cypher tracker remained at the edge of the atmosphere. The Gorgon warship kept its distance of around seventy miles. He had the feeling of many Gorgon eyes and Cypher sensors directed at the bus, as it moved slowly along the highway between cliffs banded with a dozen shades of red. They feared him, but they must have him. They would choose the time and place.

From a pocket of his jeans, Dave drew the many-times-folded and dirty Utah map torn from the road atlas. There were several mountains in the area to which they were headed; they'd have to figure out which one was the White Mansion, because he doubted very much that it would be marked with any kind of sign.

It was a slow progress southward. Hannah was afraid to push the engine or the tires too hard, but at least they were good for fuel. The land flattened out and then rose again toward a mountain range. What appeared to be rugged badlands stretched out on both sides. They passed the black hulks of a tractor-trailer truck and two cars that had collided in what must have been a terrible fireball, but otherwise the highway was empty.

Just after ten o'clock they passed through the center of the town of Monticello, which appeared to be deserted. Highway 191 became Main Street. Dave had given the map plenty of study and knew they had to get into the Manti-La-Sal National Forest, which was off to the west of Monticello. A smaller road, 101, was their way in. A weather-beaten sign in front of the post office at the corner of 191 and West 200 directed them to turn there for the National Forest. In another few minutes West 200 became Abajo Drive, which became 101 and began to climb toward the forested foothills.

Much of the forest had turned brown and died. Pine and birch trees stood bony and bare. Through them, as they continued to climb, Olivia caught sight to their left of a looming mountain with a peak of white stone. All the surrounding mountains were covered with a brown blanket of dead forests. "You see that?" she asked Dave, and pointed.

"I see it. Maybe ten miles away. I don't know exactly how the hell to get there, but that looks promising. Ethan, is that the mountain?"

"I think it is," Ethan answered. "It *must* be."

"He can sense a spaceship seventy-two miles away and a tracker in outer space but he doesn't know if that's the right mountain or not, right in front of him," Jefferson said. "*Great.*"

"The tracker is not in outer space," Ethan corrected him. "As for the mountain, I only know what's on Dave's map."

"There might not be a road," Hannah said. The engine was straining as 101 steepened. "Looks pretty rugged over that way."

"We'll keep going until we can't go any further," Dave told her. "Then we'll figure something else out."

The road crested and the mountain was in full view. It might have been majestic but for many thousands of dead trees. It was definitely the only peak of white stone in sight. Then the road descended for a stretch, with diseased forests on either side, before it began to climb once more and took a turn to the left.

"She's chuggin'," Hannah said, but everyone could already feel the bus shuddering as it fought its way up. Again Highway 101 crested, with another swing to the south, and began a long winding journey down among the foothills from which the white-peaked mountain rose. Hannah was trying to put as light a foot on the brakes as possible, but she couldn't allow the bus to get out of control descending this road. "I might be burnin' the brakes up," she worried. "They're soggy enough already, and she's pullin' to the right."

"You're doing fine," Dave said. He was alert for the smell of burning brakes, though; it would be a long way down if they gave out.

In about four miles or so 101 straightened out again and ran south parallel to the mountain in question. Everyone on the bus was looking for a way up, but there were only thousands of acres of brown trees unbroken by another road.

"I don't see a way to get any closer," Hannah said. "From here it'd be one hell of a walk."

"Keep going," Dave urged. "Could be a road up on the other side."

Another two miles passed. A more narrow road branched off from 101 to the right, and Dave told Hannah to take that one. They began climbing again, though moving more to the northwest and away from the white rock peak. Dave said, "I'm not sure this is the way but let's stick it out for awhile."

They had traveled for over twenty minutes, seemingly going in the wrong direction, when Hannah caught sight of a dirt road that went off to the left on a more southwesterly course. It was surrounded by dead forest and was likely very hard to see when the trees were full. She slowed the bus and stopped near the road's entrance. "What say?" she asked.

"You want to try this? Might lead to a dead end, but it could take us a lot closer."

"Yeah. Let's try it."

Hannah turned them onto the road and they started up again, leaving whorls of dust behind the tires. The bus jubbled over loose stones, which put them all on edge. A little more than two hundred yards up the road, they came to a chainlink fence about eight feet high. It was topped by a coil of barbed wire, and the fence went in both directions through the woods as far as they could see.

On the gate, which bore a sturdy-looking padlock, was a sign that read PRIVATE PROPERTY, NO TRESPASSING.

They sat with the engine idling. "What do you think, bossman?" Hannah asked.

"I think it's strange. This is a national forest. How can it be private property?"

"Don't know, but that's what the sign says."

"Yeah." Dave turned to look at Ethan. "What do *you* think?"

The expression was determined and the silver eyes were intense. "I think we need to go through that gate."

Dave nodded. "There's no such thing as private property anymore, is there? Odd, though, to be in a national forest. Hannah, can you push us through?"

"I could, but I don't want to. Get anything tangled up underneath or blow the tires...wouldn't be good."

"I'll do it." Ethan stood up. Hannah opened the door for him and he stepped off the bus. As the others watched, it took maybe ten seconds for the peacekeeper to take aim at the gate with the palm of his right hand and the entire gate to separate from its padlock and chain and go flying through the air; in midair it curved and sailed into the woods on the right. The coil of barbed wire hung down over the entrance but would only scratch a little paint off the bus. Ethan came back aboard and returned to his seat as if the merest amount of energy had been required, though he was opening and closing a hand whose bones and tendons throbbed with a dull ache.

"Easy enough," Hannah said. "I wish I could've done that to my ex-husband. All right, we're movin'."

She drove them through. They had taken two curves, still ascending, when another fence blocked the road. It was not made of chainlink; it was at least six feet high and made of what appeared to be a gridwork of thin white wires. Again Hannah stopped the bus before a padlocked gate, because she knew what it was even as Dave said it out loud.

"That's an electric fence. Damn...somebody doesn't want people going up this road, that's for sure."

"Which means," Olivia said, "there's something up there that's supposed to stay hidden."

"Right. Well...Ethan, can you knock that gate down?"

"I can," Ethan said, "but I think you should know that the electricity has been activated."

"No way!" said Jefferson. "All the power's knocked out, and why would anybody use up gas for a generator to run that thing?"

"Power is running through the fence and the gate. I can feel the movement of energy. Touching that would be enough to kill any human."

No one spoke for a moment. Dave scratched his beard and saw that, like the chainlink fence, this one also extended into the forest on both sides as far as could be seen. He thought it was likely the fence went around the entire mountain. Somebody had gone to great lengths and great expense to protect their property, but why?

"We have to keep going," Ethan said. "I'll open the gate." He got off the bus again and made another ten seconds' work of the gate, breaking it open and folding it back against the fence so no wires were torn. It was a minimal use of his power. He was keenly aware of the sensation of being watched by something other than the Cypher and Gorgon trackers, and scanning the trees he quickly made out two small optical devices in the branches up over his head, painted in gray camouflage. They were both aimed directly at the gate. He assumed someone had just witnessed an action that would immediately cause alarms to go off.

319

"There are cameras in the trees," he reported when he got back aboard. "Two that I saw, probably more. I would think someone knows we're here, and they're not going to like it."

With a hard edge in his voice, Dave said, "No reason to stop now. Let's go on."

Ethan returned to his seat. Hannah started them forward again and didn't breathe easily until they were way past the fence. The road steepened in its ascent and once more the bus chugged, the tires struggling for traction in the dust and stones. After a hard pull of perhaps a quarter of a mile they came to a place where the dead trees fell away and above them towered the mountain's white peak. The road leveled off. Directly ahead it ended at a guardrail overlooking the valley below, with a solid wall of white stone to their right.

Hannah stopped about ten feet from the guardrail. "This is as far as we go, folks."

They sat in silence, as the hot engine ticked.

"What now?" Jefferson asked. "There's nothing here!"

"You're wrong," Dave said, standing up. "That guardrail...what's it up here for? To keep a car from going over, so somebody's been driving that road. Damned if I know, but I can't see anyplace wide enough to turn around and it would be mighty tough to back down. Which says to me that—"

"Stay where you are," came a man's magnified voice from a loudspeaker. "If you step off that, bus you *will* be executed. Repeat: stay where you are."

The voice was flat, calm, and deadly in its resolve. It was the voice of a trained professional who Dave figured would have no qualms putting everyone on the bus to death. Whoever it was, he had a big surprise coming.

And then Dave finished what he was saying, as a section of the rock wall at least ten feet wide began to tilt inward and open up on smooth and nearly soundless machinery. "Which says to me that there's a way *in*, and it's big enough for a car."

TWENTY-SEVEN.

"ARE THEY GOING TO KILL US?" NIKKI ASKED, HER VOICE TREMBLING. Five men with weapons had emerged from the opening doorway in the white stone. Three wore regular t-shirts and jeans and carried automatic rifles, one wore gray trousers and a pale blue shirt with rolled-up sleeves and the fifth was dressed in a black suit with a white shirt and a gray-striped tie. Both these men were carrying automatic pistols. The one in the suit was a black man with close-cropped hair and the one wearing the gray trousers was Asian. All were maybe in their late twenties or early thirties, were clean-shaven, healthy in appearance, and moved quickly. They looked to Dave like very capable killers. They came toward the bus with what appeared to be deadly intent.

"Open up," said the man in the suit, who seemed to be the leader. He was used to issuing commands; his voice, though not necessarily loud, carried the demand for instant obedience. He took aim at Hannah through the door's glass. "I will repeat that *once*, ma'am: open up."

The others had taken up stations at various points around the bus. All the weapons were trained on the passengers.

"Open it," Dave said.

Hannah did. The black man came aboard, followed by one of the others with an automatic rifle. "Stand up, ma'am. Leave the key in the

321

ignition and your weapon in the seat and move back." She obeyed, realizing this was not a man to be messed with. "The rest of you stay *very* still." He was holding his pistol in a two-handed grip. His deep-set, olive-colored eyes darted here and there, taking everything in; they stopped on Ethan and remained there for a few seconds before he went on. "You're going to move slowly now and put your weapons in the aisle. If I don't like a quick movement, I *will* kill you. Everyone tell me they understand that."

Everyone told him, except Ethan who remained silent and watchful. The black man's wary gaze kept coming back to Ethan, but both the pistol and the rifle were aimed along the aisle so as to swing fast upon anyone they chose to target.

The guns were laid in the aisle. "Thank you," the man said. "Now folks...you are all going to put your hands behind your head and you are going to walk off this bus single file. Again, I don't like quick movements and neither do the agents outside. So be very, very careful as you leave and we'll have no problem. When you get off the bus, you'll be told what to do."

Jefferson had heard something that snagged in his head. "*Agents?* What kind of agents?"

"Secret Service, sir. Now...I want no talking, either. Everyone just be quiet, move carefully and slowly and follow instructions."

When they got outside, the man in the suit urged everyone along toward the entrance into the White Mansion, which was not only big enough to admit a car, but probably big enough to let a tank rumble through. He stopped Ethan by putting an arm in his way. Ethan kept his hands behind his head as instructed.

"Will, take them all inside," the man told the Asian. "*You* just stand where you are," he said to Ethan.

"Listen," said Olivia, "we have a lot to tell you."

"I'm sure you do, and we have a lot of questions to ask you as well. Please go along with the others now. Don, stick here with me for a minute." One of the men armed with an automatic rifle took a position just beside Ethan.

"Sir, would you tell me your name?" Ethan asked, as his friends were escorted through the opening.

"Bennett Jackson. Yours?"

"Ethan Gaines. Mr. Jackson, I need to tell you that there is a Gorgon warship about forty miles northeast of this position and moving closer. I don't know if they're preparing an attack or not, but it would be wise to be ready if possible."

"A human-looking boy with silver eyes who talks like a fifty-year-old man. That's a *first*. Are you a Cypher?"

"No sir."

"The cameras saw you destroy two gates without a weapon. How'd you do that?"

"I *am* a weapon," Ethan said. "May I put my hands down? This is an uncomfortable posture."

"Frisk him," Jackson told the other man. It was done quickly and efficiently. Eye contact was kept during the procedure. "Okay Ethan, you can put your hands down." Jackson looked toward the milky sky to the northeast and then back to the boy. "You're not a Gorgon or a Cypher— you say—but you're not human, either. You say you're a weapon, and I believe what I've seen. So what side are you a weapon for?"

"Your side."

"Uh-huh." Jackson gave him a thin, cold smile absolutely devoid of humor. "I have seen a *lot* of things I would never have believed possible two years ago. My wife and my six-year-old daughter are likely dead, back in Washington." Flames flickered in the olive-green eyes; they were highly dangerous, but they didn't last long. Ethan knew this man kept his emotions in a tightly sealed box, for fear that letting anything out might tear him to pieces. The loss of his wife had solidified Jackson's marriage to his job, which Ethan saw in an instant had been a constant demand to him and a point of pride. There were the memories in there of a rough background in a rough neighborhood, scenes of hard military training and a medal of some kind being presented to him. "At least," Jackson continued, "I *hope* they died before things got really bad. You're some kind of creature made by either the Gorgons or the Cyphers, is what I think. You *have* to be. Are you bringing the Gorgons here? Is that what this is about?"

"No, it's not."

"How did you find this place?"

Ethan traveled across the tortured landscape of Bennett Jackson's mind. He saw within seconds what this mountain held.

"This is the secure location for the President," Ethan said. "And he's here."

"You've come to kill him? Or guide the ship in to kill everyone?"

"No. As my friend Olivia said, we have a lot to tell you."

Jackson removed a small black communications device from within his coat. It had a keypad on it and a yellow, green and red button. He pressed the red one. "Waiting for instructions," he said into the speaker. Then, to Ethan, "If I took you inside without permission they'd put me in a rubber room before I was shot."

"If someone here doesn't listen to me," said Ethan calmly, "there will be no more *they* for you to be involved with, if you're speaking of your human race. The Cyphers and Gorgons won't stop fighting until this planet is destroyed. Even then they might not stop. Mr. Jackson, I'm here to help you and I've come a very long way. Please take me to your President."

Jackson scanned the northeastern sky once more. A muscle clenched in his jaw. "How do you know the warship's out there?"

"I can feel its harmonic signature getting stronger."

"Its *what*?"

"The composition of its matter sends out a frequency. A vibrational signal I can pick up. All matter does this. The Gorgon ships are easily recognizable from this signal."

Jackson just stood there like a statue, staring at him.

Ethan finally tapped his skull and said, "I have a *radar* in here."

"Jesus Christ," Jackson said, and narrowed his eyes. "What're we going to do with you?"

"The wise thing, I hope," Ethan answered.

Bennett Jackson wore an expression of dismay. He looked to the other man, Don, for some kind of help and got only a shrug. He then seemed to be searching all points of the compass for something to steady his own course. He rubbed at a spot on his forehead as if trying to make the gears in his brain mesh a little better.

A voice came from the communications device: "Bring him in. Room 5A."

"All right, Ethan," Jackson said. "Now when we go inside, you're not going to turn into a creature I'll have to kill, will you? I would dislike putting a bullet into the head of anything that looks like a human boy, but I'll do it in an instant. Also, there will be men inside who'll shoot you to pieces even if you're quick enough to kill me. So be careful in your movements and walk ahead of me, and I would ask that you return your hands to the back of your head, fingers locked together, and everyone will feel much better. Agreed?"

"Yes," Ethan said. He did as Jackson told him, and walked toward the opening with Jackson two paces behind him and the other man with the automatic rifle just off to his left.

They entered the White Mansion. The initial chamber looked like a spotless high-tech garage forty feet wide, with a shiny black-painted concrete floor and a ceiling about twenty feet high. Tubes of light ran along the ceiling amid industrial-looking pipes. A metal staircase ascended to a second level. Three black SUVs and a jeep were parked on the garage floor. There were gas pumps, both regular fuel and diesel, a supply of oil drums, tires in racks and batteries on shelves. Ethan saw that his traveling companions had already been spirited away somewhere, and ten or so men—some dressed informally, some in suits, but all clean-shaven and well-fed—had gathered to watch the entrance of the new arrivals, and he figured especially himself. Among them were two uniformed and helmeted soldiers with machine guns. Ethan sensed the low hum of power and felt a great source of energy here, and it both perplexed and interested him.

"What's running your power?" he asked.

Jackson ignored him so completely Ethan couldn't even read the man's mind on the subject. Jackson called over one of the jeans-clad Secret Service agents who'd returned to the area and told him to get a detail and clean the bus out of guns and whatever else was on there, but not to bring the bus inside until that order was given. Then Ethan was marched up the metal stairs by Jackson and the man named Don, along a corridor and to another set of stairs that led up to a beige-carpeted area of closed doors. Jackson unlocked a door marked 5A with a key from a keyring, reached in and flipped on a light switch. He stepped back as Ethan entered. It was a single room with a bed, a dresser, a writing table, lamp and chair and beyond that a small white-tiled bathroom. The wallpaper showed artwork of eagles in flight. There were no windows, since they were well inside the mountain. Cool air was circulating from a wall vent. Jackson closed the door and he and the other man took positions on either side of it.

"You're going to have a visitor in a few minutes," Jackson said. "He'll be very interested to hear your story."

"That's fine." Ethan looked up at the overhead tube-light and the lamp on the table before he sat down on the bed. "You have a lot of power available here. What's the source?"

Jackson again would not answer, but Ethan got the flicker of a mental image from him: a bright glowing piece of white crystal about the size of a man's hand, suspended in a transparent cylinder and slowly revolving. Cables ran from the base of the cylinder into machinery in a room that felt to Ethan to be on a lower level below the garage.

Ethan was about to remark on this when the door opened and a man in a gray suit entered, accompanied by another man in a dark blue uniform and cap with many multi-colored bars over his heart. The man in the gray suit wore a white shirt and a blue-patterned tie, he was clean-shaven and slim but healthy in appearance. He looked combative, as if he'd lived every day with his teeth clenched, his lower jaw jutting out just a little too much. He was bald but for a fringe of light brown hair with gray at the temples. He wore horn-rimmed glasses, and his eyes were so pale blue, they were nearly colorless. On his lapel was an American flag pin. The pallid eyes took Ethan in with absolutely no expression on his face, but the military man behind him had a start and actually backed up a pace before Jackson closed the door.

"Sir, this is Ethan Gaines," Jackson announced. "He tells me he is neither Cypher nor Gorgon, but he does admit to being an alien weapon in the form of a human boy. He says there's a Gorgon warship closing in from the northeast. He also says he's—"

"I'll take it from here, thank you," said the man in the gray suit, with a quick, clipped manner of speech that Ethan thought could easily become abrasive. "Ethan, why don't our radars pick this ship up?"

"They have cloaking devices that easily hide them from your systems. May I ask what your name is, and your position?" *Vance Derryman, Chief of Staff*, came the mental response.

"We're not here to interview me."

"All right, Mr. Derryman," Ethan said. "As chief of staff you have immediate access to the President. May I speak with him?"

It was a moment before Derryman answered, and when he did it was with a thin-lipped smile. His eyes were even more cautious than before. He brought from a pocket a communications device like the one Jackson had used. He pressed a sequence on the keyboard. "Ambler Seven Seven," he said quietly. "Go to code yellow and scan to the northeast. Also get a team of eyes up top." He waited for a voice to answer, "Copy that, sir," and then he put the device away. Ethan picked up *Weapons Control* from someone. He glanced at the military man, who was scared to death of him, and got the name *Winslett*, first name *Patrick*, nicknamed *Foggy* for some reason. Oh…he used to chain-smoke so much he carried around his own fogbank. Derryman took a seat in the chair and folded his hands together. Then he simply stared at Ethan as if trying out his own powers of mental perception.

"I guess," Ethan said to the silence, "that my friends have been put in separate rooms and they're also being interviewed?" He knew it was true, so he went on. "You'll get the same story from everyone, but please listen closely to what Dave McKane and Olivia Quintero will explain. Also you'll find Jefferson Jericho of interest. He's had occasion to be in the presence of the Gorgon queen."

The silence remained unbroken, but Foggy Winslett looked as nervous as if he expected either Ethan to grow two heads and six arms at any instant, or the roof to crash in on his skull.

"How close is the Gorgon ship now?" Derryman asked, almost as if posing a casual question.

Ethan spent a few seconds in concentration. The mass of this mountain was a little interference, though not enough to mask the ship from him. "Thirty miles, but it's holding its position."

"You're telling them to hold there?"

"No. As you'll learn from the others, I am a threat to both Gorgons and Cyphers. I want this war to be ended, sir. They don't understand what I am, and they both want to either capture me, take me apart on their dissection tables, or kill me. I believe they're thinking they can harness my energy in some way to create new weapons."

"Your *energy*," said Derryman. He nodded. "I've seen that in action on the visual feed. Tell me, then...what are you, and why should you want the war to be ended?"

"I have a question to ask you first, before we go any further." Ethan had been unaware of what he might find here, but his realization of what was running the power at this installation had given him a clue. "Your power source here is not of human design. Where did it come from?"

Derryman hesitated. Ethan could read his mind, but he wanted to hear it, and he knew Derryman was a very intelligent man who fully understood that.

"You're correct. It's of alien design. And you knew about that, *how*?"

"Mr. Jackson didn't realize he was telling me when I asked."

"Of course. Well, that's a very interesting ability you have there, Ethan. I like the silver eyes. They're a little disconcerting at first, but impressive. I'm assuming there's some reason for that, maybe you can see a spectrum we can't?"

"Yes."

"Nothing is purposeless in the universe, is it? The crystal that powers everything here—and seems to the physicists who have studied it to have unlimited power—comes from Area 51," Derryman said. "Do you know what that is?"

The knowledge of that, sketchy at best, was in the boy's brain, but Ethan wanted to hear Derryman's explanation of it. "I am aware that this planet has been visited many times by other civilizations. I'd like you to tell me the details."

"Sir," Winslett said tersely, "I would advise that you—"

"I hear your advice, General, and it is noted." Derryman's eyes never left Ethan. "I think our visitor here could pick out every detail of Area 51 from your mind or mine anyway. He's being gracious in not tromping around in our heads. Also he wants to hear an earthman's understanding of it. Am I correct there, Ethan?"

"Yes sir."

"This is the point where I ought to stand up and walk out of here," Derryman said. "I ought to consider you a threat of the highest magnitude and figure out some way to dispose of you, but that might be a little difficult. It also might be the wrong choice. I'm thinking that you're an energy source yourself, and you've incorporated a human body? Or is that a manufactured form?"

"A human body," Ethan replied. "I regret that the boy is gone, but it had to be done."

"Vance, I need a drink," Winslett said. Sweat glistened on his forehead and his dark brown, defeated eyes looked bloodshot already.

"Area 51," Derryman said, "is in New Mexico, about five hundred miles from here. It's a base where new fighter and surveillance aircraft are created and tested. There's a section of Area 51, called S-4, that holds what used to be lead and silver mines in the 1870s. Those mines have now been occupied, modernized, and powered as an interlocked research center. We research there any alien mechanism, device, or flesh we can get our hands on. This has been going on for over sixty years. Needless to say we've learned a lot we've been trying to keep other countries from knowing. Russia had its own program and a few other countries with the right facilities and the luck to get hold of an alien craft or artifact did as well. All that is the worst-kept secret in the world, because we can't control all the sightings or the crashes. And let me ask you this while I can, Ethan: if the aliens who have been able to reach us have such fantastic machines, why do they sometimes crash? We've helped a couple come down by pilots who got scared enough to fire missiles at close range without the proper authority, but we've seen four crashes that seem to be mechanical error. Why is that?"

"Intricate machinery no matter how advanced can sometimes fail, no matter what the propulsion system or the intelligence behind it. That's true all across the cosmos."

"My God," said Derryman, as if he'd just realized the enormity of the moment. "I'm sitting here talking to an entity who can answer the questions." He looked at Jackson and Don, who both were stoic, and then to Winslett who appeared shaken and in desperate need of his drink. For a moment Derryman seemed about to be overcome, and then he got himself under control once more, and the hard-souled, tough-minded ex-lawyer from Connecticut came back. "Now answer my questions: what are you, where are you from and if you're neither Gorgon nor Cypher why do you have any interest in stopping their war?"

"I am..." Ethan thought JayDee had captured it best. "I am a peace-keeper, comparable to the soldiers of your United Nations. I've come from a great distance. My interest in stopping their war is to save your world." Something was intruding on his mental flow...what was it? He realized in another few seconds. "Another Gorgon warship has joined the first. A third is within sixty miles, approaching from the west. There's a fourth...over a hundred miles away yet, coming from the southeast, but slowly. What weapons do you have?"

"ERAM surface-to-air missiles, fired remotely from a launcher up top about two hundred feet. A second launcher firing Patriots, and two radar-controlled anti-aircraft guns on rotating turrets at the peak." Derryman paused, and Ethan knew what he was going to ask next but did not interrupt. "Will it be enough?"

"No."

"I didn't think so. Those weapons were designed to knock down enemy aircraft built by humans, not those *things*." Derryman stood up; in spite of his steady demeanor and the movement of cool air in the room, a sheen of sweat glistened on his head. "Foggy, you and I need to get the other officers together."

"Area 51," Ethan said. "There are many alien artifacts there, removed from the ships?"

"As I understand."

"And weapons?"

"I've never been there. My briefing didn't give me the details of the layout. I really didn't *want* to know."

"Did your briefing tell you how to get in?"

Derryman was slow in replying. "Now why would you want to do that, Ethan?"

"Obviously, your weapons are not sufficient. I'm not sure, but something might be there I can use."

That statement caused silence to fall again. Derryman studied the knuckles of his right hand and then his closely trimmed fingernails.

"You're going to have to trust me," Ethan said.

Derryman looked up and asked sharply, "Are we?"

"Your world is on the brink of destruction right now. I'm your best hope, but I believe you're coming to that conclusion yourself."

"Quite a supposition, that we should trust any alien lifeform."

"Your choices," Ethan said, his silver eyes aimed like energy beams at Vance Derryman, "are limited. Your time is limited too. No, that's not a threat, sir. It's reality. Do you want to think about this for awhile? I'd like to at least have the chance to offer the idea to your President."

Derryman stared back at Ethan. His facial expression and cold eyes gave the others no clue as to what he was thinking but Ethan knew he was just as frightened as Foggy Winslett.

At last Derryman sat down again. He leaned his head back and closed his eyes for a few seconds. When he opened them again he said, "General Winslett, you have my authority to detail to this individual any information you have concerning Area 51."

"Vance...listen...I don't think we—"

"Do it," came the command, and it was final.

———❦———

Winslett's red-veined cheeks and nose already spoke of an intimate relationship with a supply of mind-numbing whiskey. His uniform and position did not shield him from terrors in the night.

He began, with an obvious effort and a distaste for the order. "I *have* been there," he said, as he stared at the beige carpet. "The base was evacuated two years ago. A security system would've automatically gone on-line. That's also powered by alien technology, so it's still active. The place is sealed up tight. Any try at breaking in would trigger defense mechanisms and ultimately blow the S-4 site to pieces. There's a nuclear device buried underneath it. I don't have the code to open the complex. The Vice President did. The Secretary of Defense had it, but I understand his plane went down over Virginia. The officials and scientists in the research group had blue badge clearances. They're all missing."

"The President has it," Ethan said.

"He does. The code gets you in, but to go deeper requires a handprint against a recognition scanner on every level."

"I believe I need to get inside and see what's there. As I asked before, may I offer this idea to the President?"

Derryman and the military man exchanged glances, and Ethan knew.

"There's something wrong with the President," he said. "Mentally wrong?"

After a hesitation, Derryman said, "He comes and goes. He's tried to commit suicide twice. One was last week, with sleeping pills. He... doesn't know the full scope of what's happened. We've kept it from him so he doesn't crack completely. The First Lady keeps it from him too."

"And the only way into the research area at S-4 without triggering the defense system is with his handprint." It was not a question from the peacekeeper, but a statement.

"Correct. We can't risk the President leaving this facility. He would lose his mind if he really knew, and we need him...as a symbol, if nothing else. We give him false military news. Hopeful news, Ethan, to keep him sane." Derryman stood up again. The interview was over. He said to Jackson, "You two stay with our visitor for awhile. You're not a prisoner, Ethan, but we would all appreciate it if you would confine yourself to this room until we get ourselves in order."

Ethan was aware of something else now, another sensation, another set of harmonic signatures from which he drew a mental picture. His human heartbeat quickened. "I have to tell you...the Gorgon ships are converging but keeping their range...and...there are two...three... four...Cypher warships taking up position ninety...eighty-six miles to the south. Not the small Cypher craft. These are battleships. Very big."

"Thank you for that." Derryman sounded a little choked. "We may need your help in weapons control if our radars can't pick up any targets. In the meantime...welcome to the White Mansion."

He and the General left the room. Bennett Jackson eased himself into the chair Derryman had vacated, his pistol still in hand. Both he and the other man seemed to want to look anywhere but directly at the alien who wore the body of a human boy.

Ethan took the opportunity to stretch out on the bed. There was no use closing his eyes; he saw Gorgon and Cypher warships hovering in the air. Would they attack each other, or the White Mansion? They might fight for him as the prize, because one would not want the other to get him. He was too valuable a research tool. All he could do now, like any ordinary human, was to wait, and for the first time in his ancient existence, he felt absolutely powerless.

TWENTY-EIGHT.

"Something's coming," Ethan suddenly said, and he sat up with a burning blue sphere in his mind. It had been only a few minutes since Derryman and General Winslett had left the room. "It's Gorgon...but not a warship. It's something else...a weapon."

Jackson was on his comm device before Ethan had finished speaking. "Ambler Seven Seven, this is Jackson. Do you read me?"

"Go ahead, Bennett."

"Sir, Ethan says there's a Gorgon weapon of some kind on the way. Coming from what direction?" he asked the peacekeeper.

"South. Launched from a ship."

Jackson relayed this information.

Ethan saw the blue sphere coming, speeding over a desert landscape. It was bright and getting brighter every second like a minature blue sun. It held a tremendous amount of energy. The warships were still keeping their distance. Ethan thought this oncoming weapon was a test of the stronghold's defenses. He realized he had seen this eye-dazzling blue glow before, and he knew what it was.

He stood up, startling both men and causing them to train their weapons on him.

"Is the bus inside?" he asked. He knew, from Jackson's mental answer: *Not yet*. "Bring the bus in right now," he said. Jackson was still on the

335

comm device with Derryman, he didn't know how to respond to this command or what the bus had to do with the weapon streaking toward them.

"You're going to be too late," Ethan said. "It's almost here. I'm going out, please let me pass."

"No, Ethan, you'll have to—"

The peacekeeper brushed them aside with two flicks of his left hand, from which he saw the slightest leap of a mild silver-colored electrical charge. Both men hit opposite walls with maybe a little too much force than Ethan had intended. Jackson's gun went off and the bullet plowed upward through the ceiling. The other man's head clunked solidly against the American eagles. Before Jackson could get to his feet, Ethan was out the door and running toward the stairs.

As he reached the stairs and started down, heading to the garage level, he heard a high-pitched alarm go off. Whether this was because of him or because of the oncoming weapon, he didn't know nor did he particularly care. He saw a soldier who'd taken a position at the bottom of the stairs. The young man lifted an automatic rifle and took a shooter's stance. Just that fast Ethan brushed him aside, and the soldier went skidding across the floor, the rifle torn from his hands and flying in the opposite direction.

Ethan ran along the corridor to the metal stairs and started down. The alarm was still going off, a pulsing sound that echoed between the garage level's walls. He saw that at least the entrance had been closed, but the bus was still outside. When he reached the garage floor someone shouted at him and suddenly there were men in his way, grabbing at him and trying to pin him down. He restrained his power, not wanting to let it flail out and possibly kill one or more of these men. "Wait! Wait!" he cried out, but they were not listening and they were full up with fear; they got him to his knees and one of them had a rifle in Ethan's face and that was when Ethan felt the blue sphere pass over, in a bright mental flash and a crawling of the flesh at the back of his neck.

He recalled when he'd seen that before. When he, within the boy, was hiding under the pickup truck in the high school parking lot. When the sphere had briefly flared out its energy beams born from the darkest territory of the Gorgon mind, and then the truck and the other abandoned vehicles in the parking lot had—

Something crashed against the slab of rock that sealed the White Mansion. A booming echo filled the garage. All shouting ceased. The hands that were holding Ethan to the concrete were gone as the men stared at the entrance.

Ethan stood up. Again something massive slammed against the stone. The alarm was going off like a madman's scream. Ethan realized that if the Gorgons could create life in a matter of seconds, they could in the same amount of time program a purpose for that life, and this purpose was to smash into the humans' stronghold.

A third time, a body hit the stone wall. Dust puffed from it. The floor shook and the vehicles jumped. Something cracked and shattered in the far reaches of the garage. Comm devices were going off, voices asking for details. The shuddering of this chamber had been felt all through the mountain, on every level. Once more a tremendous strength battered the stone. There was a cracking noise like a broomstick being broken. Pieces of rock flew from the wall and slid across the concrete.

"Give me a picture!" a voice shouted from a comm device. "What's happening?"

"We need firepower at Level Two!" It was Jackson's voice. Ethan looked back to see the man standing just behind him on his own communicator, his pistol in hand. "This is Code Red at Level Two! Send us some guns, Rusty!"

Ethan had another mental image of four huge mottled warships picking up speed. "The Gorgon ships are coming in!" he told Jackson, who relayed the information, got back a garbled voice and then said to Ethan, "There's *nothing* on radar!"

"Eyes open up top! Get your guns ready!" Derryman and Winslett had just come down the stairs. Derryman was giving the command over his communicator. Right behind them were six uniformed and helmeted soldiers with machine guns. The soldiers spread out in a fan shape. They took aim at the entranceway as it was hit again and again, and the rock broke apart in jagged cracks, and the floor shivered and moaned like a man having a bad dream.

"What is that?" Derryman asked Ethan. His glasses were askew, sweat glistened on his face and his voice was thinned by fear. "Do you know?"

"Yes," Ethan answered. "It used to be a school bus."

With the next assault the remnants of the cracked slab of rock crashed inward. From the roiling dust a huge shape crawled into the garage. It was nearly the same color yellow as Number 712 had been but was now banded with black and red striping. Ethan caught sight of a bony red protuberance jutting out several feet from a triangular head with an underslung jaw full of glistening, razor-sharp teeth. A bulbous crimson eye was set at the triangle's three points. The natural battering ram was covered with black-tipped spikes, some broken by the impact against stone and dripping a milky-looking fluid. Ethan realized it was what the life-giving energy beam had done to the iron cage the soldiers had welded onto the front of the bus in Denver.

Number 712 was a three-eyed beast now all leathery flesh and bunched, rippling muscle. It pulled itself into the garage on hooked ebony claws that carved grooves in the concrete. The body had to be at least as long as the bus had been, about forty feet and another five for its battering-ram. It was equally as thick around as the bus, the side of it that Ethan could see patterned with dark square-shaped blotches that might have been an impression of the bus's windows.

As the soldiers and everyone else in the garage looked on in stunned horror, the creature began to rise up from the concrete, a forked tail whipping back and forth behind it. Its head and shoulders crashed into the ceiling, shattering some of the glass light tubes. "Open fire!" Winslett shouted, and with a cacophony of noise and eye-startling flares of flame six machine guns and every other weapon in the chamber began to tear at the beast with bullets.

The creature drew back, swatting at the air with its foreclaws. From its cavernous mouth beneath the bony battering ram came a shriek that started loud and grew in high-pitched intensity until it broke the windows in the SUVs and caused everyone in the garage to drop their weapons and clasp their hands to their ears. A couple of the soldiers fell to their knees. Ethan too had to protect his ears; the sound was mind-stunning, an aural assault that could break the will of any human to stand before it. When the sound ceased the weapons were grabbed up again and the firing continued, but two of the soldiers and three of the other men had fallen to the floor and lay there in dazed shock.

"Fire! Fire! Fire!" Winslett shouted. Even to Ethan the man's voice was muffled, his ears still ringing with the creature's sonic weapon.

The beast's flesh was oozing dark fluid in a hundred places. Its tail lashed out and knocked one SUV into the others. Facing the humans it let out a second shriek that again drove aural spikes of pain into the head and overpowered the senses. This time Derryman was driven to his knees, and Winslett staggered back with his hands clutched to his ears. Jackson tried to withstand it and keep firing but he couldn't; the pistol fell from his grip and he went down also. Ethan was staggered too, his hands to his ears and feeling as if his entire body was enveloped in searing flame. It came to him, even in the midst of this torment, that the creature's sonic shrieks were not only at a mind-stunning pitch and volume but triggered the area of the human nervous system that registered pain. He fell to his knees and then onto his right side, his teeth clenched and eyes involuntarily squeezed shut. In spite of all the power he commanded, he drew his knees up against his chest, and his body shivered as agony beat at him in vicious waves.

Dave had felt a vibration in Room 3A and so had the man with the automatic rifle who'd been stationed there to guard him. "What the hell was *that?*" he asked. An alarm was still going off, after the sound of a gunshot which a few moments before had caused Dave to emerge from the bathroom where he'd gone to get a drink of water.

"Saber Four Eight," the man said into his communicator. "What's happening, Jonesy?"

"We're at Code Red on Level Two," came the terse and nervous answer. "Some kind of breach. Sketchy yet."

"Do tell," Dave said.

"Can't talk, I'm gone," said the man on the other end of the communicator, and Dave's guard replied, "Copy that."

"A breach?" Dave felt the floor shudder again. "Whatever's gotten in, it's big."

"Just relax. Our orders are to sit tight."

"Relax? Are you *crazy*? When do I get to see somebody who's able to listen to me?"

"Sir, now is not the time to—"

"It *is* the time." Dave took a step toward the door and his guard swung the rifle's barrel up into his face. Dave looked into the barrel with disgust and then into the man's eyes with the same expression. "I'm going out to see what the hell is happening. If you want to go, fine. If you want to shoot me, go right ahead because that's the only way you'll keep me in this room."

"Sir, my orders are clear." A finger went to the trigger.

Once again a vibration came through the floor. The alarm was still wailing. Dave said, "Shoot me if you have to." He reached out to turn the door's lock the guard had engaged and the young, hard-faced Secret Service agent stepped in front of him with the rifle still aimed at his head. Dave had the urge to throw a punch, but he thought as soon as he drew his fist back he would likely be shot, not a killing placement but one to the leg or shoulder that would instantly drop him.

A voice came from the man's comm device: "Mike, Code Red on Level Two! They need guns! Get down there, stat!"

"I'm watching one of the new arrivals!"

"Scrub that! Leave 'em locked in and get down there!"

"You're not lockin' me in!" Dave said. "No way! I'll kick that damned door down!"

"Copy that." The agent lowered his communicator but kept the rifle aimed. "Step back, sir."

"I'm going through that door one way or the other. I swear I'll kick it down. Shoot me now, if you have to."

The young man paused, his well-scrubbed face impassive. Then suddenly it became contorted with conflict. "Damn it!" he said. "You *must* be human, to be so fucking stubborn!" He unlocked the door. "I may be put in the brig for this, but come on and stay out of my way!"

They went into the corridor, where they found that Jefferson Jericho had used his skills to also talk his guard into letting him out of 1A. Jefferson and the young man were just coming through the door. Dave figured Jericho's guard had been informed of the need for guns too, and the slimebag didn't want to be left in that room while it felt like the place was falling to pieces.

The two guards rushed on along the corridor to the stairs. "What's going on?" Jefferson asked Dave over the noise of the alarm.

"Some kind of breach downstairs."

"A *breach*? What's gotten in?"

"Don't know. Whatever it is, it's making the floor—"

Dave caught a strange movement, like a disturbance of air to Jefferson's left and about eight feet further toward the stairs. Dave felt the skin on the back of his neck crawl. Above the shrill noise of the alarm something made a sound whose echo came up the stairwell and along the corridor and made both men wince with pain.

From the shimmer of air, a body formed.

It was a large man, square-built and broad-shouldered though his cheekbones and small ebony chips of eyes were hollowed out from hunger. He had a tangle of shoulder-length black hair and two month's growth of beard. He wore a dark blue t-shirt, gray trousers and dirty black sneakers.

Vope said, tonelessly, "I have come for the boy, but I have been given permission to know ecstasy in killing both of you first."

—⊗—

When the monster ceased its aural attack, Ethan got to his knees. His body was aflame, it was hard to focus beyond the pain and the feeling that his brain was about to explode. He saw the creature stalking toward them, crouched under the ceiling. Its triangular head shattered some of the light tubes, and the forked tail swept back and forth across the concrete, now hitting the oil drums and sending them flying into the shelves where the batteries were stored.

The soldiers were paralyzed, unable to pick up their weapons. Jackson was on the ground and so were Derryman and General Winslett, all of them in agony. There were other men on the stairs. They stopped where they were to fire automatic rifles at the beast, and though the bullets drew puffs of alien blood, they did nothing to halt the thing's advance.

Before the creature could deliver another assault the peacekeeper took aim, both hands outthrust. With a concentrated thought that cut through the pain, he sent bolts of crackling energy and a thousand fiery projectiles that only he could see toward the monster at nearly the speed of light. The beast was hit in the chest, which burned black in an instant and caved in, then burst into flame. The thing staggered backward, the tail crashed into one of the SUVs and sent it tumbling end-over-end into the opposite wall not a dozen feet from Ethan and the others. As its chest burned, the monster let loose another sonic scream, the power of which was nearly a physical force that flung Ethan backward to the floor and stopped all firing of rifles from the men on the stairs.

Through the haze of pain and pressure, Ethan saw the beast lurching forward once more, its chest dripping chunks of flaming meat. It was coming to crush him and the other men, and Ethan could not focus on fighting back with this unearthly scream pounding him down. Still he tried to get to his knees, to turn his power upon the oncoming monster, and still the shriek went on, exploding more of the light tubes along the garage's roof.

—∞—

In the corridor above, Jefferson spoke one word to Dave.

"*Run.*"

Vope's face rippled, as if his mask was about to fall away. In the space of time it had taken for Jefferson to speak the word, Vope's right arm had become a mottled, scaly yellow thing striped with black and brown. The hand was no longer a hand but a yellow spike covered with smaller black spikes, each one barbed and writhing.

Vope took two strides toward them and the deadly appendage shot forward as Jefferson and Dave retreated. Jefferson saw the arm lengthening and the spike coming at his chest with ferocious power. He realized he was going to be hit, even if he turned to run it was going to get him in the back...

...and then the door of 2A opened between them and intercepted the Gorgon's arm, the spike smashing through the door in a shower of wood splinters. There was a shout of terror from the Secret Service agent who was coming out, as the alien weapon had narrowly missed cleaving through his own chest. He had an instant to fully recognize the threat, turn his rifle upon the creature and get off three shots to the area where a human heart would be before the left arm with its black reptilian head and metallic fangs seized his skull and crushed it. Within the room, Hannah saw the young man's brains explode from his head and she dove like an Olympian into the bathroom, where she locked the door and pulled the shower curtain down over herself in the tub.

Between Dave, Jefferson, and Vope the other doors opened and two agents, alerted by the gunshots, came out with their rifles ready. "Shoot it!" Dave shouted. One man seemed transfixed at the sight of a creature whose arms snaked along the corridor, but the other got off two bullets that blew pieces out of Vope's forehead. What appeared to be human blood streamed down the alien's face. The shots had exposed something pulsating and malignant-looking within the wounds, like the misshapen knuckles of a leprous hand being clenched and unclenched.

The seething spike-arm had been withdrawn, and now it lunged forward again at the man who'd shot holes in Vope's head, but this human was more canny and quicker than the wretched ones Jefferson had seen slaughtered in Fort Collins. The man dodged aside and the spike crashed once more through the door at his back. The other agent had regained his senses and started firing with his own rifle at a distance of only a few feet. A bullet struck Vope's lower jaw and tore it away, a slug pierced his throat, and another ripped a chunk from his left cheek. The snake-head flailed out even as the spike-hand was retracted, but from where they stood further along the corridor behind the safety of the two rifles, Dave and Jefferson saw that Vope's actions were out of control. The snake-head's metallic fangs bit the Celotex ceiling tiles and the spike-hand did not fully retract but lay on the beige carpeting like a defeated python.

As the first Secret Service agent began firing again, aiming once more at Vope's head and piercing it with bullet after bullet, the Gorgon's ruined face rippled and contorted, one eye shot out and the nose a hole through which the hideous alien tissue pulsated.

Vope turned and fled for the stairway, dragging the spike-hand on the floor. The two agents pursued at a fast walk, side by side, both firing at the figure that staggered and retreated before them.

From below came the echo of an ear-piercing shriek that caused both agents to stop in their tracks, stunned even by the reverberation. Dave and Jefferson felt a knife-jab of pain at their eardrums and a feeling of flame burning along the spine. Dave was speechless, but he knew that whatever was going on down there, it was bad. Vope disappeared into the stairwell, and the two agents cautiously followed.

There came the sound of a crash of metal from the garage level and again the floor trembled. Jefferson yelled, "I'm going up!" He ran for another stairwell at the far end of the corridor, thinking to get as much space as he could between himself and what was attacking the level below.

Dave let him go. His concern was the condition of his friends. The echo of that shriek came rolling up the stairwell and along the corridor once more. This time the pain was so strong at eardrums and spine—like a flame scorching his nerves—he fell against the wall and clasped his hands to his ears. He made his way into the nearest room, seeking any of his companions and also shelter for himself.

———∞———

In the garage, the burning monster's scream was shrill and strong enough to shred a brain and destroy all will to resist. Ethan's human senses were overcome, his pain equally as severe as any of the men who lay nearly unconscious around him. He felt the floor shake as the creature came toward them, its claws extended to rend whatever flesh they seized upon.

The beast's shriek stopped, but the memory of it still inflamed Ethan's brain and body. The soldiers and other men were completely helpless. Ethan struggled to his knees with a massive effort, his vision clouded by a red mist. Though its chest area was burning away and liquified meat spattered onto the concrete, the monster was almost upon them. He thought it would tear the humans apart and this body too, regardless of how much the Gorgons wanted him alive.

The peacekeeper thrust both hands forward in what might have been a final attempt to blast the creature to pieces.

Through the jangled and jittery pain, he realized something was behind him.

He turned his head to see what he thought he recognized as Jack Vope staggering toward him, but a Vope whose human face was nearly destroyed and covered with counterfeit blood. The Gorgon's arms were misshapen lengths of mottled tissue that hung from the sleeves of his blood-wet t-shirt and dragged on the floor. They were changing from an approximation of human flesh and human hands to a bristle of spikes and a distorted reptilian head and then back again.

Ethan tore his focus away from that grotesque sight. From the aiming points of both palms he sent white missiles of energy at the head of the monster that loomed over him. Behind his teeth was locked an all-too-human scream.

The beast's head burst into flame and then swelled and exploded, pieces flying through the rank and smoky air. Its hind legs crumpled and the headless body crashed down upon one of the SUVs and the jeep, smashing both vehicles to junk.

One of Vope's elongated arms had a human hand at the end of it with six fingers and two thumbs, while the other still bore the snake's head. The hand flopped about like a dying fish as the Gorgon's damaged braincore tried to command it to grip hold of Ethan's neck.

From the opposite wall of the battered garage, Ethan saw the emergence of four ghostly figures. The seven-foot-tall, spindly Cypher soldiers took solid form within a heartbeat, and the one who had come through first fired his blaster with no hesitation. Twin fireballs flew over Ethan and hit Vope squarely in the midsection. Ethan looked back to see the Gorgon falling, on fire with an eye-searing red flame and torn nearly in half, but just before the body hit the floor it began to shimmer and fade out, and when it did hit the floor it was almost transparent. Then there was just the dark aura left, the faintest impression of a body imprinted upon the air, and that too faded away and was gone.

The Queen saved him, Ethan thought, his mind dazed and seemingly every fiber of this body on fire. *She took him back where they could make him whole again.*

Now he had to turn his disjointed focus upon the four Cypher soldiers striding across the bloody concrete toward him. He knew they were there as Vope had been, to take him to a chamber where their dissection blades would destroy this body in their quest to find out what he was and how he could be used.

He could not permit that. No. *Could not.*

His ears were still ringing but over that noise he heard the faint *pop pop pop* of what he realized were gunshots. He looked back and saw that two more men with rifles had come down the metal stairs and were on their bellies on the concrete, firing at the Cyphers. Jackson had also gotten to his knees, and though his ears were bleeding and his eyes were bloodshot and swollen he was taking steady aim and firing his pistol at the intruders.

Through the haze of smoke curling up from the dead monster's burned chest and ragged neck stump, Ethan saw the soldiers vibrating in and out, the bullets passing through their ghosts and ricocheting off the wall behind them. A round from Jackson's pistol happened to hit one of the Cyphers' faceplates as the soldier vibrated back into a solid but that too glanced off, leaving only a small scar on the black material. Then Jackson was out of bullets, and in desperation he went for a rifle that one of the other stricken men had dropped.

The soldiers were near enough that Ethan could make out a small red glyph at the lower right of their faceplates, what he reasoned was a mark of honor. The one in the lead wore an additional glyph, a mark of higher honor. As Jackson took aim with his rifle, this Cypher leader stopped in its advance and fired a blast with its energy weapon. The double fireballs streaked out toward Jackson, but just that fast Ethan with a resurgence of will turned them off their deadly course and sent them sizzling through the wall.

Using both hands again, he fired two blasts of his own at the Cypher leader. The effort cost him more pain and a feeling that the organs and bones of this body were nearing meltdown, but double whirling storms of a thousand fiery spheres left him and flew at the alien. The Cypher leader vibrated out at incredible speed. The soldier behind him was not so quick, and it was this creature who was blown into burning pieces by Ethan's directed energy. The two other soldiers blurred out and in again, appearing at different places and more widely spaced. Ethan sensed an electrical disturbance just to his right and there the Cypher leader vibrated back into a solid, reaching for him to clamp a spidery hand upon his shoulder. The peacekeeper feared that grip, for he thought a charge of power from it could paralyze this body with pain and render it uncontrollable, which he knew was its aim. Before the Cypher could take hold of him, it had to blur out once more because of the bullets that were being fired from both Jackson and the two men with rifles; a couple of the rifle slugs ricocheted off the concrete dangerously close to Ethan and the others who were still fighting off the effects of the monster's sonic shriek.

One of the other Cyphers vibrated back in fast enough to fire its weapon at the two riflemen, and again Ethan was able to veer the fireballs off their trajectory. A bullet from Jackson's rifle hit the soldier in the chest and knocked it backward, but it ghosted back out before it fell and did not return. Ethan sent a stream of flaming spheres and bolts of energy at the remaining soldier, who was caught before it could defend itself or dematerialize. It was blown to burning pieces as the other had been.

The Cypher leader reappeared about six feet to Ethan's left and behind him, almost on top of Bennett Jackson. As Ethan turned and summoned up the power to destroy this creature, the soldier blasted Jackson at point-blank range and the double fireballs blew the man apart.

The upper portion of Jackson's body from head to waist was thrown across the garage by the impact, and just as Ethan let loose another barrage of explosive spheres and energy bolts the Cypher leader vibrated out and the far wall was cratered by the blast, which flung pieces of rock and plumes of dust into the air.

Ethan searched the roiling miasma of dust, the breath harsh in this body's lungs and his head still full of pain. He scanned the garage, expectant that the Cypher leader might come at him from any direction.

There was no reappearance. The seconds ticked past. Ethan reasoned that the Cyphers orders had been to capture him but not kill or maim him. They had just learned he would not be taken alive. A minute passed. The peacekeeper waited, but the Cypher leader did not vibrate back into solid form. He looked at the grisly remains of Bennett Jackson. The upper portion of the body was on fire, the lower sprawled out only a short distance away. Extreme heat had cauterized both halves of the corpse. That execution had been vengeance for the death of the Cypher leader's soldiers. Ethan thought it had become a personal battle, if the Cyphers could think in that way. What the Cyphers could not capture they would have to destroy, and Ethan knew they realized that now... he was too powerful to be allowed to live, no matter what weapons they might be able to create from him.

The Cypher leader would be back at any time, and with orders to kill. Ethan was sure of it. But for the moment...his radar was clear.

Except for the ships.

He stood up, shakily, and fell again with his first step. The world seemed to be revolving around him at a dizzying speed. He pulled himself up and walked slowly, as if burdened in a dream, through the destroyed entrance to the White Mansion.

His vision was still clouded with a red mist and his ears still rang. But he could look up at the yellow clouds and see two worlds at war.

They were fighting up there. The Cypher ships had attacked the Gorgon ships. Streaks of incandescent red and blue shot across the heavens. He couldn't see with these eyes any of the ships nor could he hear any of their battle beyond a low rumble, but he could see them with his mind: the huge triangular mottled shapes of the Gorgons and the even more massive sleek black craft of the Cyphers, now pouring out hundreds of the smaller, single-pilot ships that darted in to either be destroyed by Gorgon energy orbs or, getting past those, to impale themselves upon Gorgon meat and explode with deadly force. The Gorgons were fighting back, though, because as Ethan watched he saw one of the Cypher warcraft, eight hundred feet wide, careen down from the clouds with blue-burning holes along its length and crash into the mountains ten or so miles distant. A red energy beam lanced from the sky and seared the top off another peak, throwing huge chunks of rock into the air.

The peacekeeper stood alone.

How he could stop this, he wasn't sure. Area 51 might hold the key. He realized he had been compelled to reach this place before the President of the United States could commit suicide, because that man was the only one who could get entrance to the complex.

If there was something in Area 51 that might help him...something of alien creation, that could stop this senseless war and save the planet from destruction...

Someone touched his shoulder.

He turned to face Dave, who was ashen and haggard-looking. Behind him was Olivia, and behind her, Hannah and Nikki.

His friends, on this turbulent and troubled world.

Derryman staggered out. His face and hair were whitened by rock dust, his glasses were crooked and blood leaked from his right ear. He was shaking his head back and forth as if to deny the nightmare his life had become.

Ethan started to speak to Dave, but words failed him. There was nothing he could say; the horror spoke for itself.

They stood on what seemed the edge of the earth, watching the beams of energy weapons streak back and forth, seeing explosions in the clouds, until the sky itself ruptured and rain fell upon the vast landscape of dead trees and broken rock where no human dared walk.

FIVE.

WHAT IS TO BE

TWENTY-NINE.

JEFFERSON JERICHO HAD FLED UP THE STAIRS AND NOW FOUND HIM-self standing before the automatic rifles of two soldiers who wore immaculate dark blue Marine dress uniforms, white caps and white gloves. They looked for all the world as if they were born to blast him into nothingness. Their fingers were on the triggers and the laser target-ing put red dots on Jefferson's chest near the heart. One of the Marines was using his communicator.

"Axe Two Zero," said the young man, who was maybe in his early twenties but had the hard, composed face of someone who had both seen and delivered violent death. He was having to speak loudly because the alarm was still ringing. "One of the new arrivals is on Level Four! What's the story down there?"

No answer was returned.

"Greg? Where are you?"

Jefferson had lifted his hands and put them behind his head on their command. "Something got in," he told them. His voice was weak and shaky. "That's what they said. I don't know what, but something got in."

"We know there was a breach," the soldier answered. Then, into the comm device again, "Greg? Come back, man! What's going on?"

"There was a Gorgon down below," Jefferson managed to say. "Level Three. Down below."

"Greg, answer up!"

Jefferson saw another corridor beyond the two soldiers. He had just come out of the stairwell when these men had stepped in front of him with their weapons ready. Another set of stairs continued up along the stairwell to one or more higher levels.

The young soldier pressed another combination on the keypad. "Axe Two Zero," he repeated. "Frisco, you copy?"

"The Gorgon," Jefferson said. "He looks like a man. Something else got in, I don't know what." He had the feeling of hot blood pounding in his face and cold sweat making the rest of his body shiver, and he thought he was about to pass out, but he feared any movement because he thought these two would shoot him with no hesitation. He wavered on his feet, dark motes spinning before his eyes.

"Frisco, talk to me!"

"Can I get some water?" Jefferson asked. He dared to look behind himself at the stairwell, fearful that even though shot to pieces Vope was coming after him. "Please...I think I—"

"Shut him up," the Marine told his companion, who stepped forward to spin Jefferson around and slam him against the wall. Then with a rifle barrel between his shoulder blades, Jefferson was frisked though this had already been done when he and the others had entered the garage. "Frisco," said the Marine into his comm unit, "come back!"

"He's not gonna answer," the other Marine said. "Shit's hit the fan down there."

"What's happening?" the voice of another man asked, loudly over the alarm. "Sergeant Akers, tell me!"

"I'm finding out the situation now, sir, but everything's under control."

He was a good liar, Jefferson thought. Sergeant Akers was probably scared shitless, but his voice conveyed firm authority. Jefferson turned his head to see who the new man was, though he already knew. He recognized that man's voice, and there was only one reason this installation was here and guarded by both Secret Service agents and Marines.

The President of the United States stood in the corridor.

"Jason!" Jefferson said to President Beale. The one and only time he had seen this man in person had been many years ago, when Jefferson was known as Leon Kushman and was working in Arkansas as a volunteer for Bill Clinton. Jason Beale had been a young law student in Missouri, four years older than Jefferson, and both the self-confident and rather devil-may-care firebrands had found themselves at a party where they smoked weed and talked about Leon's penchant for sneaking into porn theaters, which led to a rambling discussion of the attributes of several actresses in that profession.

"It's me! Leon Kushman! Don't you remember me?"

Jason Beale wore a dark blue suit, a white shirt, and a red-patterned tie with a knot so tight it looked near to strangulation. An American flag pin gleamed at his lapel. He was thin, the suit and the shirt a little too large for his shrunken frame. His mane of blonde hair had gone all gray and was thinning in front, but combed with careful precision and likely sprayed in place. He was still a handsome man, very photogenic, but there were circles as dark as bruises under the wary blue eyes. Deep lines cut across a high and noble forehead. His jaw sagged, and as Jefferson awaited an answer, a tic started at the corner of Beale's left eye and made that entire side of his face twitch as if he'd taken a blow there, or as if he expected a blow to be delivered and he was already flinching from it.

"Leon Kushman!" Jefferson repeated. "The party at Ginger Wright's condo, May of 1992!"

The First Lady, who was not Ginger Wright, was standing behind her man. Her name was Amanda, maiden name Gale, daughter of the president of an influential Missouri financial group and herself the founder of a public relations agency that had helped Jason Beale along to the Oval Office from the state senate. She was helping him now, it seemed, by holding onto him as if steadying him from a fall.

"Who is this man?" Beale asked his guards. There was something slow and mushy about his speech. The tic continued, getting stronger. "Why is he here?"

"Sir, please return to your quarters," Akers said. "We have everything under control."

"I *demand* to know. The alarm's going off. Vance doesn't answer when I call and neither does Bennett. I demand to know what the situation is."

"Sir, please—"

"Sergeant, I go on television within the hour to speak to the American people. They deserve to know what the situation is." He looked up at the ceiling, his face twitching badly on the left side. "That alarm. Can't you stop it?"

"Yes sir," Akers replied. Jefferson saw the young Marine glance at the First Lady and give an almost imperceptible nod. "If you'll allow yourself to be taken back to your quarters, sir, we'll get that alarm shut off and everything in order."

"They'll be coming to do my makeup soon," Beale said.

"Jason!" Jefferson tried again. "I wrote you! I asked you to autograph a picture!" He realized what name he'd last used on the several requests he'd made for a personally autographed picture to impress potential High Rollers. "Jefferson Jericho! Don't you remember?"

The President's mouth opened and then closed again. An opaque film seemed to fall across his eyes.

"Let's go back home, Mandy," he told the First Lady, who was herself heavily lined and weary-looking though she'd been very beautiful, a sportswoman as well as a business brain, back in the day. Her long dark brown hair was streaked with gray, and her eyes, sunken down into a face that carried no expression, were the color of ashes. She led her husband away along the corridor toward a set of double doors at the far end.

"Axe Two Zero," Akers said into his communicator. "God *damn* that alarm!" he told the other Marine, and then back into the comm device, "Keith, you there? Answer me, man!"

"Danny, copy that!" The voice sounded out of breath, and behind it was the noise of confusion as if people were rushing past the speaker and jostling him. "You secure?"

"Got an intruder up here, one of the new arrivals. He's babbling about a Gorgon on Level Three. What's the story?"

"We had a breach."

"Copy that. What came in?"

"You'll have to see it to believe it. I can hardly hear you, my ears are fucked up. We've got a shitmess down here. Doc's on his way. We lost Jackson, and we've got five others in pretty bad shape."

"Lost Jackson? *How?*"

"I can't talk, Danny. My head's killin' me."

"Copy that, but what am I supposed to do with this sonofabitch up here?"

"Hold him. We're gonna do a sweep on all levels, we'll get somebody there as soon as we can. Out."

"There's a dead man on Level Three," Jefferson said. "One of the agents. The Gorgon killed him."

"You sit down," Akers told him. "Do everything *real* slowly. Put your back against that wall. Keep your hands behind your head. Cross your legs in front of you and sit still."

"I know the President. I knew him when he was a law student. What did he mean about going on tele—"

"Shut your hole and sit *down*." The second Marine put his rifle's barrel right in Jefferson's face and the little red laser dot glowed on his forehead.

Jefferson sat down. There would be time later to try to contact Jason Beale, if the President *could* remember who he was, but for now the preacherman decided to ask no further questions. He wanted to stay alive, and if two Marines with rifles were standing guard over him, it suited him just fine to stay exactly where he was.

"*Damn*," said Vance Derryman as he took stock of the decimated garage level. How the hell were they going to get that carcass out of here? And how would the entrance be repaired? Bennett was dead, some of the others had been carried to the infirmary, the level was wrecked, and up in the sky the Gorgon and Cypher ships were still fighting though the boy—check that, the alien who looked like a boy—had told him their battle was moving away from the White Mansion. His head was pounding and his nerves were shot, everything was muffled, and he thought his insides had been hurt because he'd thrown up blood a few minutes ago. That alarm...piercing even through the damage to his hearing. "Somebody cut the alarm!" he shouted. His voice sounded like the murmur of someone speaking underwater. "Jesus, stop that noise!" He couldn't think, he couldn't reason any of this out. Reasoning had been his strong suit before the aliens had brought their war to this world. Everything was cut-and-dried, everything had a rational explanation. When he was briefed about Area 51, he had closed his mind to it. That was someone else's responsibility; he could listen to the briefing and hear about extraterrestrials and ships from other planets and artifacts that were being researched at S-4 for the military, but he could be masking all that with mentally replaying a golf game at Hidden Creek or thoughts on why Rachmaninoff's First Symphony had been so savagely panned by the critics in 1897. On the third day of April two years ago, the steadiness of his life had been destroyed. He'd asked his younger brother to get Linda to a shelter, because he had a duty to the President, and he had no time. He'd gotten a cell call that they'd made it and were with the National Guard in a warehouse complex outside Reston, but then the satellites had come down and the towers went out and that was the end of all communication.

General Winslett staggered up to him and said something. Derryman only caught bits and pieces of it that made no sense. Winslett's face was florid and sweating. His eyes looked like they were swimming in blood. The general stood staring at the headless monstrosity that lay across the floor, and very suddenly he turned away and made a couple of steps before he threw up. One of the soldiers came to help him, and Foggy let himself be guided to the infirmary.

They were going to have to chop that thing up, he decided. Have to chop it into a thousand pieces and haul it out of here piece by piece.

Dave McKane was at his side. He spoke, but Derryman shook his head.

Dave tried again, leaning in and speaking louder: "Can we talk?"

Derryman pointed to an ear. "I can hardly hear a damned thing!" The alarm had ceased, though; its shriek had stopped driving a spike into his brain. There were too many there already. "Give me some time!"

Dave nodded and moved away. He went carefully across the chunks of rubble and then outside, where the air did not smell of smoke or burned reptilian flesh but instead of bitter ozone. Ethan and Olivia were standing together at the guardrail, watching the distant flashes of blue and red bursts up in the clouds. Hannah and Nikki had both been taken to the infirmary not long ago. Both had been holding themselves together pretty well considering, but it was the huge carcass in the garage and the man's grisly remains that finally did them in. Nikki had collapsed soon after she'd seen the carnage and might have hurt herself in the fall if Ethan hadn't caught her, and after realizing what the monster had been Hannah said she thought she needed a little something to steady her nerves. Then the tough old bird sat down on the mountain's edge and began to sob, and Olivia had gone to find someone to help. As she was being led away, Hannah had given them a crooked smile from the wrinkled, tear-damp face, and said if she could get half a bottle of whiskey she would be as right as rain, which sounded good until you thought about what was in the rain these days.

"Has Jefferson turned up?" Olivia asked when Dave reached them.

"I'm sure he will. Bad pennies always do." Dave watched the flashes of light. In the far distance, pieces of something rippling with blue flame fell into the forest, and almost at once, smoke began to curl up from amid the dead trees. "Are they getting any closer?"

"Still moving away," Ethan said. His head pounded, the nerves of this body were still on fire and his hearing impaired, but he was able to 'hear' with his mind much more clearly than with his damaged audio receptors. "I believe they're too occupied with each other to think about me. For the moment," he added. His voice was muffled, alien even to himself. He thought also he should tell them what else he believed to be true. "They know now that they can't take me alive. The next time they come, it will be to destroy me."

Ethan let that sit for a few seconds and then he turned to face Dave. "That's why I have to get to this Area 51 as soon as possible." He'd already explained to both Dave and Olivia that he suspected—but was not sure—there might be something at the S-4 installation he could use.

What that might be, he didn't know, but human weapons would not stop this war. In fact, Ethan doubted that *any* weapon could stop the war, short of a device that would blow up the world…but then again, it was the line in space that the Cyphers and Gorgons fought over, so even if this planet was blown to pieces the contested border would still remain.

"I don't know how you think you can stop this," Dave said, as astutely as if he'd learned how to read Ethan's mind. "To do that you'd have to destroy both of them, wouldn't you? I mean…both their civilizations. Or even their worlds. How are you going to do that? Wouldn't that be…like…against your purpose or something?"

"Yes," the peacekeeper said. "My purpose is not to destroy worlds, but to save them."

"So…if you're looking for an alien weapon…how is that going to help you stop the war?"

Ethan shook his head. "What I believe…is that I was brought here for a purpose by the greater power. The only further purpose I can see is persuading your President to get me into the S-4 installation." He was silent for a moment, watching the fires of battle in the sky and calculating that their conflict was moving them further and further away from the White Mansion. "It's the only thing that makes sense to me," he said. "Something of value I can use *must* be there. Only the President can get me in, and as I told you, he's both mentally impaired and suicidal."

"I think it's hopeless," Olivia said.

"Don't talk like that." Dave saw how dark her eyes were, how they were sunken in pools of darkness, how her expression was blank with shock and grief and how close she was to falling over the edge of her own cliff. He put his arm around her shoulders, because it occurred to him that one step and she would be gone. "We can't give up," he said. "We have to trust Ethan."

"Trust Ethan," she repeated tonelessly. "There must be many millions of Gray Men out there. Around the world," she said. "China… Russia…South America…everywhere. Maybe a billion or more. Even if Ethan can stop this…what about the Gray Men? And millions more who've been driven to madness, or have had to live like animals these last two years. What about them, Dave? How can even Ethan fix that? Things can never go back to what they were, before." She stared at the guardrail, and Dave imagined she was thinking that crossing it and throwing herself from this height would at least take her away from the misery. "We've lost too much," she said. "Way too much."

Dave looked to Ethan for help, but the peacekeeper was silent. It was left up to him to bring Olivia back from the precipice.

"Yeah, we've lost too much," he said. "Me, my wife, and sons. You, your husband, and the life you knew. Look at me, Olivia. Will you do that?"

She did, and Dave thought that Olivia's eyes were nearly dead, her spirit too.

"We haven't lost each other," he said. "We've *got* to hang on. If Ethan believes he needs to get to Area 51, then I believe it too. Olivia, we've come too far to let go now." He nodded toward the flare of energy weapons in the clouds beyond. "They win everything if we let go. Please…stay with me…with *us*…just a little longer."

"Tell me," she said, still listlessly, "how we would get to that place? The cars here are wrecked. Our bus is…" She hesitated, trying to think how to phrase it. "No longer useable," she said. "I don't know the exact distance, but I'd say that Roswell, New Mexico is a long way from here. So how would we get there, Dave? Ethan? Any ideas?"

"Not just yet. We need to speak to Mr. Derryman."

They were interrupted by the presence of Jefferson Jericho, who bashed his shin against a piece of broken stone and let loose a curse as he came through the opening. He was pallid and his eyes looked dazed; he was walking like he'd gotten into the bottle of whiskey Hannah craved. "What *is* that thing in there?" he asked, and then: "The bus…where's the bus?"

"That thing *was* the bus," Dave told him as he reached them. "The Gorgons have a weapon that creates life from—"

"I don't want to know that," Jefferson interrupted. "Christ, what a mess!" He focused on Ethan. "Did you kill it?"

"Yes."

"Vope," Jefferson said to Dave. "What happened to him?"

"He—it—vanished, or transported away or whatever they do. Where have you been?"

Jefferson heard distant thunder and was suddenly aware of the battle that raged in the sky many miles away. For a moment his attention was taken by the flashes of light. "I was up on Level Four," he explained. "President Beale and the First Lady are up there. A couple of Marines played a little rough with me, but they got the order to let me go." He frowned. "Everybody okay? Hannah and Nikki? Are they all right?"

"Both in the infirmary, which I think is on this level but back in the mountain somewhere. They're okay physically, but their nerves are shot."

"Yeah, mine too." Jefferson took a long look at Olivia and saw that she was just hanging on. "How about you?" he asked her.

"I have been better. Ethan's been talking about getting to Area 51 to find…I don't know what…something he might be able to use to stop *that*." She motioned toward the flares and flashes in the yellow clouds. "I don't see how it can be stopped, no matter what he can find."

"Area 51," Jefferson said to Ethan. "Where the flying saucers are." Three years ago he would've given a good belly laugh and maybe a middle finger to the crackpots who talked about government conspiracies and the dissection of bulbous-headed spacemen in underground labs.

"I want to get into the research facility and see what artifacts are there. Mr. Derryman has told me that the only person who can get me in is your President, but he's—"

"Pretty much out of his mind, yeah. I met him once, a long time ago, when he was a law student working for Clinton. We smoked weed at a party in Little Rock. I guess we could've blackmailed each other." Jefferson had actually considered that at one point, but he figured an army of lawyers would grind him to powder and investigations into his own past could derail everything he'd built. So, to hell with the autographed picture. His blurry gaze returned to Dave. "They've got a weapon that turned our bus into that *thing*?"

"Inanimate objects into living tissue," Ethan said. "Highly advanced and rapid creation of cells using the object as a framework. In easier terms, a life beam."

"Holy shit!" said Jefferson. "And I thought 3D printing was way out there!"

"The President," Ethan said, getting them back on track. "You've seen him."

"I have. He didn't recognize me, but then again I look one hell of a lot different than I used to. I'm not sure in his present condition Beale would recognize his own mother."

"At least you have a connection to him. If we can remind him of that, so much the better."

"But you have to get through Derryman first," Dave said.

"Yes." Ethan stood silently for awhile, watching the battle drift further from the White Mansion, which was a good thing. There was a tremendous blue flash in the clouds, blue streaks seeming to shoot in all directions, and far away a huge black shape came slowly spinning down through the clouds and crashed somewhere beyond the mountain peaks. Score one for the Gorgons, he thought, but the Cyphers would have their revenge. That was another reason their war was never-ending; revenge begat revenge, and so it would be into eternity.

It wasn't long before one of the soldiers and a Secret Service agent emerged from the White Mansion Mountain and, at the point of automatic rifles, herded the group back inside. Men were in there trying to clean the place up, but it was going to be a Herculean task. What they were going to do about the destroyed entranceway was anyone's guess. The nearness of the beast's carcass made Olivia stagger and clutch at Dave for support.

"Can you get her to the infirmary?" he asked the soldier. "She's in shock, she needs some medical attention."

"Do it," said the agent, who was one of the jeans-clad, less formal men who'd brought them in from the bus. He understood shock. He'd been assigned to stand watch over the teenaged girl with the eyepatch, and he'd stayed right where he was supposed to be until he heard shooting in the corridor, and then he'd been shocked into immobility for a precious few seconds by the sight of a man-shaped thing with snakelike arms. He'd been one of the men who had gotten on his belly on the concrete and opened fire at the Cypher soldiers. After he'd thrown up blood and his ears and nose had stopped bleeding, he'd gotten some Valium from the infirmary. There had been a run on Valium. He was more in control of himself now, but his hearing was still muffled and there was a pain in his left ear that shot through that side of his face and down into his neck.

"We need to see Mr. Derryman," Ethan told him when the soldier had helped Olivia away.

"My orders are to escort you back to your rooms."

"It is *urgent*," Ethan said. "The Gorgons and the Cyphers are going to come again. The next time you won't be able to survive."

The agent could not look into Ethan's silver eyes. He stared at the dead, headless carcass for a long moment. Then he took his comm device from his pocket and keyed in some numbers. "Tempest One One," he said into it. "Sergeant Akers, is Derryman up there?"

"Affirm that. He's getting the boss ready. You okay?"

"I'm here. Listen…I'm bringing three of the new arrivals up. It's on my head. The spooky one wants to speak to Derryman."

"Ambler's in bad shape, Johnny. He needs the doc to take a look at him, but he's wanting to get the speech done."

"We're all in bad shape. The spook says it's urgent and I believe him. If you'd seen what happened down here you'd believe it too. I'm bringing them up. Out." He put his communicator away. "Let's go, but understand this: I am empowered to kill any and all of you if I don't like a single movement you make." It sounded like a hollow threat delivered from the agency's manual, because it was clear the spook had saved the installation from unrecoverable destruction. "Walk ahead of me, single file," he said.

THIRTY.

"THEY'RE ABOUT TO START ROLLING," SERGEANT AKERS SAID TO the Secret Service agent when they had reached Level Four. "Ambler won't like the interruption." He'd seen the alien's silver eyes and felt a shiver of not fear—he was far beyond fear—but wonder and anticipation. He was about to ask *Can't it wait,* but he knew it could not.

"My responsibility," Tempest One One said, and he motioned Dave, Ethan and Jefferson on along the corridor. Jefferson couldn't help but give both the Marine guards a little flippant salute as he passed them.

The group reached a door marked STUDIO and the agent told Dave to go in. Dave opened the door to a brightly lit room with softly colored green walls, a vanilla-colored sofa, a coffee table, and various overstuffed chairs. Through small speakers in the ceiling played music that Dave equated to a Main Street parade, but Jefferson correctly identified the piece as a John Phillips Souza march, all American with bursting pride and shiny buttons. He had used such music to stir patriotism and open wallets at Fourth of July celebrations in New Eden. Three rooms went off from this central chamber, all with closed doors. The Secret Service agent went to the furthermost door on the left and knocked at it. Almost at once it was opened and there stood a sharp-chinned man in a dark blue suit, white shirt, gray-striped necktie, and an American flag pin on his lapel. Ethan had seen this man on the garage level as he'd been brought in, but had not seen him since.

"They want to speak to Derryman," the agent said, moving aside so this new man could see them. "Urgent, they say."

The sharp-chinned man gave Ethan a hard, cold stare before he spoke. There were equal measures of repugnance and fear in it. "You know he's busy. Beale's just out of makeup, they're going to be rolling in about three minutes."

"Yeah, I know that. Just tell him they're here. Tell him the alien says the Gorgons and Cyphers are going to attack again."

"Hell of a time."

"Screw the protocol," said Tempest One One, reaching a ragged edge. "Everything's gone out the fucking window. Tell Derryman."

The other man withdrew into the room and closed the door without another word.

"Just wait," the agent told his charges, as the John Phillips Souza tune marched along with bass drumbeats and cymbals and shiny notes from long-dead trombones.

Nearly a minute passed. When the door opened again, Vance Derryman's face was strained with tension and pain that Ethan could feel like a blade drawn along his own spine. Behind the glasses, Derryman's eyes were red and swollen. He had changed into a black suit because the gray one he'd worn previously had been marred by rock dust.

"I said I needed time," he told Dave. His voice was slow and deliberate and a little too loud because his hearing was still impaired.

"We don't have that luxury," Ethan said. "I want to know…how did you get here?" He saw his answer in Derryman's mind in a matter of seconds. "Where's the helicopter?"

Derryman had thought the entire trip through—Air Force One from Washington to Salt Lake City, from the airport by black SUV to the secure hangar and helipad, then the flight here. He knew of course the alien would've picked it from his mind as quickly as he saw the mental images. Ethan surely already knew where the VH-71 Kestrel was kept, but Derryman spoke for the benefit of the others. "We have a helipad on the other side of the mountain. It's camouflaged. The 'copter's in a hangar there."

"That can get us to the S-4 area," Ethan said, a statement of fact.

"In about three hours. But I told you already…" Derryman paused. His jaw worked. The pain and pressure in his head were still killing him, fouling up his thought processes. "You want to see one reason he can't leave this place? Come in and follow me."

Derryman took Dave, Ethan and Jefferson through another seating area to a door with a red light above it and a sign that read ON AIR, but it was not illuminated. He opened the door and ushered them into a dimly lit space where there were a couple of rows of theater seats. Three men wearing headphones sat at a large mixing console and control panel that sparkled with small green lights. Beyond a large glass window, the President of the United States stood behind a podium that bore the Presidential seal. A bank of spotlights was aimed at him, along with a pair of professional-looking television cameras. The two camera technicians also wore headphones. Up on a ladder, another man was adjusting the spotlight beams. A gray-haired woman wearing jeans and a blue paisley blouse was dabbing powder on Jason Beale's damp forehead. Behind the President and the podium was a set of library shelves that held not only a few dozen hardcover books but items like a small bust of Abraham Lincoln, a set of praying hands cast in bronze with a Bible leaning against them, framed color photographs of Beale and the First Lady along with their two college-aged children James and Natalie, a world globe, and other items as might be found in the White House. Everything was displayed on shelves high enough so the cameras could catch them.

"What is this?" Dave asked. "How is—"

"Sit down," Derryman said. "He'll be giving his speech in about a minute." He pointed at a digital clock counting off the seconds just above the window.

One of the men at the control console pressed a button. "Kathy, he's still got some shine on his nose." He sounded tired and lackluster, as if he'd gone through this a hundred times but it was his job and he was performing it to the best of his ability. The woman nodded and applied the powder brush.

Derryman sat down in the first row beside Dave, with Ethan between Dave and Jefferson. At the end of the row sat the First Lady, who spared them not a glance. She was drinking from a glass with liquid and icecubes in it. Dave smelled alcohol.

"Am I all right?" Beale asked, looking upward at what must've been a speaker mounted on the wall on his side of the glass.

"You're fine, sir," said the console controller.

"Mandy? Am I all right?" Beale's voice was thin and fragile, a far cry from what both Jefferson and Dave remembered of previous speeches, though Dave hadn't heard many of them, and he was not fond of politics. Before the aliens had come, his opinion was that politicians disdained the public until they needed votes.

"Yes, you're all right," the First Lady said, but she wasn't looking at him and she was taking another drink.

"My most trustworthy critic," Beale announced, with a nervous laugh, to anyone who was listening. He was wearing the same dark blue suit, white shirt and red-patterned tie Jefferson had seen him in previously. He was immaculate in his clothing and his makeup was expertly applied. The dark circles under Beale's eyes and the deep lines in his face could be hidden, but no makeup could hide the feeling of sad and tragic desperation that Ethan knew everyone in the room could sense.

"Sir," said the console controller, "any glare on the teleprompter?" The way the man spoke this, it sounded like a rote question.

"No glare. It's good."

"We'll give you a countdown to showtime, as usual. Kathy, finish him up. George, you're done. The lights look fine." The makeup lady instantly stopped her work and the technician came down the ladder and folded it up to prop it against the stage set's far wall.

Jefferson leaned forward. "What's going on here?" he asked Derryman.

"The President's address to the nation. He does this twice a month."

"To the *nation*? What nation?"

"The one he believes is still out there."

"He doesn't know the *truth*? He thinks people have power and cable TV?"

"Gentlemen, I'm going to press the Talk button," said the man at the controls, as a warning that they should be careful of what they were saying.

"Go ahead," Derryman told him. "We're just here to watch."

"Ready on Camera One. Ready on Camera Two. Mr. President, let's start at five...four...three...two...one...and you're on the air."

Jason Beale stood straight and tall in the convergence of the spotlights. He did not smile at the cameras, nor was his expression forlorn. He was a politician, and he had manufactured upon his thin and sallow face an expression of the deepest, most sincere resolve.

"My fellow Americans," he read from the teleprompter, "my cherished citizens of this noble country that will never be broken by any invader earthly or otherwise, I bring you news of hope today. According to the latest military reports, your United States Army and your United States Air Force have destroyed in battle a stronghold of what we know as the Cyphers west of the Mississippi River near Alexandria, Louisiana. Your United States Navy and Marines are currently in action against a Gorgon stronghold near Seattle, Washington, and I am told by my Chief of Staff that the Gorgons are on the retreat." President Beale paused. The tic began at his left eye, making that side of his face wince. He kept his head lowered. "Pardon me," he said thickly into his microphone. "I am overwhelmed with emotion...as I'm sure we all are...all of us, in these hard days of trial and tribulation." This was not being read from the teleprompter, but was coming from the torment of his soul. He didn't speak for maybe ten or fifteen more seconds, during which the filming continued. When Beale at last lifted his face toward the lens the tic was still there but it had lessened, displaying perhaps a remnant of the man's strength of will. He began to read again from the teleprompter. "I am happy—gratified—to say that the following cities are near liberation from this unprecedented threat, though not without heavy loss of American heroes: Charlotte, North Carolina; Baltimore, Maryland; Providence, Rhode Island; Chicago, Illinois; Cedar Rapids, Iowa;

Omaha, Nebraska; Denver, Colorado; Phoenix, Arizona; and Portland, Oregon. Be advised to stay in your shelters in those cities until the All Clear signal is given, that signal to be determined at a later date. On a darker note, I am informed by my chief of staff that there is still no word from the other capitals and leaders of the world, but we will continue to monitor all satellites and send forth messages of support and the blessings of God twenty-four hours a day."

Derryman shifted in his seat. Ethan understood that of course this was all a fiction designed to give the President hope and to prevent him from finding a way to kill himself. What leader of any nation could bear to see their country—their responsibility—torn away, broken and conquered on their watch?

"We are still here," Beale went on, in his forceful and Presidential voice though the tic on the left side of his face betrayed all. "We are still the United States of America. I am receiving updates every few hours from my commanders in the field. As I told you last time we spoke, we have lost many good men and women, but just as many remain in the service of this country. We extend our heartfelt wishes for success to the other nations of this world, and we hope they are receiving this broadcast. Let me repeat as I have said many times: remain in your shelters until you are given the All Clear signal. The armed forces are fighting for you and I believe they will conquer both these threats to our way of life. I want to say to my children James and Natalie, stay in your safe area and hold onto the faith that very soon we will all see the dawning of a new day. I will say that to all the children of the world and to all the families who have bound together to withstand this assault. I will say to every soldier in the field and every sailor at sea, God be with you when you go into harm's way, and never forget that you are the pride of this nation, you are the best of the best, and we know you will not give up the fight no matter what. We too, here at this safe location, will never give up the fight." He paused for a moment, to let those stirring words resonate, and the new arrivals in the audience wondered how much of that he really believed.

The ice cubes made a hollow sound in the First Lady's glass as she took another drink.

"I will report back in two weeks, same day and same time," said the man at the podium, whose forehead had begun to show the sparkles of sweat again though cool air was blowing quietly from the vents. "This is the President of your United States, Jason Beale, signing off as always: be brave."

Then Beale stood motionless except for the tic in his face until the console controller said, "And out. That's it, sir."

"Did I do all right? Mandy, how did I look?"

"Tell him," she said between swallows, "that he looked very handsome." Her voice was just a shade slurred.

"She says you looked great, sir."

"I was worried. It's hot in here. Is it hot to you?"

"It's the lights. It's always the lights, sir."

Dave had turned his head toward Vance Derryman and leaned closer to the man's ear. "How do you get away with this? I can tell you that for damned sure Denver hasn't been fucking liberated!"

"Indeed," Derryman said.

"Yeah, *indeed*! He thinks the satellites are still up there? And people have electricity?"

"Watch your voice, he's coming out." Derryman stood up. "Excellent, Jason. That told them what they needed to know."

Beale took stock of Dave, Ethan and Jefferson, who also had risen to their feet. When he looked into Ethan's silver eyes he rubbed the back of his hand across his mouth. The tic was more severe now. "Is he safe?"

"I believe he is."

"Vance told me about the video. How you broke open the gates without any weapon," Beale said. "What are you and where did you come from?"

"I'm neither Gorgon nor Cypher, if that eases your mind. We came from Denver. Where *I* am from is hard to explain, but I am here on a mission to stop their war."

"We're winning," the President said. "It may take awhile...it may cause the loss of many thousands...hundreds of thousands...but we're winning. Aren't we, Vance?"

"The field commanders are optimistic," Derryman replied.

"Look...sir," Dave began. "I think you—"

"That's good to hear," Ethan interrupted, not wanting the plain hard truth that Dave was about to present to the President to unhinge the man's mind any further. A quick glance into that mind showed a tangle of emotions and self-recriminations, guilts, frustrations, and fears that flew like dark birds through a haunted forest. The sadness and sense of loss there was nearly crushing. Ethan withdrew, realizing that Jason Beale really did believe the lies he had read from the teleprompter to what he thought was his American people.

"We have the power grid back up in some areas," Beale said. "The northeast and the west coast. I know not very many people can see and hear my encouragement to hang on...not right now...but I think it helps. Don't you, Vance?"

"I do, sir."

Beale couldn't stop staring at Ethan. "You...look like a human boy, except for...*those*. You say...you've come to stop the war? How? And... who sent you here?"

"My commander-in-chief," Ethan answered. "Consider me a peace-keeper, like your United Nations soldiers. I need to ask you one question, sir. Will you help me get into the S-4 research facility at Area 51?"

Beale immediately looked to Derryman. "What's he talking about, Vance? Why does he want to get into there?"

"He has some idea that he can find a weapon of use among the arti-facts. I've told him we have no intention of leaving this installation. It's too much of a risk for you, sir."

"That may be," said Ethan, "but if we can use the helicopter...I think it's a risk worth taking."

"Flying through that *sky?*" Derryman cast a cold eye in his direction. "You don't know what it was like in Air Force One from Washington to Salt Lake. Now it would be even worse. That's a no-go, as far as I'm concerned."

Dave said, "Mr. President, you need to listen to Ethan. Give him the chance to do what he needs to do."

"*Ethan*," Beale repeated. "That's a quaint name for a creature not of this world."

"Sir," Ethan continued, "I ask you to believe in me. I want to stop this war, and the only way I can do that is with help. *Your* help, sir. I need to get into—"

"This conversation is done," said Derryman. "We're not letting the President leave here. Period, end of story."

"It's not the end of it. The Cyphers and Gorgons are going to attack this mountain again, once they've finished their own fighting. The next time they're going to destroy everything."

"Believe what he says, Jason," said Jefferson Jericho. "Listen...don't you remember me? Little Rock, the fund-raising dinner for Bill Clinton in May of 1992. Ginger Wright's party. I was going by the name of Leon Kushman then. Remember?"

Beale blinked slowly. He seemed to be trying to focus on Jefferson but was having trouble. "I don't...I don't think I know you. Kushman?"

"Yes."

"I've met...so many people. So many names and faces. They run together. Excuse me...I have a headache," he said to the group. "Mandy? *Mandy?*" He was calling to the First Lady as if she was no longer in her seat, yet she was no more than ten feet away at the end of the row. She finished off her drink and got up, with an air about her of weariness and despondency. Ethan thought that she had simply ceased to care, because in a matter of seconds he gathered the information that she believed both their children to be dead. The alcohol dulled a world of pain.

"I'm here," she said. "Never far away." She spoke it like a person in prison chains. She regarded Ethan as one might examine a strange form of vegetation growing from a crack in the sidewalk. Ethan knew she was about to ask *What the hell are you supposed to be* but even that seemed to be too much of an effort for her. She let the caustic question die.

"You did a very good job, sir," Derryman told him. He clasped the President's thin shoulder. Jason Beale was a shadow of himself. The President had to be reminded and encouraged to eat even one meal a day. "You always do a good job," Derryman said. "Go rest now. Listen

373

to some music. Amanda, please remind him to take his meds at five o'clock." Ethan picked up the thought from Derryman that Beale was on a number of medications, including an antidepressant, and that the First Lady's medicine was found in a bottle of whiskey. The supply of that was almost gone; she'd been going through it faster and faster. Of the original two cases there were only three bottles left. Derryman was worried about what was going to happen to the First Lady's mental health when she could no longer self-medicate.

She took her husband's arm and started to lead him out of the studio, her own balance precarious. Beale turned back toward his chief of staff. "Vance," he said, with a quick darting look at the alien peacekeeper, "we're safe, aren't we? I mean...what *he* said...about the Gorgons and the Cyphers attacking. We're safe, aren't we?"

"I told you, sir, that the breach was taken care of. We did have some intruders, as I explained, but they were turned *away*." Derryman gave extra emphasis to that word. "There is no safer place for you and the First Lady to be."

"Thank you." Beale's tormented eyes in the wrecked face found Ethan again. Like a frightened child he asked, "You won't hurt us, will you?"

"No sir. I want to help, not hurt."

"I guess...we can't lock you up, can we? What you did to the gates... no use locking you up."

"That's correct."

Beale could add nothing more to that; his mind was already nearly overwhelmed. He nodded at his wife and together they approached the door. It was unclear who was holding who up, and which was in the better shape of the two.

"Leon Kushman!" Jefferson said before they could get out. "Now my name is Jefferson Jericho! I was an evangelist, on television! Remember me?"

The President suddenly stopped just short of the door. He glanced back. "Oh...yes...*that* man. I do know that name from somewhere."

"It's me! I'm him!"

"Go rest, sir," Derryman said. "There'll be time to talk later." After the President and the First Lady had gone and the door had closed behind them, Derryman let go a long sigh. He rubbed the side of his head that was still in pain. "It has been very, very difficult," he said.

"It's not going to get any easier," Dave answered. "Do you really film him, or is it just for show?"

"He likes us to burn a DVD of the telecast so he can watch it back and critique himself. This has been going on since we got here, every two weeks. I put together the reports. He thinks there's still some organization to the armed forces, and they're out there fighting. If he didn't have that belief...he'd be long gone by now."

"When *they* come again," Ethan said forcefully, "they will destroy this mountain and everyone in it. I'll try my best to protect you, but I am not infallible. I regret the death of Mr. Jackson, that I couldn't save him. When are you going to tell the President about that?" Derryman did not reply, but the peacekeeper had his full attention. "Both the Cyphers and the Gorgons want me, because they know I'm something different that they don't understand," Ethan said. "If they can't capture me—which they can't—they'll have to make sure I am contained...another word for *dead*. This body can be destroyed, but not the essence of what I am." Ethan answered Derryman's next question before he could ask it. "No, I can't just leap from body to body...I need time to integrate myself into the form. And time is what we don't have, sir. It is important—essential—that I get into the S-4 installation. Looking for what, I don't know, but there *must* be something I can use."

"I've told you, the President can't—"

"Your world is going to die," Ethan said. "All of you—your entire civilization—will die. I can understand that you don't want to put him at risk, but there is no other way."

"Listen to him," Jefferson urged, almost pleading. "Please...listen."

"No," Derryman said firmly. "*You* listen. I have worked for Jason Beale for the greater part of fifteen years. I've seen the ups and downs, I've seen everything. He is barely hanging on, and so is she. They both know their children are probably dead. I am *not* going to send him out there in a helicopter flying to New Mexico with those things in the sky. If they're so bent on destroying you, they'll shoot that 'copter down in a matter of seconds. *No. Now...*I'll take you to the cafeteria, you can get some food. Do you *eat?*" he asked Ethan.

"The body requires it."

"If my high school biology teacher could see this!" Derryman said. His face contorted for a few seconds, and Dave thought he was close to jumping his tracks too. "I hope she died in her sleep before all this started!"

"Is this how your world ends?" Ethan asked.

"What?"

"Does your world end not with a bang, but with a whimper?"

Derryman didn't reply for awhile. He stared at the floor. Then he adjusted his glasses and said, "The cafeteria. I'm going. I suggest you come along, because the guards won't let you stay up here without me." He went to the door, opened it, and waited until they obeyed him like good little mindless soldiers.

THIRTY-ONE.

T HE PEACEKEEPER HAD DISCOVERED SOMETHING HE THOUGHT HE might miss, when all was said and done. It was called 'coffee'. As soon as he tasted his first sip, he decided this was quite a drink. It was hot and black, a little bitter, and it made him feel energized, if that was the right term. He imagined he could feel the power of this liquid thrumming through the veins of his appropriated body, and sitting at a table in the cafeteria with Dave, Jefferson, and Olivia, he thought he needed the jolt.

Olivia had joined them after a short stay in the infirmary. The doctor, a no-nonsense military man with close-cropped hair like grains of dark sand covering his scalp, had appraised her, taken her blood pressure, checked her heart and lungs, asked her to follow a moving light by keeping her head motionless, and in the end had given her a Valium and told her she could rest in one of the rooms. He had promptly gone off to give care to his many other patients who'd either been brought in or who had staggered in after the attack. Olivia had taken to a bed for about thirty minutes but had decided she was feeling calmer thanks to the Valium, and she was ready to leave. Before she'd left she had checked on both Nikki and Hannah, who also occupied beds in rooms there. Nikki was coming around, feeling better though she wanted to stay right where she was. Hannah was sleeping, looking now in repose like a very old, thin, and tired woman, and Olivia had asked one of the nurses for a notecard and written on it *Hannah, I'll check on you later. Rest while you can and don't worry about anything. Have faith. Love you, Olivia.*

The cafeteria was brightly lit and bore on its pale blue-painted walls framed photographs of American scenes: Times Square aglow with neon and crowded with people, the Golden Gate catching rays of sunlight that pierced through San Francisco fog, giant redwoods and vivid green moss-covered earth in the John Muir Woods, Boston Harbor on the day of a parade of various red-white-and-blue-decorated boats, a Kansas wheatfield that stretched as far as one could see under the blazing blue sky of summer, massive oaks lining the gravel roadway that led to a restored plantation house somewhere in the South, and other pictures of what used to be. Ethan regarded them in silence and wondered how those could possibly help the morale of the officials and soldiers who had been forced to take refuge here. This was the last stop, he thought. The last station of the line, the place to hunker down after some terrible war or disaster had claimed not only this country, but the entire earth.

There were a couple of dozen other people in the cafeteria, soldiers and civilians alike. They kept their distance from the new arrivals. The food today was chicken noodle soup in a small plastic cup, one yeast roll, and a little orange juice in a second plastic cup. There was a bin for the recycling of the cups. Dave got up for a second helping and was told by a surly cook that he couldn't have any more, so that was that.

However, there was plenty of coffee. Dave had a plastic cup of it and wondered if there were drugs in it. He couldn't figure how anybody here could get through a day, much less a week, or a month, without some kind of either stimulant or antidepressant. Without windows, the place felt like a prison; the men and the women here moved slowly and deliberately, and their expressions were mostly blank. They had all lost family members, friends, homes, and the security of their own lives. They had received their death sentence, and they were waiting for the execution.

How much longer they thought they could hold out here, he didn't know. The alien attack must've driven home the futility of this place. It was going to take one hell of a lot of effort to get that garage cleaned up, and he doubted the entranceway could be sealed again. Maybe that was how they got along from day to day, Dave thought. They just concentrated on the task right in front of them and did it, eight-hour shift after eight-hour shift.

The group ate in silence. Ethan heard their thoughts but gave no comment, not wanting to intrude. Olivia was still wan-looking and sometimes sat staring at nothing, her mind freighted with the death of John Douglas and the reality of their seemingly hopeless situation. She was fooling herself that she was doing better; she was really ready to crawl into a corner and pull the walls around her as protection. Ethan saw that two pictures played over and over in her brain: the young Secret Service agent lying in the corridor with his skull horribly crushed, and the headless monster in the garage with smoke rising from its burning chest.

She was nearly at the bitter end of her rope. Ethan didn't know what he could say to her that would give her some comfort. In fact there was nothing he could say, so he remained silent.

"Look who's coming to visit," said Jefferson.

Vance Derryman was approaching. He stopped at another table to talk briefly with a man in a gray-striped shirt with the sleeves rolled up. During the conversation, Derryman motioned toward the table of new arrivals, and the man nodded and looked at them, his face gaunt and hard and revealing absolutely nothing. Then Derryman continued on his path, and when he reached them he took a white handkerchief from within his suit jacket and polished the lenses of his glasses.

"He wants to see us," said Ethan.

"That's right."

"What does he want to see us about?" Dave asked.

"Not all of us," Ethan explained. "Only Jefferson and me."

"Right again." Derryman put his glasses back on. "Of course I'll be with you."

"Don't mind us," said Dave, with a shrug. "We'll just stay here with the peons." The cafeteria was on Level Two but further back in the mountain from the garage. Ethan and Jefferson followed Derryman out to a second stairwell. On Level Four, they were entering the President's living area from another direction. The Marine Sergeant Akers was waiting there with his automatic rifle to escort them.

They went along the corridor a short distance to the double doors that Jefferson had seen previously. "Thank you, Sergeant," Derryman said, as dismissal to the Marine. Then Derryman pressed the white button of a doorbell on the wall, and a simple, single chime sounded from within.

"I was expecting 'Hail To The Chief'," Jefferson said with a nervous laugh, but Derryman did not respond.

One of the doors was opened almost as soon as the chime ended. Amanda Beale stood there, bleary-eyed but a little more stable than she'd been at the taping an hour ago. She was wearing the same clothes, a pair of brown slacks and a white blouse that was beginning to yellow from a few too many washings. "In," she said, and turned away from them, her job done.

With Derryman going first, they crossed the threshold into a homey apartment with a dark blue throw rug on the hardwood floor, plenty of solid-looking American-crafted furniture and on the walls pieces of framed nature-themed artwork that Jefferson Jericho figured could be bought by the yard at any Pottery Barn. He couldn't help but watch the roll of Amanda Beale's hips as she walked away and wonder if she still shagged the top guy or if they played musical beds around here when they weren't thinking about aliens and the end of the world. He wouldn't mind giving that a shot, so to speak.

Then he felt the silver eyes upon him, and he ducked his head a little bit.

"Good afternoon," said the President as he came through a hallway in dramatic fashion. He was smiling, but it was a terrible thing to see because there was so much pain in his eyes. He wore the pleated trousers of his suit, and his white shirt was open at the neck. He stopped well short of them and did not offer his hand. "Thank you for coming up. Let's go in the study."

The study was off the hallway. One wall was a huge photographic mural of an aerial view of Washington, which obviously tried to make up for the lack of windows. On another wall was a large corkboard with a map of the entire United States pinned on it and also several smaller regional maps. Somebody had gone a little overboard making circles and arrows with a black Magic Marker, and Jefferson figured those were the movements of troops, tanks and fighter jets that weren't really there. Shelves held books that seemed to be more for decoration than for reading, just like the stage set, because everything was lined up and stacked just so. A massive antique desk was the centerpoint of the room; it had an American flag carved into the wood on front and two carved eagles, one on either side. A pair of black leather chairs had been pulled up to the desk and behind it was a third. There was a fourth black leather chair in the corner and a fabric-covered sofa that tricked the eye into a question of whether it was gray or green. In any case, Jefferson thought this must've been carted from the Goodwill store in Salt Lake City when they ran out of taxpayer money for black leather.

"Close the door, Vance." Beale settled himself into the swivel chair behind his desk. "Sit down here, please." He was speaking to Ethan and Jefferson, and he motioned toward the two chairs that faced him. "Is it cool enough in here for you? We can get the air turned down, if you like."

"I'm not from a frozen world," said Ethan.

"Oh…right. Well…your eyes…it's a cold color."

Derryman sat down on the sofa, crossed his legs and prepared himself for anything, because he had no idea what Beale wanted with these two other than a declaration that the President was "curious" about them.

"We have fruit juice," Beale said. "Apple and orange. I'd offer you something stronger, but we're having to conserve that." He had spoken it to Jefferson.

"Do you have coffee?" Ethan asked. Then he thought better of it, that maybe it wouldn't be good if he had any more and he had to eliminate the liquid waste up here in the President's bathroom. That just didn't seem right. "Never mind, I'm fine with nothing."

"All right." Beale leaned back in his chair and stared at the ceiling, as if something very important there had caught his attention. He seemed to be drifting away right before their eyes, and Jefferson had to follow the line of the man's gaze to see if he was studying a spider or had been mesmerized by a cobweb that wafted back and forth in the breeze from the ceiling vent.

"Sorry, I'm just thinking," said Beale, bringing himself back to the moment. "Jefferson *Jericho*. Yes, I remember you. It took awhile for that to click in. You know…there's a lot on my mind these days, you understand."

"I do."

"But we're not going to lie down and *die*," the President said. A small tic surfaced at his left eye like a disturbance on a still pond. His hand came up and, whether unconsciously or not, rubbed the offending place as if to make it stop. "Too many have died already. Brave men and women, fighting for *us*. And children…they've died too. Do you think we should give up, lie down and die? Then…what would have been the purpose?"

"We're a long way from giving up," said Derryman.

"Yes, we are. The cities are coming back. You heard my speech, didn't you?"

Jefferson nodded carefully.

"The reports I'm getting…there are people out there…not soldiers, just ordinary civilians…who are fighting back. Thank God they have guns, and two years ago I never would've said this but thank God some people know how to make bombs."

"Right," said Jefferson.

"We'll win, eventually. The Cyphers and the Gorgons…they can't grind us under. I'll tell you what's going to happen. This is being worked on right this *minute*. Should I tell them about the G-bombs, Vance?"

Both Ethan and Jefferson saw that Derryman's face had darkened. Ethan was able to know what was coming because the President's mind was a tattered flag blown full of holes, but he remained silent.

"If you like," Derryman answered, his voice barely audible.

"The G-bombs are being put together in Kentucky. In some of the caves," Beale said, all his focus on Jefferson. "There are going to be thousands when the project is finished. It's germ warfare. We're going to drop those bombs on the Gorgon and Cypher strongholds. Ordinary earth bacteria, harmless to us because we're used to them. We're immune. But the aliens…they won't know what hit them. Thousands of G-bombs, falling on them. You see?"

No one spoke.

"That's how the earth was saved in *War Of The Worlds*," Beale said. "We can make it happen. Then we burn the corpses and use bulldozers to bury what's left. *Corpses*," he repeated, and he frowned. "Would you say 'carcasses', Vance? What's your take on that?"

The peacekeeper had to speak. "Sir, where are their strongholds?"

"Pardon?"

"Their strongholds." Ethan felt Derryman about to interrupt, so he held up an index finger to gain himself another moment. "Where are they, on the map?"

"It doesn't matter where they are right now," Derryman said. "By the time the project is completed, we'll have to reassess the situation."

Ethan turned his head to take the man in. "Do you *really* believe you're doing the correct thing?"

Again, a silence stretched. Jefferson had to shift his position and clear his throat, because suddenly the atmosphere in the room had become uncomfortably heavy.

"Jefferson Jericho!" said the President, bringing up another labored smile. "I watched your broadcast a few times. Well…twice. Amanda enjoyed the music. You had a choir on from Atlanta, one time I watched. I have to say…I never would've recognized you. Even now…hard to see you in there."

"I'll have to shave and get a shower. That'll help."

"And…you said the name Leon Kushman. I was thinking, trying to remember. So many people, so many faces. But then I did connect it. The party at Ginger Wright's condo, May of 1992. We were in Little Rock for Clinton's benefit dinner. Sure, I remember you. My God, that seems like a long time ago!"

"A lifetime," Jefferson agreed.

"We kicked back. Everything going on around us, all kinds of crazy, and we kicked back. I remember…you seemed like a guy who was going places. Had a lot of ambition. And you made something of yourself, didn't you?"

"I did try."

"You did a lot more than *try*, Leon. But I guess I should call you Jefferson, right?"

"That's the name on my driver's license now."

The comment brought forth another silence. The President abruptly swiveled his chair around to gaze at the photographic mural. It was a time before he spoke again. It was his study and maybe all that was left to him in the world, so no one rushed him or prodded.

"What a great city," he said, and his voice seemed hushed and faraway. "All the beautiful buildings. All the monuments to dead people. I was thinking last night…just lying in bed and thinking…about the Library of Congress, and the Smithsonian. Those treasures…those magnificent things. What's happened to them, Vance?"

"I'm sure they're still there, sir."

"But they may not be. They may all be burned up. Everything gone. Some of those buildings were on fire when we left. By now… ashes upon ashes."

"Don't trouble your mind, Jason. You need to keep your head clear."

"My head *clear*," he said, and something about it sounded choked. His face was still turned toward the mural. His hands gripped the arm-rests. The knuckles were white. "Ethan," he said.

"Yes sir?"

"I could ask you so many questions. But I know…I wouldn't be able to understand all the answers. Maybe not any of them. And you might not want to give me the answers, because you realize I—we—are not capable. We're just children, aren't we?"

"Early teens," Ethan said.

"I want this country to survive. Christ in Heaven…I want this world to survive."

"Jason?" Derryman said. "I think you should—"

384

"Be quiet," the President told him, but gently. "I have heard enough reports." He turned his chair to peer into the silver eyes, and though the nervous tic still afflicted his face Beale looked calmer, more steady, yet older than he'd been a few moments before. "Tell me *exactly* why you believe you need to get into S-4."

"Jason!" Derryman started to get to his feet, but the President waved any objections aside.

"This is on my watch, Vance. *Mine.* I'm sitting in here like a fucking dummy on a ventriloquist's lap. Sure, I know what the commanders say and about the G-bombs and all the other stuff you bring me, but I have got to do *something.* So…go ahead, Ethan. Why get into S-4?"

"I protest this," said Derryman. "It's not necessary."

"Sit there and be quiet or leave. I mean it, Vance. By God, I mean it. One more word and you're out the door."

Derryman said nothing else, but he pressed his fingers to both temples and looked like he wanted to let go a good loud scream.

"S-4," the President prompted. "Speak."

"As I told you, I'm here to stop this war. I can't do that alone or unaided. I believe I was brought here to meet you, and to convince you to use your handprint to get me into that facility. Of the artifacts there, something may be of use."

"But you can't be certain of that," was Beale's next statement. "Why not?"

"I can read the human mind and I can sense many things. I am more powerful in my true form than in this one, but I needed the… call it…camouflage, to be able to communicate and move among you. There are many things I know and many things I can do, but one thing I can't do is read the future. That book is yet to be written." Ethan paused for the President to fully grasp what he'd just said. "I would tell you, though, that our best chance of stopping this war is not going to be found in commanders' reports or in G-bombs. It's going to be in what you would call alien technology. You have proof of the power of that, here in this installation. It's worth going to the S-4 location to at least let me *see* what's there."

"Three hours' flight on the helicopter," Derryman dared to say, "through skies ruled by the Gorgons and the Cyphers, for the purpose of a *fishing trip*?" His jutting jaw announced that he was ready for any kind of fight to protect his charge and his territory. "Jason, do you know the risk of that? This…whatever he is…admits the aliens want him dead. They'll come after the 'copter and swat us down as soon as we get airborne!"

"They *will* come after us," Ethan agreed. "The Cyphers have a tracker in the atmosphere that's aimed at me. They'll know when we leave, and they'll do one of two things: either attack us in the air or follow us to where we're going. They'll be curious about our destination, and so will the Gorgons. I believe that may keep them from interfering with the flight."

"This is a *choice*?" Derryman asked bitterly. "I'm not hearing any positives!"

"Absolutes are difficult to predict. The odds, as you might say, are stacked against us. But I'll give you two predictions: This installation will be attacked again, more fiercely the next time. And without some means of stopping this war that I don't yet have, your world is finished. But you won't care, sir, because none of you here will live beyond tomorrow or the following day."

"Because they want you. If you left here, they'd leave us alone."

"They might, but I'm sure you're already aware that neither side cares to make peace with your civilization. The reason they want me destroyed, Mr. Derryman, is reason enough for you to help me get into S-4."

"No. Wrong. We've got to stay where we are. Conserve," he said. His face seemed to have grown a harder skin. "*Conserve*," he repeated, now desperately, and his eyes behind the glassses darted between Beale and Ethan with a wet shine of not only anger but a touch of madness.

The President lowered his head. The tic was still bothering him. He rubbed at the place of its origin, where the nerves were corrupted. Ethan could read the confusion of the man's thoughts, the need to get into action against a crippling fear that he would find he could do nothing, that he was useless and ineffectual and the country had been lost on his watch. That was the worst thing in the tormented mind, the knowledge that for all the power of his office, he was nearly insignificant against the might of the Gorgons and Cyphers.

At last Beale looked up.

Not at Ethan, but at Jefferson Jericho.

"You're a man of God," the President said. "I trust you. What should I do?"

For once in his life, Jefferson was unable to speak.

He saw it then. The purpose of his being here. The real purpose, it seemed, of his measure of days. He was being given a second chance, what might be called a shot at redemption, and maybe the peacekeeper couldn't see the future, that book was yet to be written, but he remembered Ethan saying to Dave *We might need this man*, so there had been some inkling that he should not be thrown aside or executed or left to die out on the highway like a diseased dog.

At least that's what Jefferson wanted to believe, in this moment that came upon him with an overwhelming, nearly heart-stopping force. He felt pushed back into his chair as if all the old air was being forced from a small puncture in his soul.

"You should trust Ethan," he said. "Do what he asks."

The President sat silently, staring into Jefferson's eyes.

"*Jason.*" Derryman's voice had weakened. "You can't go out there. If we lose you, it's all over."

"When can the helicopter be ready?" Beale asked.

"Please...we can figure something out. You don't have to—"

"The *helicopter*. When can it be ready?"

The reply was awhile in coming, because Vance Derryman clasped his hands together and worked his knuckles and did not want to surrender. The President waited.

"Two hours, give or take," Derryman finally said. He looked like a man in severe conflict, but he'd realized that his first duty was to obey. "It's been a long time since Garrett or Neilsen have flown. I'd like to put them in the simulator first."

"Do that," Beale said. No one could mistake that it was an official command.

"If I can't talk you out of this in the next two hours," Derryman told him, "I'm going with you. No argument on that point."

"No argument, but my mind is made up. Fuel the 'copter, get the pilots ready, get whatever we need. Let's find out what's in S-4."

"Thank you, sir," said Ethan. "And thank *you*," he said to Jefferson Jericho, who also had decided to go on the flight. Jefferson had come so far, it was not something he wanted to miss no matter what the danger. He thought Dave would feel the same way, and maybe Olivia would too.

There was much to be done. President Beale dismissed them, and they left the apartment to get themselves ready for a journey into the unknown.

THIRTY-TWO.

A HEAVY-DUTY TRACTOR TOWED THE BIG, DARK GREEN VH-71 Kestrel helicopter from its hangar onto the helipad on the western side of the White Mansion. This version of Marine One carried only the identification number 'AA3' just aft of the cockpit. Small blue lamps outlined the helipad's edges. A wind had picked up from the northwest bringing an acidic smell of poisoned rain. The clouds had thickened to blot out the last of the sun's rays, and the light was cut to a dim, grayish cast.

The passengers were already aboard. Along with President Beale and Vance Derryman were Foggy Winslett, Ethan, Dave, Olivia, and sitting at the back of the cabin two uniformed and helmeted Marines armed with 9mm Colt submachine guns, frag grenades and automatic pistols. The seats were beige-colored fabric and there were two sofas along the left wall the same color and fabric. The windows were covered with dark blue curtains. Light strips glowed along the ceiling, and there was a small table with a lamp on it. The lampshade, Ethan noted, still wore its plastic dust cover. Dignifying the President's armchair was the Presidential seal. Soon there came the low growl of the three turboshaft engines warming up. The noise grew in power. None of the passengers spoke; this was going to be a trip that tested the nerves, and no one felt like talking. The two Marines had volunteered for the assignment and the pilots, Garrett and Neilsen, had flown Super Stallion transport 'copters from aircraft carriers off Iraq. Everyone knew their job and was professional, though it had been so long since the pilots had been up, they welcomed some time in the simulator.

Dave pulled a curtain aside for a look out. Beyond the window was a bleak and threatening sky, but the light show of battling warships had ceased. Either their combat had ended in the defeat of one side, or the fight had whirled on many miles distant.

Everyone was buckled in. Garrett's voice came over the intercom: "We're three minutes from liftoff, lady and gentlemen. Welcome aboard, it's our privilege to serve." To his credit, he sounded perfectly in control and perfectly at peace with the idea of flying Marine One into the teeth of the alien enemy.

The rotors started up. Their noise was muffled to a civilized rumble by the construction of the helicopter, made to allow the President to attend to business while in flight.

Though there was no conversation, Ethan could look at a person, give them his full attention, and 'hear' their thoughts like a voice in a dark room. Scanning the people here, he was nearly overwhelmed. What human emotion was not riding in this helicopter? He did the best thing he could; he leaned his head back, closed his eyes, and allowed everyone their privacy, and himself a chance to rest.

The Kestrel lifted smoothly off from its helipad and rose above the White Mansion. Keeping just below the clouds, it took a southeasterly turn and flew toward its destination at one hundred and seventy miles per hour.

Ethan, Dave, and Olivia had gone to the infirmary to visit Hannah and Nikki. Hannah was drugged and haggard. She looked ninety years old and as lost as an orphan child. She didn't make much sense when she talked, but she lay in her bed and at least seemed to be listening when Olivia had told her where they were going.

"Will you be back?" Hannah had asked in a slow murmur, as if afraid a louder voice might bring a monster back from the dead. She grasped the other woman's offered hand. "Say you'll be back, Olivia. We can't keep going without you."

"We'll be back," Olivia promised. She herself was in need of more rest and another Valium or two, but she had, as Dave had once said to Jefferson, put her balls on. No matter what was ahead, she had to be there to see it, and she thought Vincent would have approved.

"Panther Ridge can't hold on without you," Hannah continued. She shivered as if struck by a thought like a bullet and her hand tightened on Olivia's. "Where's JayDee? I need to see JayDee."

"He's around somewhere," Olivia said. "Not far."

"You're the *leader*," Hannah told her. "You've always been the leader. You *have* to come back. You and Dave both. Is that Ethan there? My eyes are so screwed up."

"It's me," Ethan said.

"I saw you...when you ran into that parking lot. The high school. I saw what happened to the cars and the trucks." She tried to focus on Olivia again. "They came *alive*," she said, as if sharing the most awesome and terrible secret. "Dave said keep that quiet, so I did. Ethan?"

"Yes?"

"Protect them. They have to come back to Panther Ridge. All of you do."

"I know he'll do his best," Olivia said. "You rest now, just try to sleep. Can we get anything for you before we go?"

"Time," the old woman said weakly. "More time." She was already drifting away from them, into what Olivia hoped was the safety of her dreams. They stayed with her until her hand fell away from Olivia's, the drugs took her down again, and for at least a little while she had left this embattled world.

"I have to see Nikki," Ethan said. "I'll be along in a few minutes."

He found her in a bed in another room where the walls were painted pale green and there were framed prints of flowers. She had a table and a lamp beside her. She was sitting up against two pillows, there was a plastic cup of orange juice on the table and the remnants of a peanut butter and jelly sandwich on a small blue plate. She'd been paging through an old copy of a magazine called *Elle* when Ethan looked into the room.

"Hi," he said, in his closest emulation of a fifteen-year-old boy's tone of voice. "Can I come in?"

Her single chocolate-colored eye stared at him. The star of her eyepatch glittered under the overhead light, which was powered by a technology a thousand times older than her. Some color had returned to her face, she had taken a shower and the waves of her blonde hair were clean and freshly brushed. The peacekeeper thought it was very good that she was drinking and eating and reading, though reading about the world that used to be and seeing the pretty pictures did nothing to lighten the sadness in her soul.

He knew she missed Ethan. She had come with him on this trip because she had trusted him, and he'd left her without a word of good-bye. It was not the boy's fault, it was his own necessity, the way the plan had always been since the moment of his arrival. It was indeed not fair, it was indeed a cruelty, and though the peacekeeper's intent was on the benefit of the Many he did have feeling for the emotions of the One.

He had existed a long time, longer than Nikki Stanwick could comprehend. He was nothing she could fully understand. But in all that time he had never faced a situation such as this, and he didn't know what to say.

He could feel her deciding whether to invite him in or not, and he almost backed off and went away to spare her any more of him, but then she said, quietly, still uncertain but willing to give him a chance, "Sure."

He went in.

"Nice room," he said.

"It's okay."

"Got everything you need?"

"I guess."

"Weird not to have windows."

"*Weird*," she said. "That's funny, coming from you."

"Yes…" He hesitated and tried that again: "Yeah, I know it is."

"Don't try to talk like him," she said. "You're not him. Don't pretend."

"Oh. Yes. Okay." He nodded. "You're right, I could never be him."

"Did you come here for some reason?"

"I did. Dave, Olivia, and I are leaving here in a couple of hours. We're going with President Beale in his helicopter to Area 51. Well…an area called S-4. It's where research is done on alien artifacts." He decided to simplify that. "Things taken from flying saucers that have crashed. I think—I hope—something may be there I can use."

"You mean…like…a ray gun or something?"

"I'm not sure a ray gun would stop this war, but I'll take what I can get."

"Hm," she said. It was a moment before she spoke again, and Ethan heard the words as they formed in her mind. "Actually…that's kind of cool."

Ethan didn't know where to rest his silver eyes. He knew they creeped her out. One had been 'kind of cool', but two were too much.

"What do those letters on your chest mean?" she asked. "Why did they come up? How come when you're touched your skin turns silver there?"

Everything came from the greater power, Ethan thought. Everything to remind him that he was in the service of that power, and though he wore a suit of skin he was not permitted to believe he was one of them, even for an instant.

"General Winslett wears colored bars on his chest to signify battles he's been in, or medals he's been given," the peacekeeper said. "These are mine. Each symbol has a meaning, and together they spell out my purpose: Guardian, in your language."

"I've seen runes like that before. Don't they come from Earth?"

"They're very ancient. I imagine they found their way to this world somehow, maybe in a crashed ship or as a gift. I'm sure other symbols did, and are considered now to be ancient or unknown languages. Sorry…I know I'm sounding kind of…" He searched for the word. "*Weird*," was what he came up with. "As for my skin—Ethan's skin—turning silver at the touch…I believe it's a chemical reaction." *Living tissue to tissue that I am keeping alive by my own life force*, he thought, but he didn't want to speak this because to Nikki this would be way beyond the boundaries of *weird*.

"I understand," she replied. Then she frowned. "I guess. Wow," she said. "What my buds at the Bowl-A-Rama would have thought about *this*!"

"They would never have believed it, even if I was standing next to you. They'd think I was made up for…" He shrugged.

"A horror movie," Nikki said.

He smiled a little bit. "Am I that bad?"

"With those eyes, you're as scary as hell," she said, giving him the truth.

"Let's hope I can scare the Gorgons and Cyphers into ending this war."

"Yeah," she said, "let's hope."

Again he searched for the right language. Communication on this world seemed to be a matter of figuring out what sequence of words would hurt someone the least. "I'm sorry I took him away so suddenly," he said at last.

"You said it was time, and I guess he knew that. You don't have to tell me you're sorry. Anyway…you're something—somebody, I mean—special. Like *astral*. So who I am to say you did wrong?"

"Because even something astral can make a mistake. You came with us because you trusted him. I took him away from you. From all of you. I should've allowed him more time."

"Well," she said, "he's out of this now, isn't he?"

"Yes."

"So I ought to be happy…but I really do miss him. He was a pretty cool guy." She gave him back a tender, wistful smile. "And you're pretty cool too, but you're not him."

"Weird, scary, but cool," the peacekeeper said. "What more can an astral entity ask for?"

She was able to laugh, and he thought it was a beautiful sound. She had a distance to go, but she was going to be all right. Now he had to find a way to do what was needed, for Nikki and Olivia, for Dave and JayDee and Hannah, for everyone who had struggled on and lived with fading hope. Even for the memory of those who had withered away and died in barren misery, and even for Jefferson Jericho, who'd fulfilled a role that Ethan had not fully realized was waiting for him.

"Can I bring you anything?" he asked.

"No, I'm good."

"Well...I suppose I should go now."

"Ethan?" she said as he started to withdraw. He hesitated. "I forgive you, if you want to hear that," she said. "But you did the right thing."

"Thank you, Nikki," he answered, because though he was not human and was far from being so he did need to hear that, just as much as if he'd been born from this Earth and not created in what seemed like a dream in the unknowable mind of the greater power.

Then he left her, and he continued on to where he needed to go.

The VH-71 Kestrel was in sure and steady hands. It flew into the gathering darkness, all its identification strobes turned off, the noise of the rotors a muffled hum within the helicopter's soundproofed cabin.

They had been flying over an hour. Ethan opened his eyes and felt the Cypher tracker on him like a hot spot at the top of his head. It was always on him, and had been following since the Kestrel had left its helipad. Now there were other things out there, too. It only took him a few seconds to process the harmonic signals of two Gorgon warships, one to the east and one to the west, on courses parallel to their flight path. They were drifting along, following the tracker embedded in the back of Jefferson's neck. Each ship was still over a hundred miles away; that distance was nothing to them, they could eat that distance up in less than ten seconds if they went to a higher speed, but Ethan sensed that they were moving slowly, not wanting to get too close. Of course, they reasoned he could feel them. There might be a specialized entity on board each craft who could sense Ethan's awareness of them. They were in no hurry. And they were being cautious too, because on his own highly-tuned mental radar, he could "see" the movements of the sleek black Cypher warships prowling through the clouds at a higher altitude. There were five of them in a precise V-shaped formation. Those also were over a hundred miles distant, yet could speed across the miles in less than the time it would take for Ethan to tell Vance Derryman that they were being stalked.

But Ethan knew that Derryman already figured the Cyphers and Gorgons were not very far away. No one in this helicopter doubted that they were being followed. So Ethan closed his eyes again and rested while he kept his mental eye open for any change of speed in the warships. It would do no good to increase the anxiety of anyone here, particularly not Derryman, General Winslett, the President, or the pilots. They were aware; that was enough.

The flight continued without incident. Everyone was free to get up, to use the bathroom, to get a drink of water or a canned soft drink from the bar. At one point the President got up and stretched, and he went through the door into the cockpit and stayed there awhile. Derryman and Winslett talked in hushed whispers. Ethan declined to listen either to their words or the creation of those words in their minds. But they were deeply afraid, that was apparent. Neither one had dared to pull aside a curtain and look out a window since the flight had begun.

Dave slept, or pretended to, while Jefferson went back to talk nervously but earnestly with the two Marines. Olivia got up to use the bathroom, then she returned to her seat and remained quiet, lost in her thoughts. Ethan once did penetrate Olivia's mind to see what was there and found the image of a lean, handsome, and sun-browned man with a gray goatee smiling as she opened a present at a party. There were many other happy people in the room, where flames crackled in the fireplace and the furniture was fine but not ostentatious. A birthday cake with pink icing sat on a table, next to the cameo of a horse's head carved into a piece of white stone. When Olivia finished opening the present—not tearing the gold-colored wrapping but being as careful with it and the white ribbon as if those too were part of the gift—she opened a box and withdrew a black sphere with the number eight on it in a white circle.

"Just what I need!" Olivia said. "A ball full of answers to every question!" She was much younger-looking and fifteen pounds healthily heavier than her current condition. She held the Magic Eight Ball up for everyone to see, and Vincent raised a glass of wine and started to make a toast and that was when the moment crumbled because Olivia was losing the memory of what his voice had exactly sounded like. So in Olivia's silent distress, Ethan had left her mind as she jumped ahead and was blowing out five white candles on a strawberry cake, her favorite.

The President returned to his seat. He had been occupying himself by trading dirty jokes with the pilots. He knew a million of them. Ethan saw that he was pallid, and his eyes were still dark-circled, but he moved with a purpose and resolve that had been reawakened by this misson; the risk actually had energized him. Ethan calculated another half hour of flight time. His body was relaxed, everything was progressing as he'd hoped. Then within the next minute, he sat up straighter in his seat and all his alarms were going off because one of the Cypher ships had left its formation and was speeding toward them to intercept.

It was coming from the southwest. The peacekeeper felt it as a human might feel a storm cloud passing before the sun. He could not hold back what he knew. He stood up so abruptly, the two Marines changed their grips on their rifles and came to full alert. Leaning toward Derryman's ear, he said, "A Cypher ship is coming. Very fast from the southwest. It's going to be here before—"

I can finish speaking, he was going to say.

But this time he had miscalculated.

A terrible bright red light filled the cabin from the right side, making the drawn curtains seem like flimsy, porous paper. Ethan's vision saw waves of darker red, nearly violet energy in it that made the air spark and tremble. The walls of the Kestral creaked and popped. Then a massive jolt took Ethan off his feet and threw him forward to crash against the cockpit door. He tasted blood, saw stars not of this universe, and felt a crushing pain in his left shoulder and along the ribs on that side. As he fought against his brain malfunctioning and sliding into darkness, he realized in an instant that the helicopter had been seized as if by a gigantic hand to slow its progress. Everyone else was buckled in except for one of the Marines, who had unsnapped himself when Ethan had stood up;

he too was thrown forward along the aisle like a boneless doll and hit the far bulkhead, collapsing in a broken heap beside Ethan.

The lamp went flying like a deadly weapon and so did everything else that wasn't fastened down by government-issued screws and bolts. Cans of soft drinks were flung out of the bar and would've beheaded people like cannonshot if the bar had been facing the other way; as it was they smashed into the bulkhead four feet away and exploded. Olivia had the sensation of being sawed in half by her seatbelt. Dave lost his breath and a burst of panic made him feel as if he were drowning underwater. Jefferson cried out as he was jerked forward and then back again, the pain making him think his bones had jumped from their sockets.

The interior of Marine One was a scene of chaos for about six seconds as everyone went through their own little experience of hell. Then, in the stunned silence that followed, the body of the helicopter was slowed to half speed...slowed half again...and then held fast by the bright red beam though both main and tail rotors continued to spin. The turboshafts screamed and cracks began snaking up the walls as the Kestrel's engines started shuddering themselves to pieces.

Ethan was on his knees. He was no longer all together. Some of the bones of this body were broken. His left shoulder burned with pain and would not obey a command for movement. His lower lip was gashed by his own teeth and bleeding. Around him the air blazed with fiery waves of energy only the alien-transformed eyes could see. Then he felt the helicopter vibrate from its nosecone sensor array to its tail rotor blade, the engines shrieked their ragged notes of despair, and the Kestrel began to be pulled sideways through the sky.

Ethan knew it was what the humans would call a tractor beam. He tried to stand up and failed. The helicopter sounded like a thousand fingernails being scraped across a hundred-foot-long chalkboard. Alarms were gonging and chiming beyond the cockpit door, and Ethan could hear a woman's mechanical voice repeating "Warning...warning...warning" but even the machine seemed not to know what the warning was about. Were the pilots conscious, or even still alive?

He staggered to his feet, lurched to the right side of the Kestrel and tore the curtains away from the nearest window. The beam was blinding. He had to sense rather than see the huge black Cypher battlecraft out there, maybe two hundred yards away, itself motionless and dragging them into its belly. Sweat had burst out upon Ethan's face and the peacekeeper was again nearly pulled down into a dark pool. His back…was something broken there too? He could hardly stand up. He had to act fast, before either he passed out, the helicopter shook itself to pieces or the Cypher ship engulfed them.

He flicked the index finger of his right hand at the window. What appeared to him to be a small white-glowing ball-bearing left the finger at blurred speed and smashed the glass into dust. Then there was nothing between him and the Cypher ship but the tractor beam and a hundred and eighty yards of night.

The pain was taking his attention. The left arm of this body was useless, broken at the elbow, the shoulder also broken. It was more than the human boy could ever have endured, but the peacekeeper would not fall.

Now, he thought, his teeth clenched and beads of sweat on his face. *Now*.

You want destruction? Now you'll get it.

He spread his fingers and formed a vision of what he needed to do. Instantly five glowing white marbles left the tips of fingers and thumb and shot away along the path of the tractor beam. He could follow them if he liked; he could *be* in any one of them. Any weapon he created came from him as its source of power, and so he *was* these five small glowing balls that now grew larger and glowed brighter and seethed and pulsed with the anger that he was feeling, the rage at the stupidity of these creatures who thought they owned Eternity, and now…now they were going to get their full measure.

The balls were each ten feet in diameter when they struck, and they glowed so brightly with destructive energy that if a human eye had been able to see these it would have been burned to a cinder, but fortunately their fierce intensity was beyond the spectrum of human vision.

They hit exactly in the places where Ethan had envisioned them striking, and they hit exactly in unison, not a millisecond apart, at a speed of over 60 million feet a second.

If an Earth scientist had calculated the effect, he might have been interested to know that a result equal to the power of a two-megaton atomic explosion had just been achieved without flame, radiation, or a blast radius. One instant the Cypher warship was hovering in place, steady as a black stone, eight hundred feet across its shiny metallic back, and the next instant, it was not there. It had been torn to pieces, dissolved, and liquified with only the noise of a high wind passing through. The tractor beam was gone. The Kestrel kicked forward again at a quarter of its cruising speed, its damaged engines still howling for mercy. A newly poisonous rain fell toward the earth. The liquid was ebony in color but carried a strong smell of the brown fluid grasshoppers shot out when disturbed by the rude fingers of boys on hot summer days. It sizzled upon the red rocks and was absorbed by the sand and low shrubs that for centuries had covered the New Mexican desert between Santa Fe and Roswell.

THIRTY-THREE.

THE KESTREL MADE TWO RAGGED CIRCLES IN THE AIR, FIRST FALLING in altitude and then rising again. On its third revolution, Garrett got his machine and his heartbeat under control once more and secretly thanked God for the simulator. Neilsen turned off all alarms and checked the systems. The electrics were okay, but he saw the fuel and hydraulic leaks indicated on the control panel. The rotors felt like they would hold up. Maybe. The ride had turned as rough as a buckboard over a cobblestoned road.

Their destination was about forty miles ahead. They were going to have to creep to it, but the two pilots were the kind of men who kept flying even when the vibration shook the fillings out of their teeth, and unless the 'copter went down hard and fast, they intended to reach the appointed place. It wasn't all bravery; where else were they going to set down, out here in this nightmare world?

"Take her," Garrett told Neilsen, and he went back to check on his passengers. He found the cabin in shambles, a Marine dead with a broken neck, the alien boy with a broken left arm and shoulder and probably more. The alien was being supported between the man with the baseball cap and the Hispanic woman. The President was all right, though he was sucking on a cylinder of oxygen through a plastic mask. Derryman and the general were ashen-faced, and from the way Winslett's eyes darted around, he looked ready to squeeze himself out the broken window. The other man, whom he'd heard was a televangelist of some fame, was sitting in his seat with his eyes shut looking like he was communing with Jesus. The second Marine was okay, he was twenty-three years old and a tough little fireplug of a guy and thought everybody in the world would die before it was his turn, so his attitude carried him through.

Garrett opened a compartment and slid the med kit out. A packet of pain pills was in there amid items such as antiseptic hand cleanser, a roll of elastic bandages, scissors, and insect bite swabs. The alien shook his head—no, no, he didn't want to ingest chemicals—but the man and the woman convinced him, and he swallowed two with a cup of water. Winslett asked for a couple, though it didn't appear he was injured anywhere, and Garrett complied. When Garrett asked the President if he needed any, he got back a "Hell, no, just fly this fucker."

Garrett decided he could help the boy—what looked like a boy—a little further, and he quickly fashioned a sling out of the elastic bandages. He didn't know whether the alien would be in more discomfort with the sling than without it, but at least that broken arm wouldn't be dangling. "Let's try this out," he said, and to the man with the baseball cap: "Help me with this. Easy with his arm…easy, easy."

They got Ethan's arm into the sling. The breath hissed out from between Ethan's teeth. The pain was severe but he would deal with it, as long as he could hold onto consciousness. It occurred to him how much of the human life involved pain; it was part of their existence, either physical pain or pain of the soul. They were strong, to inhabit such fragile bodies; to be sure, they were stronger than their bodies, for those who appeared to be weak could be the strongest in will and heart. That was why he was attracted to this body, because the boy had fought so hard to live. Now, though, Ethan realized quite certainly that the damage this body had sustained was severe, and he was running out of time. He could keep injured systems going, injured lungs breathing, and the heart pumping blood through dead tissues, but he could not repair the fractures; his left arm was useless.

And there was another thing, alarming even to him.

"They're coming again," he said, to anyone who would listen.

"How many?" Dave asked.

"The other four. And...the Gorgon ships are coming in too, very fast. The Cyphers will be here in...they're here *now*," he said. "Two on each side."

With a start of terror, Jefferson tore his curtain aside to look out. There was no movement in the dark, no lights, nothing. The helicopter juddered along on its southwesterly course.

"Let me go!" Ethan told Dave and the pilot. "Let me get to a window! They're about to open—"

The warships opened fire.

But it was not the Cyphers who began firing, it was the Gorgons, and their targets were the Cypher ships. Suddenly hundreds of burning blue streaks came from the clouds and hit the Cyphers on both sides of the helicopter. Blue explosions and bursts of shimmering flame shot up. An instant later hundreds of red streaks showed the return fire from the Cyphers, and caught in the midst of the battle was Marine One.

Fiery red spheres and bolts of blue lightning crisscrossed the sky. Blasts echoed through the night, which was no longer dark. Clearly seen in the leaping light of the explosions were the massive Cypher ships, but the Gorgons were up in the clouds and out of sight. Neilsen was dancing the Kestrel through the turbulence of alien fire. Through the window that Jefferson had uncurtained, Ethan saw a red sphere that had missed its original target coming right at the helicopter. It was going to cut them in two. He had an instant to react, and in that instant he shattered the window glass outward with the thrust of an index finger and with the twist of his hand turned the sphere aside so it sizzled past just above the helicopter's tail rotor.

"Land it! Land it!" Derryman was shouting, but there was no place to land down there.

Some of the spheres and energy bolts were hitting the earth beneath them, punching blackened craters into the ground, and throwing into the air slabs of rock the size of trucks. Hillsides either convulsed or collapsed and storms of dust plumed up. Though terrified, Jefferson was transfixed by the sight of the hundreds of glowing trails and spears of alien firepower; the battle held a mesmerizing beauty, like the most gaudy and expensive fireworks show that had ever blazed the night over New Eden. The sight of pieces of a Cypher warship burning with blue fire and spinning down two thousand feet to the ground broke the spell, but still Jefferson was held in awe.

Suddenly the remaining three Cypher ships levitated themselves straight up into the clouds, moving silently and with a speed that made mockery of any earthly aircraft. The battle continued with bursts of flame back and forth, but the crippled helicopter was out of the line of fire. Neilsen put the landing gear down and headed them toward the ground, their destination only a few miles away.

Garrett had done all he could. He returned to the cockpit, while Dave helped Ethan into a seat and buckled him up.

"Hang on!" Dave had to shout over the shriek of the engines through the broken windows. He knew it was a weak statement, but he had no idea what else to say; Ethan was sweating and shivering and obviously in a lot of pain, so—

"Yes I am," the peacekeeper answered, "but I *will* hang on."

Dave and Olivia both buckled up. The Kestrel shuddered and groaned as it neared the ground, stirring up whirlwinds of dust. Jefferson thought that there was no way this busted bird could get back to the White Mansion; whenever and wherever this thing touched down, that was where they were planted for a long time to come unless there was another 'copter or a plane they could use. But he didn't want to think about that right now. He was part of the team, and he wasn't giving up on Ethan.

"Touchdown coming up!" Garrett said over the intercom, which had been cranked to full volume. "Don't know how we'll land, so brace yourselves!"

The Kestrel went in, its rotors blowing dust in all directions. The pilot showed his mettle by touching down with hardly a thump.

"Easy-peasey," Garrett said, with what was maybe an audible exhalation of breath. "Right on target, Mr. President."

The engines were cut, the rotors whined down, the exit door was opened and the stairs lowered. First out into the dusty dark was the remaining soldier, who scanned all around through a pair of night-vision goggles and then took up a position where he could open fire on any threat. Before anyone else descended the stairs, Dave paused to retrieve the dead Marine's rifle and slide the pistol into the waistband of his jeans. Derryman, pale and shaken from the flight, started to protest but Beale said, "Tell Corporal Suarez this man is coming off the 'copter armed, and I've given my approval." The President's facial tic had returned, and he too was shaky, but his voice was surprisingly strong. Derryman went off to obey the command, and Winslett followed him.

"Lean on me," Dave said to Ethan, but the peacekeeper answered, "I can move on my own, thank you." He had to, though the pain was gnawing at him from a dozen places. He could walk but only at a slow hobble. Going down the stairs, Olivia offered him her arm, and he took it just for the sake of balance.

Then all of them—Ethan, Dave, Olivia, Jefferson, the President, Derryman, Winslett, and Corporal Suarez—stood on a flat plain that rose to rugged foothills, discernible by the flare of explosions and streaks of flame through the clouds above. Ethan noted that more Cypher and Gorgon ships were converging to the battle. Fleets of them were coming in at high speed from all directions. A blast with the noise of a dozen sonic booms crackled across the sky and made everyone in the group wince. They saw, miles away across the plain, an injured Gorgon ship punctured by red-glowing wounds drop down beneath the clouds. It was hit by a dozen more spheres and wobbled to the northwest on an uncertain and likely short course.

The President began to stride away from the helicopter. Everyone else followed. The two pilots remained with the Kestrel. Ethan doubted that they would be able to make suitable repairs, but maybe they were going to try their best. He followed along, moving like the aged human he suddenly felt himself to be, between Dave and Olivia with Jefferson walking behind him and to the left.

Beale walked a distance of about seventy yards and stopped. He faced only the flat plain, the foothills and the dark splashed with the flashes and flares of the war above them. Ethan saw him reach into his suit jacket and bring out a small black device not unlike the communication unit. He pressed a series of buttons on it.

And waited.

Nothing happened.

A blazing blue streak of energy speared down into the foothills about two miles away and tossed earth into the air. The ground trembled beneath their feet.

Beale pressed the buttons again. Still nothing happened. Ethan had to rest his right hand against Dave's shoulder for support, and on his other side he was supported by Olivia's arm.

The President looked to Derryman. His face rippled with the nervous tic and his voice had weakened. "Vance…I *know* I'm in the right place. Maybe I've forgotten the sequence?"

"Let's try fresh batteries," Derryman said, and he brought from his own pocket four small Duracells he'd taken from a package in the storeroom.

"I should've thought of that."

"My job is to think for you when your mind is full." Derryman was illuminated by the bursts of deadly flame in the sky as he took the device and popped it open. He removed the old batteries and inserted the new. "Here, try it now."

Beale repeated the procedure, a pattern of six numbers, a star, and six numbers once more.

For a moment, again nothing happened. Ethan was the first to feel the *thrum* of machinery moving in the earth.

A section of the plain was angling downward to make a ramp wide enough for a military truck. Small blue guidelights flickered on in the concrete walls. Drifts of dust were pulled into what sounded like air intakes, but it appeared that the rectangle of earth concealing the ramp was a fabrication of some kind of weather-resistant material. Fake sand and pebbles were part of the camouflage. A soft blue glow grew stronger in the opening. The ramp stopped at a fifteen-degree angle and the rumble of machinery ceased.

"Watch your step going down," Beale advised. "The surface was meant for tires, not shoes. Ethan, grab hold of someone, I don't want you falling."

"Yes sir," Ethan said, because after all Beale *was* the President of the United States. He again found support between Dave and Olivia, with Jefferson behind him to catch if either one of them stumbled. The rubbery artificial surface gripped shoe soles better than Beale had suggested. On his way down the ramp, Ethan looked up at the battle. The clouds pulsed with fire. A huge explosion sent pieces of Cypher ship whirling to Earth beyond a range of distant mountains. A few seconds after that, the triangular shape of a Gorgon craft swept over the plain about five hundred feet up. It was nearly sliced in two, fluids pouring from the hexagonal passages. Something shimmering and shaped like a child's top spun rapidly across the sky, shooting red energy spheres in all directions before it too exploded, or rather imploded because there was no sound in its destruction.

Ethan could feel them gathering, could sense the harmonics in the hundreds of warships that were answering the call of Gorgons and Cyphers. The clouds boiled like dirty yellow water in a pot. Energy bolts whipped down like jagged lightning and cracked upon the mountains. Red spheres that had missed their targets or been deflected in some way streaked on toward the horizons. Ethan thought of the last stand at Panther Ridge, and wondered if the alien forces had decided their last stand against each other would be in the sky here, thousands of feet above Area 51.

The group reached the bottom, which was a small parking garage and loading docks for trucks. Everything was illuminated in the soft blue glow. The President used his control device again and the ramp began to close. Just before the opening was sealed, Ethan and the others saw the massive underside of a Cypher ship, like a shiny black roach, pass only a hundred feet or so overhead. It was pocked with smoking holes, each one large enough to fly the Kestrel into. It moved on, its propulsion silent but an eerie high-pitched electronic chatter coming from dying systems.

The instant the ramp closed up, brighter white tubes of light illuminated at the ceiling. They were the same light tubes Ethan had seen at the White Mansion installation. Alien technology, as Derryman had explained, powered the S-4 center as well. Down here there was no sound of the war above but rather only the polite hissing of an air-filtration system scrubbing away any dust that might have drifted in. Lights had come on in a glassed-in guard's station, empty of a guard. Two traffic barriers painted yellow with black diagonal stripes stood on either side of the guard's station, but they were easily walked around. Beale led the way deeper into the complex with Corporal Suarez right at his side and Derryman and Winslett only a couple of paces behind. Twice Beale stopped to allow Ethan, helped along by Olivia and Dave, to catch up.

They came to an elevator with stainless steel doors. Beside it was an illuminated keypad and above it a flat black screen like a computer monitor. Beale keyed in a string of numbers. The attempt did nothing, the monitor remained blank. "Damn," the President said, "I can't remember all this shit." He tried again, visibly concentrating, pausing after each number.

The monitor screen brightened. An outline of a hand appeared, with palm upward, fingers slightly spread and thumb to the left.

"Good evening, Mr. President," said a cool and efficient female voice from a speaker slit along the bottom of the monitor. "Please verify."

Beale placed his palm, fingers and thumb directly against the outline. The monitor blinked very quickly, like a picture being taken, and went dark again. "Thank you, sir," said the voice.

The elevator doors opened. It was a large car, more than enough to hold a dozen people comfortably with space to spare. The numbers on the control panel went from One down to Five. When everyone was aboard, Beale pressed the Five button, the elevator doors closed, and they descended with a speed that made the stomach flip.

"You doing all right?" Dave asked Ethan.

Ethan nodded, but he was not. The body had been injured more severely than when he'd entered it. Though there'd been internal damage in that blast concussion there had been no fractured bones. The dark-haired woman with the boy—his mother, but that had to be concealed from him because it was better to let his mind work with questions rather than to be overcome with answers—had pulled him close. She and the four others had taken the full impact of a Cypher strike that had missed its Gorgon target. If the concussion of that blast in the strip mall had not ended the boy's life, this surely would have done it. His left arm was dead and cold now from the shoulder down, but his broken ribs on that side were hurting him, and pain flared through the muscles along his spine. He felt the pressure of liquid in the lungs, a sensation that they were laboring. He had to cough into his free hand, and then he regarded the ugly red scrawl of blood cupped there.

Everyone else had seen too. The peacekeeper looked at Dave and smiled tightly. "I guess I'm back where Ethan began," he said, and he wiped his hand on the leg of his jeans. Dave had to shift his gaze to the floor.

The elevator slowed and stopped. The doors slid open. Ahead of them was a long corridor that looked to be made of stainless steel and was rounded like a vein through a body. Corporal Suarez left the elevator first, then Derryman and Winslett. Beale followed them and then the others with Jefferson last.

The President led them forward. The corridor branched to both left and right. He took the group to the left and continued forty more yards to a solid slab of a door also made of stainless steel. Another keypad and a monitor screen were mounted in the wall. Beale went through the process of keying in the numbers once more and the crisp female voice said, "Good evening again, Mr. President. Please verify." The screen came on, the outline of the hand appeared and the verification was made. There came the sound of two locks disengaging.

The door appeared heavy, but obviously it was not, because Beale was able to pull it open with its rubber-coated handle using a minimum of effort. The door seemed to float open. Tube lights at the ceiling were already on. Cool air began to be circulated, but Olivia thought even before crossing the threshold—which had an electric eye implanted in it—that she smelled the dry, medicinal odor of a hospital.

They entered, and when the door closed behind them, the two locks engaged.

The first chamber was a glassed-in space with three rows of theater seats much like the President's television studio, but here the seats faced two large flatscreens. A door led into a larger room, sixty feet long if an inch. Pale green tiles covered the walls and the floor was made of gray tiles. The overhead light fixtures were round, like flying saucers. A digital clock on the wall was still running and reported the time as 20:38 in white numerals. Another stainless steel door stood at the far end of the room, with a square red warning light of some kind above it. *The surgery,* Ethan thought, picking it up from the mind of Foggy Winslett. And more from the general, a flare of fear: *Don't want to go in there hell no, no way. Too many bad memories of the bodies…*

"Here," said President Beale, "are the artifacts."

He was standing before the glass double doors of a smaller room off to the right. Jefferson figured it to be about the size of a nice walk-in cigar humidor. Within the room, under the glow of the light tubes, were lucite shelves on which eight different items rested. Below the items were little identifying letters and numbers printed on clear stick-on labels: FL12255 under what appeared to be an ordinary piece of dark-colored iron, IA240873 beneath a metallic sphere not much larger than a baseball, AR060579 beneath a featureless black cube, and so on.

"Those came from crashed spaceships?" Jefferson asked, his sense of wonder now in overdrive. *"Jesus!"*

"A couple of them," Beale said, "were shot down by missiles. The responsibility of other presidents. One collided with a private jet at night in a thunderstorm, over Indiana. The identifiers signify what state these were found in, the day, the month, and the year they were recovered. There have been seven others that self-destructed after awhile, but again that was before my time. All the records, the ships, and the bodies are kept somewhere else." Beale turned to look at Ethan. "We've gone over these things with the best possible minds available, which is not easy considering the security involved. We don't think any of these are weapons, but do you think differently?"

"I need to get closer," the peacekeeper said.

Beale opened one of the doors for him, and he hobbled through on his own power. "Come in if you want to," he told Dave, Olivia, and Jefferson. "You've come this far…take a few more steps."

They went in. Beale followed and shut the door behind him, and neither Derryman nor Winslett showed any inclination to want to enter. Ethan scanned the objects.

He didn't know exactly what each one was, but he sensed no warlike energy. "Can I touch anything?"

"If *you* can't, who could? Pick up that piece of FL12255. But before you do, think of an earthly material…a texture, the skin of something… whatever. Go ahead."

Ethan visualized water as he remembered it rising from the bottom of the swimming pool at Panther Ridge. When he put his hand on the piece of iron, it became a puddle of iron-colored liquid. When he withdrew his hand, it crawled itself back into its original shape. *Dust*, he thought, and putting his hand on the object it became a powdery iron-colored substance. As soon as the touch was broken, it turned back into what it had been…which the peacekeeper realized was a transmutable material tuned to the thoughts of whoever had physical contact with it.

"My Lord," Olivia said softly.

Ethan picked up the metallic sphere. It looked as if it were jointed together in about a dozen places. It was heavy, but not too much for one hand.

"Balance it on the tip of a finger," Beale said.

It seemed too heavy for that, but Ethan tried using his index finger. When it should have fallen, it did not; it balanced there and was perfectly weightless. In another few seconds, the ball lifted off his finger three inches and hung there. Then it started rotating. The joints began to open and close with rapid succession, but soundlessly, and suddenly there was a sixth entity in the room.

It stood slim and tall, a little over seven feet, in appearance a male humanoid albino with pale eyes and shoulder-length white hair. Jewels sparkled along the edges of both ears, which were again very much similar to those of humans but curled just slightly inward. The being wore a long white gown decorated with dozens of shining gold figures that made Olivia think of ancient Aztec pictographs she'd seen with Vincent in the National Museum of History in Mexico City. The being smiled beatifically, offered his long-fingered hands in an obvious attitude of friendship and began to speak in a quiet voice that was like no language the Earth-dwellers had ever heard; it was full of pops and clicks and what sounded like stuttering. When he was finished, in about half a minute, the entity bowed his head and faded out. The sphere stopped its rotation and settled back onto the tip of Ethan's finger, where it remained until Beale took it and returned it to its proper place.

"We've tried to decipher the message," the President said. "We think it's something to do with medicine. There's a sound in there that means the same as in a language known as 'Comecrudan', but that was extinct by the mid-1880s."

"You're exactly right," Ethan said.

"What?"

"It's about medicine. I know that language, and I know that civilization. He was offering your world the cure for cancer."

Beale didn't speak, and neither did anyone else from planet Earth.

"He was telling you," Ethan went on, "that the cure for cancer is depicted in the symbols on his gown. Is this from one of the ships that was shot down?"

"It happened a long time ago," the President said.

"I see," Ethan replied. His hand went to his left side to try to ease some of the pain there of fractured ribs and raw nerves.

He took stock of the other objects: a small humanoid-looking figurine fashioned from a metal that shimmered with many colors, a square of what appeared to be ordinary window glass but was only a few millimeters in thickness, a coil of delicately fine silver-colored wire, and the rest of them.

"There are no weapons here," the peacekeeper said. "These are gifts."

"Gifts," the President repeated, hollowly.

"Brought to you—foolishly—by civilizations wanting to make contact. You weren't ready for that. You were far from ready, and they learned that lesson."

"No weapons?" Jefferson sounded distraught. "*None?* Ethan, there's *nothing* here?"

Ethan didn't answer.

"What is that?" he asked President Beale. He lifted his hand to point at the small black cube. Arizona, the sixth day of May, 1979.

"A mystery," the President said.

Ethan picked it up. It was light, and again it could be easily managed with one hand, and could sit right in the palm. The sides were smooth and featureless, the dimensions perfect.

"No substance that we know of on Earth," Beale said, "can drill into it or leave a mark on it. X-rays can't see into it. No medical or military device we have can look inside that thing. So it just sits there doing nothing. The scientists figured that if it was going to blow up the world it would have already, but they were so afraid of it they kept it in a lead-lined vault for over twenty years."

"Maybe you're supposed to paint white dots on it and hang it from your rearview mirror," said Dave, who was beginning to realize that there was truly nothing here, that the Cyphers and Gorgons were having one hell of a battle over their heads, and there was probably no way to get back to the White Mansion, which itself was as safe as an open wound.

Ethan pondered the object. Neither could he penetrate what was inside it, but...

"This is a gift too," he said. "It *has* to be. The question is...what was it created to *give?*"

"We'll never know," said Beale.

"It looks like fear," Ethan decided.

"*What?*" This time it was Jefferson who posed the question.

"Like fear. A small black cube of fear." That statement caused the seed of an idea to grow roots. "Tell me...any one of you...what do the people of your planet collectively fear?"

"Alien invasion," Dave said. "Or for two alien tribes to be fighting over us."

"More than that," Ethan urged. "Some fear that's been a real possibility for a long time, much longer than their war."

"Total destruction," Olivia offered.

"How?" Ethan kept examining the cube as he waited for an answer.

"Nuclear bombs," Jefferson said. "Or...I don't know...The End, I guess. Like what killed the dinosaurs."

"The strike of a huge asteroid," the President added. "Even now...I mean, before all this...we know they're out there. Some have passed pretty close, but we've kept it secret. We thought that if one of those hit us again, it could be the end of all life."

"And you were defenseless against those," said Ethan, who already knew the answer.

"We had emergency plans, but we would've only gotten one chance, and if we failed, it would be all over."

Ethan felt he needed to cough up blood again. How long could he keep this body going? He didn't know.

Fear...an asteroid strike...the end of all life...one chance and if we failed it would be all over.

Something resonated within him. He could not see into the cube, could not discern its alien workings or its purpose, but like the idea of the White Mansion, he could not put out of his consciousness the progression of *fear...an asteroid strike...the end of all life...one chance and if we failed it would be all over...*

"I have to find a way into this," the peacekeeper said, his voice thick.

He had just finished saying this when a siren went off and the cool female voice said from a speaker in the ceiling: "Intruder on Level One... Intruder on Level Two...Intruder on all levels...multiple intruders... warning...warning...multiple intruders on all levels..."

Ethan knew they had come to kill him. Time was running out for everyone in this room and for every human who huddled in a shelter all across this world. They were on their way, and they would not wait for this form to fall and his true essence to break free.

The black cube sat in his palm. *Fear*, he thought. *End of all life. One chance. One.*

They were coming.

THIRTY-FOUR.

"IT'S IMPOSSIBLE!" BEALE'S EYES WERE WILD. "NOTHING CAN GET IN here!"

"Warning…warning…multiple intruders on all levels," said the female voice, its cool computerized cheerfulness now completely out of place. "Echo Sierra. Repeat…Echo Sierra."

"What does that mean?" Dave demanded.

"Worst case scenario. Everybody stays on lockdown while the Special Ops soldiers work…but there aren't any here." Beale left them in the artifacts room to confer with Derryman and Winslett, who both looked as if they were ready to climb the walls. Corporal Suarez had taken a position where he could watch the steel door, his rifle at the ready.

"He says nothing can get in here," Jefferson said. His face had become a swamp of sweat. "That's what he thought about the White Mansion too. Ethan, do you know where they are and how many?"

"Many signals," Ethan answered, but he was giving most of his concentration to the black cube. The siren was still sounding, a high oscillating noise. Pain nagged at him, pulling him away from his task. "They're not far from this room," he added. "They're fighting each other right now, which gives us some time."

Dave thumbed the safety off his automatic rifle. He offered the pistol to Olivia, who gladly took it.

"I know this cube is a gift," Ethan said. "It *has* to open up, somehow."

"By the time you figure that out we'll be dead." Jefferson looked with some consternation at the pistol in Olivia's hand. "Don't I get a gun? How about letting me hold that one?"

"I'm fine as it is, thanks," she told him.

"You can hold this." Ethan held the cube out to Jefferson.

"I don't want that damned thing. It scares the hell out of me."

"Please hold it. I need a free hand."

Reluctantly, Jefferson took the cube and held it before him in his right palm. "Echo Sierra...Echo Sierra," the computerized voice repeated, but no Special Ops soldiers were coming to their rescue.

"How much time do you think we have?" Dave asked, watching the door and the walls.

"I have no..." *Idea*, Ethan was about to say. But an idea did pierce through, and that idea was: *Time.*

The greatest gift.

A thousand permutations went through his mind in a matter of seconds. A thousand odds were weighed, a thousand combinations and possibilities. He looked at the digital clock on the far wall, which had just changed over to 20:52.

"I'm going to try something," he said. "Every civilization recognizes the concept of a positive and a null, which would be to you one and zero. In your language, binary code. Whatever happens," he told Jefferson, "don't drop it."

"What's going to happen?"

Ethan ignored him. The clock still showed 20:52.

He spoke the number calmly and clearly in binary code: "One, zero zero zero, zero zero zero, zero zero one, zero zero."

The cube did not open.

Jefferson felt nothing, no movement nor heat from the object.

Two small squares suddenly illuminated on the top. Jefferson gave a little yelp but he didn't drop it.

Within each square were two symbols that pulsed with white light. Jefferson thought they looked like Chinese markings. The other sides of the cube remained black.

"What is it?" Dave asked. "How'd you know to do that?"

"It's a *timepiece*," Ethan said. "I spoke the current time in binary code. It's set itself to recognize the time system here and react to a human voice. And…I didn't know for certain, but I assumed that the cube might respond to something other than touch." He saw that Beale, Derryman and Winslett had noticed the glowing cube and they were coming in, with the President leading the way.

"What's that thing doing?" Winslett asked, a frantic note in his voice, before Beale could speak. "Is it a *bomb*?"

"No. It's…an alien clock," Ethan decided to say for the sake of simplicity and simple minds. "I woke it up."

"A *clock*? What the hell good is that?" Derryman asked sharply.

"Warning…warning…multiple intruders on all levels," said the female voice. "Echo Sierra…Echo Sierra." It sounded now as if the computer had begun to plead for help.

"We're going to be under attack very soon," the peacekeeper said. "Cyphers are going to be coming through the walls. Before they do, I need to tell you about this." He held his hand out for it and Jefferson gladly gave it up. "I know where it came from. I recognize the symbols. And it's a little more than just a clock."

"What, then?" Beale prompted.

"This is the greatest gift you've been given, sir. It's your world's second chance."

"Explain that."

"The civilization that brought this to you is very old. They were the first to use the dimensional lightpaths. They might have witnessed an asteroid strike to your planet, eons ago. They brought this as a gift to prevent the destruction of your world in the repeat of such a strike or some other catastrophe. We can use it now. I can read the symbols, I can activate the power in this."

"Power? What power?" Beale eyed the cube warily. "What does it do?"

417

Ethan smiled faintly, in spite of the pain that was steadily breaking this body down. Oh, there was so much they did not know and could not yet understand...

"It's a time machine," he said.

No one spoke. It was a frozen moment, though from beyond the steel door there came the muffled noise of what might have been an explosion. Ethan could envision the Cyphers and Gorgons fighting out there, locked in deadly close-quarters combat.

"Such a thing doesn't exist," said Derryman. "It *can't* exist."

"This has its limitations," Ethan went on. "It can reverse time but not leap it forward. That's the point of the gift. To go back and have a second chance...a gift of time to destroy an asteroid, to avert a war, or prevent any other disaster."

"You're saying...with this thing we can *erase* what's happened?" Beale asked. "Go back in *time?*"

"With limitations. As I understand this creation, it can be used only once. And...I think going back more than two years is...how would you say...pushing the envelope. Your minds are such that the reversal of that much time may cause memory holes. Some will be able to remember and some not."

Something slammed against the steel door, but for the moment it held.

"Echo Sierra...Echo Sierra..." It was a lost voice calling out for a lost cause.

"There may be other repercussions," the peacekeeper said. "Honestly, I just don't know."

Beale drew a long breath, held it and then exhaled. "Can you program it?"

"Yes."

"For when?"

"To be as safe as possible...the latest date. The third day of your April month, two years ago. I can program the device to..." Ethan paused to study the symbols. "I think...to revert time back to within a few minutes before the Gorgons came through the portals."

"That's cutting it damned close, if it even works!" Winslett said.

"And what if it does work?" Jefferson asked. "So what if you can reel back time? You can't *stop* the Gorgons from coming through! They destroyed the armies of the world in a couple of days! What's to keep everything from happening all over again?"

Ethan nodded, the silver eyes intense but under them the dark circles of exhaustion and physical injury. A smear of blood showed at the left corner of his mouth.

"I can," he said.

"*How?*"

"In my true form...I can leave you with another gift. I can use my energy to create for you a permanent protective web around your planet. It can be tuned like the strings of an instrument to the harmonics of both Gorgon and Cypher warships. But if the Gorgons can't get through," he said, "the Cyphers will never come here. There will never be a fight for the border. Some will know it happened...some will have their memories of this erased." He looked at Dave and Olivia and then back to the President. "It'll make for a very interesting and challenging future."

"My God," Beale said. "If it works like you say, how will the world handle this?"

"I hope as what it's supposed to be, a second chance."

The President looked to Derryman and Winslett for help, but they were as lost as the lost voice and the lost cause. It was his decision to make, and what was the alternative?

He was about to say *Do it* when the first Cypher soldier blurred through the wall into the chamber outside the artifacts room. The creature was behind Corporal Suarez, who swiveled around and immediately opened fire.

The second Cypher soldier that followed blew Suarez apart with a double bolt of death from its energy weapon.

"*Do it*," Beale ordered.

What Ethan needed was his own gift of time. The two Cypher soldiers were striding toward the artifacts room. Three more of them were ghosting from the wall. Dave fired through the glass, breaking it to pieces, and Olivia opened up with the pistol.

"Take it!" Ethan told Jefferson, holding the cube out. The creature that had killed Suarez was turning, bringing its blaster to bear on them. Jefferson scooped the cube from Ethan's hand. The peacekeeper's arm thrust forward and from the palm five spears of lightning shot out, one for each Cypher. The soldiers were hit, lifted off their feet and burned into black scarecrows when they slammed against the wall, where they flowed to the floor like streams of grease.

More were ghosting in. Dave and Olivia were still shooting through the broken glass but the Cyphers vibrated so fast the bullets passed through their bodies. Two of the soldiers fired as they materialized and four red orbs of flame with white-hot centers flew at the artifacts room. Ethan was able to deflect all four, sending them sizzling through the wall, but he realized even he in this weakened body was going to soon be overpowered. Five more soldiers were sliding into the chamber. Thirteen Cyphers were there within twenty feet, and all of them aimed their blasters in unison at the seven targets.

With human sweat on his face and human blood on his mouth, the peacekeeper swept his hand in a rapid motion across the row of soldiers.

How many thousands of burning bullets left him? So many that, to him, he saw only a solid wall of them, flying outward with awesome velocity. They tore into and through the Cyphers, ripped them into flaming black pieces and splattered the walls and ceiling with clots of glistening red-and-yellow-streaked intestines. The last soldier to be obliterated was able to fire its weapon, but since half of the creature was already gone by the time the black-gloved finger twitched on the fleshy trigger, the double spheres shot up through the reinforced metal ceiling into the original rock of the silver mine. A rain of small stones fell amid a storm of dust. Two soldiers that had been coming through a wall now gleaming with Cypher guts slid away, as if deciding in their robotic logic that retreat was advance in a different direction.

"They'll be back," said Ethan, who coughed blood into a hand that was his gunsight. He staggered, and the President caught him. "I need time to program it," he said, the voice raspy and weak. "We're not safe here. Get into that room." He nodded in the direction of the steel door that led to the surgery.

"Let's go," Beale said. Then, to Jefferson, "Hold onto that thing."

They left the shattered artifact room and moved through the pall of rock dust, with Beale in the lead and Dave guarding the rear. Ethan was helped along by Olivia. He was aware of entities pressing in, of things not fully formed lurking in the haze, but whether they were Cypher or Gorgon, he didn't know. Whichever it was, a terrible danger was very close.

They were about fifteen feet from the door when Dave heard what might have been a soft whistling like the displacement of air; or maybe it was a whirring sound, like a little machine in motion.

It was coming from his left.

He turned in that direction, his rifle barrel coming up because he knew already.

Vope had materialized only a few feet away. Vope was perfect again, as perfect as the Gorgons could create the masquerade of a human being.

Dave fired into the thing's face and blew its right cheek off. Before he could take a second shot he saw the mouth hitch into what might have been a smile of triumph, just as the mottled spike drove itself into the right side of his chest. It wrenched free, and Dave fell to his knees.

There was no time for shock. With a cry of outrage and pain, Olivia emptied her last three bullets into the creature's head. Vope staggered back, counterfeit human blood flowing down the face. The spiked arm and the arm with the ebony snake-head writhed in the air, the snake's metal fangs darting out to seize and crush Olivia's skull.

Ethan did not let that happen.

His rage emerged as a massive silver whip of energy that tore Vope to shreds in the blink of an eye. The face, now devoid of emotion, disintegrated. What little remained of the body was thrown backwards into the haze, and that small part ignited into white flame and exploded into nothingness.

"Help him…help him," Ethan pleaded. Derryman and Winslett reached down and dragged Dave through the steel door. Beale slammed it shut and threw two locks.

Olivia had burst into tears, her knuckles white on the empty pistol. Ethan knelt down beside Dave, who reached out for him and grasped the front of his t-shirt.

"*Damn*," Dave whispered, more in frustration than in pain. He was a ruin. He was his own Visible Man, open to the world. His hand trembled, and his face had gone deathly pale. He had lost his rifle and the baseball cap. His sweat-damp hair was sticking up in wild cowlicks.

Ethan searched his eyes and saw the dying of the light.

"Rest," the peacekeeper said.

"I…I…" Dave couldn't speak, he couldn't get anything out. Yet he had so much to say. A coldness was creeping up. So much to say, to both Ethan and Olivia. To Jefferson, as well. He wanted to put his arms around Olivia one last time and tell her how much he loved and respected her, but he knew it was not to be. He hoped she knew; he thought she did. She knelt beside him too and took his other hand, and she held it tightly. It was getting hard for him to think, hard to realize exactly where he was and what had happened. It had been so fast. He thought as as he started to drift away…one thing he had learned…life was not fair and there were hard blows you had to take on the chin, like it or not. A test, he thought. Was that really what it was all about? If so…he hoped he'd scored at least a passing grade. His sunken eyes found the glowing cube in Jefferson's hand. He pulled Ethan close, his mouth against the ear of a human boy.

"*I believe in you*," he whispered.

And he left the world with the small sigh of a man who had worked hard all his life, seen much trial and tribulation, but had known joy and love too, in what used to be. He left the world holding tight to a being from another planet or another dimension or another reality, and as the life departed and the hand fell away, the peacekeeper stood up with Beale's help. Ethan was himself dazed and unsteady but not defeated, and he touched his silver eyes where they were wet. Then he knew fully what it was to be a human, and he was in awe of them.

Olivia got to her feet. She stared down at Dave for a moment, and when she looked into Ethan's eyes again she was stone-faced and resolute. "Do what you need to do," she told him. "Do what you *can*."

They stood in an area where surgeons prepared themselves to explore the bodies of beings from other worlds. There was a long green ceramic sink where the surgeons scrubbed their hands before they put on the rubber gloves and took up their scalpels. A pair of doors led into the operating room, and a large plate-glass window afforded a view to the two stainless steel operating tables, the concave mirror lights and the other necessary equipment. Ethan noted two cameras set up to capture all the details.

"Hold it out," Ethan said to Jefferson.

There came the muffled noise of another explosion, a massive one, from somewhere else on the level. The floor shook beneath their feet. The Gorgons and Cyphers were still at their forever war, and they would fight each other into eternity on balls of rock, ice, and fire that sat astride the border.

"Hurry," the President urged.

But it could not be hurried, because even though the peacekeeper knew the symbols, the task still had to be done with care. The creature who had brought this gift had intended to absorb the earthly languages, which would be child's play for that advanced civilization. Then detailed instruction would be given to whoever was chosen to receive it, and hopefully that person was wise enough to grasp the power in this timepiece.

But that hadn't happened, and Ethan figured the bearer of this had wound up being dissected on one of those operating room tables.

Ethan recognized that the upper symbols on the two squares stood for the representation of Furthermost Distance, which would be the year. The lower symbols stood for one and zero, again the binary code. Ethan entered the year by pressing the squares a total of eleven times. They turned from glowing white to red. That designation of the Year—the furthermost distance in time away from the present moment—was accepted.

423

The squares became white again. The upper symbols changed to the representation of Middle Distance, which would be the day. April 3rd was the 93rd day of the Earth year, thus Ethan entered the binary code of 1011101. The squares turned red, accepting the day.

Once more the squares turned white. The upper symbols altered themselves to the representation of Nearest Distance, which would be the time in hours and minutes.

Ethan recalled JayDee saying *I remember the time exactly. It was eighteen minutes after ten.*

That was when John Douglas had been alerted by a nurse to watch the explosions in the sky on the television newcasts and the Gorgon ships were beginning their ominous arrival around the planet. Ethan decided to input the time as ten o'clock, 1111101000 in binary code. The time-piece was aligned to the S-4 installation's twenty-four-hour clock and would correctly read that number as morning and not night.

"When I enter this," he told them, "the process will start. I don't know what it will feel like to you. I do know I'll have no more need for this body, and I'll release it. Are you ready?"

"Ready," said the President. His facial tic had stopped, but a muscle worked in his jaw.

"I am," Jefferson said. He was glassy-eyed. "Christ…I hope this does what you say it will."

Foggy Winslett nodded.

"Yes," Derryman said.

Ethan looked at Olivia. "Are *you* ready?"

She stared down at Dave and then she lifted her weary, shocked eyes to his. "Will…everyone who died…will they be alive again?"

"That's the plan," he answered.

"Vincent," she said, "and Dave too. All of them." The tears crept down her cheeks. "Oh, my God."

"I'm going to finish this." He sensed activity beyond the steel door. "Goodbye, Olivia," he said, and he wanted to hug her and thank her for all she had done but the river of time was moving. He quickly reached out to the cube in Jefferson's hand to input the final code.

He had entered seven digits when the enemy came.

Before Ethan could react, two Cypher energy spheres tore into the room through the door. One hit Derryman in its passage, blasting away most of the upper part of his body. Derryman's legs and lower torso staggered and the single remaining arm reached around as if searching for its missing parts, the rags of its suit jacket on fire. The next two spheres blew the mangled door inward along with much of the wall. The slab of steel and chunks of broken concrete edged with fire hurtled into the room. A shockwave took everyone off their feet and the sheet of plateglass shattered. Jefferson went down as a fist-sized piece of concrete broke his collarbone on the right side. The cube fell to a floor that was suddenly littered with flaming debris.

Ethan was on his knees. Blood streamed from a gash above his left eye, and a small fragment of concrete had scorched a streak across his left cheek. His broken arm had come out of its sling and hung uselessly. The pain that thrummed through him was nearly paralyzing. He was stunned, just on the edge of losing consciousness. He made out a figure striding through the ragged opening: a single Cypher soldier, its blaster ready for another burst of double fire. He recognized the small red glyph of an honored killing machine etched on the lower right slope of the faceplate; this was the soldier that had executed Bennett Jackson.

Deathbringer's circuits worked. The soldier was aware of its primary target ahead and slightly to the left, in a posture of helplessness though that was deceiving. But there was something else of importance here; it gave off an electrical vibration Deathbringer had never before experienced. This object was shaped like a cube and was lying near the primary target. The object bore two illuminated squares. In an instant Deathbringer's schematics identified this object as an unknown threat to be destroyed, and the Cypher soldier altered the aim of its blaster to burn this cube into melted ruin.

A piece of concrete hit Deathbringer's faceplate and caused a second's disruption.

"*No,*" the President gasped from where he'd pulled himself up from the rubble, half of his face a mask of blood. Ethan felt something else enter the room. It was behind him. It was cold, deadly, and unspeakable.

The Cypher soldier felt it too and swiveled to take aim with its energy weapon, but before that could happen a spear of liquid was already in the air and had passed over the peacekeeper.

Deathbringer began to vibrate out. It was quick, but this time it was not quick enough. The liquid splattered across its faceplate and instantly started burning through it. The vibration ceased; the Cypher ghosted back in, and as the acid melted through the faceplate material and destroyed the underlying schematics and life directives, the soldier's body began to writhe and twist as if to tear itself to pieces. The blaster fired as the trigger finger convulsed. A pair of burning spheres shot between Ethan and Jefferson and smashed into the operating room's equipment. The soldier twisted in two directions as if upper and lower parts of its body were coming unscrewed in the middle. The energy weapon fired again, and the spheres tore through the wall behind Olivia, who clung to the floor and to the tattered remnants of her sanity.

As Deathbringer spun and convulsed and the acid ate its lifeforce away, Ethan turned his head and caught sight of what stood behind him.

It was only a brief glimpse before it changed into the image of a human woman with long, lank brown hair and sad eyes in a face that used to be pretty. She wore jeans and a white blouse edged with pink around the collar. An instant before the illusion was created, the creature had been a nightmare thing whose scaly yellow flesh was banded with black and red. It had worn a shapeless, leathery black gown, and the scarlet pupils of the unblinking eyes were both repulsive and hypnotic.

The sad-eyed woman spoke.

"My Jefferson," she said, with a Southern accent. "Betrayed his lover. Such a bad boy."

Jefferson saw Regina standing there, but he knew what this really was and so did the peacekeeper. A pulsing pain began at the back of Jefferson's neck; in another heartbeat it had grown to a force that squeezed the tears of agony from his swollen eyes. He thought it was about to blow his head off.

"*You*," said the Gorgon queen. Her gaze shifted to Ethan. "Caused us concern. What are you?"

Ethan was barely able to answer. There was blood in his mouth, his lungs were hitching for breath and this body was all but done.

"Not your toy," he managed to whisper. "Your master."

She smiled faintly and with great contempt.

But her smile faltered when four more Cypher soldiers came through the broken wall, and the peacekeeper knew it was his moment.

The cube was within reach. There were three digits of the binary code to enter: three zeroes. The illuminated squares were on top of the cube; they were always on top, no matter how the cube lay.

He reached out and was able to enter two zeroes before the queen realized that what he was doing was a threat. The face rippled, and the mask fell away like a shimmering mirage. Revealed there was the hideous, cobra-like visage that could freeze the heart of any human, and as Jefferson Jericho's head pulsed toward explosion and the Cypher soldiers aimed their energy weapons, the queen of the Gorgons hissed a stream of acid from her fanged mouth, flying at the face of the boy who defied her.

The peacekeeper entered the final digit as acid splattered across the forehead, nose and into the silver eyes.

He saw the squares turn red before his eyes were burned out.

He burst free from the ruined body, a being of total energy like a writhing electrical storm that shot out bolts of lightning in all directions and grew larger to fill the room, the level, the entire installation, the sky from horizon to horizon, and to envelop the entirety of the embattled planet Earth.

The walls of reality warped.

Holes began to break through the construction that separated the Present and the Past. Olivia had the sensation of her body no longer on the floor of this destroyed room. It seemed to her that her body had not moved, but the room itself had suddenly fallen away. She was drifting in a twilight world where unrecognizable shapes and images rushed past her, and their motion caused her to spin as if all gravity had ceased to exist. She was on a Tilt-A-Whirl at a carnival, spinning so fast she couldn't catch her breath, and she wanted someone to stop it...*stop it please*...but it didn't stop, and she tried to cry out, but her voice was gone, everything had become a gray blur, and all sounds were muffled thunder.

She spun and spun and spun, and she thought she would sue someone when this was over, she would sue the owners and Vincent would help her, because nobody could stand this, she couldn't breathe, she couldn't speak, it wasn't right that someone didn't stop this, no human could bear it, and as strange and horrible pictures tumbled through her mind she feared for her sanity, and she thought in panic *God help me I'm coming apart...*

THIRTY-FIVE.

H E WAS WORKING ON THE WOODEN FENCE ON THE WESTERN EDGE of his property that the March wind had gnawed down last week. He wore his dark blue baseball cap, old comfortable jeans, a brown t-shirt, and a tan-colored jacket. *In like a lamb, out like a lion*, he thought. It had been one hell of a lion this—

And then Dave McKane staggered and dropped his hammer, because something terrible was coming. He looked at his wristwatch, a gift from Cheryl on their tenth anniversary. It was one minute after ten. Something was coming from the sky. It was crazy, yeah…*crazy*…because the sky was cloudless and blue and the sun was warming up and…

Something was coming.

He ran for the house, calling his wife's name. He ran past the pickup truck and the camper, which for some strange reason he envisioned scorched with flame and sitting on four melted tires. He was losing his mind. Right out of the blue, on a beautiful day, he was going insane.

"Dave! What's wrong with you?" Cheryl said when he burst like a wild man through the screened door and took it off its hinges on his way into the kitchen. He tossed it aside. He was all nerves, had the shakes, needed a drink, a cigarette, wow was he screwed up. Thank Christ the boys were in school, they couldn't see their old man the bad-ass scared shitless because he was, and that was God's truth.

429

"Dave? *Dave?*" Cheryl, a small-boned woman who had the biggest heart Dave had ever known, followed her husband through the house to the front room. He kept checking his watch, but he wasn't sure why. He picked up the remote control, dropped it, fumbled to pick it up again, and turned on the flatscreen.

"What is *wrong* with you?" she asked. "You're actin' crazy!"

"Uh-huh." He turned the channel to CNN. The newscaster was talking about a protest movement in Washington, a few thousand people had gathered who wanted to go to a flat tax, and spokesmen for both parties were saying they liked that idea, but Dave knew they were lying, both parties were full of liars who didn't care about anything but their own wallets and their grip on power, they were fighting all the time and it was an endless war with the citizens caught in the middle. "Wait," he told Cheryl, and he checked the Bulova again. "Just wait."

He changed the channel to Fox News. Over there two men and a woman were arguing that the President shouldn't go on his European trip with all these problems at home, he was shirking his duty to the American people, he was pandering to Europe, he was a Missouri Democrat who didn't know the meaning of responsibility, he was weak-willed and anyway his wife was no Jackie Kennedy, Laura Bush, or for that matter no Michelle Obama. Then they ended with laughter over the statement that Beale had better get ready for a "Repeal" and they went on to the stock market reports from Indonesia.

Dave turned back to CNN. The timestamp on the network said it was 10:09. His watch was one minute slow. Now the newscaster had gone on to a report of an American cargo ship being threatened by Somalian pirates last night but they'd been turned away by a patrol boat.

"Lordy!" Cheryl said. "What's so important about watching the news today?"

"Something's coming," he told her before he could stop it from getting out.

"*What?*"

"Coming from the sky. Listen...I don't know...I feel messed up."

"You're scaring me," she said. "Cut it out."

He lit a cigarette with his Bic and drew it in as if it were the last smoke he would have in this world.

"What happened out there? Dave, *talk* to me!" She put her arm around his shoulders and found he was trembling, which really put the fear in her. Her husband wasn't scared of anything, he would fight the Devil if he thought it was right. But now…

"This is the third of April?" he asked.

"You know it is! Your birthday is in two weeks, you've been—"

"*Wait.*" Dave blew smoke through his nostrils. "Wait and watch."

She waited, her heart pounding and her arm around the trembling shoulders. He made a soft noise like a cry down deep in his soul, and that sound almost put her on the cell phone for an ambulance because she had never, ever seen him like this before.

Another long and terrible minute went past, during which Dave smoked in silence and Cheryl said nothing.

The CNN newscaster then began to talk to a specialist in the housing market about mortgage rates and such, and what would happen if this or that took place and how people were going to cope.

"I don't know what we're supposed to be waiting for," Cheryl said.

Dave rubbed a hand across his forehead. Bits and pieces were coming back; it was like a big jigsaw puzzle of memories in his head, and some slid right in but some wouldn't fit. He wanted to throw up because his stomach roiled, but he was afraid to leave the TV.

That portion of the news ended, and the newscaster turned to the anti-government protests in Bangkok that had started last week and had so far caused three deaths and twelve injuries in clashes between protesters and police. A young man with slicked-back black hair and wearing studious-looking glasses came on; it was night, with a few lights burning behind him. Dave didn't know how many hours Thailand was ahead of Colorado but he figured it had to be nearly the next day over there.

The young man was asked the question, "What's the situation there tonight, Craig?"

Craig started to speak into his microphone but then stopped; his face was pale and his eyes were both dazed and terrified behind the glasses.

He looked up toward the sky and then back to the camera, and suddenly there was a noise like two or three sonic booms overlapping each other, and Craig threw up a hand as if to shield his face from some horrible sight. "Oh Jesus, oh Jesus!" he cried out, nearly sobbing, and he lurched from the scene as the camera turned from him to scan the sky. At first there was nothing in the sky but darkness. The camera searched back and forth, enough to make any viewer ill with motion sickness. It found the half moon and what appeared to be the lights of a passing jetliner.

"We're having a situation there, evidently," the newcaster said over the visual, his voice tight but measured and calm in the way that all newscasters must sound to ease the fears of their audience. "Some kind of situation. We may have just heard a bomb explosion. Craig, are you there? Craig?"

The camera jiggled back and forth, turning the nightime lights into blurry ribbons of color. It picked out Thai people on the street, some standing in groups talking, others walking around as if just waking up from a bad dream. A man who appeared to be wearing a sleep robe suddenly ran past the camera hollering and shrieking with his hands in the air.

Craig was back on-camera. "Jim?" he said. He spoke with a British accent. A lock of black hair had come free and hung over one eye. "Jim, can you hear me?"

"We can hear you, go ahead."

"This is *crazy*," Cheryl said, and Dave drew hard on his cigarette again.

"They didn't come!" Craig sounded choked. "Jim, they didn't come!"

"I'm sorry, I'm not getting that! What?"

"They didn't come!" Craig repeated, and now he had begun to weep. "Oh Christ...Jesus...they didn't come...like they did last time, and I was standing right here...right here, the very same. I heard the noise, but they didn't come!"

Ethan, Dave thought. *The peacekeeper. The alien timepiece at the S-4 installation. It worked. And he said he would keep the Gorgons from coming through, and if they didn't come neither would the Cyphers.*

"Jim, don't you remember?" Craig called out. Behind him a car rocketed along the street, its driver wildly honking the horn.

The scene went to black.

It stayed that way for maybe six seconds.

Then Jim the CNN newscaster came back on, and he was talking to someone off to the right but there was no sound. He shrugged and made a gesture with his arms that said *I have no damned idea what's wrong with Craig,* and then the network went to a commercial for SafeLite autoglass repair.

Dave looked at his wife through the screen of cigarette smoke. A little worry line between her eyes seemed to be a mile deep. He was about to ask her if she remembered any of it but of course she didn't, because if she had she would've known that time had been reeled back, they'd been given a second chance, and the Gorgons weren't coming. Maybe they were *trying* to get through, and that's what caused the noise over Bangkok, but they were hitting the protective web the peacekeeper had created. Dave checked his watch. It was 10:17. They weren't coming, because by this time on that morning of April third, he and Cheryl had been standing here watching the first amateur videos of the Gorgon ships sliding through the blasts, and then Cheryl had said *Dear God we've got to go get the boys.*

Cheryl's cell chimed. "It's the school," she said, and she answered it.

Dave turned to Fox News. "…a little confused here," said the blonde woman who sat at the desk between the two men. She was holding an earpiece in her ear with one finger, trying to get information and relay it as quickly as possible. "Okay…what we're getting is…"

"We've got to get to the school right *now*," Cheryl said. She was already going for her jacket and purse.

"What is it, baby?"

"It's Mike. That was Mrs. Serling in the office. Mike's crying, he's having some kind of fit. He's begging to come home. Dave, what's *happening?*"

Mike remembers, Dave realized. *Maybe it's not all clear to him, but he's remembering something.*

"…dementia going on," the blonde woman on Fox said. "We're getting…just a minute…reports of…I'm sorry, I've lost that connection."

433

"Hold on." One of the men also was listening through an earpiece. "We're putting up a crawl, it should be up in just a few seconds. A bit of odd news, I guess."

"What's not odd news these days?" asked the other man, and he gave a nervous laugh.

"Not an emergency," the first man went on, holding up a hand as if to restrain the audience from reaching for their cellphones in a panic. "Reports coming in of...get this, odd news like I said...multiple sonic booms in the sky over Chicago, Atlanta, and New York...well, I didn't hear anything, did you?"

"Not me," said the other man. "There's the crawl."

Across the bottom of the screen, the words were as the man had already said: *Multiple sonic booms reported over several cities, unknown origin.*

"I'm getting...what?" The blonde woman was no longer on her earpiece, but was talking to someone off-camera. She returned her attention to the audience, and she was cool and collected when she said, "We're getting preliminary reports that the sounds—and they're being identified as sonic booms—have been heard over Moscow and Helsinki. We'll be getting more details on this later, I'm sure, but we'll have to let the scientists figure this one out, folks."

"I'm no scientist but one thing I'm pretty sure of," said the man who'd given the nervous laugh. He was smiling, and for the moment he was everyone's good friend and hand-holder. "It's *not* the end of the world. We're going to go to break and then we're coming right back with investment tips from Doctor Money."

"Let's go," Cheryl urged. "Mike needs us."

"Yeah," Dave said. He turned the flatscreen off. Cheryl was alive. The boys were alive. The world was alive, and there were no Gray Men. A rush of emotion almost knocked him down. Cheryl was moving toward the door, in a hurry to go get their younger son. "Yesterday," he said before she could reach for the doorknob. "What happened yesterday?"

"What? *Yesterday*? You don't remember?"

"Tell me."

She gave him a look now that told him she was really frightened, and that either he was out of his head—unlikely, for such a steady head as his—or that...she didn't really know, but she thought whatever it was had something to do with that craziness on TV. And that hooking those things together sounded crazy, too. "We got up," she said in a quiet voice, "I took the boys to school, you cut down the rest of the dead tree, and then you went to work. You said Hank Lockhart's new porch was going to be an easy project. I talked to Mom about Ann's insurance settlement from the wreck. UPS brought that package from Amazon about two o'clock."

"Oh yeah," he recalled. "The Civil War book."

"You came home, we had dinner—meatloaf, turnip greens, and mashed potatoes, if you don't remember my cooking—and then we watched a little TV. You helped Steven with his math homework. About ten o'clock Randall called to ask you to work at the bar this weekend. Then we turned in. It was just a normal day and night." Her blonde eyebrows went up. "Am I missing anything?"

Dave looked down at the floor of the house he loved. He thought that if he started laughing he might not be able to stop and then it might turn to tears and...oh Christ, what was he going to do with the memories that were becoming clearer and clearer in his mind? He remembered the pain of that spiked arm going into him; he remembered the helpless frustration of being taken from that nightmare world before he was ready, of not being able to see the thing through with the alien timepiece. After that, he didn't remember anything...but who knew whether he might recall something of being *dead* or not?

The peacekeeper had said it: *Some will know it happened...some will have their memories of this erased.*

He wondered how many would remember. One in fifty? One in a hundred, or one in a thousand? Would the President remember, or the First Lady? And how about the unknown boy who had taken the name of Ethan Gaines? Would he ever know what he had been such a crucial part of? How many would recall that they had died, or found gray splotches on their bodies before the agony set in that transformed their

435

flesh and bones? He hoped no one would remember past that point. He hoped the greater power at least was kinder than that. He was sure he would find out, in time.

Time.

It was what Hannah had asked for. Her request in the bed at the White Mansion.

More time.

"Let me hold you for a minute," Dave said, and he took a few steps and put his arms around Cheryl, and he thought he could squeeze her so hard she could merge right into him, become so close heart-to-heart and soul-to-soul that never for a moment would they ever truly be apart again. He would hug the boys the same way, and they were going to travel and do some things that were fun, things they'd wanted to do and been putting off, because what was the point of getting a second chance if you didn't use it? He would have a good long talk with Mike, and he would make sure the boy knew those things were not coming back, not ever, and he had the promise of a very special Spacekid that it was so.

"I love you so much," he told her, and his eyes filled with tears but he didn't let her see; that would send her way over the edge. He was able to wipe his eyes on the sleeve of his jacket and then he kissed her cheek and her forehead and her lips, her body warm and alive against his, but it was time...time...time to go get their boy.

As they walked to the pickup truck from the house, hand in hand, Dave heard the tolling of a distant church bell. It carried through the bright, clear air. *Someone else remembers,* he thought. *They are telling the world, in their own way.* It was not a funereal sound, it was not a sound of sadness or loss or surrender. It was the sound of a new beginning.

Just like Ethan said, Dave thought as Cheryl got behind the wheel and he climbed into the passenger side...this was going to make for an interesting and challenging future.

He wouldn't miss it for the world.

—⊗—

Olivia and Victor Quintero were riding horses on their ranch just after ten o'clock in the morning. They had a dinner party to attend tomorrow night, a group of friends they got together with every couple of months. It was going to be at The Melting Pot on East Mountain Avenue. Olivia and Victor were talking about planning a cruise to the Greek islands in the autumn, because both of them had always wanted to see the blue Aegean and the home of the heroes.

They stopped for awhile and sat under some trees that were just about to start blooming. The world was waking up again from what had seemed like a very long winter. They had so much to look forward to. Tonight they were looking forward to lighting up the chiminea and watching the stars come out, having a glass of wine and just talking about life in the way that lovers who are also great friends do.

Simple pleasures were very often the best. Both Olivia and Victor understood that time was a gift to be cherished. And if anyone doubted that, they could always get a straight answer from the Magic Eight Ball.

———∞———

At eighteen minutes after ten, Dr. John Douglas was doing paperwork in his office, catching up with insurance forms, when one of his nurses knocked on the door and looked in.

"Can I get you some coffee?" she asked.

"No, thanks. I'm fine. Just have this *stuff* to do. Oh…will you do me a big favor and call Deborah for me? Ask her if she wants me to stop by the Whole Foods and pick up some pasta for…no, check that…I'll call her myself, in just a few minutes."

"All right." She frowned, and he knew something was wrong.

"What is it, Sophie?"

"Well…it's *strange*. It's on TV, on all the stations. They're saying people are hearing these sonic booms everywhere. Like all around the world. Just sonic booms, and that's all."

"Hm," JayDee said. "I've never heard of anything like that before."

"I know, it's really strange. It's getting people freaked out."

437

"Could be a meteor blowing up in the atmosphere, I guess. But that wouldn't be all around the world, would it? I don't know, I'm just an old doctor."

"Do you want to come take a look? They're playing videos people have taken, and you can hear the sounds."

He surveyed the dreaded paperwork. Any excuse to get up and away from his desk. But...no.

"I'd better stick with this for right now. Maybe later, thank you."

Sophie hadn't been gone but a few minutes when the phone rang. It was Deborah, calling from home. Her younger sister in San Fransisco had just phoned with the weirdest story she'd ever heard in her life, something about spaceships and aliens and a war being fought and...it was just weird. Deborah said she thought the two hits of LSD Sissy took back at Berkeley must be showing up now, after all these years.

"I wouldn't doubt *that*," JayDee said. "Listen...I may be home early. Do you want me to stop by Whole Foods and pick up some pasta?"

Deborah said that would be great, and she was going to call Sissy back to try to settle her down.

"Good for you," he told her. "And tell her if she's smoking pot, to cut back on that too." Then he said he loved her, and he hung up the phone, and there was still all that darn paperwork to get done.

———❈———

When the ungodly blast went off in the sky almost over her head, Regina Jericho dropped the pistol in the grass and looked up.

There was nothing. Only sky, with a few slowly drifting clouds.

Jefferson sat in the blue Adirondack chair, overlooking the pasture and his kingdom of New Eden. The shadows of the big oak moved in a soft wind. He looked at the gun and then into Regina's face, and she thought that something was different about his eyes...something...but she didn't know what it was, because she thought she had never really known this man at all. She thought about reaching for the gun again and finishing the job. That hadn't been the voice of God up there saving

Jefferson Jericho from paying for his sins; it had just been an Air Force jet or something breaking the sound barrier.

He said quietly, "Don't throw your life away, Regina."

She paused with her hand outstretched to retrieve the pistol. But then she straightened up, because he was right.

"I'll ruin you," she said. "I'll call every lawyer in Nashville, I'll get the detective's testimony, I'll tear you to pieces. I won't let you hurt anybody else, Jefferson. You're done. Do you hear me? You are *done*."

He gave her the faintest trace of a smile.

"All right," he said.

"I mean it! I'm going in and make some calls and there's not a damned thing you can do to stop me, you bastard! I know where *all* the skeletons are buried!"

"Yes, you do," he agreed. When she started to pick up the pistol again, to take it back to the desk in his office because she realized killing him that way would be suicide and there were other ways to kill him, he said, "You can leave the gun where it is."

"You're going to be so sorry!" she promised. "So sorry you were ever born!" Without looking at him again, without soiling her eyes on his dirty presence, she turned away and walked back along the path to the English-style mansion of his dreams, in the land of his crooked rainbows, and when she was on her cell phone in the hallway she heard a small *pop* that might have been—must have been—a car backfiring down in New Eden, where the sunlight made the copper-accented roofs glow like heavenly gold and the Church of the High Rollers might have been made of white wax, on the verge of melting.

———※———

"Kevin Austin," said Mr. Novotny. "You're up!"

The boy stood up from his desk. His heart was beating hard. He was nervous, even after all his careful work and preparation. He picked up the model of the Visible Man and took it to the front of the classroom to begin.

Kidneys, stomach. Large intestine, small intestine, pancreas. Liver, spleen, lungs. Brain, heart.

It had occurred to him, as he'd constructed the model and put the project together, that the Visible Man was lacking something very important, and it was such a vital part of a human being but it could never be shown in any science class because it was a thing intangible, unable to be weighed or measured, yet without this component Man was truly an empty shell.

That intangible thing was called a *soul*. When any of these organs were damaged and life was threatened, it was the power of the soul that kicked in to keep the flesh going. It was the driving force that said a person either lie down, gave up hope and died, or had the strength to live one more day...and one more...and one more again.

For some reason Kevin had had strength of purpose on his mind lately. He had been thinking about the soul, about how some people fell under hardship and some people got up dusty and bloody and kept going no matter what. His mom, for instance, after the very tough divorce. The Visible Man could show all the wonders of the human body, all the magnificent constructions and connections, but it could not reveal what made up a hero, who fought the good fight from day to day and never gave up.

He was talking about the brain, the seat of intelligence, when the door opened and Mrs. Bergeson looked in. She wore a frightened expression, which put Kevin and the entire class instantly on edge.

"Something is happening," she told Mr. Novotny. "It's on all the news, everywhere. Something is happening."

"What is it?"

"Strange sounds in the sky," she said. "Sonic booms. Hundreds of them, all around the world. I thought...you being a science teacher, you might want to come look at the newscasts."

Mr. Novotny paused, his hand up to his chin and a finger tapping. Then he said, "I'm sure there's a rational explanation, and I'm sure the news people will work it to death. Right now, Kevin's giving his presentation."

"You mean you—"

"Will catch it later, yes, and thank you for the information," he said, and when she'd retreated he told Kevin to continue.

Kidneys, stomach. Large intestine, small intestine, pancreas. Liver, spleen, lungs. Brain, heart.

Not nearly all that made up a human being.

Not nearly all.

He'd never thought about what he was going to do with his life, but he wondered what being a doctor would be like. He seemed to remember somebody saying—and maybe this was on TV—that *Every kid who ever grew up to be a doctor probably put that thing together.*

He couldn't remember exactly where he'd heard that said, but it sounded right.

As Kevin continued—the report was not long enough to be boring nor short enough to be skimpy on the facts, his mom had helped him time it—he had a strange experience.

Some part of his brain said he ought to go bowling one Saturday night. And he ought to go up to Fort Collins, to the Bowl-A-Rama there.

Now *that* was strange.

When he finished, he didn't know what else to say. He thought he'd done well; he'd done the best he could, and what more could anyone ask?

Kevin picked up the Visible Man. He said, "I guess I'm done."

Then he went back to his seat, and the day went on.